OUR BETA READERS
LOVED
ALAINE OF HAWTHORN

"I have read all of Eileen Raye's previous works; and this is by far my favorite! She is a multi-talented author in that she writes everything from children's books to adult books. This is her first YA book for girls, and it is so good I couldn't put it down! Her ability to put readers into the scenes and minds of the characters is outstanding. Highly recommend!"

~Danya K. (Moorpark, CA)

"The cover of this book made me look twice, because I've never seen such a beautiful book cover before. They say 'don't judge a book by its cover'; but, honestly, who doesn't these days? I am so glad I decided to read it, since I usually just collect books for their looks. This story pulls you in from the beginning, and makes you feel for the characters from beginning to end. I love it! I hope Ms. Raye writes more stories like this."

~Ivy Q. (Parkersburg, WV)

"If you want a clean romance for your teenage daughter, this is the one to buy. I read it first to make sure it wasn't full of sex and dirty words and was pleasantly surprised. So few authors write like this these days. We need more stories like this. Excellent work, Eileen Raye! I look forward to reading more of your novels."

~Julie P. (Eau Claire, WI)

"Very well written and engrossing! I couldn't put it down. This is the best book I've read in a long time. Many thanks!"

~Lauren B. (New Bern, NC)

"Wonderful story! Medieval setting, yet slightly modern attitudes I could relate to. Beautiful descriptions of clothing and setting. Relationship struggles that we all deal with (and some we don't but are relatable). Dangers on the road, enticing strangers, fantasy, lore, and romance. It's all here in *Alaine of Hawthorn*. The story was fast-paced and kept me reading until the end."

~Kathy B. (Mahopac, NY)

"I finished this novel in just under six hours, and I'm not a reader by any stretch. My interest in Alaine and Carver's relationship swallowed me whole. I was consumed with it and could not put it down! These two are absolutely captivating and thought-provoking. Although I loved the ending, I was saddened that it seems to be the end of their story. I'm hoping Ms. Raye will revive them somehow."

~Jordan R. (Lake Zurich, IL)

"After reading this, everything else seems so cookie-cutter and boring now. I need more of Alaine and Carver's story!"

~Sandra D. (Atkinson, NH)

Alaine

of

Hawthorn

FIRST ADULT BOOK BY EILEEN RAYE

Moonlight Walk on the Turtlestones

FIRST YOUNG ADULT BOOK BY EILEEN RAYE

Lost in a Vampire Movie

CHILDREN'S BOOKS BY EILEEN RAYE

A Ghastly, Ghostly Night
Backyard Secrets Lost and Found

EILEEN RAYE

Alaine

of

Hawthorn

PAGE TURNER BOOKS INC.

Henderson, Nevada, USA

Alaine of Hawthorn, 1st Edition.
Story concept, text, map design, and cover concept © 2019-2024 by Eileen Raye.
Original editing and print preparation © 2019-2024 Leanne E. Staback, Ph.D.
Revision editing by Dr. Ray Cress and Liberty Davenport.
Back cover summary by Liberty Davenport.
Map and cover art © 2022-2024 by Eileen Raye, Sloane Hybarger, Cassandra Katsoulis, Leanne Staback and Dean Sutton. (See Bibliography for downloaded artwork used on cover).

Books may be ordered through popular, online retailers, Page Turner Books, Inc.'s online store, or by contacting the publisher at:

PAGE TURNER BOOKS, INC.
170 S. GREEN VALLEY PKWY., STE. 300
HENDERSON, NV 89012-3145

Visit our website at www.ptbooksinc.com or
contact us via email at contact@ptbooksinc.com.

Page Turner Books, Inc.'s name and logo are copyright of Page Turner Books, Inc.
ISBN: 978-1-958487-03-7 (Paperback Edition)
Printed in the United States of America.
First Paperback Printing: February 2024
Library of Congress Control Number: 2022950213

For Brittany,
the red-haired princess in our family.
Do not allow anyone to
hold you back from your dreams.

Lancet Forest
Central Road
Darkwood Lodge
Timber Road
Hawthorn
Juniper Lodge
Craig Keep
Eastgreen Highlands
Fillroy Hall
Elder Tree Forest
Inn
Gillis Hall
Char Road
Central Road
Seaken Hall
Oaks Forest
Dayt Ha
Ways Hall
Owlbrook Treehold
Middleoak Falls
Old Road
Eckelform Hall
Mareview Lowlands
Leggot
Staghorn Woods
Timber Road
Sunset Manor
Trees of the Lake
Brighton Towers
Harbortown
Hollybranch Forest
Irongate
Dune
Eastwi Hall

BOOK I

❧

THE JOURNEY

1

Journey's Eve

The moon was high in the cloudless sky, sending a shaft of silvery light through the tall, narrow window onto the stone floor. Shadows were exaggerated on the circular block walls of the high, tower room. Alaine sat upright in her bed, with the quilt of soft rabbit fur, filled with goose down, pulled up around her neck. It was the beginning of the warm season, but the nights still held a chill.

Hawthorn Castle was quiet, with possibly only the kitchen mice stir- ring. All the farewell banquet guests had finally left for the night or were asleep in their quarters with stomachs full of good food and wine. Alaine knew it must be very late, well past the midnight hour.

Two large trunks sat along the far wall with the contents carefully packed for travel, their rounded lids closed. Only her hairbrush and other items needed for dressing in the morning remained on a vanity table with its oval mirror. The travel gown, of the finest wool, was hung over the back of the chair. Alaine loved its adult style for a lady of high rank, and the color of a soft, woodland tan. The trim around the high, thick collar, and wide lapels was a fern green, which also decorated a strip around the hem of the long skirt. A brown hat was perched on the chair seat with its pheasant feathers rising along one side, pointing backwards from the brim. Brown suede boots and a small tapestry travel bag rested next to the chair on the rug.

Lastly, a sash, the crest of the Eastgreen Highland Kingdom embroidered onto the thick green material, hung from the arm of the chair. The shield of her father's lands was divided into four sections. The upper left displayed a hawthorn tree, representing the House of Hawthorn, denoting her father's heritage. The upper right showed a shaft of barley with its base encircled by the common fruits of the land. The lower left, displayed a stag with antlers standing by the edge of a forest glen, representing the large regions of pristine, wooded lands that remained untouched dotting the kingdom's wide regions. The final lower right quarter pictured the golden crown of the monarch, announcing the royal blood of the one attired with the sash.

The sash, a gift from King Granth to his daughter, became an object of discussion at the evening's banquet. Sergeant Covey, who retired from the Royal Guard when Alaine was a child to become her bodyguard, put forward the argument that the Princess should not wear the sash on her travels to the southern kingdom. He insisted that it was a safety factor for her to travel with some measure of anonymity. He argued that highways could be dangerous with marauders and bands of highwaymen that may find a princess of royal blood a prime catch as hostage, to be traded for riches. Queen Iris added her voice to the fray, pleading to err on the side of prudence. So, it was decided that the sash would be packed until the Princess reached her destination, only to be worn at the court of her uncle, King Holum Targ.

Across the room, a trio of yellow candles burned the last of their stems in the candelabra on the nightstand, casting a small circle of dim light. Now Alaine could let her tears flow freely. Tears forced back during the evening's farewell celebration. Tears that were hidden through the last few weeks of hectic preparations and goodbyes. She had also suppressed a touch of anger and resentment. Why was everyone so excited and joyful, although well- meaning, as her life was being turned upside down? The lords and ladies of court made their toasts of well wishes, but she was being sent away from her home and everything she loved! Some self-pity was certainly in order.

In a few short hours she would be donning the travel gown, dressing to leave her childhood room, her home, and her kingdom for marriage and a new life. After all, she was a princess of the realm, and she had the duty of a royal match of advantage. In the past few months, Alaine pondered how different the expectations would be had she been born a prince instead of a princess. The kingdom would have passed from her father, the King, to the son. Instead, as the only child with no brothers, all the hopes for the future of her people rested on *her* slim shoulders.

Her loving parents, dreading the day when she would leave them, had postponed any prospects of a marriage over the past two years. Many girls of her rank would have been betrothed from early years, but her mother demanded that she be allowed a childhood free of a betrothal. Yet, now, at sixteen, the need for a beneficial union could no longer be ignored. Alaine was a young woman of marriable age. As sleep neglected her, Alaine's mind churned with heavy thoughts.

On this same night, another young woman was tossing and turning on her bunk in King Granth's castle. She turned over and surveyed the small, narrow cell of a room. Her father was down the hall, probably in a spacious suite. A slim chink of a window let in a dim ray of light. The single candle had burnt out in its holder sitting on an aged, wooden dresser with drawers. She sighed, as the darkness matched her dismal mood.

She had no more tears of heartbreak to fall at this point, having had the past seven days to accept her fate. Her traveling satchel rested on a rickety chair, with her cloak draped across the back. Her dress for the next day lay across the foot of the thin bed. She, the Lady Charlyn, would be traveling in the morning as lady-in-waiting to the Princess Alaine.

On an afternoon of the past week, her father, Duke Noeman of the Walls, came on a rare visit to the rooms she shared with her younger sisters. He spoke of a request that came by courier from King Granth. His Highness asked for one of the Duke's three daughters to travel with his daughter, the Princess Alaine, to the lowland court of his brother, King Holum Targ.

"My dear, you know that we cannot refuse," the Duke persuaded. "I have been friends with Granth since we were boys. I served in his father's Guard. We live peacefully due to his support and protection, *and* we owe him this small favor."

"But, Father, I do not wish to go. Send Esbeth, she is the same age as the Princess and would be happy to go," Charlyn suggested.

"No, your mother and I have discussed this. You are the eldest and this is a great opportunity for you. The Princess Alaine travels to her uncle's court to meet suitors for her hand in marriage. Eligible men will be gathering. It is a chance for you to meet many nobles that never make it north to our secluded county," said the Duke, seeing the distress on his daughter's face. "You must not worry. You will be well chaperoned, and the King's Guard will accompany the royal coach and wagons."

"Father, I do not wish to leave here," insisted Charlyn.

"So, and why is that daughter?" the father asked. "Possibly a recently arrived young squire sent to Darkwood Lodge by his father for training? He may be handsome, dear one, but he is young, inexperienced and from a poor family. It may be his hopes for a dowry and my land holdings give rise to his charming attitude toward you. We have higher hopes for you, my little one. You must learn to use your youth and beauty wisely, and not throw away all your prospects for the first handsome face."

"Father...," she pleaded, tears filling her eyes.

"It is settled. You and I will leave in two days' time for King Granth's castle. Your mother will help you gather your belongings and gowns needed for court."

Now, since her arrival at Hawthorn Castle, Charlyn had barely seen the Princess. There were only glances across the tables at the evening's banquet. The royal guest of honor retired early from the dining hall. Charlyn sighed to herself, thinking there would be plenty of time to meet Princess Alaine on the travels that would begin in the morning. She yawned, but as much as Charlyn tried, sleep would not come to her. Pictures of her younger sister flirting with her handsome squire danced in her head.

Carver Vale reached to find a niche for his fingers between stones as he climbed Hawthorn Castle's high, surrounding wall. Having grown up among old forest trees and living in the lofty treehouses used by his people, scaling a wall was second nature to him. A lock of his long, light hair fell across the side of his face as he hoisted himself upward, while finding a foothold for his soft-soled shoes. It was after midnight and quiet, as he listened for any hint of a castle guardsman moving along the wall's interior.

Carver was taller than most in his family. His brothers teased him for his lithe figure. Though lean, he was strong and fast. There were rumors that his height was not from his father, who lacked stature, but from his mother, who was said to be a tall, willowy, wood nymph. Her child, it was told, was abandoned in the care of a mother deer. Carver's father, King Alfred of Sylvan, retrieved his son and raised him within his forest home. Alfred, possibly feeling some guilt for the child being brought up without a mother, gifted him with a quickness and the magic of illusion. Sometimes, Carver could pass unnoticed, a trait often found in the sprites and faeries of the woodlands.

Tonight, was just one of the many times Carver left Hewitt's home in the village, moved quickly along the alleys of the town, and went to the high ground that held the castle, surrounded by its tall, protective walls. Tonight was no different. He, and all the village, knew that the Princess Alaine would be leaving Hawthorn in the morning. One more time, he wished to sit by the wall of her garden, if only to be near her, maybe hear her voice, or get a glimpse of her through the open arches.

Carver knelt on the top of the wall and surveyed the great field that was next to the impending stone castle. The building's irregular footprint of walls was interrupted by tall, block towers with conical roofs. After generations of living in the dim light among forest trees, the clans of the forest developed acute night vision, and his was keen. Carver saw no sign of movement prior to his quiet leap to the ground below. He took a cautious look before he started across the field to the white, limestone walls of the garden toward the back of the estate.

The sound of a horse floated through the night air. He knew that the guardhouse and stables were set off to the side of the wide, reception courtyard, but all seemed clear for Carver as he moved on to his usual spot by the garden wall. His hopes were high. Surely tonight, of all nights, the person of his dreams would come to the garden.

Sitting on her bed, Alaine soon realized the uselessness of crying. She used the back of her hand to wipe her face. Wide awake, she thought of what she wanted to do with the last few hours at her beloved castle. Time was precious, so she would spend it in her favorite place – her garden.

Leaving the bed, she slipped her feet into her slippers. Opening the heavy lid of one of the trunks, she found her everyday cloak, which was neatly folded on the top. She drew it around her shoulders, fastening the clasp near her throat. Reaching back for the cowl, she pulled it up over her head, carefully covering her braided, red hair. There were many visitors in the castle, with all of the spare rooms in use. Alaine didn't wish to be recognized by a guest that might be wandering about, as she was well known for her beautiful, red locks.

By quickly swinging the door to her chamber open, Alaine avoided the creaking noise that happened when the door was opened slowly. Tiptoeing down the curving steps from her tower, she moved with speed along the silent hallway to the winding, grand staircase leading to the lower floors. The darkness of the hall was no barrier, as every flagstone and every curve of the wall, were well known. Down, down, down she descended until she reached the lowest landing. She took the narrow passage leading to the kitchens that were located at the back of the hold. The hallway opened into a long, rectangular space, dominated by a wall of fireplaces, brick ovens, and roasting spits. For now, all was still, but soon the early rising cooks would be busy. The tall wooden benches would be laden with their food preparations, while the day's breads and rolls baked in the ovens.

Cooks and servants were never surprised to see the girl hours before the sun came up. All that lived in the castle knew that the young Princess slept little and had earned her name as the "Sleepless Princess of Hawthorn". Tales were told for years of her nighttime wanderings and antics. Annie, the old cook, would tell of the frantic Queen Iris searching the castle in early morning hours looking for her fiery-haired little girl. So frequently would she end up in the kitchen, that Annie would leave a bun or piece of cake on a low bench that the child could reach – a small, nighttime treasure. Many times, her mother would find the Princess in a kitchen corner where Brownie, the cook's dog, had her blanket.

The harried parents, after trying many methods for keeping their child in bed at night, accepted the fact that Alaine didn't seem to need long hours of sleep. As the royal toddler grew and learned how to open doors, she began to wander outside at night, only to be brought back by the guards or stable boys. Alarmed, King Granth consulted a builder and designed an enclosed garden for the child. The walled-in retreat was built off the kitchens, next to the spacious vegetable gardens. The new garden had one entrance from the exterior yard, secured with a lock and a bar across the outside gate. A small doorway was opened in the kitchen wall for entrance to the garden, having a low door handle that was easily reached by the little girl.

Now, at her full height, Alaine ducked her head as she went through the low portal into her private garden. The cool air hit her face and she lowered the cowl on her cloak. She walked down the flagstone central path, around the fountain, and on to her wooden bench where she usually sat at the far end of the cultivated plot. The roofless square gave an unobstructed view of the night sky and its luminous light. The white limestone walls glowed and the tall, open arches on an outside wall allowed glimpses of the flat, resting field and the tops of the forest trees beyond the castle's boundary wall. The sound of the soft trickle of water drifted from the fountain. Beds of various white blooms glistened, reflecting the moonlight, as statuary of small animals stoically stood guard. Alaine relaxed and tried to ready herself for the day ahead.

Carver Vale sat crouched in his familiar spot outside the garden's lime- stone wall by the wood pile. He worked on a piece of wood with a sharp, little knife. He listened quietly as the Princess hummed a tune that he had heard many times before. His ear was also trained on any noise that might harken to his discovery. His fears were not intense since he had never been discovered on his many previous visits.

Carver received his name from an elder brother, who called him the woodcarver. As a child, he spent his days in the forest making small houses for animals out of fallen logs and tree stumps. He moved on to carving sophisticated hidey-holes for the pixies and faeries. Carver's clever doorways protected the entrances and exits for the gnomes, who preferred to live underground. His brothers teased him for his wood carvings but were actually proud of his talents.

Once, at Winterfest, he took some of his carvings to Hawthorn Village and gave them to young children as toys. Talk of his skills spread through the town, when the blacksmith's wife allowed him to display small carvings for sale on her front windowsill. Soon, he was being asked to make cupboards for housewives, chairs for the firesides, and cradles for the newborns. All his pieces would be intricately carved with leaves, flowers, and forest inhabitants. So frequently was he in the town, that he became a familiar sight to the people. They believed he traveled from the countryside to bring his furniture, cupboards, and wood carvings to the blacksmith's shop for sale.

Little did the villagers know that he was a prince of the forest, being the seventh son of King Alfred. In Carver's thinking, his desire for his beloved Princess was not above his station. His father ruled over forest lands covering vast parts of the Eastgreen Highlands and the Mareview Lowland Kingdoms. Carver's older brothers had already staked out their claims to forest plots, while he remained in Elder Tree Forest with his father. Yet, Carver had no formal position, as the Prince that he was. Being a prince as the son of the woodland king was not recognized by people of the country of Hawthorn. Their peoples lived separately. He was just a part of the myths and folklore that belonged to the deep woods. With very little in worldly wealth and goods to offer, there was little hope for Alaine's hand as his bride. However, the impossible situation did not dissuade him from his desires.

Although Carver and Alaine had never formally met, he felt he knew her well - not only by the talk of the townsfolk, the glimpses of her during her daytime outings from the castle, but from the time spent next to the wall of her garden.

It was a quiet night, not reckoning to the morrow's fanfare at the castle. The air was calm, with no hint of a breeze. The frost would not be visiting. Even the dew would keep to the woods tonight. Notes of a softly sung song floated in the air.

The Duchess of Leigh knocked on the chamber door of Queen Iris. Upon hearing a soft-voiced call for entry, she went into the spacious room and was not surprised to find her sister at the window, gazing down upon the small, enclosed garden. The Queen was fully dressed, holding a finely embroidered, linen handkerchief, possibly used to wipe a mother's tears.

"She was down in the garden last night. I knew that she would want a last look before she left," Iris said, knowing that there was no explanation needed that she was speaking of the Princess.

Lady Avis joined her sister at the window and looked down upon the space.

"Where is she now?"

"Probably down with the kitchen folk for a last goodbye. You know how attached she is to all of them. I sometimes think I did wrong in allowing her to take over all the housekeeping duties for the kitchens, but it seemed to be the only way to have peace between our housekeeper and Alaine, who was always interfering with how the kitchens did things. Now, Lentil will have to take over again, and the cooks will have to adjust," said the Queen. "At least my daughter is well prepared to oversee the management of a castle. Her efforts have been efficient and kindled good will with the vendors that help supply the castle with goods. She surpassed herself with last night's banquet. Everyone seemed quite satisfied with the fare."

"I agree, sister." Then looking at the tiredness reflected on the Queen's face, "How are *you* faring this morning?"

"Well, we all knew this day was coming. I thought that I had prepared myself. It looks like the weather is fair for the traveling. I just wish that I was going along," she exclaimed, with a sigh. "Thank goodness that you agreed to go with her in my stead. Alaine is so young, and she has never been away from us except for the summer trips to your Juniper Lodge. She thinks the whole world runs as our quiet village."

"Couldn't you have asked to accompany the child?"

The Queen walked away from the window and went to her dressing table. She draped her white, silk wimple to cover most of her auburn braids hanging down her back, then added a thin, gold coronet of pearls that wrapped around her forehead and head.

"Oh, you know of that already, sister. For one thing, I wasn't afforded an invitation by my fair sister-in-law, Queen Hester. For another, no castle needs *two* queens under its roof at once. Besides, Granth would never approve of me pushing my way in. He is always so careful about propriety and respect for his brother's court."

"Speaking of Granth, where is he?" Lady Avis inquired.

"He got up early and went down with Covey. Granth insists on overseeing the preparations. He's probably sending too many guardsmen, which will surely draw attention in the countryside. Then there are the supply wagons and whatever else is needed for the seven-day journey. They need one wagon just for ladies' trunks. It will be a long train of wagons."

"I peeked my head into Nana's room. She's in a dither, and still packing. I believe she is planning to take all that she owns. Not only will I have the girls to look after, but Nana, too. She's sometimes like a child herself," Lady Avis exclaimed, with exasperation.

"Now Avis, you know how old she is getting. She never asks for anything and is so thankful for being part of the household. When she said that she wished to look upon the sea one more time in her life, how could I refuse her? Mother is probably looking down on us and smiling for giving in to her wishes."

"It is easy for you to say," she replied. "I think that mother is probably laughing out loud that now I am charged with looking after the nanny that we plagued so when we were in her care. Nana is a good, old bird, but nonetheless trying at times," Lady Avis asserted.

"What about the Lady Charlyn?" asked the Queen. "She is such a fair girl. Is she up and about yet?"

"I didn't see her this morning. She seemed not to be very sociable last eve. In fact, she looked quite miserable sitting there next to her father, Duke Noeman."

"Granth was telling me last night that there is a story about her. It seems that the girl has lost her heart to a handsome squire that came to the Duke for training. So, she was much against being forced to leave home. The Duke expressed his thanks to Granth for the opportune invitation. Her father felt that it took the lass away from a possible entanglement, while offering a rare chance to visit Irongate Castle by the sea."

"This is getting better and better," the elder sister said, shaking her head. "Seven days in a bumpy coach with a princess who believes that she is being sent to her doom rather than to a betrothal, a heart-broken, miserable lady-in-waiting, and a feeble nanny that is half confused. Is it too late to withdraw from this disastrous journey?"

The Queen giggled at her sister making a face.

"Yes, it is too late," Iris said, putting her arms around the Duchess. "Other than her father, and the doting Sergeant Covey, you are the only one I would trust to look out for Alaine's interests. I am sure that Hester has something up *her* sleeve. It would be unlike her not to find some benefit to *her* from a potential marriage. I am fearful for my girl. She is naïve and gullible. She has never been exposed to treachery. She will believe whatever she is told, never thinking that it might not be the best path for her. You must be vigilant, sister."

"You are probably right, my dear. I'll do the best that I can for her," Avis acquiesced. "Come, let's go find Alaine and Lady Charlyn. We need to be on our way."

Lady Charlyn gave up on any hope of sleep and arose from the uncomfortable cot before sunrise. She lit another candle, which she found in the top drawer of the dresser and proceeded to dress for the day of travel. Her underdress was a fine, soft linen. On top of that went the silk underskirt, layered with lace. Lastly, she put on the woolen, long-sleeved dress. The goldenrod-colored gown's bodice had gold ribbon laces that tied at her waist. The long skirt flowed to her ankles. Warm hose and black leather boots finished her outfit.

Next, she tackled her braids, using a small mirror and brush that she removed from her travel satchel. She and all her sisters had hair that flowed down their backs to the waist. Braiding and coils seemed to be the only way to tame the blonde hair and style it in a way that was expected for young ladies. Charlyn wrapped the two thick braids around the top of her head and fastened them with pins. Next, a gathered, silk scarf was placed so that it flowed down the back of her head. Then, the black velvet beret with gold braid was added, covering the top of her head with an attractive droop to one side.

She draped her cloak over her shoulders, looked around to make sure she left nothing behind, and blew out the candle. Morning's light was peeking through the slit of a window. Grabbing her travel bag, she left the room.

Alaine ran up the stairs, still eating the warm, buttered roll she had stolen from the kitchen. The scullery was abuzz. Saying goodbye to the kitchen people had brought tears, hugs, and good wishes. Annie and Oween were in the throes of last-minute preparations, since they would travel with the company going to the seacoast. There would be few places to stop along the road to the Lowland Kingdom, so food supplies and cooks would be needed for the daily encampments.

Once in her room, Alaine proceeded with dressing. Sitting on a stool at the small vanity table and mirror, she readied her braids for a coil at the back of her head. She placed the hat on her head, adding two decorative pins as anchors. Approving the reflection, she saw that her red locks were covered, for the most part. The image in the mirror portrayed a young woman older than Alaine felt.

After a knock at the chamber door, Genna, Alaine's maid, entered the room. Genna was eighteen and had grown up in the castle. Working in the kitchen with her mother at a young age, she was later trained by the Queen's maid to be a lady's maid. When Alaine turned thirteen, the Queen knew it was time for the Princess to throw off her girlish clothing and put up her hair. So, Genna came to wait on the Princess. Although they were royalty and servant, the girls had a strong bond. There were no secrets in the castle and the two were frequently laughing behind closed doors about the gossip of the day. Genna was Alaine's accomplice in frequent follies and would accompany the Princess on forays outside the castle walls, all to Sergeant Covey's dismay. There was an understanding between the young women and a history of shared secrets.

Genna was surprised to see her mistress already dressed.

"I'm sorry, milady, Rand had come to my room for my case, and I was still packing."

"That's fine, Genna. After all, you spent the day, yesterday, helping with packing my things and my preparations for the banquet."

Alaine was so glad that Genna would be going along on her travels. It was expected that a noblewoman would have a maid. She wouldn't have felt comfortable having a stranger to help her with bathing and dressing. Not to mention Genna's talent in managing and styling her hair, which seemed to have a mind of its own.

"Since you are already dressed, should I tell Rand that he can come to take your trunks down? He told me that most of the wagons are already loaded."

"Yes," answered Alaine, "and how is Rand this morning? Is he happy that you will be traveling?"

It was known that Genna and Rand had an affection for one another, but Genna's mother had been strong in her objection to any type of relationship. "It's hard to tell. You know how grumpy he can be. Today he is all about getting to his work."

"Oh, I think that he is glad you are going along," the Princess said, with a knowing smile. "He's probably happy for a chance of seeing you away from the castle and out from under your mother's eye."

"Maybe so, but mother is in no hurry to see me wed, even though I will be nineteen soon. I'm not sure why she doesn't think Rand and I would do well. He has a trusted position here."

"My father says that there will be many unattached men at my uncle's court. He says that Harbortown of Mareview is full of merchants that come there to sell their trade goods. Maybe your pretty brown eyes will attract a handsome, rich merchant that will marry you and whisk you off to a faraway land."

Genna laughed, "I'm not sure that a rich trader would be looking for a servant girl that knows nothing of the world. On the other hand, if Rand and I made a match, maybe you and I would still see each other."

"Maybe, if it is not *I* that is taken off to some far-off place," Alaine said with some sadness, as the reason for her travel to Irongate Castle came rushing back to her mind. Alaine looked around at her beloved tower room. "I think that I'm ready to go down."

"I will see to your trunks, milady," Genna said formally, sensing Alaine's sudden sadness.

The Princess descended the grand staircase, carrying her tapestry travel bag. One of the hall's immense, wooden doors was propped open, allowing a view of the bustling courtyard beyond. Wagons and carriages with their horses stood in a line as porters, stablemen, and soldiers of the Guard milled about with their last-minute tasks. Sounds of the activity echoed into the hall. The Lady Charlyn looked small, standing all alone in the great entrance foyer.

Alaine had barely seen her lady-in-waiting at the banquet the previous evening. Lady Charlyn was about her own age, maybe a little older. Though her travel clothes were fairly plain, they only accented how lovely Charlyn was. Her hair and skin were fair. Her forehead was high, above large, pale-blue eyes. Her skin was unblemished, and her cheeks and lips were pink. She did not smile as Alaine came near but lowered her head and curtsied.

"Lady Charlyn, I must thank you for joining me on my journey. I must admit that I am a novice at traveling," said Alaine.

"It is my pleasure, milady," Charlyn replied, trying to sound as if she meant it. "I too have very little travel experience."

"We will have to help each other," Alaine said, in a friendly manner. "Has your father come down yet?"

"Oh, yes," the Lady replied, "He took his leave of me some time ago. It is a long ride back to Darkwood Lodge. It will be past nightfall before he arrives home."

Out of the corner of her eye, Alaine saw her mother and Aunt Avis coming down the stairs. Behind them, Genna was assisting Nana on her trek downward. The nurse, dressed in a modest gray gown and brown cape, had a firm hold on the banister.

Approaching the two girls, the Queen said, "Well, you two appear to be ready to depart." Then, turning to the young lady-in-waiting, "Thank you, Lady Charlyn, for joining Alaine on this very important journey. It will be good for her to have a travel companion near her own age."

"I can do it! I can do it!" Nana's voice rang out, as she brushed Genna aside at the bottom of the staircase. "Now that I'm on flat ground I can walk on my own."

Lady Avis hurried to her side. "I'll walk with you Nana," Lady Avis said, gently. "We're ready to go out to the coach."

"First, I have one last gift for my daughter," said Queen Iris, holding out a small pouch that jangled when moved.

Taking the purse and shaking it, Alaine looked at her mother, puzzled by the gift of coins.

"Mother, what is this for?"

"Before you make a choice of any suitor, you must learn all that you can about them. People are not always as they seem. A well-placed coin can help loosen a tongue to gather information from attendants, and people with knowledge about a person. Your Aunt Avis will also try to learn all that she can regarding someone seeking your hand in marriage. You must promise me to listen to her advice, as you would listen to mine."

Alaine could see how serious her mother was with her words and with the concern showing on her mother's face.

"I will, Mama."

"Be safe, my little one," her mother said, before a last kiss on the cheek and firm embrace. Then, "Come, we must all go out."

As the five ladies walked down the front steps and on to the royal carriage, a kitchen girl ran up to the group, handing a covered basket to Lady Avis.

"Some treats and drink for your journey, Mistress," she said, breathlessly.

"Thank you, Hildie," answered the Lady. "It will be a long ride before we reach the inn this evening. Please give our regards to Cook."

"Let me help you into the coach," said Queen Iris to Nana, knowing that it would be a slow process.

Suddenly, a member of the Guard rode up to the royal carriage on his horse, reigning it to a halt, and dismounting next to the traveling ladies. He held a silver flask in one hand, giving it to Lady Avis.

"For your journey, madam, should any of your charges feel faint."

"And what is this?" Lady Avis asked, smiling, adding the flask to the basket.

"It is a fine brandy that will dispel any vapors. Or maybe it can be a sip for you, Nana," he said, as he winked at the aged nursemaid.

Nana smiled, enjoying the attention of the handsome young man.

"Who is this?" the soldier chided, walking around the Princess, looking her over. "What, no masses of red locks flying? No dragging petticoat and muddy boots? No smudge of grime on the cheek? Can this possibly be the Princess Alaine?"

The Queen and Lady Avis chuckled at the young man's impertinence. Alaine could feel the flush rising in her face. She set her jaw in a determined stare at the man, already plotting a revenge.

"Ah, there it is," he said, looking at Alaine. "The determined eye of an avenger, when all I am here for is to wish you well, my dear Princess." Then, in a more serious tone to the older ladies, "I have divided my garrison for some to ride in front of the wagons and some to ride at the back. Members of the castle Guard will ride alongside at intervals. Also, I have sent two scouts out ahead of us as a precaution. Board your coach, ladies," he ordered with a sweeping bow. "We will be departing shortly."

"Thank you, and safe travels, Captain Leigh," replied Queen Iris, as the soldier grabbed the reigns of his horse, and mounted it effortlessly.

Lady Charlyn was taken aback at the interactions that had just transpired, and the seeming acceptance of the soldier's arrogance toward the royal party. Mostly, she was shocked at his behavior toward Alaine. How could he be allowed to embarrass her so? She watched as he rode toward the front of the line of wagons. Even if he was a Captain in the Guard, Charlyn felt that he had breached all forms of etiquette. She was *not* impressed, even though she had to admit that her interest was piqued. Who *was* he? she wondered.

In the early morning hours, Carver Vale sped upon the well-used paths of the deep woods to the verdant copse of trees that surrounded his father's stronghold. He went directly to the woodland King's chamber and awoke him from his slumbers.

"Father, I must speak with you right away," he demanded, in a pleading voice.

The small, portly man aroused himself, propping up his head on his hand, looking at his son.

"What is it, boy?" he asked, gruffly.

"Father, the Princess Alaine is leaving the castle today to travel to the seacoast."

"Yes," the King replied, unfazed. "I am told that she goes to find a husband at King Holum's court."

"Our woodlands follow the Central Road from the highlands most of the way to the seacoast. I would ask your permission to follow her company on the journey. I could stay to the woods."

Now the regal man sat up, looking at his child with concern and some sadness. He, too, had once lost his heart to a hopeless love.

"To what end, son? Your desire for the Princess Alaine is misplaced. We have already discussed this. She is a princess that is destined to marry and produce a male heir to carry on the royal lineage. Her child will become King of the Highland Kingdom. This obsession of yours is nonsense, and I do not support it."

"Father, I wish to follow her, meet her, speak to her," Carver said with desperation. "I wish to have a chance to win her for myself. Am I not a prince, as royal as herself?"

"It is an unlikely match, even if you could somehow convince her to marry you. King Granth would never approve it. The people of the land do not recognize us. It is unheard of for a prince of the forest to marry a princess of the land."

"Just allow me a chance, father. If she chooses another, I will come home and live a solitary life. I will keep to our old woods and shun their world."

"I can see that you will not be happy unless you pursue this; so, with a heavy heart, I give you my permission to follow the Princess. Be careful, son, lest disaster fall to you both."

With that, Carver was off, leaving the old man mumbling to himself.

King Granth watched as the Duke of Leigh mounted his stallion and rode toward the front of the line of wagons already formed outside the castle gates. Except for the lack of beard, the boy looked more like his father every day. Granth still missed his old friend, and brother-in-law, Norbert Morr-Leigh, the former Duke of Leigh, who had suffered a sudden attack of illness five summers before. His son Kent had inherited his title at the young age of twenty-one.

The monarch had to admit that the young man's plan for the positioning of the Guard and the wagons would provide utmost protection during travel. Unlike the Hawthorn Castle Guard, he and his garrison were the only ones to have seen any measure of real battle of late. The Captain had recently returned after four seasons absence in helping an ally, old King Walkin, defend a far northern border from invasion. Granth was glad to have Kent and his men accompany his only child on this trip.

It was the young Duke's decision to send the scouts on ahead. King Granth thought this a good idea. He also approved the strategy for the positioning of his men and the guardsmen from the castle.

Behind Leigh's men would follow the garrison supply wagons carrying tents and rations, followed by the garrison's cook's wagon. Then would be the wagons with the sleeping tents for the ladies, and a wagon of their trunks. Toward the middle would be the royal coach, which Sergeant Covey would ride atop as a guard. Rand would drive the two strongest mares from Hawthorn's stables. The Cook's covered wagon, carrying staff and cookware, would be followed by another wagon of food supplies. Next was the largest wagon, carrying two great tents, one for use as an eating pavilion and the other for cooking and sleeping quarters for women servants. The rest of Leigh's soldiers would hover around the rear of the parade. The last two wagons, carrying firewood and extra hay for the horses, could be set on fire to block the road to defend an attack from the rear if the need arose.

With all the preparations completed, it was now time for King Granth to take leave of his daughter. He accompanied Covey to the royal coach and came to stand with the waiting ladies.

"Good morning, Lady Avis and Lady Charlyn," the King said politely, after they both curtsied. Turning to Alaine, "Well, daughter, are you prepared to leave?"

"I am, father, but I will miss yourself and mother, as I will miss this stone house and all that live here," said the Princess.

"We will miss you also, but there is the excitement of a wedding to look forward to. Soon you will establish your own household. I believe that you are well prepared, thanks to your good mother," said the King. Then he pulled a chain with large links from the pocket of his overcoat and handed it to Alaine. "A travel gift for you, my dear."

"Granth, you know that we sent fine jewels that match each of her dresses for court. They are to be part of her dowry," said Queen Iris.

"Yes, my Queen, but this is a particular gift."

Alaine examined the chain and realized that a long pendant shaped as a dragonfly was attached. The bug's eyes were small sapphires, latticed wings were embedded with pearls, and its long body was a lifelike sculpture resembling the insect.

"It is beautiful, father. Thank you."

"Find the button on the underside of the wing and press it," the King instructed.

Alaine felt around and found the metal button, pushed it, and heard a tiny click.

"Now, pull on the wing."

As Alaine pulled on the wing, a previously hidden, metal stiletto appeared – a sharp, thin blade almost as long as her hand. The surrounding women gasped as they saw the clever dagger.

"Father…!"

"The chain can be worn around your waist as a belt or around your neck. The dragonfly pendant can be removed and carried in the pocket of your cape. It is for your protection – a last resort if your life is in danger.

Should you need to use it, aim for the neck, and thrust upward. That is usually a vulnerable spot," insisted the King. "Put on the chain. Keep the blade on your person and tell no one of its secret."

Alaine attached the clasp of the chain around her waist, letting the innocent-appearing dragonfly hang by her side.

"That is gruesome, Granth," said the Queen, "but it gives me some ease. She will not be helpless, in any case."

The King leaned forward and embraced his daughter. If one looked closely, there may have been a tear in his eye.

"You must board the coach now. The line of wagons is beginning to move. All of you, climb in!" he ordered, gruffly.

The coach was loaded with its passengers, the door was closed and latched, and it began to move toward the Hawthorn Castle gates. The King and Queen stood together with mixed emotions, watching their daughter's departure.

3

The Road
to Crossroads Inn

Hewitt watched his young friend as he stood at the front of the lean-to where the forge was located – the heart of his blacksmithing work. Carver was intent on the passing troops on horses and the array of wagons as they went by. Slowly, the procession moved along the compacted, dirt road going through Hawthorn Village toward the ancient, stone bridge that made its humped roadway across the River Ways. The bridge marked the edge of the village. Once across the stone overpass, the winding road made its way through the beginnings of the rural countryside that surrounded the town.

Hewitt had come to Hawthorn years ago from his father's farm down- country. Like many young lads, he wanted to join the famous Castle Guard. Instead, being a youngster with no noble connections, he was taken on as a stable boy at the busy castle stables. He was a tall, broad, young man. His strength and gentleness with the horses were soon noticed by the castle smithy, who was on lookout for an apprentice to ease his workload. The old farrier started the boy with horseshoes and tack and was not disappointed in Hewitt's ability for the tasks of molding the iron shoes. As time passed, Hewitt grew into his manhood and his blacksmith's skills ripened.

One day, down in the village, everything changed, when a pretty young widow, with a babe in her arms, looked him up and down and gave him an inviting smile. In no time at all, the two were wed and settled into her cottage on the main street of town. Finnie encouraged Hewitt to leave the castle, build a lean-to on the lot next to the house, and start his own shop. Soon the forge was installed, and a sign of his trade was put on the roof.

Now, twelve summers and three children later, the cottage of Hewitt and Finnie was bursting at its seams, with Finnie using the front room as a shop. Not only did she sell the metal pots, spoons and bowls forged by Hewitt, but also the wood carvings, boxes, and small pieces of furniture brought to town in Carver Vale's two-wheeled pull cart. She took a penny or two for selling the wood, but Carver was always thankful for whatever price she got. The lad seemed to have little use or care for money, so it was put aside for him.

Today, the wagons of the royal caravan rattled by, kicking up the dust along the road. Hewitt's two girls ran out of the house and positioned themselves in front of Carver. They jumped up and down with excitement, waiting to see the royal coach, hoping for a glimpse of the Princess. Standing behind the girls, Carver was just as intent on seeing Alaine.

Hewitt watched Carver and his girls. He was aware of his young friend's admiration for the Princess of Hawthorn. Hewitt first met Carver Vale as a shy, curious lad who came to the village - from where, he never knew. Carver often sat on a stone by the bridge, with a small knife and a piece of wood, chipping away. Finnie took a liking to him and his little carvings that he handed out to the children.

At first, Carver spoke little, but did respond when spoken to. His clothing set him apart from the townspeople. The clothes were plain with no buttons or decorations. His long shirt was tan, with the softness of a mushroom cap, and was belted at his thin waist by a braided strap. Soft deerskin made practical pants. The vest with laces in the front also looked like some type of tanned skin. The boots that covered his ankles had soft, leather soles. On cool or rainy days, he wore a slick, green cape lined with black fur. Once, he used a coin that Finnie had given him to buy a pair of woolen socks, saying he liked the comfort they gave his feet.

At the time Carver first started coming to the village, it was not uncommon for the young Princess to come into town with her mother. Baskets of food were frequently delivered to the old or sick. It was on one of those occasions that Carver first saw Alaine with her red, flowing curls, sparkling, blue eyes, and laughing mouth.

"Who was she?" he had asked Hewitt that day.

Soon Hewitt noticed that when the Princess was about, Carver would be lurking somewhere on the sidelines.

Alaine was famous in the village for the stories of her childhood deeds, and a secret garden where she would pass the long hours. Hewitt saw that the boy would come into town with his pull cart carrying his goods for sale, leave it at Hewitt's place, and disappear sometime after dinner. In the mornings, when the blacksmith went out to his forge, the cart, Carver, and his dog, Astra, would be gone. Although it was never discussed, Hewitt came to think that Carver was going up to the castle at night to be near the Princess. He feared for Carver's safety if, as he assumed, the lad was somehow breaching the castle walls. Yet, the young man's quiet obsession for the girl seemed to grow over time. He wondered how Carver would take the loss of the Princess as she went off to find her husband and possibly leave Hawthorn Castle for good.

Today, as the royal coach approached, the girls were yelling and waving their arms, trying to get the attention of the noble passengers. Carver put hands on their shoulders to safeguard them from straying too far into the road. There was a quick peek, a tiny look, at the Princess looking out the small, coach window as the large wheels rolled by. Watching until the royal carriage was down the road, the girls turned and ran toward their father.

"We saw her, father! We saw her look out the window!" exclaimed Nells. "She was wearing a hat, and she was so pretty!"

"Yes, that was the excitement for the day," said Hewitt. "Now run into the house and tell your mother what you saw."

Carver was approaching him, as Hewitt shooed the girls toward the cottage.

"I am going to be gone for a while," Carver said, in his soft voice. "Can I leave my cart here with you?"

"You will follow her?" Hewitt asked, with no need to mention of whom he was speaking.

Carver nodded his head. "I will take Astra with me," he said, referring to his large dog. The animal had come to stand by his side, sensing that his master would be leaving soon.

Hewitt went to his cupboards, and from a lower shelf withdrew a bag that tinkled with coins and handed it over.

"If you travel to the lowlands, you may need this. Finnie has been saving it for you. It is plenty of coin for food and drink during your travels, and maybe a new suit of clothes," Hewitt said, looking down at Carver's well-used clothing. "Will you travel along the road?"

"I can travel by road but take shortcuts across the countryside and through the woods."

"Carver, why do you follow her? To what end?" asked Hewitt, with some concern.

"I don't know, but I must find out what happens to her. Maybe I can find a way to meet her. Thanks for this," he said, changing the subject and stowing the pouch in his pocket. "I'll go down the street to get some supplies and be on my way."

Hewitt slapped the young man on the shoulders in an affectionate manner. "Be careful and travel safe. Come back when your quest is done. You know that you are always welcome here."

"Thank you, Hewitt. I must be off. Say goodbye to Finnie for me."

In a flash, Carver was gone. Hewitt could never understand how the boy could move with such a quickness. There was some sort of magic about that lad, he thought, scratching his head.

Alaine and Charlyn sat quietly next to each other, thinking their own thoughts, while gazing out the side windows at the passing fields and scenery. The skies were blue, the morning sun was moving high in the sky, and the temperature was comfortable. They couldn't have asked for a better travel day.

The ride in the coach was not as comfortable as Alaine thought it would be. The interior was rather cramped with four ladies in long skirts, their individual travel bags, as well as the basket of food and drink. Once out of the town, the smoothness of the road changed to have some deep ruts causing movement to-and-fro felt by the inside passengers. Poor Nana had pulled out her knitting, thinking it would be a good way to while away the time. However, she soon relented due to the bumps and bounces that made the needlework impossible. Now, she dozed, sometimes with a slight snore, despite the rocking ride.

Alaine was feeling a pool of emotions as the carriage moved along, and her mind wandered from the country scene. When they traveled through Hawthorn Village, the people and children of the town lined the thoroughfare, cheering as they went by. She recognized all the faces and felt their good wishes for her in her heart. There was also the sadness in leaving her home, knowing that her life would never be the same. She wondered if she would ever see the town and its people again. Feeling sorry for herself, she could not hold back the tears that welled up in her eyes.

Watching Alaine's expressions, Lady Avis knew her niece well and could imagine the thoughts going through the girl's mind.

"Don't fret, dear. This is a great adventure for you. It's something you will tell your children about. It is your time to step out in the world. Try to enjoy your time in the sun."

"I am fearful that I'm losing everything that I know. Will I ever see my village again? Will I live the rest of my life away from mother and father? And also, away from you and your beautiful Juniper Lodge?"

"You are going to your uncle's Irongate Castle to be presented at court. This is to allow suitors to apply for your hand in marriage," the aunt asserted. "You will have a say in who you choose. Unlike many kings, your father has said that you will not be forced to marry against your wishes. The future beyond that will be according to the arrangements made in the wedding contract."

"Yes," replied Alaine, "but you have to admit that it is overwhelming."

"I'm sure that it is," the older woman agreed. "Yet, we are all here for you - here to support you. Let's not wish for troubles that have not presented themselves. Let's make the best of things, like today, a beautiful day." That being said, the interior of the coach drifted into silence.

Carver left Hewitt's place and went down the village road to a shop that sold clothing and other dry goods. He found a leather pouch with a flap and a strap that he could sling over his shoulder. He picked a white, linen shirt with long sleeves and ties at the neck in front. He also found a long, brown cloak with a hood and deep pockets. It was of a heavy, rustic weave that could double as a blanket at night, if he was not traveling. Lastly, he added a pair of hose – he had grown accustomed to woolen socks.

In another shop, he found a tin cup, a small pot, and a bowl. He bought bags of barley and oats. At the bakery he bought a loaf of bread, and mutton pasties for him and the dog. Astra was a big dog and needed almost as much food as Carver, so his last stop was the butcher's. There he bought salt pork, jerky, and sausage. The butcher offered some fresh steamed liver and kidney that would do Astra for a couple days.

Putting on the cloak, Carver packed all the goods into the pouch and slung it over his shoulder. Almost instantly, he was out of town, headed toward his familiar forest to begin the long walk south. He was able to guess where the royal caravan was headed today. A roadway that crossed the busy Central Road was heavily used by farmers to transport grain, produce and livestock. An inn had been there for many years and did a fair business serving travelers. Carver believed this would be the first stop for the royal party.

Carver entered his woods, using familiar pathways going south. Astra loped along at his side. Astra was large for a dog, reaching Carver's waist when standing on all fours. Carver never could have guessed how big the dog would get when he first found her as a puppy.

One day the lad had been on his way to Hewitt's, pulling the cart, when he came across a burlap bag in the road. Carver thought the bag moved and heard a smothered sound coming from inside. Curiosity got the best of him, so, retrieving the bag and opening the drawstring at its top, two dead puppies were found, and one still alive and whimpering. Surprised at the find, the weakling was put into the cart and taken to Hewitt's place. Finnie, being soft-hearted and used to caring for chickens, rabbits, and a flock of noisy geese, not to mention a husband and children, took on the mission of keeping the pup alive. She fed it barley cooked with mutton scraps and gravy. In a week, the puppy was running around the house after the kids. Astra, as Finnie had named her, grew faster than the children. In weeks, she was all legs and out of control, nipping and chewing on everything she could get her mouth on. Finnie put her foot down, sending the pup to the lean-to with Hewitt. She told Carver to take the dog with him when he left before there was nothing left in her house without teeth marks!

So, Carver and Astra became a duo. Where Carver went, the dog followed. When Carver ate, Astra ate. Carver, with Hewitt's help, fashioned a harness that hooked to his small cart, and he trained the dog to pull the cart with little effort for such a large dog. Now fully grown, and settled down, Astra was tall and sleek, with a long nose and short ears. Her hair was short and brindle in color. Finnie called her the tan ghost, with her quickness and grace. Her eyes were gold in color. Carver wondered if there was wolf blood in her heritage. She was good with children and thought that she was just another of Hewitt's brood, licking, jumping, and playing with them. Her quiet place at Hewitt's was outside the house, on a blanket next to the forge. There she would stay and wait for Carver when he went off on his nighttime ramblings.

Carver was thankful for his loyal companion. They took care of one another. Today, Astra was glad to be back in her woods. She knew that this was Carver's real domain, and her adopted home. Carver was moving quickly, but she kept up with little effort.

Charlyn was thankful for the quiet inside the royal coach. She had time to escape to her fantasies. Occasionally conversation began inside the coach, and she would take part. But soon the talking died away, and silence prevailed. Lady Charlyn had a habit of allowing her mind to drift to her favorite topic - Squire Wilken Chason, who was known to her as "Will". Her daydreams would feature her squire and herself in romantic settings. Though he was far away from her now, and getting farther away every minute, he was not forgotten. She promised him her heart, gave him her handkerchief, and told him she would return soon.

She pictured him in her mind. His tall frame with wide shoulders. His long brown hair tied at the back of his neck, with some falling onto his forehead in its carefree manner. His eyes were blue with dark lashes, under an expressive brow. They seemed to look deep into her soul. His face was tanned and serious, but when he smiled, his face lit up and made her heart pound. She relived their conversations and the occasional touch of the hand. How she longed to feel his lips on hers in a kiss – it would be a perfect kiss, she knew. These were her daydreams.

One person that did *not* intrude into her dreams was her sister, Esbeth. How Charlyn wished that it was her sister riding in the coach instead of herself. Esbeth was sixteen and only a winter her junior. When Esbeth learned that Charlyn had romantic feelings toward the good-looking squire, she took it on as a competition as to who would win the squire's heart.

Esbeth had not only matured as much as Charlyn but had surpassed her in the size of her bosom and the curve of her hip. Looking at the two sisters, it was hard to tell which was the elder. Charlyn was taller, thinner and fair. Esbeth was more voluptuous, with a pretty, round face and light brown hair.

Their youngest sister, Closin, was now fourteen and was starting to make her change to becoming a young woman. Just recently, she had put her hair up and begun wearing the more mature clothing as her older sisters. Charlyn had a closer relationship with Closin.

Esbeth was also a flirt with all the young men that came for training at their father's lodge. Her mother, more than once, sent her from the downstairs hall for the sparse coverage of her bodice or wearing her hair loose down her back with no scarf or covering as was appropriate for young ladies. Their mother frequently said that the girl was begging for trouble and that there would be no peace in the house until she was wed.

Charlyn hated the fact that Esbeth was at home and had time to pursue the one man that she wished to marry. How bad was the timing of this journey? Such were her musings as the coach bounced along the road to the inn.

For the travelers, there was only one stop of the caravan during the day. It was a chance to have some food and the ability to hold a cup for a drink without the liquid spilling out. It was also the only opportunity to answer the call of nature. So, the women of the cook's wagon and the ladies of the coach trooped off together to a nearby group of oak trees surrounded by low bushes. One by one, they took their turns while the others stood guard. It was an unhappy necessity.

Again underway, the afternoon dragged by for the ladies. Nana told stories of visits to the seashore with her family when she was young. It was surprising how detailed her remembrances were, prompting visions of running on a sandy beach, and the collecting of seashells to be taken home as treasures. But soon the inside of the coach was quiet once again.

As the sun lowered in the sky and the shadows grew longer, the inside of the coach grew dark. Not a minute too soon, it pulled to a stop in front of a long, two-story building with steps leading to a wide front porch with inviting double doors. Vines grew up the side of the porch and onto its roof, adding greenery and blooming flowers. Windows looked out from the top floor, and the roofline was riddled with many stone chimneys promising cooked food and a warm shelter. A sign over the doorway proclaimed a name:

The Crossroads Inn & Stables

Carver Vale arrived at the inn sometime after the first of the Castle Guard and caravan wagons had gotten there, with more arriving every minute. The stables were busy and overflowing. Guardsmen, wagon drivers, and stablemen were rushing about. The wagons with the tents for the soldiers were being unloaded and the tents were beginning to be set up on the large field behind the stables. All were in a race to beat the sunset and impending darkness.

In all the activity, it was easy for Carver to lower the hood on his cloak and slip into the inn for a much-needed drink. He and Astra had traveled fast through the quiet woodlands, disturbing local wood folk and surprised animals as they sped along the deep forest pathways. His arrival before the coach carrying the Princess assured him that he would be able to keep up with the traveling band as they headed south toward the sea.

4
The Night at the Inn

The travel-weary quartet of ladies went up the three, wide steps to the sprawling front porch and double wooden doors leading to the ground floor of the Crossroads Inn. All the wood on the outside of the building was weathered and worn, turning its color to shades of gray. The heavy door creaked as Lady Charlyn pulled it open to allow the party to enter.

Once inside, they stood in a line at the entrance foyer taking in the surprising interior. The place didn't look large from the outside; however, upon entering the front door there was a realization that the outside view was deceptive. The main floor of the inn was deep – a long hall with great stone fireplaces on both sides of the room. Tables of various sizes and chairs were positioned on opposite sides of a central aisle that led directly to a bar that ran across the far end of the room. A wide doorway on one side behind the bar must lead to the kitchens beyond. Lanterns hung from posts along the walls; and wide, round, iron trays were suspended from the ceiling by ropes holding fat candles, providing circles of light to the space. One could not ignore the smells of this welcoming room, heavy with a mix of wood smoke, cooked food, and the lingering odor of mead and alcohol.

The place was busy with evening guests. The sound of men's voices drifted through the air. With approval, Lady Avis spotted Sergeant Covey and Rand already seated at a table near the bar. A big man with his shirt sleeves rolled up, and a matron in a cap, stood behind the bar. Serving women and girls moved about, carrying plates of food or drink, and clearing away used dishes.

Seeing the well-dressed women standing in the entranceway, the lady with the cap left her post and hurried toward the door. She gave a slight curtsy to the noblewomen and introduced herself.

"Welcome, I'm Rose Peet. My husband and I keep the inn. We have the requested rooms ready for you. May I show you upstairs?" she asked, indicating the stairway to the right of the entrance doors.

"Please," answered Lady Avis, "we've had a long ride."

The plump hostess with a long, ruffled apron, and cap, borrowed one of the many table lamps and led the way up the stairs, not looking back, assuming the guests would follow. The stairs were steep, but a wooden handrail provided along one side assisted in the ascent. The well-worn staircase opened to a narrow hall lined with closed doors. Near the end of the hallway, before it turned on its way along the back of the building, Mrs. Peet stopped and opened a door.

"This is one of our better rooms. There are two beds, milady," the innkeeper said to Lady Avis. "And this room will do well for the young ladies," she said, opening the next door. "It also has two beds and is our best room."

"I am sure these rooms will be fine, thank you," Lady Avis said, taking the lamp and dismissing the matron, while helping Nana McNevin into the room through the doorway. The old nurse was still panting from her climb up the stairs. Then, speaking to the girls before entering, "I'll knock on your door in a little while to go downstairs for dinner. Nana needs some time to rest."

The younger women also thanked the matron, went into their room, and closed the door behind them.

The chamber was spacious, taking up the back corner of the building. It had a square layout with two windows, letting in some late afternoon light. Charlyn immediately went to the table in the middle of the room, pulled out a chair and sat down. She took off the velvet beret on her head and removed the pins holding the scarf covering her braids.

"I have to take down these braids," she explained to Alaine. "I've had my hair up since sunup and it's giving me an awful headache."

"I know what you mean," replied Alaine. "I'm not used to wearing a hat, and I need to take this thing off."

Alaine was standing at a tall dresser with drawers, just inside the door of the room. Though the room was not fully dark, it was in shadows. She lit two of the candlesticks provided and carried one to the table. The dresser held a pewter pitcher full of water, and an empty basin. The beds were large enough for two people - one on the wall next to the door, and one along the far wall. The beds were neatly made and covered with colorful quilts. Chamber pots were placed under the foot of each bed. A tall, wooden screen with three panels stood in one corner of the room and would provide a small bit of privacy as needed. An arched fireplace, filled with wood, was ready to be lit. Alaine walked to the window on the back wall and looked out.

"Come look at this. The troopers are pitching their tents in the field behind the inn."

Charlyn got up and walked over to the window, continuing to take the braids out of her hair as she went. She saw the beehive of activity taking place on the grounds below. Horses were being moved to grazing for the night. A fire was being started next to the cook's wagon. Sleeping tents were springing up like mushrooms on the expansive lot behind the inn. The sun was going down and the light was starting to fade.

"We are lucky to be inside tonight. Tomorrow night it will be our turn for a tent," said Charlyn.

"Yes, I have never slept in a tent. We'll see what it is like," Alaine pondered. Then to Lady Charlyn, "Your hair is long and thick, and you really do well at braiding it."

Charlyn had removed the two braids that had been wrapped up around her head, plaiting it into one long braid hanging over her shoulder onto her bodice. She walked back to the table and secured the thin, white scarf over most of her hair.

"I have two sisters. We all have long hair and help each other. I guess I'll have to wear this dress down to dinner. My other dresses are in my trunk," Charlyn said.

Alaine removed her hat but didn't take down her hair. She didn't have any clothes to change into either. "We'll just have to make do. Tomorrow we must be able to get to our trunks," replied Alaine.

Captain Kent Morr-Leigh took off his uniform jacket and washed the road dirt from his face and hands in a basin. He put on a topcoat over a clean, white shirt with a modest lace at the collar and sleeve cuffs. He combed and tied his hair back with a black ribbon at the back of his neck. He decided not to take the time to shave, allowing the dark stubble that had grown, simply because it was getting late, and he was hungry. He could shave in the morning.

Upon entering the busy hall at the inn, Kent quickly spotted Sergeant Covey and Rand, who were already at a table eating, and made his way to them. The men discussed the day's progress on the road and the plans for the morrow. The good Sergeant would be staying inside the inn during the night to be near the ladies, affording extra protection for the Princess and her party.

From there, Kent moved on to the table where the trio of familiar ladies was seated. Food had already been served and a pitcher of wine was being shared between them. He waved to the serving maid before taking his seat next to Lady Avis, and across from the Princess Alaine and Lady Charlyn.

"Alaine," he asked, informally, "are you going to introduce me to your fair traveling companion?"

Alaine put down her two-pronged fork. "Duke Morr-Leigh, may I present Lady Charlyn of the Walls. She is the eldest daughter of our good friend, Duke Noeman."

The Captain stood and bowed from the waist. "It is a pleasure to meet you, Lady Charlyn. I've had a friendship with your father since my youth. I hope that you did not find today's travels too taxing."

"No, we managed well," Charlyn replied.

"Where is Nana McNiven?" Kent asked, as he took his seat while looking to Lady Avis for an answer.

"Ah," answered Lady Avis. "The day may have been too much for our Nana. Once we got to the room, she took to her bed and declined my request to go down to dinner. I've had a bowl of soup and a cup of mead sent up to her lest she not eat."

"It is good that she rests," Kent agreed. "Tomorrow will be another long day with no hospitable inn waiting at the end of it. I hope that you ladies are up to a few nights in a tent," he reflected, turning to thank the serving girl who brought him a plate piled high with food.

"Actually, I look forward to it," said Alaine, realizing that the man was goading her. "I have never slept in a tent. If all the soldiers can do it, I'm sure that we can."

"I don't know…" Kent responded, smiling. "Sleeping on the ground may prove difficult even with a thick quilt. You may end up with some bruises on your royal hide."

Alaine gave him a defiant look that Lady Avis caught.

"Stop it right now, you two!" Lady Avis ordered. "I will not put up with your bickering throughout this journey!" she whispered with force, wishing not to be heard by anyone nearby.

Alaine flushed at the reprimand. "Sorry, Aunt," she said, meekly.

"I'm sorry, too, Mother," said the Captain,

"Mother?" said Charlyn, accidentally letting the word slip out with surprise.

Lady Avis continued addressing her son. "You may have taught her to ride a horse, shoot her first arrow, and catch a fish, but she's not a little girl anymore. She's a princess of the realm who may end up being your queen. You must learn to show her the proper respect, especially in public, and when we get to King Holum's court. They will be watching all of us closely, and our behavior may affect the outcome of this trip."

"And Alaine," Lady Avis continued, "you've taught Kent responsibility when he cared for you on your visits to Juniper Lodge. You taught him patience when you got into everything he owned. And you saved him from being a spoiled only child; but you too, must behave as your rank requires. You must treat him with the respect he deserves," Then, softening her voice, "You know, Alaine, he would give up his life for you."

The table fell to silence as Lady Avis took a deep draught from her cup of wine.

Charlyn suddenly understood what went on between the Princess and the Captain. They were *cousins* with a long family history. Now, their teasing of one another made sense. It reminded her of the taunting and bickering that went on with her own siblings. She gazed from Kent, who was quietly beginning to eat his dinner, then to Alaine, who was pushing a potato around on her plate. She realized that these two knew each other well, maybe *too well*. Though there may be contention between them, Charlyn felt that there was a strong family bond.

"I beg your pardon, Lady Charlyn," Lady Avis said, apologetically. "These are family matters that you should not have to hear."

"I understand, milady. I have two sisters and we do sometimes cause our parents to be distressed with the way we get along. I believe that it must be the same in all families."

"Yes, maybe so," said Lady Avis, taking another sip of wine.

Astra obediently sat by the steps leading to the inn. She watched as men went in and out. She knew that Carver was in there and had been in there for some time. She was told to wait but was becoming anxious. When the door was opened, the smells of cooked food came wafting through the air. Her nose went up. She had already eaten, yet the smells were enticing. Was Carver eating in there? Both dog and master knew that she ate when he ate. A man with a wrinkled hat came through the door from inside, belching his pleasure with his full stomach. Again, a gust of good smells came with him. He looked at Astra and held the door open for her. The dog advantageously wandered into the loud, open room, separating the scents coming through her long nose in hopes of finding Carver.

Astra knew the smell of roasted mutton, something Finnie cooked often. She always was given some. It was one of her favorites. People sat at a nearby table, with plates of food giving off the irresistible smells. Slowly she padded toward a table. Then Astra noticed another scent. A familiar scent that hung around Carver after a night away. It would be faint, but distinct, when he came to get her in the morning at the forge. The smell seemed to be coming from a girl, as the dog moved closer to the table.

"Oh, my goodness!" exclaimed Lady Charlyn. "Look at that dog!"

Conversation was interrupted as all at the table turned to look at the large animal that had come to stand next to where Alaine sat.

"She is beautiful. Look at those golden eyes," Alaine said, with admiration.

"She must be hungry," Charlyn said, as the dog's attention had turned to the plates of food on the table.

"Well, don't feed her!" ordered Kent.

Alaine looked the dog in the eyes. "Sit," she commanded. The dog sat next to Alaine's chair. The Princess smiled and reached out with her hand to pet the dog on the head between its short, velveteen ears. "She is well trained. She must be someone's pet."

"I think that she is just interested in your food, Alaine," Charlyn observed.

Alaine pulled a generous portion of bread from the loaf on the table and sopped it in the mutton gravy on her plate.

"Oh, no," admonished Lady Avis, seeing what Alaine was doing. "That dog could bite your hand off."

Alaine held the offering of bread toward the dog's nose. Astra gently nibbled at the morsel, being careful of the fingers. The bread disappeared into the large mouth, was briefly chewed, and swallowed. The dog's large tongue licked its lips. The Princess had a friend for life.

Carver Vale looked up from his chair by the fireplace, where he was finishing his ale. It was a perfect spot to observe the Princess and her companions with a series of short glances. He was too far away to hear what was being said, but he thought that he was hearing bits of her voice at times. Laughter came from the table, causing him to look that way. To his surprise, there was Astra, sitting next to the beautiful Alaine.

For a second, Carver didn't know what to do, but quickly determined that he needed to go get the dog. He put down his drink, stood up to his full height, and walked to the table before he had time to change his mind. He saw Astra take some food offered by the Princess.

"Astra, what are you doing here? I told you to wait outside," Carver's quiet voice said to the dog, putting his hand on the back of her neck. "I'm sorry," Carver apologized to Alaine, "She's been fed but she really loves mutton."

Carver stood still, hand on his dog, looking into Alaine's blue eyes for the first time. Over the past, this was the closest he had ever been to his Princess. There was no wall looming between them. It was a moment when their eyes connected. Alaine looked up with curiosity at the roughly dressed, young man standing beside her. His eyes were a fascinating color, his face was without beard, and his blond hair hung in waves down to his shoulders. Carver was fixated, knowing now, that his love for this girl was not displaced.

Kent, noticing the quiet exchange between the two, stood up as his protective habits for the Princess kicked in. Covey had noticed that something was happening at the table with Alaine and was also on his feet.

"Hey!" yelled out the matron from the bar. "Get that animal out of here! There are no dogs allowed in here! We run a clean place! Take it outside!"

"She's a beautiful dog," Alaine said to the stranger, feeling a need to say something to the dog's owner.

"Thank you, milady," Carver said, bowing from the waist. Then he put his hand in his pocket and retrieved a piece of carved wood, slipping it into Alaine's hand. "Come, Astra," he said to the dog, and without delay, was out the front door.

Hoping that no one noticed, Alaine slipped the piece of wood into her pocket for private review later when she would return to her room.

"What an odd young man," Lady Avis observed, "and it's rare to see a dog that large."

"The man was not a merchant," Kent remarked, taking his seat, and lifting his wine goblet. "He's young to be traveling alone. Maybe he's a scout for a band of highwaymen."

"Oh, Kent, you always think the worst," said Alaine. "He had manners and a kindness about him. The dog was well behaved and well trained. Surely, that speaks for something."

"He did have a certain grace about the way he moved," agreed Charlyn, supporting Alaine.

"I'm glad to see that you girls are attracted to a handsome, young lad. He will be soon forgotten when we get to court, and you have your choice of noblemen. You may both find a husband there," said Lady Avis. "But for tonight, you have had enough wine. The morning will come before we know it. It is time to retire and get some rest. Tomorrow will be another long day."

"Lady Avis is right," said Kent, "we leave early. Off to bed with you," he ordered as he stood to leave. "Goodnight, fair ladies, I'm off to the tents, but rest easy, as Covey and Rand have a room near to yours."

The two noblewomen climbed the stairs, tiptoed past Nana's door and entered their room. A large candle burned in its stand in the middle of the table. A bright, little fire burned on the grate of the fireplace. The heavy drapes were drawn across the windows, keeping out any draft. Someone had obviously tended to the room in their absence. The chamber was cozy and warm as the girls searched their travel bags for nightdresses and hairbrushes.

"I saw my dear cousin looking at you with admiring eyes," said Alaine to Lady Charlyn, as she brushed out her long tresses.

"Have no fear for *that*, dear Princess," Charlyn replied. "I believe that he is obnoxious!"

"Well, he *is* the Captain of the Morr-Leigh Garrison and a Duke with land holdings. Usually, women *do* find him attractive," said Alaine, pulling on her white linen nightgown. "I do love him, and worried for him when he was off on a recent campaign with his garrison, but he *is* obnoxious at times. Especially when he treats me as if I'm still a child."

"I am not interested in an arrogant Captain, if you'll excuse me, Your Highness. I have given my heart to another whom I hope will be waiting for me when I return home."

"Is that true?" asked Alaine. "You have a suitor for your hand?"

"Yes," said Charlyn, softening her voice. "He's a squire from the neighboring county. We were just beginning to know each other before I left home. I am sure that he cares for me as I care for him. I can hardly wait to get back to see him again. I think of him constantly. I think that I love him."

"I envy you for knowing what you want. I have never been in love," Alaine said, disheartened. "I've seen it in others. My maid, Genna, is in love with Rand, the tall man who is driving our coach. He is one of our footmen from the castle. She has been in love with him for two summers, but her mother is opposed to the match. She is hoping to have time alone with him on this journey." Then thinking of herself, "Maybe there is something wrong with me that I have never been in love."

"No, there is nothing wrong with you, Princess. When you meet the right person, you will know the feeling. Wanting to be with him will consume your thoughts."

"I hope that you are right," Alaine said, wistfully. "I am quite fearful of being wed to a man who may be approved of by my family, but one for which I have no feelings. I may never learn what it is to be in love."

"I agree that you *do* have unique pressures upon you when it comes to making a match. For once, I am glad that I am not a princess," Charlyn added, sympathetically.

Later, Alaine was lying awake on her bed, staring at the rough rafters along the ceiling. The candle on the table had burned itself out. The embers in the fireplace put off a red glow as they died. She could hear Charlyn's quiet breathing from across the room. How Alaine wished that she could find a restful sleep like her pretty roommate.

In the darkness, Alaine fingered the small, carved rabbit that the young man had placed into her hand that evening as he left her side. She thought of him and of his dog with the golden eyes. The wooden piece was carved with a little round head and the rabbit's ears folded back along the crouching body that ended with a tiny tail. Alaine rubbed her fingers back and forth across the rounded, smooth back of the bunny, thinking of the face with the piercing, green eyes that had looked deeply into hers. If she *were* to fall in love with someone, she would certainly prefer someone like him. Not necessarily because of his compelling looks, but because, for a brief moment, she felt a connection with him. Strangely, she wanted to talk to him.

Alaine had so many questions. What was his story, she wondered? Yet, it was clear by his dress that he was not a nobleman, or even a squire, as was Charlyn's love. No connection with the mysterious stranger would be allowed as a suitor for a princess. Alaine sighed a loud sigh. Morning would be coming soon. She would close her eyes, while clutching her small gift, and wish for sleep.

5

The Duke Morr-Leigh

ady Avis sat in the jostling coach on the second day of their travel. Charlyn and Alaine were in quiet conversation, sitting next to each other on the seat facing her. The aunt was glad to see that the two girls seemed to be developing a friendship. One thing that they had in common, other than their ages, was that neither of them wanted to be on this trip to Irongate. Both longed for their homes.

The early morning had gone well, actually better than she expected. Nana, after a long night's sleep, woke up spry. The nursemaid was dressed and downstairs ordering a breakfast for the travelers to be sent up to the rooms at the crack of dawn. The breakfast fare was simple, consisting of boiled oats with honey, cooked figs, rolls with butter, and tea. No one complained of the offering, as it was unclear when the next meal would be during the travel day.

Nana was the first to the carriage, assisted by Rand up the small steps. Lady Avis followed, with a basket refilled with fresh drink and lunch items. The older ladies waited in their seats as Alaine and Charlyn graced the front porch of the inn, carrying their bags. Both of the girls had declined to wear head coverings other than thin scarves pinned to cover most of their hair. The wish for comfort seemed to overrule the need for the fashion of hats.

Now, the coach moved on continuously without any stops. As the day moved on, with the tedious rocking motion, the mind would tend to wander off with its own thoughts. Lady Avis thought back to the day before Alaine's farewell banquet. Hawthorn Castle was brimming with nobles, servants, and others carrying out their particular duties when she and Kent arrived on the previous afternoon.

Mother and son had left Juniper Lodge shortly after daybreak and traveled across the Morr-Leigh lands adjacent to the King's lands. Even though they were neighbors to the seat of the Eastgreen Highlands, at Hawthorn Castle, it was a full day's ride. They reached a courtyard that was deep in shadows within the castle walls, as the sun had lowered in the cloudless sky. Lady Avis, thanks to her close ties with her sister, had her own rooms at Hawthorn, so she had no fear of being displaced. A good bed awaited her. At luncheon with Iris the following day, a messenger came to the Queen's sitting room.

"What is it, Jones?" Queen Iris asked the man.

"An urgent request from the King, Your Majesty," he answered.

"All right, bring it here."

"It is for Lady Avis, Your Majesty," the footman explained.

"Oh," said the Queen, surprised as the servant held out the tray with the note to Lady Avis.

As she broke the seal on the paper and read the message, Lady Avis looked at her sister with confusion on her face.

"I've been summoned to the council room at once by the King," she said, her voice questioning the message.

"Well, don't look at me," said Queen Iris, "Granth said nothing to me about it. That's odd, though. I knew that he was taking advantage of all of the Council members being here for the banquet to hold a meeting, but even *I* never attend those meetings." After a pause, she continued, "He *has* been pre-occupied of late. I knew that something was going on with him. This whole thing with Alaine leaving has focused him on the future of the kingdom. Also, the sudden loss of your dear husband was a shock that made him consider his own mortality over the past few winters. Lately he's been mumbling about his age, and the fact that there is no male heir to the throne. It seems that much will depend upon Alaine's choice in a husband."

"Possibly, it is something about the marriage agreement as to why he's summoned me," Lady Avis put forward a supposition.

"We've already finished all that," the Queen said, dismissively, "The terms for the marriage contract have been written and sealed. We have a copy and there is the copy you will deliver to Granth's brother, Holum."

"I have been told to escort you to the council chamber, milady," the footman interrupted the sisters.

"You'd better go, Avis," the Queen said. "Come back and tell me what is going on."

"Yes, sister," replied the Lady, as she rose to leave with her guide.

The footman Jones led Lady Avis down the castle's grand staircase to the main floor. The King's Council of Hawthorn met in the Tapestry Room, which was used for all formal ceremonies involving the King. The room was massive and held the great chairs of the King and Queen on a dais opposite the door. One wall contained a large fireplace; opposite was a wall with three arched windows containing rare, stained glass. The name of the room came from the several detailed tapestries which hung on the stone walls, chronicling important events in the lives of the past two kings, all of the House of Hawthorn.

As the tall, wooden door swung open, Lady Avis waited on the threshold to be formally announced prior to entering the room. This was the seat of the Eastgreen Highland's government, and formalities were observed.

"Your Majesty and nobles of the land, please admit the Duchess of Leigh, Lady Avis," the footman called out.

"Welcome, Duchess," called King Granth. "Duke Seaken-Char, would you please escort our guest to a chair?"

Duke Seaken-Char was a crooked stick of a man, and he leaned on his cane as he rose from his chair. Slightly hunched over, some of his tall height lost with age, he gallantly offered an arm to the

Lady and brought her to an empty chair, which he pulled out from the table, allowing her to sit.

Duke Seaken-Char was one of the three older dukes who were members of the Council, all with sons awaiting their inheritance. These Dukes, Seaken-Char, Gillis, and Filroy were originally pledged to King Granth's father, King Holmes. They had lived through the warring and the times of unrest; they were veterans all. They embodied the living history of Hawthorn and offered wise advice to the throne.

The Council consisted of the Dukes of the Eastgreen Highlands, the landholders, responsible for the local government within their districts. All held garrisons of troops sworn to the King. They had the ability to enlist men and raise men-at-arms at the request of the King. Though the King was the ruling monarch, the Council had great influence. King Granth knew that only strife could be had by going against the majority.

What went on in the Council was held secret by the members, so it was rare to admit outsiders, let alone a woman. Lady Avis noted the heavy, wooden tables arranged in the shape of a square with King Granth sitting in the middle of the top table. Next to him sat Scribe Dilford with his quill and parchment, the keeper of all royal records. The faces around the tables had turned to look at her, causing a brief flash of self-consciousness. Yet, all of these men were familiar to her. She had been a Lady of the Hawthorn Court since her marriage, thirty years heretofore, to the Duke of Leigh. Her husband had grown up with the King and, when he died, all in the room had attended his funeral. Over the years, as she aged, she watched all of these men age with her. It was her generation that now ruled the kingdom.

At once, the door to the room opened again, and the footman Jones announced another guest.

"Your Majesty and nobles of the land, please admit Kent Morr-Leigh, the Duke of Leigh."

"Welcome, Duke Morr-Leigh," said the King. "Thank you for your prompt reply to our summons. Please take a seat next to your mother."

The young man crossed the room. He had come from the guard house next to the armory, down near the stables, where he was in discussion with the soldiers assigned to the journey to the coast the next day. Called to come at once, he knew he wasn't appropriately attired for such a meeting, but there was no time to change his clothes. He was surprised at the summons and more surprised to see his mother seated at the council table. The two exchanged a look as he took his seat.

"We, the Council, agreed that you should both be here today," the King began, directing his words at the two visitors, "as an important vote has been taken regarding the lands held under the former Duke. Please stand, Duke Morr-Leigh."

Mother and son were stunned. Were their lands to be taken from them, which was a thought racing through their minds? Was Kent considered too young to manage the district? The young Duke stood and faced his King.

King Granth continued, "As you know, since the death of Duke Norbert Morr-Leigh, this Council has overseen the lands of his district, and administered the judiciary for the people of his lands. This continued during the time that you, Lord Morr-Leigh, were away at battle supporting our good ally, King Walkin. However, now that you have returned, we all agree that it is time that you take up your position. Today, we are inviting you to take your place on this Council, as well as taking over the responsibilities for your lands. Are you prepared to take the oath of the Council?"

Relief flooded through Kent's body. The solemnness of the occasion struck him. Not yet of thirty years, he would become the youngest member of the Council. His father's wishes would be granted, as this was always his hope for his son. He noticed the stillness in the room. All were awaiting his response.

"I would be honored to take the oath of the Council of Hawthorn, Sire," Kent replied.

"Good man!" called the King, as "ayes" rang out around the tables, with the pounding of fists.

Tears came to the eyes of Lady Avis as Sir Dilford administered the oath. Hearing her son's clear voice, so similar to his father's, touched her heart. She held a handkerchief to her face and gave the King a grateful look for allowing her to be present for this moment.

Soon the room settled, and the King resumed the Council business. "The second topic for discussion today is an issue that has long been on the minds of myself, this Council and the people of our land," the King began, as a hush fell over the hall. "We all know that Queen Iris and I were blessed with only one child, the Princess Alaine. There is no obvious male heir to the Eastgreen Highlands, as our laws require. Today we are gathered at Hawthorn Castle to wish the Princess well as she leaves for my brother's court at Irongate Castle. King Holum and Queen Hester will sponsor Alaine as she entertains suiters for her hand in marriage. We have had diplomatic exchanges regarding possible royal matches. Two princes have been rejected due their age, being over forty winters. At least two other potential noble suitors will be traveling by sea to Irongate Castle; therefore, it made sense to have the initial introductions at the Mareview Lowlands, rather than here.

"It is the wish of the Queen and me that Alaine will marry and have a male child who could succeed me to the throne. As she may end up living far away from us, and a first-born son may be in line to succeed his father, we have voted today that *any* male heir, my grandson, could lay claim to the throne. Upon my death, it would be up to this Council to approve any heir that would apply to succeed. If the boy is under the age of eighteen, the Council will appoint a regent from among the Council members, until the child is of age to rule.

"However, if there is no male heir of Alaine, it is my wish that the throne be offered to King Holum's son, my nephew, Prince Stenson. He is now an age of twelve winters and being prepared to assume his father's throne. As our king, he would have the ability to reunite the Eastgreen Highlands with the Weston Mareview Lowlands as Hawthorn was during my father's reign.

"I am ordering Squire Dilford to prepare a document be drawn up with my wishes for succession. It will be signed by me and signed by all Council members. Once sealed, it is to be opened only upon my death. A copy will be prepared, sealed, and delivered to my brother by Lady Avis, as she chaperones the Princess to the Lowland Court."

Thinking back to that recent day at the Council, it had been an eventful day for Lady Avis and her son. Tears came to her eyes once again, as she thought of the oath-taking and Kent's future. It was a day that she would always remember, with his parents' wishes fulfilled. The traveling coach rolled along, with the King's document for King Holum carefully packed at the bottom of the good Lady's trunk.

The cook's wagon was covered with tarps stretched over iron rungs. The inside ventilation was poor, with openings only at the front and back. The air was warm as the four occupants rode along at the rate that their two horses moved on the rutted road. They sat upon bags of flour and grain. Pots and cooking utensils hung on ropes above their heads, making noise as they clanged against each other. Every inch of floor space was filled with something, so foot space was minimal.

Annie, the experienced cook, was thinking of the preparations that would be needed for the evening's supper. Even though the Garrison's cook would help with the cooking, she did a quick sum of the number of people she would need to feed tonight: at least fifty soldiers, fifteen waggoneers, the nobles, various footmen, and stable boys. The experienced cook put Oween to work on peeling a basket of carrots for the stew as they traveled along. Annie mixed up four large, wooden bowls of yeast dough, something she could do in her sleep, and covered them with cloth so the dough could rise and be ready to be made into biscuits when they made camp. Clara was set to work on peeling potatoes.

Genna was the lady's maid to the Princess, so she was not expected to help with food preparations. She rode in the cook's wagon, as there was no room in the royal coach, and because the cook staff were the only other women traveling in the group. She was a good-natured girl, who had worked beside her mother, Ellen, in the kitchen from the time she was a young girl. Her mother beamed with pride when the Queen selected Genna for training as a lady's maid three years ago. Genna's status had risen among the castle servants but remained friends with all of the kitchen folk. She offered to help with the food, just to have something to do. Annie gave her a sharp knife and a bag of green beans with a cauldron to put them in, once cut. The cook knew that any extra help would save time later.

The girls chattered as they worked. Genna remained quiet, with only one thought dominating her mind - when would she have time to be alone with Rand? With him driving the royal coach and sleeping in a room within the inn the previous night, Genna had barely seen him since they left the castle. She wondered if he would have time for her.

Feelings of insecurity swamped her thoughts. Had his interest in her cooled? Would he be avoiding her on the journey? She pushed a tassel of curly, brown hair away from the side of her face as she worked on the beans.

After a while, Annie made her way to the front of the wagon and called to the driver. A stop was needed. The sun was high in the sky, so it would be a good time for a snack and to take care of the needs of nature. The wagon master was glad for a chance to get down from his post. He needed a drink, and so did the horses.

Genna was the last of the women out of the wagon. She saw that the royal coach had come to a stop behind them, and the ladies were piling out of the carriage. Covey was helping Nana, who was last to reach the roadside. Rand got down from his perch as the coach's driver and walked to the water barrels roped to the side of the cook's wagon. He gave Genna one of his shy smiles. How could she have doubted him, she thought? Smiling herself, Genna hurried to join him, brown curls escaping her scarf.

As Kent rode his horse from the front of the caravan toward the rear wagons, he came to a break in the line. The second half of the train, including the royal coach, was nowhere in sight.

"What the hell?" he cursed to himself. He spurred on his mount. Roadside emergencies filled his head – a broken wheel or axle? Maybe there was a problem with one of the horses, or a sudden illness of one of the travelers. He moved quickly along the road, not knowing what he might find.

He was confounded when he arrived at the wagons stopped in the middle of the road. Four of his guards were sitting on fallen logs, eating and drinking, their horses grazing not far off. He saw Covey sitting with Annie and her two helpers, also taking a leisurely rest. Alaine and Lady Charlyn were off to the side of the road, doing what, he was not sure, but nothing appeared to be amiss. Dismounting, he walked over to the young noblewomen.

"Princess Alaine," he addressed her formally, "what is going on here?"

"Look at this, Kent," she answered, with enthusiasm. She was holding what appeared to be a hollowed-out piece of bark filled with berries. Charlyn came from nearby to join them, adding two more handfuls of blackberries to the collection.

"You look charming with your mouth all purple. They must be good," Kent said, sarcastically. "You too, Lady Charlyn."

The Lady's name rolled off his tongue with a softness, and he raised his hand to remove a bit of berry stuck to the corner of her mouth with a gentleness that was unexpected. Surprised by his touch, she could feel the color rise in her cheeks.

"Why are the wagons stopped here?" Kent asked, with a renewed, business-like tone. "The forward wagons are way up ahead and still moving. This stop has split the caravan."

"Ladies cannot go from morning to evening without a stop, Kent," Alaine explained. "The cook's wagon stopped, so we all stopped."

"All right, but we're going to have to make plans for stops. *This is not safe!* Take the berries over to Annie. Get yourselves cleaned up and get back in the coach," he ordered. "Where's Rand? We need to get going."

"He's over there with Genna, having lunch. They look sweet together, don't they?" Alaine answered.

Kent shook his head. "Does no one have any concept of security here? *This is not a picnic!* Ugh!" Kent replied, throwing up his hands and taking off toward the cook's wagon.

"I think that he wants us to get back in the coach," Lady Charlyn said, watching his retreat.

"I think that he likes you or he would have done a lot more yelling," replied Alaine. "That lot over there are going to get the brunt of his wrath."

"We had better do what he says. We don't want an angry Captain on our hands," said Charlyn, thinking of Kent's gentle touch in spite of his dismay with the travelers. For the moment, thoughts of her squire, back home, were forgotten.

In the late afternoon, Captain Leigh was riding up to the front of the line of wagons when he quickly reigned his horse, seeing one of his sergeants and two guardsmen on foot at the side of the road speaking with a man on foot. He motioned to the wagon driver next to him to continue moving forward on the road as he stopped to investigate. With half of the wagons lagging behind, the day had been frustrating so far, due to the slow pace of travel even though the road was dry and the weather fair.

Kent recognized the man in the long, brown cloak standing with his men. At his side was the large dog that had gingerly taken food from Princess Alaine's hand the previous evening at the inn. Had the man flagged down his troops? What was it he wanted; the Captain wondered? Quickly, he dismounted and walked to the side of the road to join his soldiers.

"What's the problem, Miles?" he demanded of his lieutenant.

"He waved us down, sir," answered the man, indicating the traveler with the waving of his hand toward Carver Vale.

"You were at the Crossroads Inn last night," Kent said to Carver. "Are you traveling on foot? How did you get ahead of our wagons?"

"I travel across the land and fields and follow along the forest," replied Carver. "The road winds through the fields and the wagons are slow. It wasn't hard to move ahead of your line."

"Did you wish to travel with our protection?" Kent questioned, wondering why the lad had stopped his men.

"No, I wanted to warn you of a group of men that are following your trail."

"What?" Kent asked with suspicion. "What do you know of this?"

"I slept in the woods near the inn last night and left early this morning. I came across a group of men. I heard them talking. They know that you are escorting the Princess. They are traveling along the edge of the trees and staying out of the sight of your guards."

Kent gave the man a stern stare. "What do you know of the Princess?" Kent questioned.

"I was in Hawthorn Village yesterday. All the townsfolk were talking of the Princess leaving," Carver stated factually.

"Who do you know there?"

"Hewitt, the blacksmith, is my friend. I stay with his family when I go to the village."

Satisfied with the answers, Kent asked, "How many horses do they have?"

"What?"

"How many horses do the highwaymen have?"

"Ten or twelve horses."

"Sergeant, take Stone, with three of the forward guard and ride back to the rear guard. Warn them to be on the lookout for riders coming up from behind or from the side. Try to get those back wagons caught up with these. I'm going to look for a safe spot up ahead for us to camp for the night."

As his troops left, Kent took in the figure of the young man before him. Despite the rather odd clothing, he was well spoken for a working man. His hair, face, and hands were clean. He stood straight and looked into your eyes when he spoke. There was no subservience there, thought Kent, even when addressing a Captain of the Garrison. Did he think himself the equal of a soldier, he wondered? At any rate, if his warnings of the highwaymen were true, he had done them a service.

"What name do you go by?" Kent asked the stranger.

"Carver Vale, sir."

"What is your business on the road? To where do you travel?"

"I travel to Harbortown in Weston Mareview Lowlands."

"And why do you travel there?"

"I go to meet my bride."

"You go to be married?"

"Yes, if she will have me."

"That is a quest similar to our own," mused the Captain. "It is the time of the year for weddings, I suppose. Be that as it may, thank you for the warning of the highwaymen. I ask that you do not speak of the Princess and her travels to anyone."

"I will not speak of it," swore Carver.

"Safe travels to you."

"And to you and your company, sir," replied Carver. Then to the dog, "Come, Astra."

When Kent got to his horse and mounted, he glanced back over his shoulder for a last look at the stranger, but he and his dog had already vanished from sight. Kent looked afield and wondered how the man with the dog had seemed to just disappear.

Later, as the air began to cool with the retiring sun, the royal coach finally arrived at the campsite. The ladies in the carriage remained entrapped as the proceeding wagons were being directed into the formation of a wide circle on an expansive, recently harvested oat field. It was a while before the coach came to a stop in what was thought to be a good spot for the night. The travel-weary women disembarked into a manic fury of activity. They stood watching the goings on, getting their bearings. A great tent was being erected in the middle of the ring of wagons. The cook's tent was up, and their fires were burning alongside. Horses were being unharnessed and led away for food and a night of rest.

Lady Avis took control. "Nana and I will try to find someone to help get our tent set up. Covey is probably already taking care of it, so we'll try to find him."

"Aunt, can you ask him to bring our trunks? We would like to change our clothes," Alaine requested.

"I'll see what I can do. Where did Rand get off to?"

"I saw him take the horses," replied Lady Charlyn.

"All right," said Lady Avis, developing a plan. "You girls go over there and stay with Annie until we can sort this out. I don't want you wandering around in this turmoil."

With that, Avis and the old nurse turned on their heels and went off to the outside of the circle of wagons, where all hands were either caring for livestock or setting up tents.

When Alaine and Charlyn appeared at the cook's tent, Annie was in no mood to take care of nobility while trying to get out a large meal. Her cap askew, she grabbed two wooden buckets with rope handles and went to the girls.

"Dear Princess and Lady Charlyn, we need a favor," said the mindful cook, not wanting the two underfoot.

The young ladies' eyes widened, fearful of being forced into the havoc of the food preparation.

"See those trees over there? Well, there's a stream running there. Take these buckets, fill them with water, and bring them back. We need to fill our water barrels before we leave in the morning."

With some relief, the girls took the buckets and headed toward the trees. It would be good to have a little freedom to stretch their legs and explore the place. So off they went.

The large tent now dominated the center of the field within the ring of wagons. Wooden planks were being removed from the sides of wagons to set up tables for serving food inside the great, fabric structure. Men were moving in and out, carrying whatever. Once beyond the wagons, the girls saw areas that were roped off for the horses. Then there were the soldiers' tents, which were small, two-to-three-man cones with openings in the front. These brown tents were set up around the perimeter of the camp. Men were milling about, vociferous, calling out to one another. It seemed that everyone was busy doing something to prepare for nightfall.

As the girls walked away from the camp toward the line of trees, the noise diminished. They tramped slowly through the uneven ground of the field. Twilight was upon them, and branches of the ash trees swayed gently in the evening breeze. As they reached the tree line, the ground dropped in a slope leading to the stream bed which hosted a pool at the far, downstream end.

Yet, it was not the alluring stream and the forest lands on the far bank that stopped the girls where they stood. It was the man in front of them, who was a short distance away, facing the flowing water while pulling on his trousers. His back and lower legs were bare. He shook his head, with water droplets flying outward, and grabbed his hair at the base of his neck, ringing out the residual wet. The diminished light came from the west, but it was enough to show off the muscles of his arms and back. He stooped to put on leather sandals and take up his shirt from the leaf-covered ground, throwing it over one shoulder as he turned to face the two girls.

"Oh, my lord," the words escaped from Lady Charlyn, dumbfounded by the man before her.

Alaine, familiar with her cousin's physique throughout her growing-up years, waited for him to speak as he walked up the bank toward them.

A look of surprise on Kent's face had quickly changed to a smile. "Ah, we have spies, I see," he quipped, as he stopped in front of them.

Charlyn remained speechless. Her mother was overly protective of her girls, so there were strict rules at their hall regarding contact with men. Even the young men who were in training with her father were kept at bay. Chaste social rules were followed by visitors to the lodge whenever the girls were about. Now, standing within a foot of Kent Leigh, she had never seen a half-naked man, let alone, at such a closeness. She suddenly felt naïve and overwhelmed.

"Annie sent us to get water," Alaine said, holding up the bucket.

"Well, you can't go down there now," Kent insisted. "Some of my men are taking advantage of the pool and are bathing."

Neither of the girls knew what to say as thoughts of unclothed soldiers filled their heads.

"Here, give me the buckets. I can fill them where the stream runs over those rocks before the water gets to the pool."

Kent took the buckets and headed down the sloping ground toward the rocks. Alaine looked at Charlyn, noticing her flushed face as she watched Kent walk away.

"Now you see why the women fawn over him. He *is* quite a handsome man, is he not?"

Charlyn managed a one-word answer, "Yes."

They waited at the tree line, hearing the voices of the soldiers drifting up from the pond, poised to run should any of them appear. Alaine took in the landscape, looking at the woodlands beyond the stream.

"Look over there," she said, pointing toward the edge of the far trees. "I thought I saw the dog that was at the inn last night."

"No, it can't be. I don't see it," said Charlyn.

"Now it's gone. Maybe it was just a deer coming down for a drink at the stream," Alaine surmised.

By then, Kent was returning, carrying two full buckets. One could not help but notice his chest and arm muscles at work, with his shirt still hanging over his shoulder.

"Here you go," he said, handing a bucket back to each girl. "Now get back to camp and give them to Cook. It's almost dark and you needn't be out here. I'll go try to find my mother and check on your tent," he ordered as he took off toward the back side of the oat field, pulling on his shirt as he went.

The girls began their trek back, trying to keep the precious water from slopping out of their buckets. Charlyn remained quiet, with nothing to say. She was still trying to manage her feelings. They walked as quickly as they could, but the night was overtaking them.

That same night, Alaine lay on her featherbed pallet, waiting for sleep. She was tired from the day's travels, but as often happened, sleep would not come to her. She decided that living in a tent was something she *could* do, but not something she would *want* to do for any period of time.

Earlier, when Alaine and Charlyn found their assigned spot, it was already dark. A small campfire was lit in front of the tent; it was just beginning to flare. Nana, in her wrap, was sitting on a wooden box next to the fire, staying out of the way of the movements inside the tent.

Voices were heard coming from the structure, and silhouettes on the canvas showed activity on the interior.

Covey stood by the tent flap that was tied back to allow an entrance. When he saw the Princess and Charlyn walking toward him, he straightened to his full height, which was taller than most of the men in the camp. The old soldier threw his shoulders back and pushed out his chest.

Unfortunately, his rather robust stomach stood out a way beyond his chest. Alaine was familiar with the stance and what would be coming next. These two adversaries knew the situation as well, as in any game of chess.

The Princess was the knight, with unexpected moves and outcomes, and Covey was the bishop that could sweep in diagonally to check her or elicit help from the Queen and King. At heart, Alaine knew that the man was more the beloved uncle, always underfoot, protecting her interests, but not afraid to enlist her parents' authority when the need arose.

"Princess Alaine where have you two ladies been?" he demanded.

The girls stood silent, while Alaine prepared a response in her mind.

"Two young noblewomen wandering around in a dark camp full of men?" Covey questioned, in a quiet voice that did not take away from the sting of the sense of impropriety.

"Annie sent us to get water. When we got back it was already dark. Then it took us some time to find our place between all of the horses and soldier tents. We're sorry," Alaine responded, contritely.

As usual, Covey was taken in by the regret voiced by the Princess.

"I was worried when you were nowhere to be found," he said. "Next time we will try to let you know where the tent will be, or you can always stay with Nana or Lady Avis. No harm done, I guess," he relented.

"I'll stay here with them," Nana said. "You go get some supper, Covey. By the time you get back, the housekeeping should be settled. Then you can walk us all over to the great tent for dinner."

"All right. I'll be off, then," the big man called back over his shoulder, already on his way.

"Where's Lady Avis?" Charlyn asked the old nurse.

"She went to the privy tent that was set up for the ladies."

"What's a privy tent?" Charlyn questioned.

"The soldiers dug a hole, put a small bench over it, and pitched a little tent around it. It provides us some privacy, so we won't have to use chamber pots in the tent," Nana explained.

"What a good idea," Alaine added, trying to imagine the convenience.

"We'll be sharing it with the cook's ladies, but it will be good to have," Nana went on.

Alaine heard Genna's voice coming from the tent.

"Now, put the last one over there."

"Let's go see," urged Alaine to Charlyn, pulling her forearm.

Stepping just inside the opening of the tent, the two girls watched as the thin, featherbed mattresses were being unrolled onto a rug covering the ground. Three wooden poles held up the center of the fabric structure, providing enough head room for Rand to stand up straight. Two of the large trunks with flat lids were aligned with the poles, dividing the tent's interior into halves. A lantern sat atop one of the trunks, lighting the space. More poles held up the fabric on both sides. This canvas structure was far larger than any of the soldiers' tents. Genna saw the girls and decided to explain how she was dividing the space.

"I'll sleep back here," Genna said, indicating a slim mattress on the floor at the back center of the tent. "Nana will sleep here." Another featherbed lying on the one side perpendicular to the poles in the center. "And Lady Avis will sleep here, with this trunk giving each of them some space."

A trunk sat between the two mattresses, with another trunk near the tent opening. The other side of the tent was set up in the same manner, with a trunk separating the sleeping space for the girls. But that was not what caught the interest of Alaine and Charlyn.

"*The trunks!*" they both exclaimed at once, running to them and opening the lids.

Realizing what was taking precedence, Genna said to Rand, "You better leave so that I can help the ladies dress for dinner. I'll see you later."

The girls were both rummaging through the contents of their trunks with glee. What should they wear? Two days in the same clothes was *not* something they were used to enduring. After all, they *were* nobility. Genna smiled and waited to help with the dressing.

By the time Covey returned to escort them to dinner, Lady Avis and Nana waited outside the tent while Genna helped put the finishing touches on the young ladies. Charlyn had chosen a rose-colored gown with green piping around the bodice and on the sleeves, which flared at the wrists. The dress was gathered at the waist, accenting the bodice and laced neckline. To her head, she added a fillet – a cloth-covered, narrow headband - which matched the piping on the gown. The air outside had cooled, so she added her embroidered, green shawl.

Alaine chose one of her comfortable morning gowns - an old friend of cornflower blue - simply trimmed in white lace at the ends of the sleeves and around the neckline. She added the metal dragonfly belt to her waist, more in a tribute to her father's love than for fear of danger. Alaine grabbed her favorite cloak, and casually wrapped it around her shoulders. Then, just as they were ready to leave, Alaine remembered she always wore a certain broach with this dress.

"Go ahead," she urged Charlyn and Genna, "I need to find my broach. Tell Aunt that I will just be a moment."

The Princess dove her head into the large trunk, searching for a box with a cross-stitched image of a hawthorn tree on the top. Once she found it, down near the bottom of the packing, she pulled it out and opened the brass clasp. Within was her everyday jewelry, not as elegant as the gems in the velvet-covered box, which were gathered as part of her wedding dowry. For those precious jewels, gowns had been made to be worn at her uncle's court at Irongate, all to highlight the gems. This little box held sentimental pieces worn for comfort and a reminder of home.

The search was for a pin that had been given by her mother the day she turned sixteen. It was diamond shaped, in pounded gold, and attached in the center was an opal that was acquired from a merchant. His story was that he had purchased it from a sailor who had brought it back from a long voyage to the South Seas. Alaine liked it because the stone reflected many colors and seemed to complement the color of whatever dress she was wearing, in this case, shades of blue. Once found, she hastily attached it to the lace just below her throat. Straightening her cloak, the Princess felt renewed with the change of clothes and went to join those waiting outside.

As the escorted ladies walked toward the giant tent set up within the circle of wagons, they could hear the loud commotion of men's voices. Peals of hollering and laughing rang out at intervals. Undaunted, Lady Avis took Covey's forearm, leading the party into the tent. It took only moments for a hush to fall over the room. Soldiers, waggoneers, and stablemen, most with a cup or bowl in their hands, fell quiet when the noblewomen entered.

"The ladies would have some dinner," Sergeant Covey announced. "Make way for them, gentlemen."

Men cleared the way from the long, wooden planks set on barrels to make up a serving table for food. Alaine realized she was very hungry, and the smell of food made her mouth water. Annie rushed forward with bowls and cups for them. Luscious biscuits and hearty stew comprised tonight's meal. The food was still warm as it was ladled out of the iron cauldrons. Men gave up their seats for the ladies, who sat on makeshift benches to eat their food. Alaine ate all of her bowlful and returned to the table for a second biscuit. Cups of cider came from a large barrel providing a cool drink after the meal. All was good.

Covey and Rand walked along with the ladies back to their tent after dinner. By now, Nana and Lady Avis were ready for a lie-down. For a while, it was busy within the confined space of the ladies' small lodging. The women took turns walking out to the little privy tent. Nightgowns were put on and garments were draped over trunks in preparation for morning.

"We have our Princess to thank for these nice feather mattresses," Nana told Charlyn as she brushed her hair, sitting on one of the trunks in the middle of the space. "Some time ago, when she was but a child, mind you, Alaine insisted, 'we must save all the feathers' to the overworked kitchen staff. At first, the idea was resisted, but soon they were putting aside a crate of feathers a week from all of the fowl going through the place for the ovens and spits. It was not long before we had more feathers than we knew what to do with. Today, all of the beds in Hawthorn castle have wonderful pillows and down comforters. Then, seamstresses began making feather mattresses, better than sleeping flat on the ground, I suspect. Clever girl, our Alaine. Lucky the man who marries her."

"That is a good thought, and useful," said Charlyn. "I shall have to suggest it to my mother."

"Come, Nana, we all must try to get some rest before morning. Turn out that lamp and settle in," Lady Avis advised from her bed on the ground. Soon all was quiet, and darkness filled the tent. Still lying awake, Alaine wished for the freedom of her garden. Charlyn had fallen asleep shortly after the lamp was put out, as did Lady Avis. Occasionally, she could hear Nana's gentle snoring coming from the other side of the tent. The night was creeping by.

Alaine let her mind wander to the meeting at the stream with her cousin, and Charlyn's apparent response. The girl had barely said a word during the walk back to the camp. Later, she noticed Charlyn's eyes seeming to search through the faces in the food tent. Had she been relieved that Kent was not there, or was she looking for him? Alaine's instincts told her that her handsome cousin had a strong effect on her new friend.

The quiet was broken as she heard Genna rustling about at the back of the tent. She remained still as her maid tiptoed by Charlyn's feet and then her own on the way out. Alaine assumed her maid was probably going to the privy; but, as time passed, she realized that it was not so. Her mind jumped to the most obvious conclusion…Genna was probably meeting Rand. Alaine worried for the couple, who so longed to be together that they were willing to risk getting caught. Both could be shamed and tossed from their positions at Hawthorn Castle for any inappropriate behavior. In the morning, Alaine would warn her friend and then hope for the best. A while later, relief came when she heard Genna creep past her to the mattress on the floor.

Alaine dozed in a shallow haze, never quite reaching the plane of sleep. Some horses were neighing in the near distance, and her eyes flew open when she heard footsteps going by outside of the tent. Someone else was also awake in the depths of the night. The sudden alertness settled into wakefulness. She wondered how long until morning, as everyone else slept. Alas, she decided to get up. Even though it was dark, she fumbled to find all of her clothes and silently dress. On went boots and cloak, and she quietly escaped into the night.

Breathing in the cool night air was so refreshing after the stuffiness of the canvas structure. Alaine gazed around at the surrounding campsite. The small fire had long since burnt itself out.

There were fleeting sounds coming from the areas holding horses; otherwise, everything was still. Taking advantage of the privy, she saw no one else afoot. Walking toward the back of the camp, one lone soldier appeared to be awake and on guard over by the men's tents.

Standing in the shadows, she wondered what to do. The girl had no wish to go back inside. She turned and looked at the empty field behind the camp, knowing that walking that way would lead to the little pool of water and the stream that ran into it. Restless, Alaine made a decision, and it was to go off for the stream.

She had not gotten very far on the field when a large bird on the wing startled her. An owl, probably, silently swooped down, snatched its prey from the ground and flew off toward the woods. Undeterred, on Alaine went, enjoying the night. The moon was at its quarter phase, providing little light. Stars could be seen in the sky between fat, lumbering clouds.

There was no breeze; the air was still and heavy with moisture in the early hours.

As the Princess approached the area where the water was located, the ground descended toward it. Walking along the bank, Alaine gazed down at the tranquil pool. She almost missed the wooden bench stationed among the bushes on the slope. Thinking that maybe a farmer had built it and set it in this prime spot in order to sit and view the stream, the girl walked toward it.

Taking a closer look, Alaine saw that the bench was made of branches and twigs twisted to make its shape, providing a seat and back. The construction had to be recent, as some of the wood still had green leaves attached. Small, white wildflowers, still on their stalks, were woven along the top of the backrest and into the armrests, adding specks of light against the darkness of the wood.

The bench was so inviting that the sleepless Princess could not resist it. Taking the seat that overlooked the stream and the vista beyond, she strained her eyes, seeing a doe with her fawn moving along the water's edge at some distance. The soft, distant tinkling of the water made gurgling sounds as it moved over the rocks, rushing toward the pond. It reminded Alaine of the fountain and of the noise that it made in her small garden at home. Taking in a deep breath, letting it out in a sigh, her muscles relaxed, and her mind floated as a leaf on the pool.

Her eyelids felt heavy and would close… just for a moment.

When her eyes opened, they quickly adjusted to the dim light. Alaine was startled as she realized that she was no longer sitting alone on the bench. An arm's length away sat the young traveler she recognized from the inn. Just last night, she had tried to hold onto his image in her mind. Adding to the reality, his dog sat on the ground by his arm. The man's rustic cloak was gone, and his hair was tied back. His face was smooth with no beard and his profile was handsome, even in the shadows. He sat quietly with his hands resting in his lap. There did not appear to be any threat from him, and strangely, Alaine, was not surprised to see him… just curious.

"Who are you?" she asked him.

"I'm Carver Vale," he answered, in the soft voice Alaine remembered.

"Where do you come from?"

"From the forest lands near your home at Hawthorn Castle."

"Why are you here?"

"I follow your travels."

"Why would you follow me?" Alaine asked, innocently.

"I wanted to talk to you."

"Do you know who I am?" the Princess asked.

"Oh, yes. Everyone in Hawthorn knows who you are."

"Do you also know why I travel to the seacoast?"

"I hear that it is to seek a husband," he answered.

The conversation went quiet. Together, they sat looking at the scenery. The sound of a bird called out, interrupting the hush of the night.

"Then why is it that you wish to speak to me?" asked Alaine, resuming the narrative.

"Because I am a friend that you know not. I may be of use to you," Carver answered.

Again, they sat in silence.

"It is peaceful here," Alaine observed, after a pause. "It makes me realize how tired I am."

"You can close your eyes and rest, dear Princess. Astra and I will stay to watch over you."

Believing him sincere, once again Alaine allowed her eyes to close. Her mind drifted off into a light sleep.

When the Princess awoke, the sky was lightening in the gray haze that filled the horizon before the sunrise. Now, alone on the bench, she gazed at the peaceful scene before her, searching for the man and his dog. They were gone. Had he really been there, or was she just dreaming? As she looked on the seat of the bench beside her, she found a tiny wood carving of a dog… *his* dog. It had not been a dream, she thought, turning the small figure over in her hand.

Suddenly, standing and walking toward the tents, she hurried, fearing that early risers would see her crossing the field. Alaine felt refreshed after the short nap. She headed straight for the privy tent, thinking to use it for an excuse for being out and about early. In her haste, the thoughts of Carver Vale were pushed into the recesses of her mind.

Moments later, the wayward Princess entered the tent, finding a rush of activity with the last of the dressing and hair styling being done. Genna was already rolling up the feather mattresses and closing trunk lids, readying them for packing onto a wagon.

"Where have you been?" Lady Avis questioned, when she saw Alaine come in slightly out of breath.

"I went to the privy," Alaine said, severely stretching the truth.

She was taken at her word by all but Genna, who gave her a look that the Princess knew well.

"Have Genna fix your hair. Your red braids are disheveled and coming undone. I don't suspect you'll be wearing that cloak all day," instructed the aunt.

"Yes, Aunt," Alaine replied, relieved that there was no further questioning of her whereabouts.

The camp was abuzz with the process of getting ready to proceed with the day's journey. The field that was transformed to a small city of tents was once again plowed farmland. By the time the ladies walked back from a breakfast at the cook's tent, they found their small habitat gone, already packed away. The horses were being harnessed to the wagons, as well as to the royal coach, with the morning sun still low in the sky, putting out rays of gold.

They stood in a huddle, waiting to board the carriage. Lady Avis carried a restocked basket of drink and scones made with berries collected the previous day. They all set their travel bags on the ground near the wheel of the coach.

Sergeant Covey motioned for Lady Avis to join him as the wagons were being prepared for departure. Avis saw the concern on his face and took Nana's arm while walking the short distance from the royal coach.

"What is it, Covey?" she asked when she reached him, and a guardsman she identified from her son's garrison.

"It is a warning, milady," the Sergeant replied. "The Captain sends a message for you. It seems that highwaymen have been seen in the area. He has assigned two extra guardsmen to ride with the coach, so there will be six. Rand and I are also armed in case of an attack."

"The Captain asked me to give this to you for protection. He says it is small enough to be hidden in your food basket," said the guardsman.

He handed her a sword hilt dagger, with the familiar letters of 'ML', for Morr-Leigh, cast in the silver of the hilt. Lady Avis recognized it as the dagger that her son usually carried at his belt.

"Thank you for the warning, Covey. We will remain alert during the drive."

Walking away, toward the coach, the two older women put their heads together.

"There is no reason to scare the girls with this information," Nana put in. "But we will have to keep them from straying away from the coach and the wagons as they seem to do."

"Yes," agreed Lady Avis, "we will have to keep an eye on them."

"Speaking of keeping an eye on them," said Nana, "where are they off to?"

"There they are, crossing the field. Where are they going?"

The ladies watched as the young women walked toward the far end of the field.

"They are quickly becoming partners in transgressions," observed the aunt. "I'm not sure you and I are up to reigning them in." Then, wistfully, "Ah, to be young again."

Previously, as Lady Avis and Nana moved off a way to speak with a guardsman and Sergeant Covey, Alaine and Charlyn were engaging in small talk when Charlyn asked, "Where is the broach that you were wearing with that dress last night?"

Alaine's hand flew to her chest where the broach had been. "Oh, no!" she exclaimed. "I've lost it!"

"When did you last notice wearing it?" Charlyn asked, trying to be helpful.

"It was pinned to my dress last night," she replied, trying to think when she last felt it there.

"If it had fallen off in the tent, Genna would have found it this morning," Charlyn offered.

Alaine thought through her movements during the night. She could have lost it any time, walking across the back of the field toward the stream, or even on her way back. Looking around desperately, did she have time to go look for it, she wondered?

"I went for a walk over to the stream bank this morning," she confided to Charlyn. "Will you go with me to try to find my broach?"

Charlyn sensed a small conspiracy.

"Yes, let's hurry," she said, glancing over at Lady Avis and Nana.

Alaine scanned the ground while quickly retracing the path she had taken in the darkness. When at the bank of the pond, she followed it along to the brace of bushes where the bench sat.

"Oh, look. A little bench," Charlyn pointed.

The Princess thought the rustic framework of the bench looked less inviting in the daylight, almost as if it would fall apart if one tried to take a seat. The leaves and strands of tiny wildflowers were either closed or wilting on their stems. All was rather sad looking, Alaine reflected, remembering how enchanted the bench had seemed during the night.

"Let's look around here on the ground," the Princess encouraged.

Yet, as much as they searched, the elusive broach was not to be found.

"We had better get back," Charlyn reminded, at last.

"Yes, it is gone," Alaine bemoaned, in a defeated voice.

Rushing back to the coach, the girls continued to search the ground on their way, all for naught.

Carver Vale stood on a ridge at the end of the woods watching the last of the royal escort wagons leave the farmland. His hope of gaining the hand of Princess Alaine was renewed. The admirer believed that there was the basis for a friendship. The object of his passion had spoken to him as an equal and had shown him trust.

He looked down at the diamond shaped broach that he held in his hand. Carver felt an irrepressible urge to have something that belonged to her when he gently removed it from the lace near her throat. His intention was to somehow return it to her; but, for now, he reveled in having something of hers, normally worn close to her heart. Carver tucked the keepsake into his own breast pocket.

The day was fair; the roadway was straight and dry. He would need to hurry to keep pace with the caravan.

"Come, Astra," he called to the dog that was rummaging in the undergrowth.

7
Dangers on the Road

The morning coach ride was quiet after Alaine and Charlyn received a severe dressing down by Lady Avis for returning late from their walk, which held up their departure. Neither girl offered any reason for their gallivanting. Yet, all in the carriage were keeping their secrets. Lady Avis and Nana agreed that the Princess and Lady Charlyn should not be told of the rumors of highwaymen. The dagger from Kent was hidden in Nana's knitting bag.

The weather was warm, the roads were good, and the caravan was moving along at a faster pace. The brief stop for lunch allowed for a short meal, care of the horses, and other necessities.

Later, the loss of the broach was still bothering Alaine, who chewed on a fingernail as the coach bounced along. She did not regret the sojourn to the bewitching bench and the encounter with the attractive stranger. She now knew his name – Carver Vale. It was an odd name, and not one she had heard at court or in the village of Hawthorn. As she thought back, trying to remember every detail of their brief conversation, he had called himself a friend, but she didn't remember ever seeing him before the night at the inn. The Princess thought she should have been afraid, or at least surprised, when she found him sitting next to her, but for some reason it felt like he belonged there. When she tried to remember what he looked like, the thought of his profile, sitting in the shadows, was captivating. Alaine knew she wished to see Carver Vale again. She wanted to talk to him - about what, she wasn't sure. Maybe just to know his story. He'd given her two small gifts, the carved figurines, nestled in her jewelry box. Maybe she was just being foolish, she thought, as she straightened herself against the seat. They couldn't *really* become friends. She was a princess, and he was not of her class, which was the nobility. A world with demands upon her, such as a marriage. The need was, though regretful, to put him out of her mind and forget about him – but could she?

In the middle of the afternoon, the coach came to a stop – a surprise to its occupants. Alaine and Charlyn craned their necks to look out the small window in the door. A large, barn-like building filled the view beside the road. There was a faded sign over the door:

Farmer's Merchant

"What is it?' asked Charlyn, referring to a large structure along the almost deserted road.

"I think it's a store," answered Alaine, with some doubt.

"Whatever it is, Annie and Smyth are on their way in there," observed Charlyn.

"May we go in, too?" Alaine asked her aunt, curiosity driving her request.

"If Annie's in there, she'll probably be a while. I guess we can all get out and stretch the stiffness out of our backs," the Lady replied.

The girls needed no further encouragement. They bounded out of the coach and, with zest, followed the flagstone path leading to the roadside emporium.

Inside, the building consisted of two large rooms, one with a high ceiling. The larger room was stacked high with bags of animal feed and stocked with farming tools, harnesses, and other items of use for farmers. The room near the door was crowded with loaded shelves, counters and tables holding all sorts of things for sale. There were baskets, bins, boxes, and containers holding food items and an array of dry goods. Annie was at the long back counter speaking with the storekeeper. Smyth, the garrison cook, stood next to her, holding a bag of coins in his hand. The prices for various food goods were being discussed. In the meantime, two lads walked past carrying giant sacks of flour, potatoes, and barley.

"How much for that lug of apples?" Annie asked the storekeeper.

"Mmm, apples," Charlyn whispered to Alaine.

"These ribbons would be nice for our hair," Alaine said, pulling out the narrow strips of fine fabric from a bin, choosing some of the colors that would go with her dresses.

Nana and Lady Avis were also walking through the aisles, taking in the offerings, picking up items, examining them, and replacing them.

"Look at the blue of this yarn," Nana said, holding up a skein for review. "It's such a pretty shade."

"Here are some cards," Charlyn said to Alaine. "We could play cards while riding. It would help pass the time."

"We'll take this basket of onions and these mushrooms," Annie called to the clerk, from a nearby table.

"Are you sure those are the right kind of mushrooms, Annie?" Lady Avis asked.

"A body can't call themselves a cook, lest they have a good knowledge of mushrooms, milady. These will be good in a thick barley porridge."

Smyth was asking about any stores of meat that might be on hand, knowing that the men wanted at least one meal with meat every day. He tried to oblige the soldiers when he could.

"A twelve-point stag hangs in the locker," the storekeeper answered. "It came in yesterday. It's not yet skinned, because I've not had time to get to it. There are also four geese brought in by a local farmer this morning."

"We'll take the lot. So, what's your price?" asked the cook, with a grizzled beard and grin, showing gums with missing teeth.

Later, when the ladies once again took their seats in the coach, all were pleased. Alaine was sorting the new ribbons and Charlyn was looking at her pictured playing cards. Nana tucked her four skeins of azure wool into her bag - enough for a shawl - she mentioned with satisfaction.

Lady Avis put a piece of honey-spice candy into her mouth, while offering some to everyone. The horses pulled away and they were on the road once again.

Kent was pleased with the day's progress as he rode forward to meet his two scouts returning from their exploration of the road ahead.

"Good place to camp a few leagues ahead, sir," reported Lieutenant Proden, one of Captain Leigh's most trusted men.

"Can we circle the wagons as we did yesterday?" Leigh asked.

"It's a large plot of grassland. There are pine groves on each side off the road, and the lot has forest lands along the back side," the lieutenant reported.

"How thick are the woods? Can horses come through it for an attack?"

"These woods are old forest, too thick and overgrown for horses. It would be hard enough to pass through it on foot."

"How much further is it?" the Captain inquired.

"At this pace, we'd be there and have the camp set up by dark."

"Good," said Kent. "Stay here at the front of the wagons and guide them to the spot. I'll ride back and check on the royal coach."

The Captain turned his horse and spurred it into a trot back down the road.

The royal coach was quiet, with Nana dozing, only to be startled awake by loud shouts from outside the carriage. Suddenly the horses pulling the coach took off, severely jolting its riders. More horses could be seen running along both sides of the coach, some carrying unfamiliar men. Indistinguishable shouts and yells were heard over the noise made by speeding, rattling wheels. Scenes of the roadway fled past the window.

Alaine gasped as she saw Rand fall from the coach's driver seat and hit the ground. He was left in the dirt as the jostling ride continued. Was Covey holding the reins, Alaine wondered, or anyone? The sudden awareness of being under attack brought terror to all of the captive women.

After a few moments that seemed like forever, the coach came to an abrupt stop. Through the windows, they could see horses and riders in combat on both sides of the coach.

"Stay in the coach!" Lady Avis had time to yell, over all of the clamor going on outside. "Nana, give me the Morr-Leigh dagger!"

Nana began desperately digging in her knitting bag. Alaine was reminded of her own small weapon hanging from her belt. Grasping the dragonfly, she pressed the metal button on the underside of one wing, allowing the sharp blade to come free in her hand.

Amid the havoc, there was no time. The door of the coach was wrenched open beside where Charlyn and Nana were sitting. A large arm thrust its way into the interior, and a beefy hand grabbed Charlyn's wrist, tugging her toward the opening. Alaine reached up and tried to get her arms around Charlyn, who was screaming and resisting the pulling force. But out the girl went, unable to resist, landing awkwardly on the ground. From inside the coach, Alaine saw Charlyn being dragged away by a man twice her size.

By now, Lady Avis had her hands on the hilt of the dagger, but Alaine was on her feet going out the door to follow Charlyn.

"Alaine, stay here!" her aunt yelled, but the girl was her impetuous self.

"Come back! Help! Help us!" she screamed out the door of the coach.

Alaine was acting on instinct, without thinking of consequences. Once out of the coach, she dodged the fray of four horses involved in combat between two guardsmen and two highwaymen. Running around the back of the carriage, Alaine saw Charlyn being dragged by a highwayman across the road by one arm. The girl was screaming and trying to resist the brute of a man, but it was hardly slowing the progress. He pulled her up the dirt bank toward a saddled horse that was waiting.

Covey was on the ground in front of the coach, fighting another man, both with short swords drawn. Realizing no one was available to help, Alaine took off across the road. As she climbed the dirt bank, she saw that the big, shaggy man was trying to get Charlyn onto the back of the horse. Charlyn was fighting for her life, batting her aggressor with both fists. Alaine watched as the villain, having had enough of fighting with Charlyn, drew back one arm and punched the young noblewoman in the face. Her body crumpled to the ground. Alaine let out a scream of outrage at the sight. At once, the man bent down and picked up the girl like a flour sac and tried to throw her unconscious body across the back of the horse. Now, pure anger and determination fueled Alaine. While the blackguard had his hands full with Charlyn, Alaine ran to the back of the horse and plunged her little dagger into its back flank.

The horse immediately reared up on its hind legs, throwing off Charlyn and the man holding her. Spooked, the stallion ran off the roadside bank, and down the road. Alaine froze, as the burly man dropped Charlyn and took a stance, staring at her in fury.

The headstrong Princess immediately realized her own jeopardy. Alaine feared that her small knife would do little against this angry lout, who could easily overpower her. She took steps backward, away from the menace before her. Suddenly, his approach stalled, and his look of anger changed to one of fear as he stared at something behind her.

With a loud snarl, Covey bolted up from the road, sword raised in his hand. The gruesome attacker, unarmed, turned, and took off running through the trees lining the highway. Covey gave chase at first, but soon returned to the young noblewomen for fear of leaving them without protection.

As Covey approached, he found Alaine on the ground, cradling Lady Charlyn's head on her lap. There was no movement from the girl. Her dress was torn, and her blonde braids had come undone from their pins. An angry, red knot was rising on her forehead above closed eyelids.

Alaine softly repeated her name, but Charlyn was unresponsive. It was a relief that at least her breathing was steady.

Now, feeling safe with Covey by her side, tears came to the eyes of the Princess. She quickly wiped them as they fell to her cheeks, frustrated with her own crying as she recounted the recent danger. The outcome could have been far worse. As Alaine stroked Charlyn's hair, there was a thankfulness they were both alive and neither of them had been taken by the attackers. Now, talk of dangers on the road was no longer just a discussion over the dinner table, but a stark reality.

Riding toward the coach, Kent saw a cloud of dust coming from the road ahead, partially obscuring his view. Then he heard the shouts resonating and spurred his horse to a gallop. Two dead men lay on the ground by the carriage. Stopping at the coach, he saw that his mother and Nana were shaken but unharmed.

Lieutenant Miles, seeing his commander, rode to meet him. "What happened here and where is the Princess?!" he demanded.

"Highwaymen came out of the trees on the side of the road. There were at least ten of them on horses. They went after the coach. The girls are over there with Covey."

"Where are these rogues? Do we have them?"

"There are these two here, and we have three more tied up over there, with Teran guarding them. Some of the guards chased the others down the road and have not yet returned."

"Stay with the coach, Miles. I'll be with the Princess," Kent yelled.

Kent saw that both girls were on the ground with Covey standing by them.

"Oh, no," he shouted aloud, fearing what he might find. Dismounting, he ran across the road. As he approached Alaine and the fallen Lady Charlyn, he fell to his knees beside them.

"The man pulled Charlyn out of the coach and dragged her over here where he had a horse waiting," Alaine explained to Kent. "He hit her, and she hasn't woken up since then."

"Did you catch who did this?" Kent demanded of Covey, in a strained and angry voice.

"He ran off. I didn't want to leave the Princess and her Lady alone, so I didn't chase him," Covey responded.

"Well, get some men and go after him. He needs to be brought to justice. He shouldn't be too hard to catch if he's on foot. Find him!" the Captain commanded.

As Covey went to get help, the rest of the wagons that had been left behind when the royal coach started on its wild ride, pulled up on the road. Alaine saw Rand sitting in one of the open wagons, with Annie and Smyth next to him. He was conscious, but obviously injured.

"Let's get Charlyn to the cook's wagon. She'll need to remain flat. You can stay with her until we get to where we're going to stop for the night," Kent ordered.

"Is it very far?" Alaine asked.

"I don't think so, but we'll let the others go before us and I'll stay with the wagon. We can go slowly to keep the jarring as little as possible."

Kent carried the unconscious girl while Alaine ran ahead to the cook's wagon to get a spot ready for her. They laid her on the piled flour sacks, placing a rolled cloth under her head. Nana brought a compress for the angry welt on her forehead. The girl looked comfortable but remained lost to the world.

Beales took off into the trees lining the roadway to escape the sword- wielding soldier chasing him. His plans for holding the Princess hostage for five hundred pieces of gold had failed. The game was at a dismal end, as well as his thoughts of shipping out to a warmer land to start his life over using his share of the coin.

He and his men had followed the royal coach for two days, taking care to stay out of sight of the scouts and guards. A chance had been taken for the surprise attack to take place on the lands of Duke Seaken-Char, well known for his loyalty to the King. Beales knew the Duke had his own force of troops that patrolled the main road. The noble's large keep, Seaken Hall, had rumors of deep dungeons.

Now, an outlaw on the run, his horse was gone, thanks to that wench who came from nowhere to thwart his efforts to get the Princess onto his mount for a getaway. Sweat was dripping from his face onto his unkempt beard. Not used to running any distance, he went as fast as his large bulk would allow. His clothes were heavy and clung to him as he fled. Twisting his neck to look back, he saw no one in pursuit. That only allayed his fears temporarily. Knowing the number of soldiers in the royal escort, he thought they would soon mount a hunt for him.

The trees near the road were thinly placed, but now the landscape was thick with brush and older trees as he moved inland. Beales decided to make for the dense forest, seeking a place to hide until the sun went down and throughout the night. He would make his way north toward his hovel of a farmhouse at first light.

A while later, deep in the thick forest, Beales was spent from his run, and looking for a place to hide and rest within the thicket. As he looked around for some kind of landmark, the hairs on the back of his neck prickled. *Which way was it back to the road*, he wondered? Then the realization struck him that he was lost in an inhospitable wood. His eyes and ears were starting to play tricks on him. There were rustling sounds of movement. *Animals*, he questioned? Then a flash of something passing nearby was seen from the corner of his eye, forcing him to turn for a closer look, only to find nothing there. Next, a buzzing sound flew by his ear, so close that he raised a hand to bat it away. Again, something flew by the other side of his head and made a "thunk" as it embedded itself in the trunk of the tree beside him – an arrow.

Without time to think, Beales took off again, stumbling over branches and fallen logs. No path could be seen as he moved blindly from one spot to another. More arrows whizzed by at close range, inflicting terror. A red fox sped across in front of him just before he fell over a jagged tree stump, bringing him to the ground in a heap.

"Well, he's a big one," Flecher commented, bow still in his hand with another arrow notched.

Bole had the hemp rope around the wrists before the downed man could catch his breath.

"On your feet, man! These are *our* woods," the short, stocky woodsman proclaimed.

"So, you try to kill a man?" Beales growled, holding his ankle in pain.

Slim, blond Flecher straightened to his full height, his long bow almost as tall as he was.

"Had I wanted to kill you, you'd be dead, trespasser."

"We'll take him back to the road. Surely, he was running from something, or someone," said Bole.

The three twisted and turned their way through the thicket, the bulk of a man limping along, being led by a prince of the woods on each side.

Astra was the first to hear the small group headed for the road and led Carver to them with a bark as she bounded ahead.

"Carver, it is good to see you!" Bole greeted his kin, speaking in the language of the forest. "Yet, we aren't surprised to find you. Word in the trees is that you travel south."

"Who is this?" Carver asked. "One of the band of highwaymen who were following the Princess? I fear that they may have already made their attack and I am too late."

"We found him tromping through the trees. You know how these field people get lost and go in circles," Fletcher relayed. "Soon they become food for the foxes and bobcats unless we, or the moss faeries, lead them out."

"Why your travels, Carver?" Bole asked his brother, changing the subject.

"I follow the Princess of Hawthorn to the Weston Mareview Lowlands," Carver replied.

"Is she the one with the flying red curls that used to play near the woods with the noble boy?" Flecher asked, remembering the carefree girl.

"Yes, but she is grown up and is ready for marriage. I want her as my bride," Carver announced.

"It seems that you have grown up also. We have heard of your dealings with the village people," said Bole, spoken in the manner of an elder brother.

"This is not our way, Carver. Does our father know of this?"

"He's dismayed with my choice, but he has given me permission to seek out the Princess."

"Then we wish you well, brother," Flecher said, with support.

"Look up ahead. Now there come more visitors to our woods," alerted Bole.

Sure enough, Covey and Miles approached with swords in hand. Two more soldiers followed, carrying spears. Carver and Astra walked forward to meet them, holding up a hand in greeting.

"This is the lad that gave us the warning about the highwaymen," Miles told Covey.

"This man was found in the woods alone. He was one of the highwaymen following the royal escort," Carver explained to the soldiers.

"He and his men attacked the royal coach. We were sent to find him and bring him back by order of the Captain," Covey stated, sternly.

"How does the Princess fare?" Carver keenly wanted to know.

"She fares as well as can be expected," answered Covey, "but her lady- in-waiting was injured by this lout. So, we'll take him from here."

Covey signaled to the two guards to take hold of the prisoner.

"We will leave you, then," Bole proclaimed, now standing next to Carver. Flecher silently stepped close behind them.

Covey observed the woodsmen with suspicion, wondering who they were. The trio made a mystical picture, standing close together. All were different in stature and coloring, yet there seemed to be a family resemblance. Maybe it was the striking eyes, beardless faces and unusual clothing that made them look part of the same clan. They seemed to know what they were about and appeared to have no fear of authority.

One waved a hand in salute as they took their leave, seeming to dissolve into the surrounding brush. Only the bark of the dog was heard from the wood beyond.

"Odd lot," Covey observed to no one in particular. "Come, let's get this man back. Sunset is upon us."

When Charlyn first regained consciousness, she thought she heard faint voices nearby. She became aware that she was lying flat on something uneven, but firm, with a gentle bouncing, indicating ongoing movement. Not yet ready to open her eyes, she took inventory of her body and how she felt. Starting at the top, there was a rather bad headache, her forehead hurt, and her neck was stiff. She could feel her arms, legs, fingers, and toes. Yes, other than the headache, she felt fairly normal.

Her mind began racing, thinking back to the last thing she remembered. Fear - it was fear she remembered. The terror of being taken by a villain. She remembered struggling to get away. Then, there was nothing. She winced and brought a hand up to her sore forehead where a damp cloth was resting.

"I think she's waking up!" whispered a familiar voice next to her right ear. "Charlyn …," called Lady Avis, quietly. "Charlyn…," she repeated.

Opening her eyes, Charlyn tried to take in her surroundings. She was inside a moving wagon with a tarp overhead, allowing some light to filter in. Cooking utensils hung about, jostling with the movement. Turning her head slightly, she saw three figures sitting in a line, squeezed together next to her. All looking at her with their full attention, the Princess, Lady Avis, and Nana were awaiting her first words.

"How are you, dear?" Lady Avis asked, gently.

"What happened? How did I get away?" Charlyn stammered, weakly.

"We were attacked by a gang of men. You were pulled out of the coach. Alaine went after you," Nana explained, with drama in her voice.

"Yes, and against my wishes, Alaine followed after you," explained Lady Avis. "She was able to spook the outlaw's horse, so it ran off. Fortunately, Covey was able to get to you both and scare the man off, but not before the lout hit you."

"You've been unconscious for some time. Kent put you in the wagon, and we've been traveling slowly lest we injure you further. Most of the others went on ahead to prepare a place for us," Nana revealed, with concern. "How do you feel?"

Charlyn tried to sit up, but only got as far as raising herself on one elbow. "I don't know… I feel kind of dizzy." She laid back down.

"Well, just stay flat, dear. When we get to the camp, we'll make a comfortable spot for you to recover," promised Lady Avis.

Alaine reached out and held Charlyn's hand, knowing that it could have been *her* lying on the flour sacks. Charlyn sighed. She felt nauseated and would be happy when the wagon stopped moving. How much further, she wondered?

It was already dark when the wagon carrying the noble ladies pulled into the campsite. The tents were erected, the horses were untethered from their loads, and the campfires were blazing.

Smyth was manning grills heavy with venison. Annie and her crew were busy making pan bread and fried asparagus. The chores of camp life went on despite the drama of the day.

Covey and Miles made it back to the camp prior to the lagging wagon. Their prisoner, Beales, was added to the rest of the captured highwaymen and tied into a wagon that was sent with guards on a trip to Seaken Hall. Backtracking on the main road to the sidetrack leading to Duke Seaken-Char's Hold, they should arrive before sun-up.

When Covey saw the cook's wagon pull in, he went to meet it. He offered to carry Lady Charlyn to the tent that was already prepared, thanks to Genna and a group of willing soldiers she enlisted into service for the tasks. Yet, Lady Charlyn insisted on standing and trying to walk despite the dizziness she felt when she was upright. With Covey on one side and Alaine on the other, the group slowly made their way to the waiting canvas retreat.

Feeling better upon lying down, Charlyn gratefully drank a small cup of wine and soon drifted off to sleep. Nana was at her side while the others went off to the great tent for some food and their own cup of wine. All were weary and would be glad to see *this day* come to an end.

Carver Vale traveled through the night to find the latest encampment of the escort party. He had taken some time to share a meal and a brief interaction with his brothers, Bole, the eldest, and Flecher. Carver's six brothers were dispersed throughout the upper and lower kingdom's wooded lands, which made finding chances to meet infrequent. It was the family's tradition to gather at their father's arboreal keep among the elder trees at the time of the fall leaf change.

That was the last time Carver had seen all of his brothers in one place; and, as usual, endured their chidings, he being the youngest of the seven. Their father, King Alfred, was always elated to have a feast under the trees with all of his offspring and their families at his side.

After a time, as he stood at the edge of the forest land, Carver could see the tents and fires of the camp not far afield. There were the occasional sounds of horses, but for the most part, all seemed quiet. He took a seat on a log and gathered his cloak around him. Astra settled on the ground at his feet, sprawling out her long body. A layer of mist hung just above the ground over the grasslands. Carver thought that the Princess Alaine might still be awake. He wondered if she was troubled after the attack by the highwaymen. If she couldn't sleep, maybe she would walk out to the meadow. He longed to see her, but for now, all he could do was wait.

Predictably, later that night, Alaine was lying awake on her mattress. How she wished to leave the tent, if only to visit the privy and a chance to inhale the cool night air. Yet, she felt that she couldn't leave Charlyn, who might awaken and need something. She had heard Genna when she quietly slipped out some time ago. Her maid was probably on her way to find Rand.

Covey told them earlier that the footman had dislocated his shoulder in his fall from the royal coach during the wild chase. Smyth took him in hand, being used to helping members of the garrison with battle injuries. First filling the lad with hard drink, Smyth popped the bone back into its socket. Then the arm was tied to Rand's chest to keep it in place. Surely, he wouldn't be driving the coach for some days to come.

Now, where was Genna? Alaine worried. Was she alone in a tent with Rand? Unable to sleep, Alaine waited for the girl's return.

When morning came, Lady Avis and Alaine helped Charlyn walk to the privy tent. The young woman was still dizzy and unsteady on her feet. Once they returned to the tent, Lady Avis went off to find her son. According to the concerned matron, there would be no traveling today!

Charlyn was not well enough to ride in a wagon for any distance. They would have to postpone their travel, at least until the next day.

Genna returned and was sitting alone, combing her hair outside the tent. Alaine went to her.

"Genna, what are you up to?" Alaine whispered, having an opportunity for a private talk. "I know that you are leaving the tent at night, and you barely made it back before Nana awoke this morning!"

"I can't stand being away from Rand. He was almost killed yesterday. Last night he was in a lot of pain. I need to be with him," Genna pleaded. "I love him, and I almost lost him. He says that he wants to marry me."

"Yes, but you are not married yet. You can't be found in his tent. Some of the soldiers may have turned a blind eye, but the nobility will not stand for an unmarried girl staying alone with a man. Even though you are my maid, I would have little to say if you were caught. You must be more careful!" Alaine warned.

"I know, I will try," said Genna contritely, tears of embarrassment welling in her eyes.

"I think that you should go to the cook's tent to see if Annie needs you to help with anything," Alaine suggested, using her authority.

Genna walked away with her shoulders hunched. It was rare for the Princess to scold her, and Genna knew it was only Alaine's care for her that prompted the rebuke. She tied her hair in a knot as she walked, pondering her fate, and doing as she was told.

Lady Avis and the Princess decided to take a walk around the camp and get some lunch, leaving Nana to work with her new wool, while watching over Charlyn. Nana helped the young lady put on a beige morning gown with ribbons at the high neck and lace flowing from the sleeves ending below her elbows. Nana gently brushed the girl's hair, allowing it free of braids, to cascade onto Charlyn's shoulders. The old nurse made the Lady comfortable, rolling a mattress pad so that she could sit leaning against it. Nana then supplied Charlyn with needles and wool, giving her something to do. It was early afternoon when the visitor came to the ladies' tent. Kent had washed, shaved, and neatly tied his hair back. He wore his garrison jacket over a clean shirt. His trousers were dark, smooth, and tucked into the tops of his tall, black boots. He came with gifts – a small, illustrated book with the words to well-known songs and a used wine bottle stuffed with wildflowers. Both Nana and Charlyn were surprised when he came to the tent flap and requested entrance. He settled himself on the ground next to where Charlyn had stretched out her legs.

"How are you feeling?" he asked her, after Charlyn had accepted the gifts.

"Much better, today," she replied, shyly. "I am sorry for being the cause for the loss of a day's travel. I remain a little dizzy when I stand or walk. I'm hoping that it will be less by morning."

"If anyone should be sorry it is I for not being where I was most needed yesterday. I should have been near the coach. Please accept my apology."

"There is no apology needed," she responded, graciously. "It is impossible for you to be all places at once. I believe that we must be thankful for Sergeant Covey. From what Alaine told me, he saved us from being taken as hostages."

"I agree. The man is good, and loyal to the Princess. If only he could have gotten there before you were injured. At least he caught the lout, who is probably facing Duke Seaken-Char for punishment by now."

"Why Duke Seaken-Char?" Charlyn questioned.

"These are his lands, his district, held intact since before my father's time."

"Oh," she said, while sneaking a look at the handsome Captain.

"What is it that you are doing there?" he asked, referring to the needlework, while noticing the girl's delicate hands.

"Oh, it's from Nana. She thought that I should have something to do, so I'm practicing knitting. I'm not very good at it, but Nana insists that if I know how to knit wool, it will be useful all my life."

"Our Nana is very wise. You know that she was nursemaid to both my mother and Queen Iris from the time they were small. She's quite the fixture in our family," he whispered to Charlyn, lest the old nurse overhear. "She's tried her best to get the Princess proficient in needlework. Possibly when Alaine is older, she will take to it, but for now, I think she would prefer a more active pastime," he laughed.

"I, too, need practice. It is quite calming to knit, and you end up with a prize at the end."

"What is it you are making?" he asked, looking at the tail of knitted wool on her lap.

"It is a scarf. I always make a scarf. It's the one thing that I can make. But don't ask me to make socks," she laughed, "socks are beyond my skills."

They were both laughing when Lady Avis and Alaine entered the tent to find the visitor sitting on the floor next to Charlyn. The girl looked charming and flushed despite the terrible bruise on her forehead. Kent quickly rose to greet his mother, after which he gave an excuse to leave, wishing Charlyn well.

Alaine followed him out and caught up with him, walking between empty garrison tents.

"What do you think you are doing?" she demanded of her cousin. "Dressed up in the middle of the day? Flowers stuffed in a wine bottle? Seriously?"

"It was the best I could do under the circumstances," he replied, not slowing his pace for her.

"You are flirting with my lady-in-waiting!" she exclaimed, rushing to keep up with his long strides.

"No, I was assessing her health and our ability to continue our travels in the morning."

"Don't put up a pretense to me. I've seen you romance the ladies before. You broke Lady Loren's heart and left her."

"I couldn't help leaving. There was a call for troops and a war afoot," he said, justifying his actions. "Besides, she couldn't have been too broken hearted since she was married and ready to have a child by the time I returned to court."

"Well, my lady-in-waiting should be off limits. By the way, you are too old for her."

"I am not too old," Kent replied, with indignation. "Most men are my age when they take a bride, and she is of marriageable age."

"So you are speaking of marriage?"

"No, we hardly know each other yet."

"So leave her be," Alaine demanded.

"You can't tell me what to do. You are barely past childhood yourself," Kent retorted, now deliberately trying to annoy her.

"But I am someone who has your mother's ear," she replied, playing her last card.

He stopped walking and faced her.

"Stay out of it, Alaine," he demanded in a warning voice, then stomped off, dismissing her as he would a bothersome bug.

As Alaine returned to the tent after her bout with Kent, she walked into an emotional scene. Genna was sitting on one of the trunks, crying. Nana, unsure of the problem, was trying to comfort her.

"What's happened?" Alaine asked at once, dreading that she already knew.

Before anyone could answer, Lady Avis entered the tent, obviously upset.

"What is it, Aunt?" the Princess asked, while Genna looked up with a pause in her sobs.

Lady Avis walked over to Genna, prepared to ask her own questions. "Is it true that you spent the night in Rand's tent?"

"Yes, milady," Genna answered, clutching her handkerchief.

"Did you also spend the night before with him?"

"Yes," was the meek response from the maid, "but nothing happened. We just talked."

Lady Avis put up her hands in defeat and turned away. She was disappointed in the trusted servant. She was so focused on her responsibility for the Princess and Lady Charlyn that she never expected Genna to be the cause of any troubles.

"What is it, Aunt? What has happened?" Alaine prodded for details.

"I just spoke with Annie. The whispers are all over the camp. We surely didn't need this," the Lady espoused, while pacing the limited space.

"Whatever is going on?" the confused Nana demanded.

"According to the gossip, Genna has been seen going into Rand's tent at night. The soldiers of the guard were speaking of it, and now it's been spread about. It's quite the scandal, it is! The cook's girls were afraid to speak to Genna for fear of being dragged into it. Annie sent Genna back to our tent."

"What must we do?" Alaine asked, worried for what would happen to Genna.

"For now, all of you stay here. Genna, you are not to leave the tent except to go to the privy, and then Nana or Alaine will go with you. I had better go speak with my son. I will tell him that we will keep Genna with us."

Once Lady Avis left, it was quiet in the tent. Charlyn and Alaine did a bit of small talk, which soon lapsed into silence. All realized the seriousness of the situation.

Genna went to her mattress, lying with her face to the canvas wall. Her sobs had ceased, but a deeper depression took their place. She feared that she had foolishly ruined her life. She would lose her position as Alaine's lady's maid and be cast out. She worried about her mother, a widow, who was so proud of her daughter. How would she tell her, Genna agonized? And Rand, what would happen to him, she wondered? Would he lose his place at Hawthorn Castle? In misery, Genna's mind drifted to the extremes. Maybe she could go away, get a job in Harbortown at a shop or one of the many inns, and never return to Hawthorn. She foresaw a lonely life ahead as she drowned herself in pity.

Time within the tent passed slowly for its occupants. Alaine wondered what was happening when Lady Avis didn't return in what she thought was a reasonable time. She knew that her aunt was a fair woman and would support Genna as much as propriety would allow, but Genna's fate seemed to hang in the balance.

Lady Avis found Kent in the great tent, speaking with some of the men of his garrison.

Kent was not surprised to see his mother approaching in a state of distress. The rumors about Rand and Genna had already reached him. He had spoken with Rand, who swore his love for Genna and refused to answer any questions about her visiting his tent. The young man, still injured, with his arm incapacitated, was told to remain in his tent. Kent placed a guard at the front flap, with the strong suggestion of communication being off limits.

Lady Avis, Covey, and Kent huddled together at a table of wooden planks, discussing the best way to manage the situation. All in the camp would be waiting to see what actions were taken. Unfortunately, it was Genna's reputation that was the most under attack, primarily because she put herself in the delicate position. Someone had been watching and the secret was too inflammatory to be kept.

Suddenly, shouts were coming from outside.

A man ran in and yelled to Kent. "Captain, we have visitors. You're needed out front!"

"Now what?!" Kent exclaimed, on his way out of the tent.

Kent and Covey strode toward the front of the camp, which was near the main road. A black coach, with the door emblazoned with a duke's crest, pulled to a halt in front of three loaded wagons. The wagons were dotted with people, and a clutch of guards reined their horses and dismounted by the coach.

The coach door opened and out came the tall, gray-haired figure of Duke Seaken-Char, who walked toward Kent, while leaning on his stick.

"Duke Morr-Leigh, what is it that you have for dinner?" he hailed and patting the dumbfounded Kent on the shoulder. "I heard that you were in the neighborhood. Are we welcome for supper?"

"You are certainly welcome. We are just surprised to see you," Kent answered.

"I did bring plenty stores of meat, vegetables, and baked pheasant pies. Also, a couple of vats of our aged wine will add to the festivities. We even loaded on extra cooks and serving hands."

The old Duke gave the order for the wagons to be unloaded before he was led to the great tent by Kent and Covey. Seaken-Char was pleased to greet Lady Avis, and promptly called for a cup of tea.

Soon, the nobles sat on make-shift benches, sipping tea from tin cups, with biscuits and jam, discussing everything from the weather to the roads. Kent finally asked about the surprise visit.

"Oh, the tedious carryings-on at my great hall have been so mundane that I retire to my rooms before sunset. The neighborhood's in such a quiet routine as to bore one senseless," the elder Duke complained. "Then, last night, as I was finishing my sherry before I retired, my footman announced *your* lieutenant requiring my urgent attention!

"Well, the tale he had to tell - villains, a chase, sword fights, distressed noblewomen about to be carried off. Damned exciting, except for the poor girl who was hurt, of course. Duke Noeman's daughter, was it not? How is she doing?"

"She is recovering. We did not set on the road today to allow her to rest," reported Lady Avis.

"I thought that I would come to meet you. You might want to know the fate of the prisoners you sent us. Besides, an excuse was needed to get out of that pile of rocks of mine."

"You have already dealt with the highwaymen, Duke?" asked Lady Avis.

"Call me Rengard, dear lady. Yes, we handled them first thing. The scoundrels hardly had time to get comfortable in the dungeons. They are already off to Duke Noeman, with signed contracts of servitude for the next five winters. You know how Noeman is always complaining about getting strong lads for his timber works and sawmills. The men agreed that working for Noeman would be better than rotting in our cells. My guards are escorting them with my letter to Noeman and the signed contracts. Seemed a just end."

"What about Beales? You sent him also?" Kent inquired, with the lift of an eyebrow.

"Sad story, that Beales. His father kept sheep herds on my lands for years, that went to the son when he died. Good man was the lad, carrying on with it. But two years ago, his wife died in childbirth. Last winter his sheep herd had sickness and all of the animals had to be put down for fear of the disease spreading. That left Beales alone, with nothing. The man took to the drink. A dairy farm hired him on for work but let him go in the end. That was the last that I heard, and now this. Maybe some hard work is just what Beales needs. At least Noeman will get the time out of him, and some revenge for his daughter's injury."

Lady Avis had been quietly listening when a thought came to her mind.

It was possibly a solution to a problem.

"Duke Seaton-Char, do you keep records of the births, deaths and marriages for your district?"

"Oh, yes, it is required by the King. Each town and village have a scribe for that. We record all births, deaths, and marriages," replied the Duke, after a last sip of his tea. "We do our own census at Winterfest. We also do the livestock count at harvest time. It is all on record."

"That is interesting," commented Lady Avis. "As the Magistrate of the district, do you perform weddings?"

"No…no, there is a mayor in each town that usually performs the marriages. It has been years since I've officiated at a wedding. Used to do them, though, when it was family or friends."

Kent suddenly realized where his mother was going with the conversation. "We have a very recent situation whereby you may provide a helpful solution…" Kent began to tell the story.

Elated, Lady Avis rushed into the tent with her gown flowing behind her. The atmosphere was dismal, as all were sharing in Genna's melancholy. Going straight to the prostrate girl, the Lady clapped her hands with excitement.

"Genna, are you sure that you wish to marry Rand?" she asked, while pulling the maid up to stand before her.

"Yes," Genna answered, as a wisp of hope appeared, "more than anything."

"Well, then, would you marry him today?"

"Today?" Genna asked, in disbelief.

"Today?!" Alaine echoed, standing next to Genna.

"Yes, today! You will not believe what has happened!" Lady Avis exclaimed, as Nana came to stand beside her. "The Duke Seaken-Char has come to the camp and brought with him a feast for dinner. We spoke to him, Kent and I, of your wish to marry. He is the Magistrate of the district, *and* he has offered to marry you!"

Genna looked at Lady Avis with amazement on her face, still grasping the meaning of what was said. Nana's mouth fell open at the prospect of a sudden wedding. Charlyn got up from her seat and joined the small group of women as dismay turned to exhilaration.

"Marry today?" Genna repeated, "But what about my mother?"

"Yes, it is too bad that she will miss the wedding; but Duke Leigh and I will explain it to her when we return to Hawthorn. You are almost nineteen, and of age to marry the man of your choice. You could have no finer prospect than Rand, a footman in the house of Hawthorn. *And* she should be pleased that her daughter had the honor of being married by Duke Seaken-Char, himself!"

"I think your mother will forgive you, Genna," added Alaine. "It will be quite a tale to tell your children one day."

"Now, we must get you ready," insisted Lady Avis. "The old Duke wants the wedding to take place before dinner. He desires a festive supper. Kent and Covey will help prepare Rand.

"Alaine, you go fetch some wildflowers that we can use to make a wreath for Genna's hair. Nana and Charlyn, find a dress for her to wear – something light. Oh, this will be fun!"

"I have the perfect dress!" exclaimed Alaine, running to her trunk. "Where is my yellow morning dress with the lace bodice? We can use the new ribbons. Charlyn can weave them into Genna's hair."

"We shall all dress our best for the festivities in honor of Duke Seaken-Char," said the Lady, going to her own trunk for a glamorous gown. "Alaine, you may wear one of your new dresses made for Irongate court. A wedding - who would have guessed?"

Duke Seaken-Char took charge of the festivities while Kent and Lady Avis were off preparing the bride and groom for the ceremony. And what a job he did, with help from many hands. The gregarious, crooked stick of a man had a way with managing people, and his wish was their command.

He ordered pine branches to be brought inside to line the canvas walls as decoration. Lanterns were strung high and flickered with light. A long table was set up for the happy couple and the nobility. Garrison shields were used to line the floor, leaning against the front of the table. The troops' flags, displaying the Morr-Leigh colors of blue and gold, provided background on the wall behind the table. More wooden planks were used to make counters for food, lining both side walls and two great wine kegs were set up, ready to be tapped. Serving girls and lads began laying out the food platters, while cooks were at the grills and open fires, busy with their cooking.

Late in the afternoon, crowds began to gather in the great tent. There would be standing room only, as people moved closer together. The morning's whispers were forgotten, replaced with the anticipation of a celebration with fine food, wine, and good company.

Duke Morr-Leigh and his mother, the Lady Avis, escorted the glowing bride, followed by the Princess Alaine and the fair Lady Charlyn, arm-in-arm. They paused at the threshold of the tent, allowing people to provide a pathway to the front, where Duke Seaken-Char stood in elaborate conversation with Covey, and a quiet, somewhat nervous Rand. As the bride was walked to her place beside the groom, Nana and Annie pushed their way to the front of the male-dominated crowd for a good view of the impending nuptials.

Genna was a picture in a flowing, pale yellow gown with lace on the bodice and at the ends of the long, flared sleeves. She carried a small bouquet of lily-of-the-valley with luscious green leaves surrounding the tiny white, bell-shaped flowers. Charlyn had woven a crown of wildflowers for Genna, and white and yellow ribbons shimmered in her braided, chestnut hair. Her cheeks and lips were rosy, and her large, brown eyes saw nothing but the man she loved standing before her.

Rand stood straight and tall; his bronze curls brushed back. His face was smooth, and freshly shaven. He wore an untucked, oversized, white shirt, lent to him by Covey. His left arm hung in a sling of brown cloth. He wore black pants shoved into the tops of his well-worn boots.

Despite his injury, he made a handsome groom who could do nothing but stare at his soon-to-be bride.

Duke Seaken-Char, a bit of a showman who was enjoying the limelight, called for quiet and initiated the ceremony with a tale of his own wedding, years ago. He told of the many nuptials he had performed, and gave simple advice to the bride, but more pointed instructions to the groom, inviting laughter from the crowd. At last, he called for each to pledge their vows of love and faithfulness to one another. Rand, having no ring, presented Genna with his mother's small, circular broach containing three white pearls – one for each of her children. He delicately fastened the pin to Genna's bodice. Finally, the Duke joined their hands and pronounced them husband and wife for all time. At that point, cheers filled the tent as the Duke led the couple to their place of honor at the dinner table.

The wedding ceremony produced a sense of happiness that filled the crowded space and spilled out onto the campsite. The evening was gay. Everyone ate to their fill, with leftovers hauled off for later use. Annie and her girls then produced a freshly baked cinnamon cake layered with fruit jam. The bride and groom enjoyed it all as they sat at the middle of the top table.

Surprisingly, the soldiers produced a practiced group of musicians from among their number. Their musical skills had been honed during the long stretches of time awaiting battles in the field. Some were proficient in pipes, flutes and mouth organs. Several of the men held small drums covered with skins for keeping time, while various fiddles and stringed instruments produced lively folk tunes. The few available ladies were in demand for the dancing, but the men without partners danced in a circle around the newlyweds, grasping arms and prancing about.

Alaine sat quietly next to Genna for the meal. As the highest ranking noble at the festivities, she looked every bit the Princess and was given respectful glances from all. Her deep purple gown was of a color rarely seen in a fabric and was stunning against her skin. The ruffle at the neck dipped with a circular pattern, slightly exposing cleavage. Amethyst crystals sparkled, dangling from the coronet nestled in her golden snood covering her netted, upswept braids. Listening to the music, she fingered the golden chain at the base of her throat where more of the purple jewels danced. She smiled as she heard the old Duke shamelessly flirt with Lady Avis, who seemed to be enjoying the attention of the nobleman.

Charlyn did not dance but remained in her seat between Alaine and Kent. She wore a blue silk gown with long, slim sleeves, and a bodice with a tapestry of flowers. Her black beret drooped low on her forehead, concealing an angry bruise. Kent didn't join the dancing but stayed at the table sipping the good wine while making small talk with the young lady-in-waiting. Shortly after the meal, it was he who supported Charlyn when she asked to retire and walked her back to the ladies' tent. Kent's gallantry was not missed by the Princess.

Later, Alaine kissed Genna on the cheek as she was leaving the festivities with Rand. She watched as groups of the celebrating men departed the great pavilion to spread out toward their own places within the camp, well sated with food and drink. Sitting alone, her thoughts went to her own future nuptials. Berating herself for her envy of Genna, Alaine felt her maid was lucky to marry the man she loved. Looking forward to her own future, there was more dread than happy expectation. The Princess, dressed in finery, gazed around the thinning crowd. She could hear the Duke Seaken-Char deep in conversation with her aunt. Suddenly, Alaine felt a deep loneliness. Quietly, she got up and left the table and slipped out of the tent. It had been a long day.

9
Into the Woods

The night was dark, and it was a quiet walk back to the ladies' tent as Kent led Lady Charlyn. The girl leaned on the forearm of the Captain. Her dizziness with walking had lessened over the day, although a dull headache remained. Charlyn was thankful that Kent had gone out of his way to make the evening pleasant for her. He sat next to her during dinner and put her at ease with conversation about comfortable topics. Each was learning more about the other.

As they approached the front of the peaked dwelling, Kent was unsure of what to say to end the evening. He saw that the inside of the tent was dark.

"Looks like no one else is back yet. Will you be all right by yourself?" he asked Charlyn. "Would you like me to wait out here until Nana or Alaine return?"

"No, that will not be necessary. I just want to lie down. It has been an emotional day."

"To be sure," Kent agreed. Then, thinking ahead, "Do you feel that you will be able to travel in the coach in the morning? I can plan for extra stops. If you are not feeling well at midday, we can look for a place to camp and end the day early."

"I am sure that I will feel better in the morning," answered Charlyn, determined not to be the cause of another day's lack of travel.

"Then I will bid you good night, milady," Kent said, with a slight bow at the waist before he turned to leave.

"Good night, Captain, and thank you for your considerations," she replied, with a brief curtsy, then turning to face the darkness of the tent.

Alaine stood as still as a statue among the trunks of the tall pine trees, looking out over the spacious grass meadow flanking the back of the camp. Moments earlier, she returned to the tent and found it empty except for the sleeping Charlyn. Alaine hadn't changed her gown, but quickly removed the tiara and let down her hair. Putting on comfortable boots, she grabbed her cloak and tiptoed out. A mind busy with emotions and leftover images of the day would never allow for sleep. Returning to the cool night air, the sleepless Princess wandered through the trees to the edge of the field.

Alaine heard the occasional sounds from men continuing to celebrate the evening, but most of the tents were occupied with their sleeping tenants. Horses' neighs echoed from the other side of the camp, where they were freed to graze on the ground cover. As she observed the meadow, the tops of the grasses moved here and there. Alaine imagined small animals moving about unseen, carrying out their nighttime errands.

All at once, she saw a movement across the grass, near the tree line. At first it looked like a deer, until the animal took off running in long, bounding strides across the field. Then, Alaine felt her heart start to pound – it was not a deer, but a dog – *his* dog. Carver Vale must be near, just across the grassland, in the wood.

A sharp whistle split the silence of the night, followed by the far-off call of the dog's name, "Astra". A dark figure could be seen awaiting the returning animal. At once, common sense was thrown away, and the hood of her cloak flew off as Alaine ran through the tall grass toward the woods and the alluring stranger.

Kent left Charlyn and ambled back to the great tent, finding its interior almost empty of celebrants. Just a few groups of two or three men had settled in with cups in their hands. There at the top table remained his mother and Duke Seaken-Char. A stab of irritation hit Kent for the way the old man had monopolized his mother throughout the evening…and now, into the night. Yet, as good manners required, he suppressed his annoyance and put a smile on his face as he went toward the table.

"I have come to offer you my quarters for the night, sir," Kent respectfully said to the Duke.

"No need, man," answered the elder. "Your mother and I were just about to take a moonlight carriage ride. My men are harnessing the horses for us now."

"What?" Kent questioned, with surprise, looking from the Duke to his mother. He felt his irritation resurfacing.

"We're just going for a short ride, Kent. Ren has redone the inside of his coach and put on new wheels. I wanted to try it out," Lady Avis added in a persuasive voice, followed by a small giggle.

Kent looked at his mother with disbelief, and then at the Duke. Immediately, it dawned on him. They were not ready to end the night. The two of them wanted some time alone, away from the eyes of others. Frustrated, he could do nothing but respect their wishes.

"Ah, well, enjoy your ride. I think I'll just go get some sleep," he offered, politely. "Thank you, Duke, for your gracious visit, as well as the fine food and wine. We will be on our way at early morning."

Kent turned and left the tent to the goodnight greetings from the two elders following in his wake. He trudged through the darkness, between wagons and tents, thinking about his mother and the old man. "Ren" she had called him, instead of his full name of Rengard. His mother was using the man's familiar nickname, sometimes heard at court. A carriage ride in the moonlight, he thought skeptically, while glancing up at the night sky. There was no visible moon tonight, or any stars for that matter, only a thick blanket of charcoal clouds.

As Kent reached his tent, he was still in an ire as he removed his jacket and shirt in the darkness. Opening his bedroll, he sat down to pull off his boots. The man had to be twenty winters older than his mother, he brooded. Was the Duke taking advantage of his mother, still a grieving widow? Kent stretched out his tall frame and pulled his blanket up to his chin. Then, calming himself, he realized that there was really no reason to be distressed. His mother had had an enjoyable evening after the stress of the morning; and, it *had been* five summers since his father's passing.

Kent knew that she was lonely at times. Tomorrow, they would break camp early to continue their journey, and Duke Seaken-Char would be on his way back to Seaken Hall.

His thoughts turned to his own evening, which had been very good, having Charlyn's attention almost entirely to himself. As much as he tried to find fault with the girl, he couldn't. She was gentle, kind, and surprisingly unspoiled for a daughter of a duke. She had a very pleasant posture and looks by any standard, yet she did not seem to be aware of it. Kent thought Charlyn would do well at the Hawthorn court.

Charlyn seemed to also have a good mind. She spoke of her enjoyment of reading, singing, and helping her mother manage the accounts for the household. The Lady spoke with pride of her father's rule as the Forester for the kingdom. Wood from his mills built the houses and barns, provided wood for everyday home goods, and the hearths and stoves of the villages. Duke Noeman's best logs went to the shipbuilders in the lower kingdom. Kent was surprised at the depth of Charlyn's knowledge regarding the management of the northern forests under the control of Duke Noeman.

"For every tree taken, a sapling is planted. Dead, fallen and burnt trees could be logged, but the older trees – determined by their girth – could not be cut", the girl reported. "Of course, the dukes could manage the trees on their lands for a wood supply."

Kent smiled in the darkness as he thought of his evening with Charlyn. Yet, as delightful as thoughts were of the lady-in-waiting, pangs of responsibility struck the young man. He was charged by his King to escort the Princess Alaine to the court of King Holum. The company was already a day behind, and he feared what would be said as word of the attack by highwaymen reached Hawthorn Castle. Already a messenger had been sent to assure King Granth and Queen Iris that everyone was all right, but he worried the attack may raise questions or reflect on his leadership skills. Tomorrow, they must continue their journey and try to make up for lost time. The Irongate court in Harbortown awaited their arrival. His mission, and not a pretty face, must be his priority. Kent sighed into the darkness and resolved to get some rest before the dawn was upon them.

Surprised and pleased, Carver recognized the Princess running across the field to meet him. His first thought was to run to her, grab her about the waist, while lifting her into the air and twirling her about. Yet, he suppressed any action, standing still with his arms at his sides.

By the time Alaine reached Carver Vale, she was out of breath. The breathless girl came to an abrupt stop just in front of the woodsman. Once there, the Princess didn't know what she should say to him.

His stance was relaxed. Astra stood by his side and gave a short bark of welcome. Carver's hair was loose, framing his face, hanging in waves almost to his shoulders. He wore a shirt open at the neck, and pants. Absent was his rustic cloak. Even in the darkness, Alaine could see that his eyes were on her. Those serious, strange eyes, with tiny flecks of gold that remained visible in the dim light of the night. His mouth was closed, with the hint of a smile, expressing his pleasure in seeing her.

How beautiful she was, he thought, even in the darkness. It was Carver who broke the silence between them in the elongated moment.

"Good eve to you, Princess. How do you fare? I know that your company didn't travel today. Earlier was heard the ruckus of an assembly, as well as sounds of music coming from the campsite."

Just the sound of Carver's voice was welcoming, and relaxed Alaine's fears for the boldness of her coming. Somehow, she knew that the decision to see him again was right. The small gust of a breeze flowed through the meadow grass and cooled her warm face. Her sense of adventure was high.

"Yes, it has been an eventful day for us after our attack by the highwaymen on the road yesterday. My lady-in-waiting was injured and is still recovering, so we could not travel this morning," Alaine began to explain. "Then, after midday, Duke Seaken-Char arrived, bringing a feast of food with him from Seaken Hall. He offered to marry my maid, Genna, so the dinner turned into a sudden wedding celebration. It was all unplanned, but everyone seemed to enjoy the festivities."

"I was very sorry to be told of your encounter with the vandals but was glad to hear that you were unharmed. I wished that I had been there to help you. How is your lady faring now?"

"Charlyn is much better tonight. She is asleep in our tent. How did you hear of our troubles?"

"Word travels fast in the woods. My brothers found one of the villains and handed him over to your troops yesterday. They told us you were unharmed."

"Yes, thank goodness there was no great harm done to our people. We will be ready to proceed with our travels in the morning."

Carver glanced up at the sky and gave a short laugh. "I doubt that you will be traveling in the morning, Princess. Look at the sky. Feel the breeze. The coming storm is heavy in the air. Breathe it in. The animals and birds all know it. They've been going about all afternoon and evening gathering food and shoring up their dens and nests. The deer are secreting their young."

"It is the spring season, so a shower is not unexpected. Despite a little rain, I am sure that we will continue to travel south tomorrow," Alaine insisted.

"This will not be a brief morning shower, Alaine. Your travels will need to be postponed."

Alaine shivered. Not so much caused by Carver's prophecy of the storm, but the fact that he said her name for the first time. It was his use of the familiar address usually reserved for family and those close to her. She had no objection and felt a thrill as her name fell from his lips.

"So, if there is a storm, where will *you* stay?" she asked, picturing him holed up under a tree.

He laughed again. "Have no fears. Our people have tree lofts throughout the forested lands. Would you like to see the one nearby?"

Alaine hesitated. The woods behind Carver were black. So dark was the scene that she could not make out the individual trees. Little barbs of fear were poking at her. Suddenly, the cozy tent back at camp seemed very far away.

"Is it very far?" Alaine asked, with trepidation. "It looks awfully dark in there."

"No, it's not far, just well concealed. Don't be afraid. I will lead you," he encouraged, while holding out his forearm for her to grip.

Alaine stood rooted in her spot, only a step from the extended arm. Just that morning she had lectured Genna about propriety. Now, here she was, alone with a stranger, thinking of going off into a dark wood. She didn't *really* know who this person was yet, though she felt so attracted to him.

He could have harmed her previously had he wanted, so she had no fear of him. To steal some time with him now was so tempting.

Gingerly, Alaine reached out her hand and placed it on Carver's shirt sleeve. As if magically, Alaine suddenly found herself in the woods surrounded by darkness.

"I feel lost already," she fretted, looking around. "How can you see where you are going?"

"We have lived in the dim light of the woods since early days. Our vision in the dark is acute, much like the owls and other animals that live here. We are fortunate in that way. It gives us quite the advantage," Carver related. "Come this way," he directed.

Alaine kept a tight grip on Carver's sleeve as they moved through the darkness of the dense woods at an amazing pace. There didn't appear to be a defined pathway. Their passage involved many turns, which led to Alaine's total disorientation. They stopped in a small clearing where a shining lantern hung from a low branch.

Alaine watched as first one, then two, then a cluster of darting green, glowing orbs of light surrounded them. A humming noise filled the quiet air as they flew about in constant motion.

"Oh, look. Green fireflies!" she exclaimed. "I've never seen any that big or that color."

"Moss faeries. They're not fireflies, they're moss faeries."

As Alaine looked closer, she could see the translucent, flitting wings and the tiny bodies within the green glimmer.

"They know where we're going," Carver commented, casually. "They've come out to greet us."

"Faeries? Real faeries? There are so many of them!"

"They always fly in clusters for protection. You'll hardly ever find one by itself. Unlike some of their cousins, they are kind-hearted, and never play tricks on people. They are known for leading the lost out of the forest to safety. They are friends to our forest clans. If our children stray, they guide them home."

"Where do they live? Do they ever come out of the forests?" Alaine asked. "That may be why I have never seen them before."

"I've never seen them outside of the forest," Carver answered. "They live in the trees. In fact, that is how they got their name. They sleep in groups in the moss that grows on the north sides of the trees deep in the woods. When they are still, with their wings closed, they blend in with the green moss."

The dog bounded past them around another bend and was followed by the swarm of moss faeries. As Carver and Alaine followed, the loft came into view. A platform was suspended above the ground, built between the trunks of three giant pine trees. A large glowing lantern hung from a railing lining the ascending steps. Astra was already climbing the roughly hewn stairs toward the level wooden deck.

"C'mon," said Carver, leading Alaine by the elbow.

Alaine climbed the steps following Carver. The crude railing provided handholds, making the way easier than expected. Another lantern hung from a peg at the entrance to the floor of the loft.

The deck was a half-circle and the spaces between the immense trees were open to the night, as well as the front portion that resembled a wide porch with a railing, exposing a view of the forest.

An irregular table was surrounded by stools and a couple of well-built chairs.

On the table Alaine noticed Carver's short carving knife beside a miniature figurine of a fawn lying in leaves.

Alaine looked around in wonder. Staring upward, she saw slats of wood in a fan-shaped arrangement providing a see-through roof high overhead. On the deck, a wide, metal basin was set into a hole in the flooring,

"What is that for?" Alaine asked, pointing to the blackened metal bowl.

"We use that for making a fire. You can't be too careful with fire in the woods," replied Carver.

"Where would you sleep?" she asked with curiosity, looking around the space.

Carver walked to one of the tree trunks and pulled on a latch that opened a door. Inside, two flat shelves were hollowed out inside the tree, one above the other, covered in matting and furs, providing places to lie down and sleep.

"This one is the biggest," he said, walking across the loft to the largest tree trunk with a similar door and opening it for Alaine to see.

Alaine walked over to look at the larger shelf-bed in the tree trunk closet. "That does look comfortable," Alaine commented. Then, "Do you mind if I remove my cloak? This gown is warm after our walk here."

Alaine removed the cloak. Carver took it and laid it across the foot of the hidden bed and turned to admire the girl's gown.

"That dress is fine," he said, with admiration.

"It is, isn't it?" she replied, doing a twirl around. "It is one of the gowns made to be worn at my uncle's court. It is part of my dowry. My mother had several new dresses made for this trip."

"It is said that you go there to meet the suiters for your hand in marriage. Is that so?"

"Yes, there are several noblemen I am to meet there. A frightening prospect, really. I feel that I am not ready to marry, but my position requires it. I must not disappoint my parents."

And so it began - the conversation between Carver and Alaine. They talked. Each spoke of their families. Alaine spoke of her life at Hawthorn Castle. Carver spoke of his father and brothers, woodworking, and his friendship with Hewitt and Finnie. After a while, the long, emotional day caught up with Alaine.

"Suddenly, I am *so* tired," the girl said, with a sigh.

"Would you like to rest?"

"Usually I can't sleep, but so much has happened today. If I could just lie down and close my eyes for a few moments."

"You can use the bigger bed in the tree. Just close the door. I have many things to do before the rain begins if you don't mind."

Alaine went to the tree trunk cabinet and sat down on the bed. The moss faeries that had lit upon the deck railing followed her into the hollow and settled themselves on the inside of the tree trunk. With closed wings they appeared to be green leaves hanging on the carved-out wood.

Alaine sighed and nestled herself on the pad. She had barely lain her head down when her eyes closed, and she sank into slumber.

As the Princess slept, Carver went about the tasks of preparing the loft for the rain that was coming. Untying the ropes, he lowered the slatted roof, which moved the pieces together, making a solid ceiling over the loft. The roof was latched to the tree trunks and vertical posts. He smiled with approval, knowing the rainwater would run off onto the ground behind the structure. Then, he lowered the rolled, leather flaps between the trunks, closing off the space, and secured them to the platform. Lastly, he went down to the storage sheds below the loft, to collect firewood and other necessities. When the loft was prepared for the coming storm, Carver went to the sleeping closet that Alaine was using and quietly opened the door. The Princess was lying on her side, deep in sleep, her crescent eyelashes resting on her cheeks. He quickly slipped the carved figurine of the fawn into the pocket of her cloak. Carver bent over her sleeping figure and gently brushed a lock of red hair away from her face when he saw the necklace. Without much thought, he unclasped the string of jewels and put it in his pouch of coins. Gently, he closed the wooden door and went off to collect food for himself and Astra.

Alaine awoke from a velvety sleep to the humming sounds made by the moss faeries circling above her head within the tree hollow. She pushed the silken covers back and sat up while pulling on her cloak. Opening the portal in the tree trunk, the buzzing cloud of green faeries flew out. How long had she slept, she wondered, as she stepped out onto the planks of the loft floor? She looked about and was surprised at the changes to the loft. The lowered roof made the space feel smaller. She could no longer look out onto the forest due to the coverings between the tree trunks. Ragged logs of wood now sat at the bottom of the metal basin. A cozy rug was laid out on the floor for Astra.

"Carver," Alaine called. "Carver," she repeated, in a louder voice.

There was no answer. The woodsman was gone. She tried to remember what he was saying as she went to the bed and quickly dozed off. It was something about things he needed to do before the rain began. She remembered trying to hold the softness of his voice in her mind.

The moss faeries flew to her and then to the railing leading to the ground. When she didn't follow, they returned to her *en masse*, and again rushed to the threshold. Alaine realized that they were waiting for her to follow them. What had Carver said? Moss faeries led people out of the woods? She realized that Carver was gone, and she had better follow the faeries or she would be lost in the woods. Feeling a sudden urgency, she needed to get back to the camp.

Alaine held the bottom of her gown as she descended to the forest floor. She raced to keep up with her little guides that were speeding away ahead of her. The trek through the woods seemed to take much longer then when she had Carver to lead her. After many twists and turns the faeries stopped in front of her. The Princess looked out upon the vacant field and the campsite across the meadow. At the edge of the woods, she turned to the faeries with a curtsy and a wave.

Alaine noted the darkness of the sky as she made quick strides through the tall grass. *En route*, a drop of rain hit her forehead. It was not a misty, little thing, but a heavy plop of water. A strong breeze came up, blowing out her cloak. The girl began to think that

Carver was right about a storm as she heard the distant rumble of thunder. She began to run. Though there would be no sunrise, the sky was turning a lighter shade of gray.

10
Rain Delay

Charlyn, clearly worried when Alaine returned in the early morning, asked her, "Where have you been?"

Alaine began to hurriedly remove the wrinkled, purple gown. "I couldn't sleep so I went for a walk," answered the Princess. "Where is Nana?"

"I think that she might have had too much wine and ended up sleeping in the cook's tent with Annie and her girls."

"Where is my aunt? Last I saw her, she remained at the table in the great tent with Duke Seaken-Char," questioned Alaine, wondering if Charlyn was left alone all night.

"As far as I know, she has not returned. When I awoke, no one else was here."

"Really? That doesn't sound like my aunt. I hope that she has not taken ill," said Alaine, as she draped her gown across a trunk to allow the damp hem to dry. Then, reaching to remove her amethyst necklace, Alaine raised her hand to her throat and realized that it was gone.

"Oh, no, I've done it again! My necklace is gone! I've lost it!" she moaned in misery.

"What?" asked Charlyn, at first not understanding what Alaine was talking about.

"I've lost my necklace. How do I keep doing this?!" she cried in frustration. "The necklace is part of my dowry. I'm going to be in so much trouble when my aunt and mother learn of it."

"When did you last notice wearing it?"

"I remember that I still had it on when I removed my tiara and stored it away. I should have taken it off then, but I didn't. Since I knew that I would not be able to sleep, I was in a hurry to leave the tent and was trying not to wake you," Alaine explained. "I don't know what is wrong with me! I should not have any jewels if I can't take care of them!"

"Look around the floor of the tent while I get dressed. We'll go out and search the grounds," Charlyn offered.

"Yes, let's get dressed. We'll have to hurry. It's beginning to rain outside, so put on your older boots."

Moments later, Alaine and Charlyn searched the ground around the tent, the privy, and the path to the great tent and back. Finally, they were forced to return to their tent empty-handed as the rain turned from frequent, bold drops to a steady downpour.

Thunder was heard as the Princess stood at the tent opening, scolding herself for the loss of the necklace; but something else was nagging in the back of her mind. As Carver predicted, she watched the rain coming down, preventing another day's travel. Alaine tried to remember if she was wearing the necklace at the forest loft. She believed that she was. Twice, now, she had met Carver. Twice, she was alone with him and had fallen asleep. And twice, the jewels she was wearing went missing. She had to ask herself, was she just a naïve girl being charmed by a handsome thief? Would he really steal from her, she wondered? Longing to see Carver again, she hoped not, with all of her inexperienced heart.

The Captain's day started with a bang…literally! A nearby clap of thunder announcing the impending storm spooked the horses in the nearby field. The stampede that followed had horses running through the camp. Some were stopped by the wagons and remained in reach, but others took off through the towering pines lining the road and headed up and down the highway.

Barefoot, Kent was out of his tent, pulling on his shirt. After seeing the fleeing steeds, he shouted orders to the men peering out of their tents.

"Gather some men and go after them, man!" he called to a sergeant stumbling out of a nearby tent.

After collecting his boots, Kent made his way from tent to tent arousing those who were still sleeping off the previous night's wine. Once all of the nearby horses were rounded up, he designated an area behind the wagons, under the trees, for gathering and corralling them.

Wagons were relocated and log barriers would be needed, so he set another team of men at it.

Then, under what was beginning to be a steady rain, he saw Annie approaching in a bother, seeking him out.

"It's starting to rain, and we won't be able to keep the cooking fires going. I can't light fires inside the cook's tent!" she said with frustration, her arms waving up and down as she spoke.

"Where's Smyth? We're going to need him," the Captain said, as he rushed toward the cook's tent with Annie. Thunder rolled overhead and the rain increased in intensity. He stopped one of the stable grooms running by. "Go find Smyth, and tell him to come to the cook's tent," he ordered. "I don't care how bad his head feels!"

Not long after the unsuccessful search for the necklace, Nana returned to the ladies' tent, bringing a pot with tea and some cups. She put the pot down and shook out the shawl she was using to cover her head and shoulders during the trip from the cook's tent.

"What a mess it is out there!" she exclaimed. "The men had to set up a tall pavilion between two wagons so that Annie and Smyth could have cooking fires under the tarps. I was lucky to be able to make this pot of tea. We may all end up with a cold dinner today."

112

"Thank you for thinking of us," said Charlyn. "A cup of tea sounds good."

"Where is Lady Avis?" asked Nana, looking about. "She's not in the cook's tent."

"It is a mystery, Nana. My aunt has not been back all night. Has the old Duke left yet?"

"Yes, he is gone. He and his band left before the first light and the rain, but I doubt that they reached Seaken Hall before the downpour," replied Nana. "I've been helping Annie and the girls. They are quite harried over there. She has asked us to come help once the rain lets up."

"At least that will give us something to do," Alaine said, feeling confined. "Otherwise, we will just be sitting here all day."

It was a short time later that Lady Avis returned to the tent. Looking tired, little was said other than that she needed to sleep. After removing her evening gown, the Lady took to her sleeping pallet. Alaine and Charlyn exchanged a look but said nothing.

The tea that Nana brought was lukewarm, but there were no complaints. Rushing about, Nana put a basket near the tent flap and told the girls to put their wet boots in it so that mud would not be dragged into the tent. She emptied a box of pine needles that were being used for kindling for their outside campfire onto the ground in front of the threshold where a puddle was already collecting.

A dripping Captain called into the ladies' tent, and poked his head into the opening after Nana called an answer. His hair was hanging wet around his stubbled face, with a streak of mud accenting his jaw.

"You can't come in here!" Alaine ordered at once. "You'll just get everything wet."

Nana, ignoring Alaine, pulled Kent into the tent and sat him on a nearby trunk. She hurried to wrap a blanket around his shoulders, which was something she may have done when he was a child in her care many years ago. He smiled a small, grateful smile.

"Would you like some tea? We have some left that I was saving for your mother, but she is sound asleep," Nana offered.

"Let her sleep," said Kent. "She had a long night. I just stopped by to tell you that we would not be able to travel today. Tomorrow is also unlikely as the roadway is under a foot of water."

Alaine and Charlyn giggled, both at the miserable sight of him, and the obvious statement about travel.

"We were pretty sure that we wouldn't be going anywhere today," Alaine replied, with a touch of sarcasm.

For Kent, it was good to wrap his cold, wet fingers around the warm cup of tea. Through a wet lock of hair hanging over his forehead, he glanced at his cousin and her Lady Charlyn. Alaine's impatience with the constraints caused by the weather was clear on her face as she gazed out the tent opening at the rain showers. Tendrils of hair hung down on both sides of her face from her upswept red curls, trying to burst loose of their pins. Her sage-colored gown with long sleeves was fitted at the waist. A finely knit, vermillion scarf was loosely tied around her neck. Charlyn stood beside her, slightly taller, with her hair neatly coifed and a calm expression on her face. She wore a simple, woolen dress with flared sleeves. A lace collar, with two sharp points, accented the bronze broach of flowers pinned at the base of her throat. The Lady's gown had straight lines, with few folds, and was short enough to show off her thin ankles as she stood in her stocking feet. A sudden wish for intimacy went through Kent as his imagination took flight.

The pounding of the rain increased on the canvas roof.

"Do you think this tent will hold up?" Charlyn asked Kent, sounding worried due to the ferocity of the storm.

"It should," Kent reassured her. "So far, there is little wind out there, and it is wind that usually brings the tents down during a storm. We have already lost some of the garrison tents due to flooding water. Men are stretching their tents over wagons so that they will be able to sleep off the ground tonight. Others may end up in the big tent. We'll do the best we can, but for now, I must request that the great tent be off limits to the ladies, except for serving dinner."

Kent finished drinking the cooled tea with honey. His stomach growled, but there was no time for eating. Horses needed to be found and brought back. Once the horses were settled, it was important that all would have at least one good meal for the day and a dry place to sleep.

"Thank you for the tea, Nana. I must get back out there. I will try to see you all later."

"Be careful," warned Nana, as the busy Captain left the tent, giving a smile to Charlyn and Alaine over his shoulder.

The cook's tent was as busy as Nana warned when Charlyn, Alaine, and the good nurse arrived. Annie and Smyth were already working at preparing food for a warm dinner. Outside, Smyth was boiling several pots full of venison bones to provide rich stock for stew. Two of Annie's girls were preparing root vegetables. Annie decided to use the occasion to tutor all of the young women on the task of turning flour, water, and lard into biscuit dough. Placed into iron pans with domed lids, the results were scored loaves with fluffy centers, ready to be pulled apart.

If there was any fun during the rainy day, it was when Genna joined the ladies in the cook's tent. Almost at once she was subjected to chiding, and very personal questions from the girls, until Annie put a stop to it. Genna's face was blazing with embarrassment. She sought refuge with Alaine and Charlyn.

"How are you?" Alaine whispered, in a more delicate manner. "Does marriage with Rand suit you?"

"I love being with him after waiting so long," Genna answered quietly, "but it is more than I expected. Even though we have known each other for years, we have never been allowed to spend much time together, alone. It's wonderful, but a little overwhelming."

"Where is Rand now?" Charlyn asked.

"He's outside with Smyth, who has put him in charge of keeping all of the fires lit. Smyth is getting some men together to find more wood, then get it into a dry place, and chopped into small enough pieces for the fires."

"That sounds like a terrible job in this rain," Charlyn said.

"They are stacking whatever they find inside the big tent and using saws and axes to cut it," Genna reported.

"Where have you been all morning?" Alaine asked.

"Well, we were woken up by horses running next to the tent. As they were collecting the horses, Rand was sent back by Sergeant Covey lest he injure his shoulder further. By then, the rain was pouring, and the water was starting to flood into the tent. So we had to move everything into a wagon and try to spread the tent over it. Both of us are wet through. Rand is frustrated because he can hardly move his arm without having a lot of pain. Smyth thought that he was overdoing it, so he brought him over here to help with the fires."

"The big tent has been given over to the men for now," Alaine announced, loud enough for all to hear. "So, this will be the place for the ladies. At least this tent is larger than our sleeping tent."

"That is fine," said Nana. "We can help with the food. In the after- noon, Charlyn can bring her playing cards. I have plenty of extra yarn and needles, so I can help you all with your knitting."

Alaine groaned, and Nana gave her a disapproving look. The thought of days spent in cooking and knitting lessons was not her idea of a pleasant way to pass time. She envied the men who were allowed to carry out their tasks between the rain showers.

Yet, before the afternoon was over, the ladies were enlisted in a new task. Suddenly every length of rope or cord became the most valuable commodity in the camp. With the rain came the wet clothing. With the need to hang clothes for drying came the need for clothesline. Annie's spools of thick twine used to truss fowl and meat for cooking, were being cut into long lengths by the ladies and being braided to make lines for hanging wet garments. So the girls, noble and not, sat in a circle making thin, but strong, lines for drying wet clothes.

On the afternoon of the second day of almost continuous rain showers, Alaine felt the need to escape. The restraints of the wet, dampness and mud left her in need of some solitary time after being trapped in the close quarters of one tent or another. She was desperate to get away.

Genna was spending most of the day with the noble ladies either in the cook's tent or their smaller abode. Knowing the Princess so well, she could almost feel Alaine's building anxiety and restlessness. The maid was not surprised, when during a lapse in showers, Alaine donned her damp boots and cloak and slipped out of the tent without so much as a word to anyone.

Charlyn also noticed Alaine taking her leave, assuming that she was going to the privy tent. The Lady was passing the time practicing playing a small, stringed harp lent to her by one of the soldiers. As time drifted by, Charlyn became aware that Alaine had been gone for some time.

She looked out of the tent opening to see that the light drizzle of rain had temporarily stopped.

Alaine was elated as she made her way through the camp to the edge of the tall pines, side-stepping puddles of water as she went. She breathed deeply the damp air as she looked over the wet field before her. The pounding rain had flattened the tall grass, and the taller plants hung their soggy heads. A mist rose from the wet ground as if the warm earth were exhaling into the cool air. The horizon remained gray with the promise of more rain, but for now, the deluge was over.

The Princess stood very still, unconsciously gazing, looking for someone, as she fingered the carving of the fawn that remained stashed in the pocket of her cloak. Alaine remembered her surprise at finding it as she was walking to the cook's tent in the rain. She left it hidden there. It was a reminder of the tree loft and the woodsman.

It was Astra that she first saw running along the tree line across the field. Alaine kept her eyes near the dog, seeking the sight of Carver, who she knew might be nearby. Not far beyond the dog, she saw him, wearing his brown wrap. The hood was up, covering most of his head, and an archer's bow was slung over one shoulder. She willed him to look across the field toward her.

As if in answer to her wish, Alaine saw his head come up and look toward the edge of the camp. She knew that he saw her when he raised his hand in a wave to her. Before she could respond, she saw him wading through the wet grass on his way to her. He came to her with no hesitation, as if rushing to meet an old friend. Alaine tried to compose herself before he reached her, but she couldn't control her quickened heartbeat or the flush she could feel coming to her face as he approached. She could not look at him enough. There was the way he walked, his face, and his captivating eyes, all intriguing to her.

"You were right about the rain," she said, when he came to her. "We seem to be seriously delayed in our travels."

"I fear that it is not over yet," he responded, in his friendly way. "There are no blue skies in sight."

"I was so tired of sitting in tents that I just wanted to get outside and breath the air."

"It was the same for me. The tree loft is comfortable but not a large place. Also, Astra hates the long hours of not going out. There is only so much sleeping to be done."

"What were you doing?" she asked, indicating the bow and the bag slung over his shoulder.

"I was trying to find a rabbit or a bird for our dinner. Astra needs something to eat. The mushrooms, berries and roots are not very appealing to her. Before I could stop her, she ran over to your camp last night and came back with a large bone in her mouth."

Alaine laughed. "Yes, our cook boiled down a lot of venison bones yesterday."

"To Astra it was a treasure. She chewed on it all evening."

After a moment of silence, Alaine felt she had to speak to him about the thoughts that were bothering her.

"I need to ask you about something," she began, in a serious tone. "When I came to your tree loft the other night, I believe I was still wearing a necklace that went with my gown. When I got back to camp in the morning, I couldn't find it. It may have fallen off."

"Do you wish me to look for it?" Carver asked, innocently.

"Yes, if you would. It is part of my dowry when I marry. I am afraid to tell my aunt it is missing. It was specially made for me and is very valuable."

"I will search around the woods. I don't remember seeing it anywhere in the loft," he lied, while looking at her with a sincere expression on his face.

Carver felt a pang of guilt as he saw her brow furrow in worry. He knew he was the cause of her distress. Alaine fretted to herself. She considered that Carver seemed to be telling the truth. She *wanted* to believe him. Then, remembering her manners, she changed the subject, wanting to continue talking with him.

"I wanted to thank you for the little carvings. They are very realistic. I've seen something like them with the children in the village."

"My friend Finnie sells them in her shop in Hawthorn," he explained, relieved to be off the subject of the necklace. "It's a way to pass the time. I look at a piece of wood and see something in it. Then I whittle to bring it out."

"That is a praiseworthy skill. I fear I have no such creative talents."

"I'm sure you have many talents. I've heard many good things about you from the Hawthorn townsfolk," he said, looking at her with admiration.

"It is kind of you to say so."

Suddenly, Astra came bounding toward them, mouth filled with a pheasant. She dropped her prize at Carver's feet.

"This is a fine cock," Carver said, bending to pick up the bird.

"How do you know it's a cock?"

Carver pulled a tail feather and stuck it in Alaine's hair. "The hens don't have these feathers. Astra, it looks like you found your own supper."

"Supper! Oh, dear," Alaine proclaimed. "I'm sorry, but I must be getting back."

"Wait. When will I see you again?" he asked, seeing her turn to leave, the thin scarf she was wearing slipping to the ground.

"I don't know," she called back at him. "Maybe soon."

Carver watched her go.

"Maybe soon," he repeated to himself, bending to pick up the piece of red cloth.

When Alaine entered the ladies' tent, out of breath from her run, she was not expecting to find Lady Avis in a temper. Her aunt met her at the threshold and addressed her directly, hands on both hips.

"Where have you been, Alaine? I was worried, and Sergeant Covey is out searching for you."

"The rain stopped, and I went out for a walk," the Princess answered, meekly.

"Look at you!" Lady Avis continued. "It takes me back to when you were twelve summers old and would come in after a day out with Kent. Your gown and cloak are wet at the bottom and your boots are caked with mud. What is this feather doing in your hair? And look at your hair! Alaine, you are no longer a child. You are the Princess of the Upper Kingdom with great hopes resting upon you. You need to begin behaving as the royal lady that you are."

Then speaking to the maid, "Genna, help her change her clothes, and do something with that hair – cover it with a scarf if needed."

Lady Avis turned back to Alaine, "I am going to tell Covey we have you with us. When I return, I want you to be presentable and we will go to the great tent for dinner."

The largest tent had taken on a masculine air. Piles of cut wood were stacked by the front entrance. Garrison bedrolls were piled along the side walls. Men's shirts and pants were hanging wherever possible, for drying. Only the long table remained and was given up to the ladies of the camp for meals.

The dinner, reflecting the lack of any meat stores, was a thick potato soup and rounded loaves of rye bread. Steamed puddings were sliced onto plates so that everyone would have at least one helping.

Unfortunately, the outburst of Lady Avis toward Alaine had cast a dark cloud over the meal. The cook's girls whispered at the far end of the table. Annie and Nana spoke quietly between themselves. Alaine sat between Genna and Charlyn, with Lady Avis on the other side of Charlyn. There was a silence at that end of the table, except for the clink of a spoon or cup. Alaine ran her spoon around the bowl. She tasted the heavy soup in small sips, finding it warm and tasty. Though she had had little to eat during the day, Alaine felt no need for food. Holding back her emotions, she felt a lump in her throat. There was the sting of truth to her aunt's admonishment. She pictured her mother and felt that she would also agree with her sister. Was she behaving as her rank required? She admired Lady Charlyn, who seemed to effortlessly act as a lady of nobility. Alaine felt she should not be the cause of upset for her aunt or Nana. Covey shouldn't have to go around the camp looking for her as if she were a lost child.

Alaine thought she must strive to improve her behavior.

That night, as Alaine lay awake on her pallet, she heard the raindrops once again begin to fall on the roof of the tent. Holding her pillow to her, in the privacy of the darkness, she allowed her tears to fall. She wondered what it was about Carver that made her want to dismiss all of the barriers of propriety she had been taught. Maybe her desire to see him was a rebellion against the restraints that would not allow it. No, she decided. It was more than that. She was drawn to him in a manner she couldn't explain. He was like a friend, but more than that. For now, she resolved not to try to see him again. She would save her memories of him. Those, no one could take away. Her mind wandered to the three little carvings hidden in her trunk, and to visions of the moss faeries leading her through the trees.

A bath day came out of necessity and hinged on the finding of the opportune wooden tub. It was also welcomed due to the general boredom with the daily routine forced upon the camp by the ongoing rain. Oween, one of Annie's girls, noticed a large, low-sided tub set out to collect rainwater. It had appeared at camp filled with cooked dishes and meat pies brought by the cooks of Seaken Hall. Left behind, it was put into the use of collecting water. The girl got the idea of bringing it into the cook's tent, heating water, and using it to take a bath. Oween spoke to Annie, Annie spoke to the noble ladies, and all agreed that being able to take a bath and wash their hair would be a much-needed diversion.

So, a partition made of blankets on lines was set up in the back corner of the cook's tent. The tub was brought inside. Water was heated in large soup cauldrons. Additional buckets of rainwater were added until the right temperature was reached. Laundry flake soap and the soaps brought by the ladies were used for washing. The men were all banned from the area of the cook's tent to allow the women to take their turns with washing. It was a laborious process, with heating the water, but thought to be worthwhile by all. Alaine and Charlyn had their heads together giggling quietly as they listened to the voices of Nana and Genna coming from behind the blanket partition as the maid assisted the old nurse with her bath. It went on for some time.

"This water is getting cold," Nana complained. "And don't pour that over my head. I'll catch my death if I get my hair wet."

"I'll fetch more warm water if you would like, nurse," Genna offered.

"No, I just want to get clean and rinsed. This tub is not made for one of my girth. I need to get out as soon as I can. I'm already chilled."

Alaine and her lady-in-waiting sat together on a low bench, combing out their damp hair to allow for drying.

"It does feel good to be clean again," Charlyn commented, gently teasing out a snarled lock.

"Yes, it is probably the last chance for a bath before we reach Irongate Castle – *if* we ever get there."

"The rain is much less today. Maybe we will travel on the morrow."

"It cannot be soon enough," insisted Alaine. "I'm very tired of this place and of being confined to tents. How I wish to be back home! Do you not miss your home and family? What of that squire to whom you wished to return?"

A pensive look came over the young Lady's face as she moved her comb to the blonde tresses on the other side of her head. She did not answer at once but pondered her feelings.

"It is odd," she finally answered. "I feel that I have changed my thinking just in the past few days. Suddenly, I feel so much older."

"I, too, am feeling older, dealing with thoughts that I have never had before. My world seems wider," commented Alaine.

"I was trying to remember what Will looked like last night, but I had trouble remembering any details. Details with which I was previously obsessed. What was it about him that made me think he was the one I wanted? It reminds me of something my father said to me before we left home. Maybe it was that he was a handsome man who, for the first time, paid attention to me. Now, I'm not sure I loved him. With all that has happened on this journey, he seems to have faded in my thoughts."

"Could my cousin have something to do with that?" Alaine asked, knowingly.

"The Duke has been very considerate towards me, but I'm not sure that either of us have developed strong feelings. After all, it has only been a few days since we met. I am but a noblewoman he is charged with protecting as we travel. As you once said, the ladies of the court find him attractive, and, right now, there is a shortage of other ladies for him to admire. Only time will tell…"

"I do believe that he admires you," Alaine replied, "but as you say, it is early days."

"Turn around, and I will comb out the back of your hair for you," Charlyn offered, glad to change the subject away from herself.

Alaine turned around on the seat, facing away from her pretty companion. "I have a confidence I am longing to share, but if I tell you, you must pledge to me your secrecy," Alaine disclosed, with all seriousness.

"I have come to feel close to you and believe we have become friends on this journey. I'm sure that I could keep your secret," Charlyn encouraged, as she combed through the long, red tresses.

"You could not share it with anyone, even Kent or, least of all, my aunt," Alaine insisted.

"You can put your trust in me, Princess. Your secret will be safe."

Alaine hesitated. Should she tell Charlyn about Carver Vale, she wondered? She longed to speak of him, about him, to someone. Inside, her feelings were askew. Maybe sharing her thoughts would help clear her head. Was she also attracted to the first handsome man who showed her some attention?

"Do you remember the young man with the dog that night at the inn?" Alaine began her tale.

"Yes, briefly. He was there and gone quickly, as I remember."

"I have seen him in the days since," Alaine admitted.

"You have?" Charlyn asked, with surprise.

"Remember that little bench overlooking the stream behind the camp? I met him there. I was unable to sleep, as usual, and walked out across the field to the stream. I found the bench and sat. Soon, I dozed off for a short time and when I awoke, he was sitting on the bench next to me. We talked as if old friends. His name is Carver Vale, and he is a man of the woods. He seems to be following our journey."

"That is amazing, Alaine!" Charlyn whispered.

"Also, on the night of the wedding, I came back to the tent, and you were already asleep. I was wide awake, so I went out. I was walking by the edge of the camp, and I saw him across the field. I should not have, but I ran across the field to see him. He took me into the woods to the tree loft where he is staying. It was magical. We talked. He is soft-spoken and kind. I can't help but like him, and he seems to like me. He warned that we would not be able to travel due to the coming storm; I argued, but he was right."

"Is he still there?" Charlyn asked, truly surprised at Alaine's revelation.

"Yes, I saw him and his dog yesterday at the edge of the camp by the tall pines. He came across the field when he saw me. I can't help but be drawn to him, yet he is not a noble and not of my world. There is no allowance for me to be friends with him. After what my aunt said last night, I fear that I must try not to see him again."

"Maybe that is for the best," consoled Charlyn, "especially when we are on the way to meet the man you will marry."

"In my head I know that is what I should do. But in my heart, I long to see him again, talk to him, and spend time with him. It is as if we have known each other for a long time."

"Soon, we will be leaving here. We must focus on our journey. You must be careful, Princess. Think of what almost befell Genna. You must protect yourself from any dispute."

"Of course, you are right," Alaine sighed. "I must put him out of my mind. As difficult as it will be, I must forget him."

As Nana and Genna emerged from behind the barrier, Alaine and Charlyn were left to their own thoughts regarding the rights and wrongs of romance.

11
The Wayward Hunt

The rain had finally stopped but the sky remained overcast with clouds and no visible sun. The morning was fraught with turmoil for Captain Leigh as one concern after another presented itself. He sat in the big tent at the only table, usually reserved for the ladies, taking stock of the issues prior to deciding what actions to take.

Speaking with Annie first thing this morning, they discussed the state of the food stores. The original plan was for a seven-day journey down Central Road, the fastest and best route from Hawthorn Castle to Irongate Castle. This was the morning of their eighth day of travel, and they were far from their destination. When the rain had slowed to a drizzle the previous morning, it was decided that Smyth would take two men and a wagon back up the road to the mercantile.

The hope was to purchase more foodstuffs. The roads were wet with mud, filled with ruts and puddles of standing water. Smyth said that the going would be slow, and as of this morning he had not yet returned. Annie and her girls were doing the best they could to put out two meals a day with what was on hand.

Fortunately, the soldiers were used to scrounging for food when encamped awaiting battle. A team of men had searched the nearby woods on the other side of the roadway the previous day. They returned with some fowl and rabbits for Annie's pot.

Headed up by Lieutenant Miles, two spearmen and four archers had also left to search the woods south of the road. It was deer that they were hunting, maybe a stag, that would supply meat for the company for three to four days. This morning's problem for Kent was that the men failed to return the previous night – seven missing men. A search party was being prepared.

In the great tent, Kent was putting on his jacket while stuffing a hard bread roll into his mouth, knowing that it would be a while before he would have time for a meal, depending how the search went. Men were milling about the tall, canvas room, attending to their own tasks, providing the background noise for the Captain's thoughts. Through the tied-back tent flaps came the two men he wished to see prior to taking out on the road. His scouts had returned. The men approached their Captain with some fear as they had no good news to report.

"Proden, Felter, what news do you have of the way up ahead?" Kent called to the men. "Will we be able to break camp tomorrow and continue on our way? Yet, first, I must attend to a search for the soldiers that failed to return last night. Smyth and his team have also not returned, so tomorrow will be the soonest we could leave."

"The conditions of the road ahead are so wet with mud that the going will be slow with the wagons, sir," Felter reported. "We did find some good fields just off the roadway that will allow us to camp before we reach the River Falls."

"But that is not the problem, sir," Proden broke in.

"What *is* the problem?" Kent asked, impatiently.

"The entire town of Leggot, by the Stonelink Bridge, is flooded and under water. The River Falls has overflowed its banks and the people of the town have been forced to flee to Duke Eckelform's Hall with their animals, and whatever they could carry to higher ground. We would be able to camp a half day's ride away from the bridge, but it could be many days before the water recedes enough to allow our crossing."

126

"Seems that our seven-day journey has turned into an undetermined time stranded on the road," the Captain complained, while rubbing his beard with his hand. "There must be another way that we can proceed. Yulup," Kent called to a passing man, "Go fetch the maps from my tent."

The Captain began to pace back and forth with the new problem. The two scouts spoke with the nearby men, leaving Kent to his own council.

Knowing the terrain, the scouts doubted any easy solution, as they moved away in search of food and drink.

As the maps were brought to the great tent, Covey and Sergeant Ash followed, having heard of the scout's return. News of the flooding was quickly spreading among the men. Maps of the Upper and Lower Kingdoms were unfurled on the table. Furled corners were secured with the cups and wooden bowls at hand. Kent and his soldiers bent their heads over the parchment, searching for alternative ways of passage to the Lowlands. It became clear that other possible routes would take them far out of their way. The other choice was to camp near the River Falls and wait for the water to recede.

It was at this inopportune moment in the Captain's frustration that the Lady Avis, Princess Alaine and Lady Charlyn entered the tent and made their way to the table holding the maps. Lady Avis was distressed to see the degree of her son's untidy appearance. Hair hung in clumps, uncombed around his face. His beard was growing out, unshaven since the wedding feast. He wore his older, well-worn garrison jacket. The open front of the garment revealed a once white shirt with dirty cuffs, left open at the neck. His trousers showed signs of smeared mud, as did his boots.

The soldiers all looked up as the ladies approached. Alaine took the lead in speaking first. "We have come to ask of the travel plans, good sirs."

Kent was in no mood for dealing with the women. He straightened, looking at Alaine, his mother and the Lady Charlyn.

"Travel plans. You ask of travel plans, milady?"

"Yes, we wish to know if we should plan for travel today," Alaine responded.

"Let me think," Kent voiced, with sarcasm. "The roads could not be in worse condition for horses and wagons. We are low on supplies and Smyth, who went out yesterday for goods, has not yet returned. A party of seven of my garrison men went south to hunt deer and didn't return last night. Our search party for them will be leaving soon," Kent reported, his voice rising with each statement. "Felter and Proden have just returned after scouting the road ahead, where camp sites have been found. But the River Falls has overflowed its banks and flooded the countryside. The days that will be needed for floodwaters to recede enough to allow for crossing is unknown. So, no, milady, we will not be continuing this ill-fated journey today, and possibly not tomorrow!"

The background noise within the tent had ceased. There was a quiet after the Captain's loud rant.

Taken aback, Alaine said nothing, but straightened her back while fighting back tears after Kent's unexpected rudeness toward her.

The face of Lady Avis reddened. Her ire came up as she stepped closer to her niece.

"You are speaking to the Princess Alaine of Hawthorn, sir," Lady Avis admonished, in a lowered voice. "Your tone lacks the due respect of her rank, and yours."

Alaine turned to face her aunt. "It is clear that we have interrupted important matters. I will take my leave."

The silence in the air prevailed as the Princess strode from the tent with her head held high. Charlyn made a move to follow her, but Lady Avis put a hand on her sleeve.

"Leave her alone, dear. She needs some solitude," said Lady Avis. "Come, we will see what the ladies are up to in the cook's tent." She gave her son a look that only a mother can give, prior to leaving the tent.

Alaine made a hasty walk to her tent. The thoughts of continuing their travels were dashed. Having suffered Kent's wrath many times throughout her life, she knew that his tirade was fueled by frustration that had nothing to do with her personally. He was obviously dealing with many obstacles important to them all.

She retreated to a dark corner beside one of her trunks and sat with her back against the damp, canvas wall. She was but a head and arms sticking out above the pile of her heavy skirts. Tears ran down her cheeks. She couldn't get away from the thought that none of this would be happening, and none of the people would be on this trip, but for her, the Princess of Hawthorn. It was because of her that this escapade had begun. It was because of her that Charlyn had almost been fatally harmed. And it was because of her that seven men were now missing. As Kent said, it was an ill-fated journey, all for the need to get *her* to Irongate Castle.

Alaine's depression over the situation quickly turned to frustration, for she knew that her tears were for nothing. The annoyance quickly turned to anger. She didn't want to sit in a tent as a frail girl totally dependent on others for determining outcomes. Alaine wanted to *do something*! An anger of pounded copper and determination rose within her. Thoughts racing, there was nothing to stop her from taking action. After all, *she* was the highest ranking noble in the camp. Kent could lead, but so could she!

The Princess looked at the clothes she was wearing. What would she be able to do so dressed? Ride a horse? Shoot an arrow? Run? Her mind raced. Clothes! First, she needed different clothes, she decided.

Alaine came out of her corner a determined woman with purpose. Out into the camp she went, trying to walk casually as she went from one empty garrison tent to another. Returning to her own tent, she stripped off the heavy, woolen day gown, leaving only a thin, sleeveless chemise. She pulled on the stolen trousers, tucking in the undergarment, and pulling the drawstring at the waist. Then, donning the smallest shirt she could find hanging to dry in a tent, Alaine pushed the tails into the pants. The chain with the dragonfly was hung around her neck, providing a certain comfort of having the small dagger close at hand. Next, she dove her head into the trunk with her everyday clothes, looking for a particular item. A jacket was needed, and the short beaver cape that had slits for her arms would allow for easy movement.

Just as Alaine was securing the cape at her throat, Genna came into the tent. A look of surprise appeared on her face as she saw the way the Princess was dressed.

"Milady, what are you doing?"

"That is just it, Genna. I'm *doing* something! It is time for me to quit sitting around. Here, help me with my hair," Alaine demanded. "I want a single braid and I'll tie this black scarf around my forehead and cover my hair with a knot at the back."

Genna knew well how Alaine's determination could push her into action, sometimes ending in calamities involving Sergeant Covey and her royal parents. Yet, Genna knew that it was impossible to hold Alaine back when she set her mind to something. Alaine's hair confined, Genna stood back to look at her mistress. Alaine almost had the look of a lad, and surely not a princess of the realm.

Alaine grabbed the stolen, small bow and quiver of arrows, securing them on one shoulder.

"I am ready," she proclaimed. "Wish me luck, Genna. I am off," Alaine said with determination, stopping to hug her friend.

"Princess, please do not do this. I am in fear for you. You should not go."

"I'm not helpless, Genna. I *can* do this!"

With that, Alaine left the tent and sped to the corral under the pines. It had been hastily constructed to hold the horses during the rain showers and overnight when they were not in the pasture behind the camp. She was looking for a horse from the Hawthorn Castle stables, many of which she knew or had ridden previously. Settling for the gray, spotted mare called Cloud – how in tune with the overcast day - she quickly bridled the horse. Alaine knew that she could not go out to the roadway without being seen, so she led the horse to the back field, thinking that she could follow the tree line south until she could get out to the road.

Guiding the horse by hand, the Princess heard a rustling coming from the trees. Cloud's ears perked up and the horse gave a snort.

"Where is it you are going, Princess?" came a soft voice from behind her.

Alaine knew who it was at once and turned to face him. He wore his long cloak and carried a walking stick. His satchel and, like her, a bow and arrows were slung over his shoulder. His hair was drawn back, his eyes were as piercing as ever, and his expression was serious.

"We have seven missing men that may have come to harm. The soldiers went south yesterday hunting for deer, as our food stores are dwindling. I am set to find them," Alaine announced with resolve.

"Well, if you wish to find them, you must leave the horse here. The forests south are far too dense for riding. There could be many reasons your men have not returned, and I can guess at some of them. Our people believe that the forest lands were deeded to them many seasons past, and they con- sider the trees their territory. They do not take well to men encroaching."

"My cousin, our Captain, is taking a search party out to find them. They have probably already departed. I will not sit here and do nothing. It is due to me that these things are happening. I wish to help set things right."

"Circumstances are not due to you, Princess. It is not your fault that your parents seek a stately and beneficial marriage for you. The attack of the highwaymen happened in spite of a strong escort. The enduring rain was surely not your fault, just a happenstance common to this season," Carver conveyed in support. "As to the missing men, if you are determined to join the search, I will go with you, if you will allow me to guide you through the woodlands."

Alaine stood quietly, considering his offer.

"Did you bring food and water for yourself?" he asked.

"No, I was trying to get away before being seen," she answered meekly.

"Never mind, I have some that I can share. Astra always finds the streams, many of them swollen since the rains."

A call came from across the pasture that turned Alaine and Carver's heads to see Sergeant Covey striding toward them.

"Looks like you have been found out, Princess."

"Genna!" Alaine surmised.

The well-meaning maid must have gone to Covey for help. It was hard to believe that the man could walk so fast when he found the need. Momentarily he was before them.

"What is it you are doing, Princess? And what is this attire? You must return with me at once. Lady Avis will be worried," the man insisted, rather breathless.

"I am not going back!" Alaine stated defiantly. "This man knows the forest lands and will guide me in the search for our missing soldiers."

"You cannot go, Princess. It is not fitting. The Captain's search party has already left," countered Covey.

"If I am old enough to be taken to Irongate Castle and used as a pawn in a royal marriage, I am old enough to make some decisions for myself. *I* am the royalty here and you are my liege. I *will* take action! You do not rule me, sir."

"I have sworn fidelity to my King and Queen, Princess. If I cannot dissuade you, then I must come with you."

Alaine looked at Carver for his approval. He understood the man's dilemma. He nodded his head to Alaine in assent.

"Suit yourself, Sergeant Covey, but we are leaving now," insisted Alaine.

Kent and the other five men of the search party kept their horses trained on the center of the roadway in order to avoid any deep ruts hidden by the muddy puddles. Even so, they could not gallop, but proceeded at a trot. As they moved along, the trees lining the road became bigger, primarily oaks and ash, leafing-out in their spring foliage. The Captain knew that the missing garrison men had gone south on the road, riding their horses, so the roadside was being searched for horses left behind by the hunting party. A dim sun had broken out, forcing its light through the clouds. It was high in the sky. Kent judged that the morning was gone, and this was an afternoon sky.

"Look, sir!" called Sergeant Ash. "There's one of our horses."

The company came to a halt. Indeed, a brown garrison mount, still with saddle, grazed at the tall grass by the edge of the road.

"Go get it," the Captain ordered the man next to him.

The group continued along the road at a slower pace, searching for the other horses. Not far along, gathered together in a small cove of grass, were the rest of the hunting party's mounts.

"Here they are," the Captain called. "Miles and his men must have entered the woods nearby."

It was decided to leave all of the horses together as Kent led his troops into the woods. They called out for Miles, hoping for a return call that was not to come. Kent came to a halt and looked around. After only a short distance, they found themselves enveloped by trees and foliage. Less light was filtering through the tall trees, and the forest floor was shaded with growth. The underbrush was thick, allowing no discernible pathway. The colors of everything in sight merged into shades of green and brown. Tree trunks were covered with moss and clinging vines. Mounds of berry brambles were as tall as the men. The atmosphere was quiet and eerie.

"Our men could be lost anywhere in here. We need to take care, or we will never find the road again. You two, use your short swords to cut a pathway through the brush. Ash and I will follow watching for any signs that our fellows have passed here. You two follow us and cut marks on the trees so we can find our way out. Let's move. I don't want to be caught in here after the sun goes down. That's probably what happened to Miles."

The group carefully picked their way through the forest, breaking the silence by calling out for the missing men. They found open spaces which could be quickly traversed, but not a man or deer was to be seen. It was when they were in the middle of one of these grassy meadows that they were suddenly overtaken.

Men with arrows already notched in bows stepped out from the trees, completely surrounding Kent and his soldiers. There was no time to react. Any battle was lost before it began. There were at least thirty men from the trees all poised for the assault.

"Drop your weapons and make no movement," Kent urgently commanded his small party.

The soldiers stood close together in a bunch, keeping their eyes on their captors. The archers held their places as two of them came out of the trees and walked toward the encircled soldiers. One man was short with dark, graying hair tied in a knot at the back of his head. The other was a little taller, and thin, with fair, straight hair.

Both were wearing clothing in shades of the woods, camouflaging them with the background. The older man seemed to know that Kent was the leader of the troop and approached him directly.

"These are our lands by treaty. Why do you come into our forest?"

"Yesterday some of our men came to hunt deer in the woods and never returned. We have come to find them," Kent replied.

"Yes, we have your men. They are unharmed. You will come with us," ordered the woodsman.

The woodsman turned and barked orders to his men in an unfamiliar language. The archers lowered their bows and stowed their arrows. They collected the soldier's weapons from the ground. Then, Kent and his soldiers were herded by the forest men along some unknown path leading them even deeper into the inhospitable undergrowth.

"Put your hand on my arm and we will travel faster through the woods," Carver instructed Alaine.

"What about Covey? We can't leave him lost in the trees," Alaine asked, with worry.

"Astra will stay with him and lead him along. She always knows how to find me," Carver replied, without concern.

Alaine placed her hand on Carver's forearm, and they began to move through the trees with haste. Alaine looked back and saw the dog leading Covey, who was trying to keep them in sight. On they went as the density of trees increased. At one point Carver stopped, allowing for Astra and Covey to catch up. Once they were in view, Carver took Alaine's hand and rushed forward, seeming to know where he was going.

After what seemed like much time and a long distance into the thick underbrush, Carver and Alaine broke into a large open space of an encampment of structures, many of which were off the ground within the trees. These tree houses were not unlike the small loft that Carver had shown her, but larger, with greater detail. Alaine's eyesight had already adjusted to the dim forest light. When looking ahead, she saw Kent sitting on the ground, tied to a nearby tree. He didn't appear to be harmed. The other soldiers were sitting nearby in a fenced enclosure under one of the tree lofts.

"Oh no, I believe that we may be too late," said Alaine.

"Let me handle this," Carver whispered, as he bent to talk softly into Alaine's ear. "This forest hamlet belongs to my brother."

Bole was notified of the visitors as soon as Alaine and Carver stepped out of the trees. He came down the steps of the treehouse, carrying a lantern in one hand. Flecher followed closely behind his brother. The two walked to meet Carver and the guest he brought.

"Farewell, brother. What lad is this that you have brought into our woods?" Bole demanded.

"Hail, brothers. May I present to you Alaine, the Princess of Hawthorn. Princess, these are my brothers, Bole and Flecher."

Alaine reached up and removed the scarf she wore, exposing her red hair. Kent had been watching the activity from his spot on the ground. He was shocked to see what he thought was a boy with the familiar stranger but was actually the Princess Alaine confronting his captors.

"We are honored, Princess," Bole said, bowing deeply from the waist. Flecher did likewise. "Carver, why have you brought the Princess to our homestead?" Bole asked.

Not waiting for Carver to answer, Alaine spoke with authority, "Carver has assisted me. I have come in search of my missing men. They are part of my escort to the Weston Mareview Lowlands and Irongate Castle."

"Your men are all here and unharmed," responded Bole. "We were just discussing what to do with them. They have trespassed deeply into our forest."

"I am requesting their release, sir. I apologize for their foray onto your land. If your companions could lead them back to the road, they could find their way back to our camp. I will promise you that they will not stray onto your lands again."

"As you wish, milady," said Bole. He turned and spoke in his language to his men, who made way to release the soldiers.

It was at this time that a loud bark was heard as Astra came bounding out of the trees, and behind her stumbled the exhausted Covey. All eyes turned to the tall man.

"This is my bodyguard. He is pledged to the King and Queen for my protection. He insisted on coming with me," Alaine explained to Carver's brothers.

"We will release your men, Princess, but first, come to my lodge and take a drink with us," Bole offered, wishing to learn more of this girl, for his brother Carver's sake.

Alaine looked at Carver, who put her at ease with a smile. Alaine knew that it would be rude to reject the offered hospitality.

"I would be happy to attend, sir, but I would request that Duke Morr-Leigh, the captain of our expedition, be allowed to join us."

"Ah, so he is the Duke now," said Flecher. "We had heard rumor of it. Today we did not recognize him."

A man came to untie Kent, who stood as soon as he was able, and came to join Carver and Alaine.

Lanterns had been lit along the curved, wooden staircase leading up to the treehouse. Darkness came early to the deep woods. Only the last beams of afternoon sunlight came through the canopy of trees. Bole led the way up the wooden planks, followed by Alaine and Carver.

Flecher walked with the somewhat astonished Captain.

12
The Treaty of the Trees

Genna ran to the great tent seeking Lady Avis, who was not to be found. Next, she hastily made her way to the cook's tent where the Lady was in conversation with Annie. The need for a hot dinner was being discussed – the prospect of a root vegetable stew flavored with one small ground quail for each cauldron. The smell of bread loaves steaming in their domed pans over low fires filled the air.

Interrupting, "Lady Avis, I must speak with you…" Genna insisted, breathlessly.

At once, Lady Avis noticed the distress on the maid's face, and a pang of worry went through her.

"What is it, Genna?"

"The Princess has gone off by herself to find the missing garrison men!" Genna blurted out.

Everyone in the tent stopped and turned to listen to what was happening.

"What!?" Lady Avis exclaimed, with disbelief.

"It's true, milady. Alaine dressed herself in men's clothing and took herself away. I was there just before she left. She demanded that I help her cover her hair. I tried to stop her, but she would not listen."

"Oh, that girl!" Lady Avis declared, as the women in the tent gathered around. "As if I'm not growing enough gray hairs on my head. We must find Covey to go after her. Which way did she go?"

"I have already told Sergeant Covey. As soon as the Princess left, I ran to find him. He has gone after her," Genna related.

"Did he find her?"

"I don't know. I did not see them returning. I ran to tell you that she left. She was determined, milady. I tried stop to her."

"It is not your fault, Genna. You did right by alerting Covey of her leaving. We all know how headstrong Alaine can be at times."

"What else should we do?" asked Nana, with concern.

"Stay here," the Lady answered, formulating a plan. "I'll go to the big tent to find the two scouts who returned this morning. They know the landscape. Genna, you come with me."

The two women soon located the guides resting against their bedrolls in a corner of the great tent. They immediately stumbled to their feet, as Lady Avis called them out.

"Genna, tell them what you know of the Princess leaving," the Lady demanded.

"The Princess Alaine dressed herself as a lad and said that she was leaving to find the missing garrison soldiers who did not return from the hunt yesterday."

The scouts looked at each other and one of them let out a groan, knowing that they were being called to duty.

"I know that you have only recently returned, but would you set out again to find Princess Alaine?" Lady Avis asked. "Covey has already gone after her, but he does not know the roads as you do. My son has already departed also, so it is you that I must ask."

"Did she leave on foot?" Proden asked Genna, knowing that they couldn't refuse the Lady's request.

"She left the tent on foot, but she is skilled on horseback. She may have taken a horse," Genna answered.

"We'll leave straightaway," said Proden, beginning to gather his things. "Make haste, gentlemen, as I do not want her alone at nightfall; and keep an eye out for Sergeant Covey," ordered Lady Avis.

"Fear not, Mistress, we will find her. We'll take an extra horse with us." Felter said, trying to console the two worried women as they left.

The disheveled young Duke sat at one end of the table with a recovered Sergeant Covey while all of the attention was focused on his fair cousin. So far, he was surprised at Alaine's ability to manage the encounter with these alien woodsmen. He had watched from the balcony of the large tree house as his men were being released and led off into the woods, hopefully toward the roadway and their horses. They should return to the camp by nightfall and take word of himself and the errant Princess back to his mother. He could only guess at his mother's reaction when she found Alaine gone. The longer it was that no one returned, the more distraught the Lady would be. After climbing the stairway to the elevated platform home, the group was led to an interior space used for eating in the large, open floor plan. Alaine sat on a floor pad at the middle of a long, irregularly shaped slab of glossy wood. Across from her sat the supposed leader of this hamlet, known as Bole, with his brother Flecher sitting next to him.

Kent recognized Carver Vale, who was sitting next to Alaine - too close for Kent's comfort. Who was this man who kept popping up, first at the inn and later on the road, warning of highwaymen? Was he following their travels, as Kent suspected? But why? With a closer look, there seemed to be a familiarity between the two as they leaned closer to one another. Kent felt that he was missing something. He wondered what Vale was doing here with Alaine, as it appeared he was the one who led her to this place. For now, Kent kept silent, somewhat anxious, letting the encounter play out.

Watching the strangers, Kent was not surprised to learn that the three men were brothers. There was a similarity about them in looks and manner. At times, they spoke in their own language, yet all spoke the language of the kingdom with no accent. The small cluster of tree houses represented a society of families living unseen and separate. Kent wondered how this could be so, but he was sure that the long-standing restrictions on the kingdom's forested lands had something to do with it. He wondered if his uncle, King Granth, knew of these forest clans living out of sight.

During this lapse of quiet, Kent's thoughts were interrupted by two giggling girls. They wore the multicolored clothes of these people and spoke in whispers to each other. They brought cups filled with liquid, setting one by each person at the table. They went to stand by a carved partition, their eyes focused on Alaine.

"These are my daughters," said Bole, "Belfrie is the elder and Leebis is her younger sister.

"What are they laughing about?" Alaine asked Carver.

"It is your hair, Princess," answered Flecher. "They have never seen that color of hair."

Belfrie said something to her father in their language.

"They are asking if you would unbraid your hair so that they can look at it," Bole interpreted.

Alaine removed the ribbon at the end of her braid and loosened the hair from its constraints. She combed through the mass with her fingers as it spread out across her shoulders. Kent watched with uneasiness as Carver brushed aside a red tendril that strayed onto Alaine's cheek. The Princess rewarded him with a small smile. Watching them, Kent was suddenly alarmed. How could she even *know* this person Vale, he wondered? Had the two somehow spent time together? No, he thought, thinking back over the last few days. That wasn't possible.

One of the girls ran off, and soon returned, offering Alaine a delicate, copper coronet for her hair. Alaine put the circlet onto her head, the coils of copper highlighting her forehead while securing her flowing locks away from her face.

"Thank you," Alaine said, nodding to the girl. "It's beautiful and fits perfectly."

"That was made by one of our craftsmen," said Bole. "You must keep it as a gift." Then, after a slight pause, "So, Princess Alaine, how is it that you came to us today with our brother, Carver? We understand that your journey was taking you to Irongate Castle for a possible marriage."

Kent and Covey both turned their attention to Bole and Flecher, wondering how it was that these men of the forest knew this detail regarding their journey to the coast.

"Yes," said Alaine, looking straight at the elder woodsman while preparing her response. "It is true that our travels have not gone as well as originally planned. Initially the weather was fair and the first night at the inn was cozy. The second day we traveled far and made camp in a field by a stream."

"We know of that farm," Flecher interrupted. "The farmer's oat fields border our woods. He has been a good neighbor, with respect for our trees."

"Despite the garrison of soldiers, we were attacked by highwaymen on the third day," Alaine continued, "and my lady-in-waiting was injured. Such was her injury that we could not travel the next day."

"We knew of this attack, as we found one of the scoundrels lost in the woods," said Bole. "We handed him over to your good man here," indicating Sergeant Covey.

"Then came the rains. The roadway filled with water. Day after day we were unable to travel," Alain explained. "Although we were well stocked for a seven-day journey, with a large company, our food stores began to dwindle. Yesterday some of our garrison soldiers went out to hunt deer, and the rest you know. Today the Duke came in search of our men. I also wanted to join the search. It was helpful that Carver offered to guide me here."

"Duke Morr-Leigh, what are your plans for continuing your journey?" inquired Bole, using Kent's formal title.

Caught off guard, Kent sat up straight and set the cup of mysterious drink on the table as he gathered his words.

"The days of rain have certainly hindered our travels," Kent began. "We sent out our cook with a wagon yesterday to travel back to the farmer's market for supplies. It is my hope that they made it back to our camp today.

"This morning, our scouts returned with news of the way ahead. The roads are bad, and we have many wagons, but the scouts found a good place to camp about a half day's ride from the River Falls. Yet they also reported that the river has overflowed its banks and flooded the countryside. The Stonelink Bridge is under water, as is the village of Leggot. The townsfolk have fled to higher ground. How long it will take for the waters to recede enough that we can cross the bridge is unknown."

All was quiet at the table after Kent painted the dismal picture. The three peculiar brothers exchanged glances. Kent got the feeling that they were already aware of the flooding.

"I have reviewed our maps, and it appears that our choices are limited," Kent continued. We can travel Eckelform Hall Road north and cross the Duke's lands to Timber Road. That road later merges with Central Road on the other side of the river going south. Depending upon how far we can travel in a day, it will take us three to four days out of our way. I'm not sure that it may not be wiser to wait for the river to return to its banks. Either way, it is a further delay."

"This is awful," Alaine moaned, her voice reflecting misery.

It was then that Bole's daughters brought plates of food, a bowl of berries, and a stack of flat, round cakes that appeared to be some sort of bread. Eying the food, Kent thought that it was a plant-based fare. He was hungry, having not eaten since the previous evening, so he picked up a wedge of unknown wafer and began to eat. Soon quiet prevailed, as all were eating. The woodsmen spoke softly among themselves in their foreign tongue. They seemed to be having some disagreements among themselves. At last they finished most of the food provided.

"Duke, we were wondering why it was that you brought such a lot of men on this journey?" Flecher asked.

"Ah, yes. That was King Granth's idea, to have the full garrison escort the Princess," Kent replied.

"It seems that traveling with so many men led to more hardships," Flecher observed. "I mean, how many men would you really need? What if you were to send half of the men and wagons back to Hawthorn Castle before you move on?"

Kent considered the suggestion. There would be half the people to feed, half the supply wagons and horses to drag through the mud. It *would* make the travels easier, especially if they decided to take the detour.

"If there was another way to get the Princess to the seacoast, what is the fewest number of people and wagons that would be needed?" asked Bole.

Just that morning Kent had studied his maps, and he knew that there was no easy way to the coast. He thought about the smallest group of people needed for the escort. Maybe twelve guardsmen, the royal coach and three supply wagons. What was the woodsman suggesting? Kent wondered.

"Do you know of another way to reach the seacoast?" Alaine asked Bole, interrupting.

Flecher left the table and returned with a rolled, thin hide, which he unfurled onto the table. "Here is one of *our* maps," he said, pointing to the soft leather.

Everyone peered with intent at the map. The degree of detail was unexpected by the visitors. In fact, the map represented the entire landmass of Hawthorn. It included the upper and lower kingdoms prior to the division by King Holmes, which split the lands between his two sons.

"This is an old map," Covey observed, "there is the old Craig Castle built by King Ardan. It's partly in ruins now, but the surrounding walls are sound. The old soldiers have taken it over as a place to live out their days."

"This map goes back to the days of the great-grandfather King of Princess Alaine," advised Flecher.

"Before Craig Castle, it was the time of invasions and war. Boats landed at the coast, and legions of raiders came onto the land and wreaked havoc with the people. It was a time of hardship and death," Bole spoke with emotion, recounting the history. "Then Ardan was made King. One of our forest people, named Caslyn, led Ardan and his men to a place where there was a great cleft in the side of the mountain, which was hidden by a large wood. Standing on the site, overlooking the valley, the strategic positioning was apparent, because no one could approach from any direction without being seen. There was no possibility of attack from behind. It was King Ardan that cleared the land and built his stronghold - Craig Castle.

"Our people developed a network of pathways throughout the forest lands and would bring early warnings to the King when the invader's boats would come. Arden's men would be ready to attack the plunderers, taking them by surprise. The stragglers of battle would retreat to their ships and sail away. After some time, the raiders stopped coming and the land of Hawthorn settled into peace. After years of supporting the kingdom, the old King rewarded our people with The Treaty of the Trees, granting us control of the forest lands throughout the kingdom. Only the northern forests were kept by the King for the needed timber. Later, it became the lands of Duke Noeman of the Walls, which is now in the hands of his son."

Kent, Alaine and Covey were transfixed hearing this perspective of the history of their lands. Covey, being of an older generation, was more acquainted with these events, knowing some of the stories from his youth. The younger nobles were reminded of some of the old stories told at court when the older men were deep in their cups of wine.

Kent continued to stare at the elaborate detail of the old map - detail that had probably never been seen by any outsider of the forest. Not only did the map name all of the villages and townships of the kingdoms, but it showed all of the trails, hamlets, and homesteads of the forest peoples. Everything was carefully labeled in a black script. All rivers, lakes and the shoreline were labeled in blue. The great halls of the landholding dukes throughout Hawthorn were denoted.

"This map is far more specific than anything I've ever seen," observed Kent, continuing to study the hide. "The forest lands show little on our maps. Let's see, it looks like our campsite is about here along the Central Road, and we are about here in the forest."

"Yes," replied Bole, "this is my holding of the forest lands. These are my trees, and this portion belongs to Flecher," indicating the forest land west of Bole's.

"What is this by the River Falls?" asked Alaine, pointing to a labeled emblem on the map.

"Translated from our language, it is Middleoak by the Falls. It is approximately in the middle of all the land. It's the very old, sacred place for our clans. We have our binding ceremonies there, or weddings, as you would call them. Most of all, it is where we seasonally honor all of our forefathers. Our father was born there but chooses to live at his Manse of the Woods here," replied Flecher, pointing to another emblem on the map that was in the forest very near Hawthorn Castle."

Alaine continued to question, "I see that all of our roads are shown as black lines, but the roads through the forest are shown in broken lines. Is this a road?" indicating a broken line that ran almost from the Central Road, along the River Falls, through the forest land all the way to the sea in the south.

"It is an ancient passage to the south used by our people. Actually, it is the way the invaders used to come into the land from their boats on the shore," said Bole.

"If we could have your permission to use this passage, it would solve our travel dilemma," Alaine put forward.

"There is no way our people would allow your full company to travel that route. Our roads are narrow and only for our use," said Bole.

"We would have to get permission to lead you along that path," said Flecher. "And if we *did* get permission, it would only be for a small portion of your party."

"Permission might be granted for the daughter of King Granth?" queried Carver, to his brothers.

"Would you seek permission for us, if we abide by your laws?" asked Alaine.

"It would take two days before we could receive an answer," said Bole, "but an allowance *might* be made for a princess of the land. We can make the request."

Kent and Covey were surprised by the offer. Bole went on to discuss the terrain along the passage, pointing to various spots where the going with the wagons could be difficult. He also knew that letting the people of the land into their forests could cause unrest among his people. It would be controversial. There would have to be some appeasement.

The negotiations began…

Kent, Lady Avis and Covey huddled in the busy cook's tent, deciding on the details of their travel plans. The cook's tent, filled with the aroma of baked bread, was being used because the great tent was already packed and loaded for the move.

After much thought, Kent made the decision to send thirty of the garrison soldiers back to Hawthorn Castle with a letter of explanation to the King and Queen. They set out the day before, taking their horses, tents and half of the wagons. With them went a certain weight off of the young Duke's shoulders.

The other twenty guardsmen and stablemen would be guided by Felter and Proden to the wide field a half day's ride from the River Falls. There, the men would set up camp and wait for Kent's small party to return from the coast. By then, the flood waters should have receded, and they would finish the trip back to Hawthorn.

Smyth returned to the camp the day that Kent and Alaine were away in the forest. The cook brought back a wagonload of supplies. Dry goods of flour, meal, and beans were bought. The merchant at the store directed them to nearby farms where they were able to buy butter, sheep, chickens and eggs. With fewer mouths to feed and the town of Leggot nearby, the supplies should last.

"If the forest people do give us permission to travel across their lands, what is the least number of people and wagons needed?" asked Kent, primarily of his mother who knew what was needed for the ladies.

"There is the royal coach, of course, and we must take all of the trunks," replied Lady Avis.

"I would want to go," said Sergeant Covey. "I could drive one of the wagons and Rand could drive the coach, as usual."

"We should also bring Genna. It would look poorly if we did not have one lady's maid for Alaine," Lady Avis offered.

"Thinking of the coach," Kent said, fingers to his forehead, "maybe we should not bring it, but send it along to the camp site with the remaining guard. When we reach the seacoast from the forest road, we will have to travel along the shore road for some ways before we reach Harbortown and Irongate Castle. The royal coach would be very conspicuous and draw the attention of the locals. Remember, we will no longer have an escort of guardsmen."

"That is true," agreed Covey, always thinking of the safety of the Princess.

"But how else would we go?" asked Lady Avis, not sure of giving up the comfortable coach.

"We can take three of the covered wagons. One would be driven by Rand, carrying supplies and a trunk, also where he and Genna could sleep. A second wagon, driven by Lieutenant Miles, could carry the rest of the trunks, where you and Nana could sleep. The third wagon would be driven by Covey and carry the ladies during travel and used by Alaine and Charlyn for sleeping. The men can use tents.

"The forest people should not object to such a small party. Bole said that the smaller the company we have, the better. We would have five women and four men. Actually, we should take one more from the guard, just for caution. I have no fear while traveling through the forest, but the Shoreline Byway may be another story. There are inns and places to stop for food, but we must take care to conceal our identities. We can dress without finery or garrison clothing."

"I guess that would be better than waiting for the flood waters to recede or dragging wagons through the hill country for days," relented Lady Avis. "When will we know if the forest men will guide us?"

"They should be here by morning," Kent replied. "Prepare all of your ladies for travel. At best, it will take two days to travel through the woods and two more days along the coast road before we reach Irongate."

"And if they don't come?" asked Covey.

"If they don't come, we will know that they could not get permission, and we will move with the rest of the company to the new camp site. Covey, you speak with Rand, and I will talk to Miles. Rest well tonight, mother, for tomorrow will be a long day."

13
Middleoak

Genna decided to ride on the stoop beside Rand, who was driving the first wagon for the diminished royal party. They were preparing to cross the forest lands to the seacoast. The maid could have chosen to ride in the last wagon with the rest of the ladies but, being a newlywed, she valued the time with her husband. Genna also preferred being outside in the open air, where she could see the scenery, such as it was.

Four of the men from the forest had shown up at their camp just after dawn that morning. To Genna's surprise, they came on foot and proposed to lead Kent's troop without horses. The small band of three wagons was ready to travel. The ladies were assisted into the last covered wagon, to be driven by Sergeant Covey. After speaking with Flecher, Kent told Rand to follow the man with the bow and arrows, and then took up his position at the back of the procession on horseback.

The rest of the camp - what was left of the men, cooks, horses and wagons - was packed and ready to follow the royal party down the Central Road until Kent's group were led off into the woods.

The royal coach would stay with the garrison. It would act as a decoy for anyone set on malice following the Princess.

The morning air was fresh, and Genna wrapped her shawl tightly around her shoulders as she shifted on the seat closer to Rand. Her husband made a comment of admiration for the forest men's ability to effortlessly stay out in front of the horses pulling the wagons. Admittedly, the roads were still muddy, with the horses needing to be held back, lest they be injured or cause a wagon wheel to be damaged. So went the morning ride.

It was early afternoon when Flecher went to the side of the road and signaled for the wagons to follow him up a shallow, muddy bank toward the trees. These were mature fir trees that presented a thick border, but to Rand and Genna's surprise, passages were found that allowed for the horses and wagons. Their forest guide was as skillful as a seamstress threading a needle.

The trail was narrow, as bushes and branches tore at the wooden sides of the wagons and their canvas coverings. The further they proceeded into the woods; the less daylight seemed to make its way through the canopy. Other than the noises from the horses and the movement through the brush, an eerie silence penetrated the forest. Here, the party's fate was in the hands of the inhabitants of this tree-laced land.

As the wagon jostled along, Alaine's thoughts were all about Carver Vale. Her resolution to forget him was dashed the moment she had seen him again. Seeing her determination to join the hunt for the missing garrison soldiers, he had offered to guide her. Alaine now realized how foolish believing in her own ability to navigate the thick forest by herself had been. Thinking back, it was exciting going through the trees with Carver. With her hand on his arm or hand-in-hand, they traveled so swiftly that it felt like magic. Carver was her ally, supporting her quest. It was only poor Covey that paid the price of stumbling through the woods, trying to keep Astra in sight.

When the trees parted and opened to the forest village, Alaine was surprised to see the large, multilevel treehouses. These were much greater than the loft that Carver had shown her. The raised habitats were arranged in sight of each other but spread out enough to leave a cleared, central space to be used for gatherings around the great stone fire pit. Adding texture were the lights glowing from every structure.

Entering the clearing, Alaine was shocked to see Kent sitting on the ground, tied to the base of a tree. She could only wonder how that had come about. Not far off, the other garrison men were being confined in a fenced-off space under one of the lofts. How relieved she was to have Carver beside her to help face what came next.

The supposed leader of the place approached them almost immediately. Bole had certainly shown respect for her rank as a royal princess. He released the soldiers upon her request. He opened his home to them and provided her, Kent and Covey shelter for the night. Most of all, Flecher and Bole were willing to request permission for them to cross their forest lands to the coast, using the ancient road. That was an unexpected happenstance.

Yet, as important as these matters were, Alaine's thoughts kept straying back to the handsome woodsman whose green eyes seemed to sparkle and change colors with the light. This morning, she was disappointed when he was not among the men who were to guide them. Why hadn't he come, she wondered? When would she see him again?

In her mind, Alaine went over every bit of the time she spent with Carver at the treehouse. She had reveled in sitting next to him for such a length of time. There had been easy conversation between them. Being close to him felt right. She relived how he had supported her in his quiet way. Looking into his eyes and wanting his touch made her feel that these were forbidden pleasures. Maybe there was a way that he could be her friend, she pondered. But no, it was more than just his friendship that was longed for. Round and round the circle of thoughts went as the wagon bumped along, denying the hopelessness of her feelings.

The dim light inside the ladies' wagon gradually faded to darkness. Lady Avis longed for the day's travel to end. It was sorely wished to put one's feet on the ground. The noble aunt was proud of her girls, as she now thought of them, who had shown their true nobility, issuing no complaints throughout the day. Nana also gave no protests even though the rocking of the wagon was pounding on her old bones. Lady Avis kept reassuring herself that this was the fastest way to reach their destination, taking days off of their travel to Irongate, so it must be endured.

At long last, the wagon came to a halt. Sighs of relief could be heard from within the wagon. Kent and Covey came to the back opening to assist the ladies. Nana and Lady Avis were first to descend. Then Kent helped Alaine and was there to put hands around Charlyn's waist for an assist to the ground with a smile on his face. Flecher came to them, carrying one of the bright, beautifully designed lanterns, and led them out of the thicket. Yet all movement stalled as the newcomers took in their first sight of Middleoak.

Immediately they saw the many lighted structures - treehouses near and far - in all directions of the surrounding forest. There were so many lofty houses that they couldn't be counted, lighting up the trees. Nearby, lanterns lined the pathways ascending to the multiple platforms in the trees. It was obvious that this was not a hamlet, or just a village of tree lofts in the forest. *This* was a city of importance. As the shining emblem implied on Bole's forest map, Middleoak was the capital city of the forest clans.

Flecher led the weary travelers to a nearby loft and led them up a wide staircase. The many lights in the house were already lit.

"This is my father's house," Flecher explained to Lady Avis. "There are many rooms for all of you to rest. Nourishments are in the pantry. A supper has been prepared to honor the visit by Princess Alaine. Many of our people have traveled a long way to take part. I will return to escort you to the dining court in a little while."

After he left, Lady Avis realized that an important diplomatic dinner with the forest people was upon them. Suddenly attentive, she went to Kent and Covey.

"Are you prepared to publicly thank the forest clans for allowing us to cross their lands?" she asked her son.

"Yes, I have written and signed the deed, and will present it to Bole," Kent replied. "Hopefully, the small gift will appease any grumblings due to our passage."

"We will need all of the ladies' trunks in order to dress for dinner. You, Covey and Miles must wear your best, also."

"We'll get the trunks," Covey said, already on his way, grabbing Miles by the arm.

Alaine stood at the railing of the small balcony, looking out onto the night. She and Charlyn had chosen a large, airy room with two beds on the second level of the opulent treehouse. Alaine marveled at the vista before her.

"Come, Princess, the trunks are here and Genna is coming to help us dress for dinner," Charlyn said, as she came to join Alaine on the balcony.

"As long as I can remember they have always called it the River Falls. I never knew why until now. I have heard speak of waterfalls, but I have never seen one. Now it all makes sense."

"It *is* beautiful."

"Beautiful and peaceful," answered Alaine.

The moon was rising in the east, causing the sky to glow behind the tree-covered hills. The river water plunged over the sharp, granite ledge and fell from a great height into the inky, black water of the lake that bordered Middleoak. Moonlight danced off the mist like diamonds before the droplets plunged to the dark pool below. Sounds of the water splashing into the lake below could be heard in the distance.

"Look at that trail of lanterns moving through the trees. There seem to be many people gathering in that building by the lake. That must be where the dinner is going to be. We must get ready."

"What should we wear?" Charlyn asked.

Turning away from the magical view, "I *know* what I'm going to wear," Alaine proclaimed.

Later, Kent, Lady Avis, Covey and Lieutenant Miles waited for Alaine and Charlyn to come down from their room. Nana pled weariness and had already taken to her bed. Flecher arrived. He stood apart and waited patiently by the stairway. He knew that the dinner would not begin until the Princess arrived.

Charlyn was the first to descend the stairs, drawing the attention of all. She wore a velvet rose gown with a fitted bodice and a two-toned, flared skirt. The dress had the modern styling of long sleeves lined with pink silk, sleeves with tails which hung down below her fingers. The upswept coils of her blonde hair were wrapped in a beaded, golden netting. She was lovely, but those waiting were soon distracted by Alaine, who followed Charlyn.

Alaine's red locks flowed onto her shoulders, confined only by the copper coronet that circled her forehead. She was a vision in dark green, fitting for her forest hosts. She named the gown "The Dandelion Dress," as sharp dandelion leaves and stalks with seed puffs were embroidered in silver thread on the bodice and filmy, layered skirts. Around her waist hung her chain-link belt with the jeweled dragonfly. Yet the most stunning accessory, aside from her red mane, was the necklace hanging around her neck. The pendant on the chain – a square-cut stone – was the greenest emerald, surrounded by sparkling diamonds. Once again, the Princess had raided the trunk holding her dowry.

"Alaine, your hair…," Lady Avis voiced, with disapproval.

"This coronet was given to me by Bole's daughters. It is only fitting that I wear it tonight," Alaine answered, with dismissal. It was her wish to please the people of the woods.

Flecher, approving of her appearance, came forward and held out his arm to the Princess. Alaine laid her hand on his arm, and he led her away. It was not a long walk to the Middleoak pavilion. The noble procession entered the great open-air space filled with large, round tables, with every seat occupied with people of the forest clans. Flecher led them to the top table, where Bole stood. After introducing his lady to the group, Bole faced the crowded room to introduce the guests in the language they understood. "Dear friends, visiting us tonight are representatives of the Eastgreen Highlands. Lieutenant Miles is of the famous Morr-Leigh Garrison. Sergeant Covey is the bodyguard of the Princess Royal. Lady Avis, the

Duchess of Morr-Leigh, is here, as well as her son, Duke Morr-Leigh.

"Lady Charlyn, lady-in-waiting, is the daughter of Duke Noeman of the Walls, the good Forester of the Kingdom. Lastly, we are honored to present Princess Alaine of Hawthorn," declared Bole, bowing slightly toward the Princess before offering her the seat next to him.

The audience at the lighted tables clapped politely and stretched necks for a look while murmurs of curiosity floated through the room. Almost on cue, servers appeared carrying trays of food and drinks. Alaine scanned the room and all of the adjacent tables, searching for a familiar face, but she didn't see Carver Vale anywhere.

After the meal, Alaine asked Bole if she could thank the forest people for allowing their passage through the woods on the Old Road. Bole agreed and said that he would translate her words to the gathering. He stood and called the audience to attention.

"The Princess Alaine has words for you," he announced.

The room became quiet, waiting to hear what the girl had to say. Alaine stood and prodded Kent to stand next to her.

"I, Princess Alaine, would like to thank the clans of the forest for this historic gathering, not only for myself, but for my parents, King Granth and Queen Iris of Hawthorn."

Alaine's voice rang out loud and clear across the pavilion. She paused to allow Bole to translate.

"I would also like to thank you," she continued, "for the permission to travel across your lands to the seacoast. Duke Morr-Leigh would like to present your people with a small gift of good will and a reminder of our meeting."

Once Bole finished the translation, Kent handed him a rolled scroll of parchment.

Kent stood tall and began to speak. "I give you a deed to Morr-Leigh land located at the edge of the forest near Hawthorn Castle. On this plot is a crystal-blue lake fed by two mountain streams. The water is cool and sweet. The fish in the lake and the game that frequent the land can be used by your people. This is a gift of appreciation and friendship."

Once Bole translated, the gift was well received, with clapping of hands and expressions of approval.

Shortly after the speeches, people began to mill about the room, some leaving the pavilion. Many came forward to speak to Alaine, and Bole did his best to translate. Flecher, seated next to Kent, discussed plans for the next day's travels. Leaving with the early morning light, they could reach the edge of the forest closest to the road running along the seacoast by nightfall. To Kent's relief, once on the shore road, the travelers would be able to reach Irongate Castle within two days' time. It was at this point that Lady Avis requested to return to the treehouse so that they could all get some rest.

The night was passing, and the borrowed treehouse was solemnly quiet. Most of the lamps and lanterns were put out. Earlier, the walk back from dinner held little conversation other than the thought that things went well for the travelers. Charlyn, obviously ready for sleep, removed her gown, put out travel clothes for the morning and repacked her trunk. She encouraged Alaine to get ready for bed, but finally retired herself after the Princess remained out on the balcony taking in the view. Charlyn could only wonder what Alaine was thinking about but suspected that it had something to do with the illicit woodsman.

Outside, the Princess felt no need for sleep, as usual. Alaine was lost in the anticlimax of the day as she gazed out at the waterfall and surrounding trees. She had been so sure that she would see Carver again as they traveled through the woods. Instead, Flecher had appeared and become their guide. When they had arrived at Middleoak, Carver was nowhere about. Again, she had looked forward to seeing him at the dinner. There had been several hundred people at the gathering of the clans, but she hadn't seen Carver. Why would he not come to help guide them with his brother, she wondered? And why was he not at the gathering in the pavilion? Alaine felt herself a novice at these games of the heart, but she had felt a closeness with Carver. Maybe she had overestimated his feelings for her. He was friendly, kind and helpful towards her. Yet, there was nothing from him that suggested anything more. The growing intimacy may be feelings only on her part.

A breeze went through the trees as her head was filled with doubts. It was then that Alaine heard a rustle in the dark bushes below, which drew her attention. In the shadows was a figure, one that she recognized. The dog sat as still as a statue. A sprig of hope sprang up within her.

Surely Carver was near; her eyes were searching the ground below for the one she longed to see. Then he was there, joining Astra and signaling her toward the stairs. Excitement consumed the girl as she made the decision to go to him – possibly her last chance to see him.

Alaine quietly went through the room where Charlyn slept, taking up her cloak on the way, and treading softly down the stairs to the first level. She reached the outside steps and found Carver waiting for her. At once, he took her hand and they escaped to the forest floor and into the trees.

"Where have you been?" Alaine asked Carver, with impatience.

"Why, did you miss me?" he asked, smiling down at her.

She laughed at his question.

"Actually, I wasn't chosen to help guide your people through the forest. You're crossing land held by my brothers, Bole and Flecher, so it was decided that Flecher would be the guide."

"But why weren't you at the dinner? I didn't see you."

"I was there. I was sitting with my family, but I left after you spoke. My people seemed to be very pleased with you and the Duke," said Carver, "and you looked very beautiful."

They were walking through the trees toward the lake. Alaine was glowing inside after his comments. She wanted to dress well for his people, but she could not deny that her wish was to look her best for Carver as she had dressed for the dinner.

"Are there no moss faeries here?" Alaine asked, searching the bushes for them.

"Not here," he answered. "They are shy and prefer the deep woods. There are far too many lights and people here."

"Where are we going?"

"To the lake. It's not far. I have something to show you."

"It's at the lake? What is it?"

"Something that I've been working on for the last few days. Something especially for you," Carver responded.

Alaine's curiosity was piqued, unsure of what to expect. They walked casually along, with Astra roaming nearby. They were not rushed, probably because each one realized how fleeting the time was that they could spend together. Carver held Alaine's hand in his, lightly but possessively.

"We leave in the morning, and Kent told me that we should reach the coastal road by nightfall. Tonight, when I did not see you at the dinner, I thought that I would never see you again."

Carver stopped and turned to face her. He stood very still, looking at her. The moonlight making its way through the trees highlighted his hair and the side of his face. Alaine believed that she could see a glint in his dark eyes. Slowly, he bent his head toward her, with his lips brushing against her forehead. Then, his hands encircled her waist, pulling her to him. Alaine's whole body responded to Carver's touch and his closeness. The anticipation of what he might do made it almost unbearable for her to remain still.

"I promise you," Carver said, in a husky, soft voice, "you *will* see me again."

With that said, looking at her upturned face, he bent to kiss her on the lips. Afterwards both, filled with emotion, stood still in the darkness, taking pleasure in the moment.

"Come, I want to show you my surprise," Carver urged, at last.

The two walked a short distance, where the trees and shrubs began to thin. The lakeshore came into view before them. From a nearby tree limb, hanging by ropes, was what looked like a bed. Alaine was expecting something small, a keepsake that she would be able to remember him with, not a full-sized bed!

Alaine walked over to the suspended bed that did not touch the ground. She could see Carver's work, in the headboard, footboard, and side boards that were all intricately carved. The panels were stained, but even in the darkness the woodgrain could be seen. There was a forest theme in the carvings – trees, leaves, and flowers. Alaine ran her hand over the headboard, finding animal figures added here and there. A luxurious quilt covered the mattress and pillow.

"I've never seen anything like this," she said, amazed. "What made you do this?"

"It is for the Sleepless Princess of Hawthorn," he answered. "A bed that will swing you to sleep."

"How do you know that I do not sleep very well?"

"Alaine, I have met with you several times, like tonight, when you should be in bed, asleep. Besides, everyone in Hawthorn has heard tales of your sleeplessness and your nighttime garden within the castle walls."

"Yes, I know that the townspeople tell stories about me," she agreed.

"I had to borrow the mattress and covers, but the bed can be taken apart and sent to Hawthorn Castle. Do you want to try it?"

Carver held onto the frame of the bed as Alaine gingerly climbed onto the mattress and settled herself.

"It *is* very comfortable," she said, lying back against the bedding.

"Now, I'm going to give it just a little push and it will swing," Carver told her, as he demonstrated.

Alaine leaned back with her head on the pillow, red locks flowing around her. Her cloak and the green layers of her skirts flowed around her. Moonlight flickered down through the leaves, and the still lake was in her view. Muffled water sounds could be heard. Carver leaned against the tree and played a tune on a small, carved flute as Astra sprawled out on the ground.

It had been a very busy day, and for the first time, Alaine felt her muscles relax. Her mind wandered to relive the bliss of Carver's kiss. So this was love, she thought. She was happy and content. He promised that he would see her again. Not sure how they could ever be together, Alaine knew it was what she wanted. The lulling motion of the bed held her in its grip, and as much as she didn't want to sleep, she was straining to keep her eyes open. She didn't know that Carver played the flute, Alaine thought, as her mind drifted off.

Later, a rustling in the bushes and the sound of foxes coming to the lake's edge for a drink, woke Alaine. The sky was just turning light in the east beyond the lake. She sat up and looked around. Just as had happened on other encounters with Carver, he was not there when she awoke. Confused by Carver's disappearance, Alaine got off the bed, gauged her directions, and began walking toward the large treehouse where her companions were sleeping.

It was not until she was halfway up the winding stairway leading to the first level of the lofty house that she put her hand to her throat and immediately realized that the emerald necklace was gone. At first, she was stunned with disbelief, before the realization sank into her consciousness. Alaine grabbed the handrail by the stairs, standing still, as her eyes filled with tears and her heart broke into a hundred pieces. The necklace was lost and, besides herself, there was only one that she could blame.

Once she caught her breath, she continued her flight. Kent was up and standing in the big, open room of the loft. His mouth opened in surprise as Alaine ran past him to the stairs leading to the second level. He noticed that she was still wearing the same clothes from the night before. He called to her, but she didn't turn around.

By the time Alaine reached the room that she was sharing with Charlyn, she was blinded by tears. She rushed to the bed, flinging herself face-down, sobbing into the pillow. Charlyn awoke and quickly went to Alaine with concern.

"You've gone to see him again?" Charlyn asked, not really needing Alaine to answer.

"Please, leave me alone," Alaine pled, between choking sobs.

Charlyn quickly dressed in the gown that she had laid out the night before. She packed the trunk with the rest of her things and closed the lid. She left her travel cloak and valise on the bed, leaving Alaine to herself.

When Charlyn came down the stairs, Kent and Covey were already up and dressed. Kent went to Charlyn.

"What is wrong with her?" he whispered to the lady-in-waiting, not wishing Covey to hear.

"I'm not sure. She is too upset to speak about it," Charlyn replied, securing her wimple to her head with pins.

"She just came in from outside and she was still wearing the gown from last night. Where has she been?"

"You know that she doesn't sleep well," Charlyn answered, trying to defend Alaine. "She was still awake when I went to bed last night. I didn't hear her leave. She probably went out for a walk."

"In the dark?" Kent asked, in disbelief. "There is something more that is going on here. Remember, I've watched her grow up. She has not been herself lately."

"Whatever it is, I cannot say," Charlyn replied.

"We need to get ready to travel. We don't have time for a storm of temper. My mother and Nana are in the pantry preparing a basket for the trip. Can you go get her?"

But there was no need. It was then that Alaine came down the stairs, carrying her travel bag. She was dressed in a dark gray, long-sleeved woolen dress. Her hair was braided and secured at the back to her neck. She wore a black lace scarf that flowed over her shoulders. Her back was straight, and there was no sign of tears.

"Covey, the trunks are ready to be brought down," Alaine said to the Sergeant. She walked past Kent and Charlyn without a word and left the treehouse for the forest below.

The Duke and the lady-in-waiting exchanged a glance but said nothing.

The day had begun. Kent went to help Covey with the trunks.

When the wagons were loaded, Flecher and his men appeared. The women were loaded into the last wagon, except for Alaine. The Princess demanded to ride alone in the second wagon by herself. Kent tried to speak to his cousin; but in the end, her wishes were met. As the wagons rode away from Middleoak, everyone had memories to take with them.

BOOK II

IRONGATE

14

Irongate Castle

The Princess of Hawthorn rode in solitude as the wagon jolted along over the forest terrain. Lost in her thoughts, she ran through all of the emotions related to her meeting with Carver the night before. There was the expectation, the excitement, the feelings of a dawning love, and the unsurpassed experience surrounding the kiss. It was her first kiss, leaving her yearning for more. Alaine's affection for Carver Vale was stronger than she had ever felt for another person, other than her parents. Innocently, she believed he returned her feelings.

But with morning came the heartbreak. She had been deceived. Now, she had to believe that Carver pretended to care for her in order to steal her necklace. Circumstances pointed to the fact that he probably took the amethyst necklace and her opal broach, also. Why would he do that to her, she wondered? Yes, the pieces of jewelry were worth a lot of gold; yet the Carver she knew so briefly didn't seem to care about money or material things. How could she be so wrong?

Alaine had to admit to herself that she hadn't *wanted* to believe the truth. Maybe she was just a silly girl wishing for the taste of love before she went off to a mundane life with a stranger.

For now, she was done with it! It was a heartfelt lesson learned. From now on, she was resolved. Woe be it to the next man that tries to win her heart, including those waiting at Irongate Castle.

Later, toward the end of the afternoon, the wagons stopped. Alaine stuck her head out the back of the wagon to see what was happening. Genna was already walking towards Charlyn, as Lady Avis and Nana were helped down from their wagon by Kent.

"What is it?" Alaine called to Genna, struggling to climb out of her wagon.

"There is a break in one of our front wheels. Rand is going to change it, but he needs help from Miles and Covey."

"Come, help me get down," Alaine asked.

Lady Avis, Nana, and Charlyn headed off into the brush for an opportunity to take care of necessities. Genna went to get Covey, and Alaine went her own way. The Princess walked alone, taking a last look at the forest. Without thinking, she looked for moss faeries, but they didn't seem to be around. Charlyn, seeing her chance to speak to Alaine, approached her new friend.

"Pardon me, Princess. I need to ask if I have offended you in any way?" the lady inquired.

Alaine was shaken out of her world of thoughts, "What? Oh, no, of course not."

"May I ask, are you displeased about the woodsman?"

"Displeased is one way of putting it. Yes, but I don't wish to speak of it. That is over and I will be glad to leave this place and those strange people."

Kent walked over to join Alaine and Charlyn. He knew that something was wrong since Alaine was riding alone. Flecher followed Kent, coming to say his farewell.

"The guides are going to leave us," Kent reported. "It is a short distance out of the woods and down the trail that leads to Shoreline Byway. That road runs along the coast and will lead us to Mareview Harbortown."

"There is a good inn not far along. You could rest there tonight," offered the woodsman.

At this point, Genna came to join them, reporting that the wheel was changed, and they could get moving. Kent turned to Flecher, who was ready to take his leave.

"Once again, we would like to thank you for your help. Please thank Bole for us. I hope that we will meet again in friendship," Kent told Flecher.

"I do believe that we will meet again, probably sooner than we both would think," Flecher replied. "Princess Alaine, it has been very pleasant to meet you. I wish you and your company well on the rest of your journey," he said, gallantly bowing at the waist.

"Thank you," Alaine responded, hiding any current ill feelings.

"One last thing," Flecher said, "here is something that my brother asked me to give to you." He handed Alaine a small, wooden box.

Alaine accepted the unexpected gift, recognizing the style of the engraved wood. Immediately, her face reddened, as hurt and anger rose within her.

"Your brother...your brother...ugh!" Alaine stuttered with exasperation, as words failed her, looking at the wooden cube in her hand. Trying to get control of her emotions, she turned away and stomped off toward the covered wagon.

Knowing that it was time to leave, Flecher saluted them all with a knowing smile. Within a moment, he vanished into the woods behind them.

"What was that about?" Kent asked Charlyn, referring to his cousin's behavior. "What has gotten into her?"

"I think that you don't know Alaine as well as you think you do. Men are so blind to the feelings of women," Charlyn said coolly, walking away to rejoin the other ladies, shaking her head.

"What?" he called after her, not knowing what he said that was wrong.

The travelers arrived at an oceanside inn very late that evening. The matron explained that there was only soup left in the kitchen of the evening's prepared food, which was accepted without complaints. The tavern didn't have enough rooms for all in the party. Lady Avis and Nana were given a room with two beds. Rand and Genna took another room. Charlyn and Alaine were provided the last two small, attic rooms. It was decided that Kent, Miles and Covey would stay with the wagons in the stables.

Alaine's room was sparse, with no window, and a ceiling of roof rafters. There was a slim bed and a small table for her candle. She was physically and emotionally tired, so she took no notice of the humble accommodations. Slipping out of her gown and under the quilt, Alaine was glad to stay by herself, since she did not wish to talk about Carver Vale, not even with Charlyn.

The Princess clutched the carved gift that Flecher had given her, waiting until she was alone to examine it. She prepared herself prior to opening the lid, holding it in one hand. With an intake of breath, she opened the box. Inside was a little wooden heart, resting in a nest of fern leaves. It was smooth on the surface, front and back, and the wood had been stained, probably with a red berry juice.

Alaine held the little heart in her hand as her feelings ran rampant and tears stung her eyes. Anger came first. How dare he? she thought. She reminded herself that she hated him for his deception. Next, she felt a profound sadness about a lost love that could never be. A sadness to be carried with her for some time. Then, to Alaine's dismay, a tiny spark of love, still holding on, pushed its way up from somewhere deep inside. It was a moment remembering Carver's kiss. Finally, depression seeped in, and she blamed herself for it all.

Thankfully, exhaustion and lack of sleep overtook her as she drifted off on the narrow bed in the tiny room, still holding Carver's heart in her hand.

The sun was high in the sky on their second day of traveling on Shoreline Byway, as Lady Avis sat on a rug thrown out on the sand, staring at the beach before her. Nana and Genna's boots and stockings sat in a clutter next to her, along with a small pile of preciously collected seashells.

The Lady felt good, in that she was able to keep her promise to her old nursemaid - Nana would see the seashore once again. Lady Avis watched, chuckling to herself, as the suddenly lively nurse and the maid tripped in and out at the water's edge, tempting the waves. Both women were comical, holding their skirts high and squealing with delight when the sea foam caught them.

As for Charlyn, the Lady's affection for her grew steadily. She was a noble girl of good character. Not far off, Charlyn and Kent sat with their backs against a fallen tree truck, viewing the beach. Kent remained with the women as Miles, Covey and Rand took a meal at the tavern across the road. Lady Avis was not sure if he was being thoughtful of the ladies or had seized the opportunity to have time alone with Charlyn. The Duchess noticed that her son seemed to migrate to wherever the girl went.

The two young people had developed a friendship, always finding something to talk about. Occasionally, Lady Avis would hear sounds of their voices drifting by, or the fleeting laugh as they watched Nana and Genna. She sincerely hoped that Kent was not leading the girl on, only to turn his attention to others when they returned to Hawthorn court. Only time would tell. It was probably premature for her to imagine fair-haired grandchildren running through Juniper Lodge.

Yet her niece, Alaine, remained a concern for her. Their party should arrive at Irongate Castle later in the day, and Alaine had been out of sorts since leaving Middleoak. She was polite, but barely spoke to anyone in the company unless spoken to. The girl kept her to herself and was currently walking alone along the shore. Even Charlyn said that she was unsure of Alaine's complaint. Possibly the fact that their destination was within reach, Alaine was beginning to face the impending marriage before her. Lady Avis was determined to protect the girl from a disastrous match as she had vowed to her sister, Queen Iris. If only Alaine's disposition would improve, and the sooner, the better.

Later that evening, just after sunset, the trio of wagons reached the outer gates of Irongate Castle. True to their name, the metal barricade was high and foreboding, attached to tall, thick, stone walls on both sides of the blackened gateway. The sentry guard refused entry at first. It was only when Kent came forward identifying himself as Duke Morr-Leigh, that one side of the heavy barrier was pulled back for their passage.

After an uphill ride on a long, curving lane, the front of Irongate Castle came into view. Rand, driving the lead wagon, went directly to the front driveway, beyond the obvious main entrance, and reined the horses to a stop. The weary travelers soon assembled themselves on the front steps, with Kent and Lady Avis taking the lead through the heavy, wooden portals. Once inside the immense stone entrance hall, they stood in a huddle as servants went off somewhere to tell of their arrival.

At last, a tall, thin lady approached them from the interior of the building.

"Welcome. I'm Lady Sculpter, greeting you on behalf of Queen Hester, who is completing her evening preparations. The Queen has been informed of your arrival and is on her way to meet you."

Upstairs, from her rooms in the East Wing, Queen Hester sat at her dressing table. Her maid placed the last of the pearl-crested combs into her perfectly coifed, black hair in preparation for the evening's activities. The sudden interruption of a footman brought notice of the newly arrived guests.

"What?" the Queen asked, obviously annoyed. "Whoever heard of arriving at this time of day? Amy, you are dressed for dinner. Run down and greet them. Give my apologies while I finish dressing. March," she said to her lady's maid, "send Celia to fetch Mistress Ronan to meet me in the main entrance hall."

Queen Hester had been awaiting the arrival of the Princess Alaine every day for over a week. She was beginning to think that they weren't coming, wondering how her husband had made these haphazard arrangements with his brother, King Granth. The noble suiters awaiting the girl's arrival were there for at least a fortnight. At last, the matchmaking for Alaine could get underway. Shrewdly, Hester planned to use her influence to see that this betrothal might line her own pocket.

"Hurry, March, help tighten these laces and fetch my black evening slippers!" Hester demanded, while fastening the clasp on her pearl necklace. Momentarily, Hester hurried along the lengthy corridor, down the staircase, and through the hallway toward the front doors. The Queen saw Lady Sculpter exchanging pleasantries with the visitors when she arrived.

"Duke Morr-Leigh at your service, Your Majesty," Kent said, with a deep bow of respect to the Queen. "This is my mother, the Duchess Morr-Leigh, sister to Queen Iris. May I present the Princess Alaine of Hawthorn, and her travel companion, the Lady Charlyn."

The ladies all curtsied in unison. The Queen was appalled at the look of the band of travelers. Observant of propriety, she took in their appearance. How could they present themselves in such common attire? she wondered. Was this example of inferior standards what has become of the Northern Kingdom and its court? she wondered.

Alaine stepped up to retrieve the moment from awkwardness. "My parents send their salutations and appreciation for your generous hospitality."

"You are very welcome, my dear. In honest, we were expecting a much larger party, but we are pleased that you have arrived safely at last. We did have word of flooding on the roads," the Queen said, sounding sincere. "It is wonderful to see you again, Alaine. You were still a child when we last met. What a charming young lady you have become."

"Thank you, Your Majesty," Alaine answered, lowering her head at the compliment.

"You may call me Aunt Hester, child. After all, we are family. Your cousin, Prince Stenson, has been looking forward to seeing you, as is your Uncle Holum."

Meanwhile, a gray-haired lady in a brown gown and a fluffed cap appeared, still out of breath from her run to the hall. She lurched to a full stop, awaiting her orders from the Queen.

"This is Mistress Ronan, our head housekeeper," the Queen indicated, with a wave of her hand toward the lady in the cap. "She will show you to your rooms. Food and refreshments will be sent up. Chamber maids have already been assigned to meet your needs. Please let Mistress Ronan know if there is anything you require for a comfortable stay. Tomorrow, after you have had an opportunity to rest, the ladies are invited to a luncheon in my quarters in the East Wing. Then, we will get to know each other better. I am anxious for your opinions of my garden.

"Tomorrow evening, King Holum and I will host a dinner in your honor, Princess. It is then you will be introduced to the three esteemed gentlemen that have traveled a great distance to meet you. Now, if you will excuse me, I must see to our dinner guests. Have a restful night, and we will meet on the morrow."

With that, the Queen left, leaving the visitors to the hands of Mistress Ronan.

Genna came to the suite of rooms provided for the Princess Alaine, followed by a troop of footmen and servants carrying trunks. The wooden door opened into a small anteroom with a chaise lounge, a long, high table holding an oil lamp, vase with fresh flowers, and a silver tray. The archway ahead opened into a spacious sitting room with a fireplace, couches, chairs and tables. The room was well lit with wall scones and table lamps. There were bedrooms on either side of the main living space, and Lady Avis took the lone bedroom on the left. Next to it was a small dressing room with a large, copper bathing tub. Alaine and Charlyn were in discussion regarding the two remaining bedrooms on the right of the communal space.

"If I take this room," said Alaine, pointing to the larger, well-furnished bedroom, "then this one is too small for you. We will have to request a larger room for you elsewhere."

"Not at all, Princess. This room is fine for me. It has a nice bed, a wardrobe, and a dressing table. Remember, at home, I share space with two younger sisters. It is pleasant to just have a private space."

"Well, I would like you to be with us. Also, it is better that we are all together when Genna is helping us with dressing. So it is settled?"

Charlyn agreed.

"As to arrangements, I would like to say a word," Lady Avis interrupted, entering the room.

But before she could speak, she waited for trunks to be placed in rooms and the footmen to leave. Then came two chamber maids bringing wash basins and water. Fires were lit in the living room and bedrooms. Just before the maids finished their tasks, Mistress Ronan appeared at the doorway.

"Will these rooms be spacious enough for your stay?" she questioned, speaking to Lady Avis.

"Yes, very much so. However, where are our nurse and our lady's maid to be housed?"

"They have been provided rooms on this floor a little way down the corridor."

"And my son, Duke Morr-Leigh and his companions?"

"The gentlemen have been provided rooms in the West Wing of the castle with the rest of the noble guests. If there is nothing else, I will go to the kitchen and direct them to send up the hot food."

Once the housekeeper left, Lady Avis settled herself into one of the comfortable, plump chairs. Alaine and Charlyn took up the padded couch. Lady Avis motioned for Genna to join them, so she took another fat chair. The young women remained quiet, awaiting the comments of Lady Avis.

"With the Duke in the other wing of the castle, our party has been divided. Communication between us may prove difficult," Lady Avis expressed her worry. "While we are here, we must be wary, and carry out our activities so that we are put at the best advantage. We must all keep courtly manners, leaving nothing for criticism.

"Regarding the rooms, Genna, whenever we are not here, I want you to be here. You are to supervise the chamber maids when they are here. You can be friendly toward them, but don't leave them alone. Gather whatever you can about the castle gossip. Girls, your trunks are to be kept locked at all times. Genna, you may take out the clothing for the day and hang it in the wardrobes but keep all of the accessories and jewelry in the trunks. Also, be sure to leave no written notes lying about.

"Be on guard and don't be fooled by this clever queen. She may not be out for Alaine's best interests, especially if there is something in it for her. She will have her spies and accomplices. So, we must all be careful of what we say in public or what could be overheard and reported back to the Queen. Genna, speak to Rand and I will speak to Kent. We need to gather as much information as possible about the royal suitors and anything else that might affect a betrothal. Charlyn, I will trust you to stay close to the Princess whenever possible. I'll not be surprised if they try to occupy and divide us.

"Alaine, your father has been in communication with two royal princes, and it seems that they have traveled here to meet you. The third man is unknown to me, but we will meet them at the dinner tomorrow evening. Meanwhile, the proposed marriage contract from your father is rolled at the bottom of my trunk, to be unsealed by your uncle, the King, once you make your choice."

Lady Avis had just finished speaking when the food was delivered and spread out on the tea table. A pitcher of wine was included. They ate quietly, all thinking about the warnings of Lady Avis. Alaine excused herself to her room after eating and closed the door. The mood of the evening was one of apprehension.

15
The Queen's Plan

Carver arrived in Harbortown as the sun was setting over the water. He watched the busy waterfront from across Shoreline Byway. What was surprising and slightly intimidating was the size of this town and the crowds of people scurrying about. Inns, taverns and small shops lined every space on the row overlooking the harbor full of ships and the smaller fishing boats. After a brief search, he was glad to find a quaint inn on one of the cobbled side streets that would give a room and allow for Astra. Once settled, food was needed, not just for himself, but extra to bring back for the dog. For now, Carver made for a tavern he had previously passed on the main road.

Inside the Last Mast Public House, Carver found the place to be loud and filled with smoke. The kitchens were open at the back of the crowded room, billowing cooking fumes into the air. A seat was found at one end of a long table as Carver surveyed the people around him. Most appeared to be sailors, many speaking in unfamiliar languages. The clothes of some were soiled and ratty, making his forest attire look acceptable. Yet there were also groups of men who were well-dressed, making him look at his own clothes.

He decided to buy new clothes tomorrow at the shops, as Hewitt suggested.

There were snatches of conversations from a nearby table of the arrival of the Princess of Hawthorn at Irongate. Carver listened greedily, overhearing talk of the two princes that had traveled here for a chance to marry her. Lastly, there was gossip of a very rich Marquis, whose merchant ship dwarfed the other boats moored in the harbor. It was said the noble was related to the Queen, and sure of his ability to claim the royal girl.

Deep in thought as he ate, Carver resolved a visit to Irongate Castle was needed on the morrow. A way into the castle must be found. The forest Prince was determined that there were no gates too strong or walls too high to keep him from his Princess. A plan to ask for her hand in marriage at Irongate was also needed, but the question of how to make that happen was the challenge.

It was the morning after their arrival at Irongate. Kent was wandering about in the spacious suite of rooms provided on the second floor of the west wing of Irongate. Last night, the two leather cases containing his belongings and clothes were temporarily misplaced as the wagons were unloaded. The footman who delivered his breakfast was set on the task of finding them. In the meantime, the plan was for a bath and a shave. He watched as the parade of chamber maids carried in hot water and poured it into a metal tub.

Once dressed in some of his last clean clothes, he planned to find his way around. The footman told him that Miles and Covey were housed down the driveway at the guardhouse, but where Rand was stashed was still unknown. The servant's quarters? Kent wondered. For sure, the small group that supported Alaine was separated, and communication among them would be stifled. Already the young noble had sent a note to his mother via a manservant, letting her know his location. Another message went to Miles and Covey, for them to meet him in the front hall at midday. It was time to get the lay of this courtly battlefield and divide allies from any potential adversaries; *and* it was time to learn the motives of these noble men that wished to marry his cousin.

After a quiet night's rest, Nana got up and dressed, not knowing what would be expected of her during the day. Although she was not considered a servant, she was also not part of the nobility. She would not be included in any of the activities planned for Alaine, of that, she was sure. With no expectations, she was satisfied with the thought of a quiet day, possibly working on her needlework. Maybe she should work on that half-embroidered collar she had put into the trunk at the last minute.

Breakfast arrived in her cozy room at the hands of a chamber maid and was laid out on a round wooden table in front of the one comfortable armchair near the fire grate. Most of the room was taken up by the bed, and her trunk protruded at the foot of it. While eating the warm fare, Nana wondered if she should go down the hall to give assistance to Lady Avis, but she felt no pressing duty.

A knock came at the door, and Mistress Ronan entered after Nana called out.

"I thought that I would see how you were doing, Mistress," the housekeeper inquired.

"You can call me McNiven, and I am quite comfortable, thank you," Nana answered.

"This room is small, so I wanted to offer you the use of my sitting room. It is the last door on the left, at the end of the hallway. There is a fire going all day, and you can take your lunch there."

"Thank you. I would like that."

"I need to attend to the Queen's luncheon, but afterwards possibly we could share a cup of tea. My father was a servant at Hawthorn Castle and came here with King Holum. I would enjoy hearing about the castle and the village."

Nana was a wise old bird and knew that information flowed both ways. Chatting with Mistress Ronan could provide valuable tidbits about life at Irongate and the men who were here to meet Princess Alaine.

"That sounds like a wonderful idea. I am in want of a quiet day to recover from the travels."

"I will see you later, then, McNiven" Mistress Ronan assured, making for the doorway. "Have a pleasant morning."

Alaine was beginning to believe in Aunt Avis' fears related to Queen Hester and the possibility that Hester had her own plans regarding any betrothal. As she wandered alone in the perfectly manicured garden, the Princess reflected on the luncheon, which went well with a few unexpected occurrences. With Mistress Ronan as their guide, the arrival of the ladies at the room used for gathering prior to entering Hester's dining room was timely. Initially unexpected, was the number of ladies from court who were also invited to the luncheon. They were of all ages, spread out across the room in their own little groups. Alaine somehow thought the gathering would be a more intimate affair. Self-conscious, she immediately felt that she was on display; and, of course, she was. Curiosity about the Princess of Hawthorn was not to be contained. Alaine was glad of the time spent on her hair and dressing.

Also, the opulent dining room was larger than expected. The walls were covered with a heavy, mint-green material, allowing the long, white table and chairs to stand out. Tiny crystal pots of yellow flowers lined the center of the table. Occasional small, rectangular windows showed the green backdrop of a garden beyond. The seating at the luncheon separated the Princess from Lady Avis and Charlyn, as Hester insisted that Alaine sit next to her at the top of the table. She was on her own to respond to the Queen and her ladies throughout the meal. The food was served in courses and was light and delicious, as Alaine concentrated on her manners. At one point, she glanced down the table at Lady Avis and Charlyn, both submerged in conversations with the ladies around them. Lady Avis gave her a small smile, showing some concern by a wrinkled brow.

After the lunch, Alaine found herself being whisked off by Hester and a few of her favorites to a smaller tearoom, where punch was served with small cakes. Hester and the older ladies sat on highbacked chairs, while Alaine and the younger ladies had cushions on the floor. The informality of the setting gave the noblewomen permission for more personal questions for the Princess of the Eastgreen Highlands.

Lady Avis and Charlyn were taken off elsewhere by their new acquaintances. Not worried, Alaine knew that her aunt was well-versed in the intrigues of court. Lady Avis would be using the opportunity to glean all of the information she could about the men requesting Alaine's hand.

Finally, when all others were dismissed, Queen Hester took Alaine into the garden that ran along the entire east wing of the castle. Hester pointed out several of the plants and trees that had been brought across the seas and were now thriving in their new home. Tall and short hedge rows divided spaces. Alaine reflected on the landscape, thinking how small her own little garden was at Hawthorn. She meandered along by herself after the Queen was called away.

Queen Hester was in a small salon, one she used for quiet conversations with one or two guests. Soon she would have to begin her preparation for the banquet, introducing the courtiers and royal suitors to Princess Alaine. The crowd expected for this evening was larger than usual. Many of the nobility had to be excluded, as the seats at the table were limited. For now, there was time to relax and reflect on the luncheon and her time with the girl. In her mind she was already making plans for the preferred outcome of the matchmaking.

"Well, dear cousin, what is she like?" asked the Marquis de Locke. "Please tell me that I am not to be wed to a girl with the face of a boot. I have heard that the party arrived last night in some farmers' wagons. Hardly what one would expect for a princess. Have they not a royal coach to spare?"

Hester brought her teacup to her lips, took a sip of the delightful Asian blend and returned the cup to the saucer prior to responding to the handsome Marquis that she knew well.

"You will see for yourself tonight, dear sir. I must say that I was rather appalled at the sight of them on their arrival, but I have since changed my mind," Hester replied. "When the ladies arrived for the luncheon, they looked every bit of the nobility that they are – well dressed, poised and well-spoken. The Princess Alaine is truly lovely and as well-mannered as her station requires."

"Does she have a good mind?" Locke asked, his dark brows expressive over heavily lashed brown eyes.

Not yet at the prime of his life, the Marquis was a man of good looks, with straight, black hair, and sideburns jutting down along his strong jaw. His clothing, the best that gold could buy, clung to his lean form, as he stretched his long legs out from the Queen's upholstered couch. At the top of his game in shipping, it was time for him to take a wife and have a family.

"So that is a little story, my dear," Hester answered, with intrigue. "Though she is young and unexposed to the world; Alaine probably has a mind as sharp as yours. We were sitting in a small group with my ladies after the luncheon, with Alaine next to me. Everyone was fixed with curiosity to learn about the newcomer. I asked her how she spent her time. Did she do needlework? Did she sing or play the harp? To all of these questions she answered 'No'. So I asked her to explain herself.

"It seems that King Granth felt that the girl should be educated, so she has been taught to read and write. She says that she can read all of the royal documents and has a basic knowledge of maps, but that she prefers tales of history and enjoys scrolls of poems. She is proficient in horseback riding, archery and - of all things for a lady - fishing with a rod in streams. Yet, according to Alaine, her greatest talent is doing sums and managing money. It is so fitting a wife for a merchant such as yourself, Felix," Hester said with a laugh. "Alaine says she runs the kitchens at Hawthorn Castle and has been doing so for two winters. She does all of the purchasing of food goods that flow through the place. Impressive, don't you think?"

"That is amusing, Hester," the man replied, with a haughty smile, "but you know that my estate is twice the size of Hawthorn Castle.

Not to mention that my mother would never allow a child to interfere with the housekeeping."

"Yes, I forgot about Aunt Maris. She may have a difficult time adjusting to having another woman in the house. Your mother will not give up her place easily."

"Mother will put the girl in her place and teach her our customs. It is mother's wish that I marry and have a family, and I will remind her of that if she is too hard on my new bride. The Princess will settle in, and when a child is born, she will be too busy to pine over her cold, stone castle."

"It sounds as if you have it all well-planned, Felix. Just remember that you promised me my own merchant ship once the contract is signed and the marriage is completed," Queen Hester insisted, taking another sip of tea.

"Have no worries, cousin. You shall have your ship," the Marquis said, with assurance.

Alaine began to feel chilled as she walked alone in the garden. She was still wearing her pale-blue morning gown with its sleeves flaring at the elbows. It provided little warmth. Alaine stood gazing at the side of the building, wondering which door she could use to get back inside. Suddenly hands came from behind her and covered her eyes. *Carver*, she immediately thought and whirled around, irrationally expecting to see him. Instead, she saw a tall, young man with a smiling face that was vaguely familiar.

"Stenson!" she exclaimed, as recognition dawned on her. "How tall you've grown! Not the little boy I remember."

The young Prince laughed. "You have changed also, cousin. With your hair up and your fancy dress, you really *look* like a princess."

"It is so good to see you. You must be as tall as your father,"

"Not yet, but I have been keeping his tailor busy. Mother says that all of my pants are too short. I've had two suits of new clothes made just for your visit."

"Two?"

"Yes, one for this evening when you are the guest of honor at the banquet. Mother said that since you are family, I would be allowed to attend."

"And the other outfit?"

"I will wear it in four days, when you are formally presented at court. That is the day the men wishing to marry you will offer you gifts and ask for your hand in marriage."

"Oh, your mother didn't mention that to me. I haven't even met the men yet. How am I to make a choice so quickly…?" Alaine murmured, more to herself than to the Prince.

A shudder went through Alaine's body, and her facial expression changed from the happiness of seeing her cousin to one of concern.

"Are you cold?" Stenson asked, noticing the change in her.

"Yes, it's getting cool, and I was unsure of how to get back inside."

"Come, I will show you," he offered, gallantly.

Stenson led her to a set of double doors after crossing a wide, flagstone pad.

"Mother uses this space for evening gatherings outside when the weather is fair," he said, motioning with the sweeping of his arm. "They set up chairs and have music for the courtiers."

Once inside, the Prince led Alaine through the castle, explaining the layout as they went. The hallways were wide, and the ceilings were high.

There were many closed doors, keeping the secrets of what was behind them.

"Most of the Queen's rooms are in the east wing of the building, and unmarried ladies are given upstairs bedrooms on this side. Here is the stairway that leads up to your rooms."

"Yes, I remember," Alaine said, as they proceeded.

"The middle of the castle is primarily the assembly hall, the grand dining room, the kitchens, and some of the servant quarters. This is where we will meet before dinner tonight," he explained, pointing out two sets of double doors.

As he led on, they came to the front hallway with the great portals Alaine had passed through the prior evening to enter the castle. Soon, they came upon another staircase leading to the second floor, after Stenson explained that they were now in the west wing.

"This is the ceremony room, and the largest room at Irongate," he bragged, while opening a door so that Alaine could look inside. "We call it Majestic Hall and it's used for all of the formal events."

"It *is* larger than our Tapestry Room at Hawthorn," Alaine stated, while observing the room's size and elegance.

Stenson led the girl along the deep corridor.

"These are the rooms my father uses to conduct the business of the kingdom. He spends most of his time here," the young Prince explained, "but this is my favorite room. It's called The Map Room. My mother calls it the library because it holds father's book collection."

Stenson opened the door and pulled Alaine inside. The long, rectangular room was quietly impressive, with large racks from which hung intricately painted maps. Windows allowed light to flow in, illuminating a great wooden table upon which parchments were spread. Floor to ceiling shelves held piles of neglected scrolls.

"Father collects maps. All of the captains of the merchant ships bring them. They know the King will pay them gold for a good map. My tutor, Master Papopolis, is from the south and knows much about maps and geography. He is teaching me Latin and Greek and how to read the maps. He tells stories of all the different lands and peoples. He is visiting his homeland now but will be back at the end of summer."

"It is good that you are learning these things, since you will be King one day. For myself, I sometimes wonder why my father thought that it was so important for me to be educated. I am not sure that it will be put to much use," Alaine responded, wandering to the map table and bending to study the map of the country of Hawthorn.

Alaine studied the details of the well-drawn chart, showing the two kingdoms, and the divisions of the dukedoms. All of the towns and cities were noted, with roads and rivers carefully depicted. She noticed what was there and what was *not* there. Comparing this map to Bole's map in her mind, Alaine noticed that all of the vast tracks of forest land throughout the country were shaded in green and empty of any detail. It was as if the forest clans and their communities were unknown or deliberately concealed. She thought of Carver and his people.

"What are all of these buildings along the seacoast?" she asked Stenson, as he joined her at the table.

"Three of the dukes of the Mareview Lowlands have fortresses along the coast. They have the fire towers, and if you see here," he said, pointing to small images of fire, "more towers are set along here, where the land juts out into the sea. Fires are lit at night so the ships will not run into the rocks. Father says there is also a signal system in case of a hostile invasion."

"The fire towers are quite impressive. My captain pointed them out when our ship was sailing toward Harbortown at night," came a voice from the back of the room.

A man stepped out of the shadows. He was as tall as the young prince. His receding hairline, brows, and close-cropped beard were fair. His brocade waistcoat was trimmed in a dark fur at the collar and cuffs, with gold buttons descending from his neck. Light trousers made his high black boots stand out; the leather adorned with golden medallions at the outside of the calf. The royal held two books in his hands. A red jewel was the focus of a heavy, golden band encircling a finger on his right hand.

"Prince Sturgrom!" Stenson exclaimed with surprise, as he stood to attention.

"Excuse me for interrupting," said the Prince. "I couldn't help but overhear. I was borrowing some books. Your father gave me permission to enjoy his collection while I was here. I must say his library is better stocked than my own."

He paused, "Prince Stenson, would you introduce me to the lady?"

"Oh, yes," said the adolescent, remembering his manners. "Prince Sturgrom, may I present my cousin, the Princess Alaine of Hawthorn."

The Prince bowed from the waist, and Alaine curtsied, as they were of equal noble status.

"I heard that you had arrived, and was looking forward to meeting you this evening," Sturgrom said, addressing Alaine. "I trust that you have recovered from your journey. The Queen mentioned that you were met with some bad weather along the way."

"We were delayed, but happy to arrive safely," the Princess replied. "I had luncheon with Queen Hester today. Afterwards, I was rather lost in the garden when Prince Stenson rescued me. He has been showing me around Irongate."

"The Queen's garden is beautiful, but I enjoy walking through the parklands on the west side of the castle," he said, waving his arm toward the windows and scenery beyond. "There are many types of trees, a pond, and much birdlife. I've been walking there every morning."

"That sounds refreshing," Alaine replied, not sure what she was expected to say.

"I was wondering," the man began, "if you would care to join me for a walk after breakfast in the morning? It would allow us to become better acquainted."

Alaine was startled. She was feeling very unprepared for these games of courtship. She didn't want to insult the man or appear rude. He was a prince who traveled far to meet her. Stenson shifted from one foot to another as she pondered the correct reply.

"That would be very nice. I would like to see the pond," Alaine said, then felt that her answer sounded childish.

"Then I will meet you in the front hall in the morning. I hope to see you this evening. In the meantime, enjoy the rest of your afternoon. It was a pleasure to meet you, Princess."

Prince Sturgrom bowed again, gave a small salute to Stenson, and retreated out the door.

"Are you alright?" Stenson asked, looking at Alaine's pale face after Prince Sturgrom left the room.

"Yes. It was just an unexpected encounter with the Prince. I guess that I will have to try to get to know the suitors so I can make a choice for a husband, but I believe that this will be more difficult than I thought. The Prince seemed much older than I imagined."

"My mother said that he is just past thirty winters. He was married once before, but his wife died."

"Oh, that is sad."

"His position demands that he marry again," Stenson reported, as if he knew of all these things. "He does seem to be a kind man. I have met him here before, and we had a long talk about maps and his country in the north."

"I am sure that I will learn more of him tomorrow," Alaine replied, feeling the need to be alone. "Well, I had best get back to my rooms and prepare for this evening."

"I will walk you to the stairs," Stenson offered, wishing to put his worried cousin at ease.

16
The Suitors

As the afternoon waned and the preparations for the banquet moved along, the upstairs hallways of Irongate were filled with servants carrying out their ongoing tasks. King Holum stood before his mirror in his dressing room, accepting his reflection with his mind full of anticipation for seeing his niece. She was an energetic girl, with red tresses flying, on their last visit to Hawthorn. Yet first, he must speak with Hester regarding some changes needed in the dinner arrangements. He knew that she wouldn't be pleased as he made his way through their shared rooms leading to the Queen's closet room, where he paused in the doorway.

"Another new gown, my dear?" he asked, watching her maid while she adjusted the golden ribbon laces at the back of the dress.

"Yes, it is new, made especially for tonight. Do you like it?"

"It is a novelty. The ladies will all be running to their dressmakers in the morning asking for strips in their skirts."

Hester wasn't beautiful, but she was a handsome woman with good features and lustrous, black hair. The Queen also made the most of her good figure with close attention to her clothing.

Tonight's gown had a fitted green bodice, billowing sleeves of golden lace, and wide ribbons of golden silk sewn between green panels of the flowing skirt.

"They aren't stripes, Holum. It is just a new way of using the silk cloth." she claimed, while putting on her gold and emerald earrings. "I will need a few moments to finish dressing before I'm ready to go down. Is Stenson ready?"

"He is ready and waiting for us. It was good of you to let him attend the banquet," the King answered. "It seems that he met Alaine in the garden this afternoon. He was showing her the Map Room when they ran into Prince Sturgrom. The man works fast. He has already committed Alaine to spend the morning with him tomorrow."

"Oh, I didn't expect that. I planned for her to spend time with me and the Marquis in the morning," replied the Queen. "No matter. All of the suitors will be able to spend time with the Princess prior to the betrothal ceremony."

"Right, but that is not the reason I'm here, my dear."

"What is it?" she asked with concern, turning to face her husband.

"Duke Seaken-Char arrived this afternoon. I've sent his men to the guardhouse and put him in his usual rooms next to the Duke of Leigh. So we will need to set another place at the table."

"Oh, no!" the Queen responded, with annoyance. "What does that old goat want? *And*, as usual, he shows up unannounced."

At the back of her mind she thought of a further complication to her plans for the betrothal of Alaine to the Marquis. Hester knew that the old Duke was a meddler.

"Now Hester, you know that he was one of my father's greatest friends, as well as giving Granth his support. He is always welcome in my house. However, he does have one request for tonight. He wishes to be seated next to the Duchess of Leigh at dinner."

"So, of course he shows up today! Which of our nobles should I displace for a seat at the table?" complained Hester, with exasperation and a sigh of resignation to her husband's request.

"Don't worry, I will take care of it. The Duchess of Leigh?"

"He says that he came to escort the Duchess back to Hawthorn once the betrothal is complete."

"There is no end to that man's demands. You would think *he* was a king. Soon we will have half of the Hawthorn court under our roof," she added, with sarcasm. "Now, go out and let me finish dressing," she said, waving him off.

Genna ran from room to room, helping with clothing, hair, and accessories. All the while, Lady Avis was a beacon of calmness amid the preparations for the banquet. Previously, she sent a message to Kent to meet them at the bottom of the east wing staircase so they could enter the assembly hall as a group.

She was somewhat anxious to finally meet the suitors for Alaine's hand. Through conversations during the day, she learned a lot about the two princes who traveled to Irongate after communications with King Granth. Nana also brought vital information about a rich Marquis, who, it turns out, was the cousin of Queen Hester. Lady Avis smelled a plot of intrigue, in that the man was here at court, at the time of Alaine's arrival. Through Genna, Lady Avis passed the word to Rand, who was housed in the servant's quarters, to learn all that he could about the suitors, no matter how trivial. The wish for power or wealth was frequently the influences behind marriages among the nobles. The Duchess of Leigh would also trust her own instincts when she observed the men asking for the hand of a princess. At last, the ladies gathered at the door, ready to go downstairs. Lady Avis gave an admonishment to Genna to care for the rooms in their absence. Entering the wide hallway, the ladies found it empty. They hurried through the shadows between the few lighted wall sconces. Only the swish of the material of their skirts could be heard in the silence. Leading the descent of the staircase, Lady Avis was surprised to see the tall, slightly bent figure of Duke Seaken-Char standing next to her well-dressed son. The two noblemen bowed as they came down the steps to stand next to them.

"Duke Seaken-Char, finding you here is so unexpected," Lady Avis remarked, with a sincere smile.

"And miss this opportunity to escort such a collection of beautiful ladies? Not to mention a chance to watch Hester at her games," he replied, with a smile. "Actually, I was down helping

Duke Eckelform after the flood waters receded. The town of Leggot was damaged, especially along the main road near Stonelink Bridge. So, being almost in the neighborhood, I couldn't resist supporting the Princess in her choice of husbands and I made my way here," he explained, smiling at Alaine.

Then turning to Kent, "I also put some of your men to work helping the villagers get back into their houses. I hope that you do not mind, Captain. Your troops were camped nearby, with little to do awaiting your return. For their help in removing the mud and rebuilding the animal pens, they received food for their company. The exchange was working well when I left."

"Good use of them, Duke. I'm sure that the men were glad to have some activity to pass the time," Kent acknowledged.

"Where is your walking stick, Rengard?" the Duchess asked, using the man's first name.

"I thought that I would try to hobble along without it for tonight. I'm sure that you would allow me to lean on your arm, if need be," he remarked, with a wink of the eye, causing the Lady to blush.

Meanwhile, standing next to Kent, Charlyn was taken aback by seeing her handsome Captain dressed in his best attire. She suddenly feared he might be more taken with the better dressed, more refined, ladies of King Holum's court.

"Shall we go in?" Kent asked, extending his arm to Charlyn with admiration in his eyes. Charlyn smiled back at him as a gush of relief flooded her heart. How could she doubt him?

Immediately after Alaine and her company entered the elegant assembly room, a hush fell across the chamber. Bodies shifted their stances to improve their view of the new entrants. A couple of hands shot up in salute to Seaken-Char, who seemed to have admirers wherever he went. But most of the attention was for the young lady who sparkled from the top of her head to her toes – the Princess of Hawthorn.

Conversations around the room hardly began to resume when King Holum, Queen Hester and Prince Stenson were announced, and the nobles bowed and curtsied with respect. The King rushed to the side of his niece, embraced her, and bent to kiss her on the cheek. With Stenson smiling at his side, he was thrilled at the sight of the girl who had grown into a lovely young woman.

"I am so glad to finally see you, my dear. Hester has been keeping you all to herself," the King teased, keeping his arm about Alaine's waist. "However, Stenson said he had a chance to speak with you this afternoon."

"It is good to see you again, Uncle," Alaine answered, responding to Holum's affection. "Yes, my towering younger cousin rescued me from the garden and gave me a little tour of Irongate."

Stenson, enjoying his time in the adult setting, beamed at her words. "I see that you made it down, Rengard," the King observed, acknowledging the older Duke. "Welcome Duchess Leigh and Duke Leigh. And who is this beautiful lady on your arm?" he asked Kent.

"May I introduce the Lady Charlyn, daughter of Duke Noeman of the Walls, Forester to the Upper and Lower Kingdoms," Kent presented with propriety.

Charlyn's cheeks flushed as pink as her gown as she curtsied.

"That old fox! I knew he had daughters, but clearly, he has been hiding them," Holum joked. "Please give your father my regards when you return home," he directed Charlyn. "He and his family are always welcome at our court."

"Thank you, Sire," Charlyn managed.

Queen Hester stepped into the conversation, "Alaine, your gown is remarkable. Cloth of that color is rare; but I'm not sure that belt goes well with it. What is that pendent hanging down, an insect?"

Alaine had chosen to wear her midnight-blue gown with long sleeves. The layered skirts were studded with crystals that caught the rays of candlelight as she moved. A chain of silver and sapphires glittered at her throat, accenting the modest bodice of the dress. The braided coils of her red locks were held in place at the back of her head. A delicate coronet, laced with crystals and sapphires, spoke of her royal status.

"The belt was a gift from my father," Alaine replied to her aunt. "I promised him I'd wear it."

King Holum lifted the decorated dragonfly and examined it. "This is quite intricate, with exceptional workmanship. Let us hope there is no need for you to use it while you are in my house," he said, with a wink to Alaine.

Obviously, the King had guessed the secret of the hidden dagger. "Come, we must make our way around the room. These courtiers would all like a good look at you; *and*, you must be properly introduced to Prince Sturgrom and Prince Brannon, who have been waiting for you."

For Alaine, the next hour was a whirl of faces and names as the royal party moved from group to group. Some of the women were familiar, having attended the Queen's luncheon. Most of the men's eyes seemed to hold admiration and approval of her.

As they approached Prince Sturgrom's group, Alaine noticed laughter and friendly bantering going on among the nobles. The man seemed to have gained some friends and admirers since his arrival at Irongate. He was attired in a black tunic with the obligatory gold buttons and braiding. He looked very stately and assured, his red and gold ring glinting in the candlelight whenever he moved, his hands in animation as he spoke.

"Good evening, Princess. Your gown is quite handsome; however, I'm not sure that it would be warm enough at my court in our northern climes."

"Is your palace cold, Prince Sturgrom?" Alaine asked.

"It is certainly cooler than it is here, and very cold in the winter, but we manage with layers of clothing and warm fires," he replied. "I will tell you more about my land when we walk in the park tomorrow morning."

"I am looking forward to it, sir."

King Holum moved the royal party along, only allowing for introductions and a bit of small talk before leading on to another group of curious courtiers. He was clearly a master of managing his people.

Alaine made eye contact with Prince Brannon as the King led them toward the group of young nobles surrounding him, most of them being the younger ladies of the court. His dress was more casual than expected for a formal banquet, but the man was younger than Prince Sturgrom, and handsome. His wavy hair was auburn,

cropped just beneath his clean-shaven jawline. His eyes were a striking blue, shining out from a tanned, freckled face. When he smiled, showing rows of white teeth, dimples appeared in his cheeks. He was not a tall man, but had a strong, athletic build.

"Prince Brannon, may I present the Princess Alaine of Hawthorn," Alaine heard her uncle say.

The Prince bowed and stood straight, giving her his best smile as she curtsied in return. Alaine waited quietly as her uncle made all of the other introductions. At one point, she thought that the Prince was looking at her, but noticed that his gaze drifted to the fair Charlyn, and lingered longer than was appropriate. Alaine looked to Kent and noticed that he had also seen the look from the Prince, as Kent's mouth formed into a straight line of distaste.

A distant bell rang, and two footmen opened the doors to the adjacent dining hall as the King led them to the last group of people awaiting introductions. This time, it was Queen Hester who made the introductions, with special attention paid to her cousin, the Marquis de Locke.

"It is pleasant to meet you, Princess," the tall man's voice proclaimed. "My cousin has told me much about you and the Eastgreen Highlands. I'm sure that Hester is planning some activities while you are here. I would like the opportunity to show you my ship, which is moored in the harbor."

"That would be interesting," Alaine replied. "I must admit I have never been on a seafaring ship."

"That might be a good outing for you and your ladies, Alaine," the Queen chimed in. "And I'm sure that it would be nice to see the ship and visit some of the merchants along Shoreline Byway. We receive goods from many distant lands here in Harbortown. Well, it is settled then. I will make the plan for an outing tomorrow afternoon," she added, smiling up at the Marquis and back to Alaine, pleased with her own quick thinking.

At once, a second round of bells rang out and most in the assembly turned toward the King, waiting for him to lead the way into the dining room. He held out his arm to the Queen and turned toward the open doorway.

"May I escort you to the dining room, Princess?" asked the Marquis, the gentleman with the honey voice and diamond tie pin.

For some reason Alaine resisted the good-looking noble, who had the look of a man who always got what he wanted.

"Actually, I have already promised my cousin, Prince Stenson, that he could escort me to dinner," she replied, turning to the young man.

Stenson proudly stepped forward and proceeded to follow his father with Alaine on his arm.

Alaine's response brought smiles to the faces of two men who overheard – King Holum and Duke Seaken-Char. They admired the Princess for standing her ground.

It was late, and by the time the ladies returned to their rooms after the evening's entertainment they were all ready for bed. Opening the door to the suite, they found Genna asleep on the couch by the door in the small anteroom. A light sleeper, Genna awoke instantly and was ready to assist with the undressing, but Lady Avis and the girls waved her off.

Pleased with the events of the evening, Lady Avis went straight to her room, wishing to be alone with her thoughts and observations. It was time to write a letter to her sister, Queen Iris, to tell her of the happenings, and send it via courier in the morning. She also reflected on the arrival of Duke Seaken-Char. He provided strong support and had the ear of King Holum. It was a good turn of events.

Charlyn went to her room, focused on her own little world of feelings, relishing the evening with Kent by her side. The old Duke, Lady Avis, Kent and herself had been seated as a group at one end of the table, while Alaine was seated next to the King at the head of the table. Duke Seaken-Char had made sure that the dinner conversation was lively, making for an enjoyable meal. After dinner, a musical performance had completed the close of the day. Glowing in Kent's attention, Charlyn dreaded the day that she would return home without him. As she readied for bed, she was thinking that Kent seemed to enjoy her company. Yet, she reminded herself, there was no promise of a future once their tasks for Alaine were finished.

Alaine also retreated to her bedroom and immediately kicked off the tight slippers that had been hurting her feet for hours. She fussed with her gown, loosening the ties and slipping it off onto the floor. Stepping out of the dress and a slip, she draped them over the back of a chair. The Princess had learned her lesson when it came to the care of her jewelry, gently removing the necklace and tiara and carefully packing them away in her trunk and remembering to turn the lock. She spent some time removing all of the pins from her hair, allowing the red tresses to fall in waves onto her shoulders after a good brushing.

Alaine went to the head of the bed to retrieve the nightgown that Genna usually folded and placed under the pillow. Suddenly her eye was caught by something sitting on the cushion. It was a small feather - an intricately carved, wooden feather. Breathlessly, she picked it up for closer examination. Her heart began to race. Carver! Feelings flooded back as she wondered how the feather had gotten to her bed, *inside* of Irongate Castle.

Alaine ran to the front room where Genna was almost back to sleep on her settee.

"Genna, did anyone come into the rooms while we were gone?" Alaine asked, with urgency.

"What?" Genna responded, groggily.

"Did anyone come into the rooms while we were gone?" Alaine repeated.

Genna sat up and gathered her thoughts before answering the question. "Nana came to the rooms, and we had dinner together in front of the fireplace," Genna began. "Later the chamber maid came in and emptied the pots and brought fresh water to the rooms. When she returned to take care of the bedroom fires, I went with her to each room. Then she left. Why? Is something missing?" Genna asked, now awake and alert.

"No one else?" Alaine persisted.

"No, Princess, I stayed by the door and made sure that no one else entered."

"No, there is nothing missing. I just found something changed in the room and thought that someone had been there," Alaine said, keeping the disappointment out of her voice.

"What is it?" Genna asked perceptively, with concern for Alaine in her voice.

"It is nothing...," Alaine answered, lowering her head and walking back to her room, deep in thought.

Maybe Carver had paid the chambermaid to bring the feather and place it on the pillow, she wondered. How else could it have gotten there?

Genna knew that it was not "nothing". It was something important to Alaine. Genna wondered what was causing the unusual moods of the Princess from the time they were camped along the roadside. The maid thought Charlyn might know something of the matter as she nestled herself back into the couch for the last time.

Later, awake and unable to sleep, Alaine allowed herself to go through every memory involving Carver. She couldn't understand how all of her time with him seemed so easy and comfortable, while she felt no such comfort in choosing between the men who wanted to marry her. Although she didn't really know the suitors for her hand in marriage, she couldn't imagine being with any of them for the rest of her life.

There was also the issue of the missing jewelry. Was the man that made her wish for a future just a thief? How was she ever going to make a choice between the princes, when all of her thoughts were for Carver, no matter how much she tried to put him out of her mind? How *did* the feather get here? she thought, turning it over in her hand.

An owl hooted outside as the night droned on...

17
Harbortown

Alaine spent a pleasant morning with Prince Sturgrom. Although she was still intimidated by the man's age, she found him to be kind and very knowledgeable about almost all of the things they talked about. The Princess actually enjoyed their walk along the dirt trails of the parkland on the west side of Irongate Castle. Lady Avis and the slower Nana lolled along behind the couple, allowing for some privacy. The clouds remained low and misty as they strolled on a path. The natural greenery was thick and ran all the way downhill to the guardhouse and stables. Birdsong resonated through the moist air. A mist hung over the pond that was surrounded by reed grasses and dotted with ducks. As they moved along, the Prince related the names of trees and flora, as well as some of the resident birds. He showed Alaine where some ground quail nested and where a fox tended her kits near a fallen tree.

The Prince spoke eloquently of his homeland, painting pictures in the mind of snow-filled winter landscapes, and views of blue waterways kissed by sloping green hillsides as the seasons warmed. Alaine spoke to him of Hawthorn Castle and the surrounding countryside, so familiar to her, and now so far away. The Prince also talked about his father, the King of Swerd, who was aging and wished for his son to remarry. The man spoke of his homeland with great pride, while carefully describing his castle home and its attributes to Alaine.

After their walk, Prince Sturgrom took Alaine to King Holum's map room. On an unfurled chart, he showed her the route his ship would take on his return voyage. Seeing the map, Alaine had a much better idea about the northern location of the land of Swerd. Her fears and a touch of sadness were hidden from the amiable man. The Princess knew that if she chose this man as a husband, it was unlikely that she would ever see her homeland, family, or her beloved Hawthorn Castle again.

Now, past midday, the sun was making its way out from the morning's overcast skies which were not unusual at the seacoast. After a light luncheon, the entire afternoon was available for a pastime. As arranged by the Queen, the purpose of the outing was to tour the Marquis' opulent ship and allow the ladies to visit some of the Harbortown shops. As it turned out, five people crowding into Queen Hester's carriage was not a recipe for comfort. Alaine, Lady Avis and Charlyn were packed together on one seat, with Kent and the Marquis on the other. Between the long skirts of the women and two tall men with long legs, foot space was limited. Fortunately, the drive was not long from the Irongate grounds to Shoreline Byway, which ran along the coastline leading to the harbor.

During the ride, Alaine kept her eyes cast down or peered out the coach window to avoid encountering the Marquis' relentless stare. She felt uncomfortable with the man's seemingly constant gaze upon her. Were his intense looks an examination in suitability or a search for flaws? Alaine wondered. It was as if she were an object, and he was inwardly debating how she would fit into his collection.

So, it came as a relief when the carriage turned from Shoreline Byway onto the wide, stone wharf. Merchant ships, fishing trawlers, and many smaller boats were moored in a long row. The horses and coach moved slowly along the harbor front, which proved to be a bustling place of noisy activity. Wagons and carts of all sizes were parked, waiting to unload their goods or receive the commerce being off-loaded from the anchored vessels. Groups of men moved about, intent on their labors. Ropes and pulleys of all sorts were being employed to move their loads. This was a world belonging to men, alien to Alaine, but curious to the observer.

At the end of the wharf, the coach stopped, and the group of nobles unloaded in front of a wooden gangplank. All eyes were trained upward, taking in the massive ship, by far the largest in the harbor. The immediate issue for the ladies was how to board the forbidding wooden structure. The gangplank was long and steep with no railings to assist in the ascent. The Marquis stepped forward, offering an arm to each of the fearful girls.

"Come, Princess Alaine and Lady Charlyn," he encouraged. "It looks worse than it is. We'll proceed slowly." Then looking back over his shoulder, "Duke, will you assist Lady Avis?"

Up they went, with Alaine and Charlyn keeping a tight grip on the shipowner's arm. Kent and his mother followed cautiously behind. Soon, they were safely standing on the main deck taking in the three towering masts. The sails were stowed at the crossbars and ropes were everywhere meeting a need. The decks, the wooden railings and doors gleamed in the afternoon sun.

"Welcome to the Galeecia," the Marquis pronounced, with a wave of the arm. "She took three summers to build. Now, she is the gemstone of my fleet."

"There's a fleet?" Charlyn asked, sorely impressed.

"Yes, I own several merchant ships, all smaller than this, used to move cargo up and down the coast. My three larger ships are able to carry more goods and are used for longer voyages at sea. What do you think of her, Princess?"

"I could not have imagined the size of the ship," Alaine answered honestly. "It is very clean, and the wood is very well polished."

"I am in luck to have good Captain Salone and his crew who take great pride in the ship. Wood exposed to the salty sea air needs constant care, requiring devotion from the men. Fortunately, the crew treats the Galeecia as their home.

"Up there," pointed the Marquis, "is the wheel deck, on the stern. That wheel is what helps to steer the ship. When at sea, that deck is always manned. Our Captain navigates using his instruments and the stars. He has the most recent charts of the coastlines. The Captain's cabin is through that door. The galley is on two levels, through that door. There are food storage and sleeping areas for the cook and his boy. The rest of the crew sleeps below decks."

"What are your defenses on this ship?" broke in Kent, being a military veteran with a concern for threats. "Have you a need to be fearful of pirates?"

"We do have six cannons on board," the Marquis replied, happy to point out prestigious features. "They are on the deck below, three on each side. The cost was a small fortune; I assure you. As to your questions about pirates, we haven't experienced a challenge with this ship, as this is its first major voyage, but we have had encounters along the southern coastlines with some of my other ships. That is why I felt the need for the cannons. The larger the ship, the less the maneuverability on the water. A pack of smaller pirate ships must be taken seriously. Of course, we do carry arms for the men perchance we are boarded, though that is unlikely. Now, come this way," he said, motioning toward the bow of the ship.

The Marquis opened a narrow wooden door, leading into a small corridor with two more doors.

"Here is *my* cabin," he announced, opening the door on the left.

One by one they filed into the irregularly shaped room, only to be overwhelmed by wood – wood walls, wood floor, wooden furnishings.

"Space is the most coveted commodity on a ship. Everything must be fitted for the practicalities of living at sea and the constant motion of the ship. It takes a little getting used to. I designed this cabin for me and my future wife," declared the Marquis, looking at Alaine.

Pink rose to Alaine's cheeks after the Marquis' comment. Looking away, she observed how cleverly every bit of space was used. There were two small windows looking out from the bow. Lanterns were set in holders on the walls. A little writing desk and a shelf with rails needed to hold items in place made up the rest of the triangular space. A great bunk bed, also with a low railing, took up most of one wall, with a cupboard at the end.

"This bed was especially made for me," the Marquis said, following Alaine's gaze, "long enough for my height. Also, it is wide enough for two people. Several travel trunks will fit underneath, held in place by this net."

The proud shipowner walked to the other side of the cabin where a wooden partition closed off one corner of the room.

"Behind here is a convenient water cabinet; and this partition allows for privacy when dressing. *This* cupboard is big enough to hold several ladies' gowns." And pointing to a small, upholstered chair with padded arms, "I had this comfortable chair made for a lady. Here, you can see that its feet fit into holes in the deck to keep it in place when the ship is in motion at sea."

There was a small table, folded and hung on the wall, with two folded chairs that took up the rest of the wall space and could be taken down for meals in the cabin.

"Well, you have certainly thought of everything, sir," Lady Avis complimented, running her hand over the smooth, red material on the back of the fancy chair.

The Marquis smiled at her words and continued to point out other special features of the room.

Alaine thought differently of the space. She imagined many long days and nights secluded here during a sea voyage. The sight of the cabin only renewed her pondering of the intentions of the merchant shipowner. Was he hinting at a request of her hand in marriage? That would not have been part of her father's original plan.

Later that afternoon, Kent stretched out his legs in front of him while sitting on the comfortable settee. He was sipping a hot cup of tea while he looked out the shop window onto the busy byway. It seemed that all types of people and business traffic could be seen moving before him in a diverse parade. Looking around, he appreciated that the shop owners made a comfortable spot for gentlemen to wait while ladies went about their shopping.

The collection of stores was divided into sections, all connected with seamless passage from one shop to another without the need to go outside. Yet there were several doorways that could be entered from the byway. These shops were dedicated to goods that would normally be purchased by female customers. The corner shop featured all types of laces and ribbons and other accessories for gowns and hair. There were scarfs of silk and lace, as well as some of warm wool for cooler days. There were many sorts of combs, pins, and nettings for hairstyling. Elaborate head dressings lined shelves on one wall.

Another shop contained rows and rows of bolts of gown-making materials to meet all occasions. One merchant specialized in ready-made stockings and undergarments. Slippers, shoes, and boots filled the next store. Who knew where Charlyn, Alaine and his mother went off to with so many options?

"My estate is over a hundred years old, but we *have* modernized with rich furnishings, rugs and draperies," the Marquis was saying. "The site is on a hillside overlooking the sea. From my balcony, I can actually see my ships when they are in the harbor." He paused with the thought, "My mother is there now. She is anxious for me to take a wife. She would like grandchildren while she is still young enough to enjoy them."

"Yes," agreed Kent, "I am sure many mothers of men our age think that way. I have been musing about possibly taking a wife myself, lately."

"Any woman I marry will live in luxury the rest of her life. She would have the finest clothes and jewels. She would associate with only the people of highest esteem in our society; *and*, with my ships, there would be the possibility of travel. I visit this land every other summer, not only for trade purposes, but to see my cousin, Queen Hester. These visits have always been profitable and pleasurable."

Kent was getting the feeling that the Marquis was doing more than just trying to impress him. The man seemed to be focusing on his own attributes, first on the ship, and now. Did the Marquis presume that as Alaine's cousin and a representative for her father, he could influence Alaine's choice in husbands? Obviously, the Marquis was not aware of Alaine's distaste for being told what to do. But for a man who believes wealth and security were the most important factors for a marriage contract, the Marquis seemed to be making a case for himself.

The rich shipowner continued to chat on, while Kent gave an occasional nod of the head or grunt of agreement. Kent's gaze focused on the street traffic before him, and eventually glazed over. There was the hum of women's voices somewhere in the background. It was in this comfortable haze that Kent watched as a beardless young man, dressed in rustic clothes, walked by the window. He had a satchel over one shoulder and was followed by a large dog. It took a moment for the vision to sink in before Kent was on his feet. *It can't be*, he thought! He ran for the closest door to the street, stepping out onto the walkway. Neither the man nor his dog was anywhere in sight.

"What is it?" asked the Marquis, who had followed after Kent.

"I'm not sure," said the confused Duke, continuing to survey the street and walkways. "I thought that I saw someone who *should not* be here."

"You look alarmed, man. Come back and sit down."

Kent complied, following the Marquis back to the sitting area and taking his seat. But as he sat there, Kent's mind was racing. He knew what he had seen, or *who* he had seen, in this case. He was *sure* that it was Carver Vale, and the dog added confirmation. What was he doing here!?

Kent remembered when he had first spoken to the man on the side of the road. Carver said that he was traveling to Harbortown to meet his bride, or something of the sort. But Kent knew that the forest people stayed to themselves and didn't marry outside of their clans. Then Carver had shown up in the woods with Alaine dressed as a lad, with her saying that Carver had guided her through the forest to Bole's hamlet. How could he conveniently show up to be a guide? How could Alaine even *know* the man? Kent thought back to the intimate moment he had observed between Alaine and Carver while sitting at Bole's table. It was obvious that they *did* know each other, but how? And what was all of that odd behavior of Alaine's after the evening of the dinner at the Falls? She stayed to herself and hardly spoke to anyone all the way to the seacoast. Could that have had something to do with the strange woodsman? Thinking about Alaine's behavior, the pieces of the puzzle were starting to fall into place for Kent, and the picture they were forming was not good. What if it were *Alaine* that the forest man wished to wed? No, that can't be, he thought. What about Alaine? Did she have romantic feelings for him? Kent knew that Alaine could be obstinate when she got something in her mind. Was Carver here to steal her away? And would his cousin go willingly?

"Oh, no," he thought. This could be a disaster!

Suddenly, Kent got to his feet. "Where are those women?" he shouted to the Marquis. "We must collect them and get Alaine safely back to Irongate. That man that I saw…I fear that the Princess may be in danger of being kidnapped. Come man, we must make haste!"

Carver walked back from the butcher, where he'd bought sausages and a large soup bone for Astra. The dog knew that the meat was stowed in the satchel, as she followed closely behind Carver on the walkway. Carver carried another package wrapped in brown paper – a new shirt, purchased at the gentleman's tailor. Turning the corner, he made his way up the short street to the rooming house where he was staying.

He was barely inside the downstairs doorway, when the landlady approached him, her scarf lopsided on her graying head.

"I made allowances for the dog, but all of those ruffians can't stay in your room! They'll have to find their own lodgings!" she demanded.

"What?" Carver asked, with a lack of understanding at her dismay.

"Those men in your room," she asserted, "they can't stay here. You hear me?!"

"Ah, yeah, I'll take care of it," Carver said, just trying to appease the woman.

"See that you do," she scolded in a huff, and off she went, mumbling to herself.

Carver went up the narrow wooden stairs two at a time and hastily walked the hallway to the door of his rented room. As he opened the door, his mouth dropped open as he saw not one or two of his brothers, but all six of them.

"Are you here for father?" he assumed, falling into the language of the trees and thinking King Alfred had sent his brothers to fetch him.

"No," replied Bole. "We are here for *you*, and to talk about this mess that you may be dragging us all into. Just what are you intending to do?"

Without answering the question, Carver posed one of his own, "How did you find me?"

"Are you making a jest?" asked Delle. "You stick out with your clothes and beardless face. You would not be taken as a sailor or a fisherman, and certainly not a noble. There aren't many on the byway with a hound like Astra following after them. You were only too easy to find, Carver. There was talk of you in the tavern."

"So, now that you are here in Harbortown, what are your plans, brother?" Flecher demanded, leaning on his longbow.

"My plan is to ask Princess Alaine to marry me," Carver responded, calmly. "I have already found my way into Irongate Castle and have been able to reach the rooms being used by the Princess."

"Have you thought beyond getting to the Princess?" queried Jute, who was next to Carver in youth among the brothers. He had the look of his father, with his stocky build.

"So your plan is to get into Irongate and take the Princess out, willingly or unwillingly," proposed Lignin, the second in the birth line and most intellectual of the brothers. "And after she is taken? What do you believe will be the consequences of those actions? A search for her by the castle guard going into our forest lands? Armed conflicts with deaths among us or them? Hostile actions that lead to a war between the forest clans and the people of the fields?"

Carver was becoming annoyed and feeling set upon. He threw his bag onto the bed and turned to face his brothers, running a hand through his hair.

"Of course, I would not take her away *unwillingly*. I believe that she has a sincere affection for me. I know that she will say 'yes' to my proposal."

"I don't know, Carver," piped in Flecher, shaking his head. "The last time *I* spoke to the Princess, which was the day after the dinner at Middleoak, she had no kind words for you, brother. In fact, just the opposite."

"That was just a tiff that I can mend," Carver responded, waving a hand in dismissal.

Lignan continued his questions, "Even if the girl *is* agreeable to a match, do you really believe that King Granth and the nobles of the land, both from the Upper *and* Lower Kingdoms, will allow the taking of the royal Princess of Hawthorn by a forest clansman without some sort of retaliation?"

"I am a prince! I'm as good as any of those vying for her hand," Carver blurted out, defensively.

"Yes, you are a well-loved prince among our people, and will inherit the forest lands where father now resides; but the people of the fields know little of us and do not recognize your title," reminded Bole. "You don't seem to have a detailed plan, brother. Which leads to the question, what are you offering her? A life with conflict between our people?"

"It is beyond me how you convinced father of such a cockeyed notion as to follow after the girl," Nocken said sarcastically, wondering why his brothers had dragged *him* into this conflict.

Carver was stung by the words of his brothers. Maybe because they had made a good point. He hadn't thought of the potential outcomes of his actions to gain the heart and hand of the Princess. He moved to the bed and sat down. With elbows on his knees, he cradled his head in his hands, slipping into a despondency over his lost dreams of a life with Alaine.

Quiet filled the over-crowded room. Astra had fetched her bone from Carver's bag and was chewing on it in one corner. Carver's brothers looked to Lignin. As forest princes who were all responsible for their own regions, they were members of the Assembly of the Groves, the governing council of the forest clans. None were involved as much as Lignin. The popular Prince was known for his speaking skills, participation with policies, and having great influence in resolving problems that came to the Assembly. He was a natural leader among the forest people. The handsome diplomat was well-respected throughout the wooded lands. Lignin knew it was up to him to talk to Carver.

"Carver, you have spent almost all of your life among father's trees near Hawthorn Village. It has been an era of peace in the land for us and the people of the fields. Both peoples have remained separate in their own spaces, as agreed in the Treaty of the Trees. Keeping the peace is actually a hard fight and an ongoing pursuit. How is this done? How is it that there have been no invasions by enemies in your lifetime? Old King Holmes had the country divided into the Upper and Lower Kingdoms, making each of his sons a king. How is it the two Kings built and kept their governments intact since the time of their father? With the seven landholding dukes of the Upper Kingdom and the five of the Lower Kingdom, how is it the two Kings have not been challenged or overthrown? How is it that there have been no wars among the dukes? Is it possible there is nothing but harmony for so many years?

"It will not be surprising to you, Carver, that you are not the first of our people to stray into a nearby village. It happens from time to time. The people of the fields may be surprised to know how many of us live among them. Fortunately for us, the loyalties to their clans usually remain with our people, allowing for information to flow to us.

"How is it that we know of what goes on at Hawthorn Castle? I will tell you. Years ago, a young clanswoman made a friendship with a rich sheepherder on the lands of Duke Seaken-Char. They married and had a child. When her husband died, the woman appealed to the Duke to care for her son if she surrendered her husband's land. The Duke agreed and she returned to the forest. The Duke sent the boy to a northern country, to a philosopher that needed an apprentice. The boy not only learned to make the paper of scrolls and ink, but he learned languages and learned to write.

He returned to his homeland and is now known as Squire Dilford, King Granth's scribe. Our Assembly is aware of the happenings at the Council of Hawthorn soon after the ink is dry on the parchment. King Granth could never plan for war without our knowing.

"Another instance is a young clansman that left the woods at about your age and joined the guard of Duke Dayton, whose lands have the mines and the stone quarries. He became a famous archer and rose to be the Captain of the Guard. The Duke's lands extend to the far east of the land, where the high cliffs overlook the Strait of Meteran, through which the ships must pass coming from the north. Our Captain would warn, not only the Duke, but our people, of an approaching enemy armada days before the ships could be seen from the Irongate harbor.

"The point is, the network of agents that report to our Assembly is spread throughout the land. Not to say, King Granth and King Holum don't have their own legions of informers. Keeping the peace requires diligence and information from all corners.

"Carver, you may believe that this has nothing to do with your quest for the love of a royal princess, but you are wrong. It is just this kind of thing that can lead to unrest and maybe even lead to war in our peaceful land."

"So, you all wish me to give up the Princess and return to my father's woods," Carver reasoned, defeated.

"No, that is not what we wish for, lad," Bole responded, with compassion. "Carver, *if* you are to ask for the hand of the Princess, it cannot be done in the shadows. You cannot just take her away, even if she is willing, without causing an uproar," warned Lignin. "You must proclaim yourself the son of a king and ask for her hand in front of King Holum at the betrothal ceremony. She must accept you in front of her family and the royal court."

"But what about the unrest and the war?" Carver asked, confused.

"The marriage contract for Princess Alaine has been written, and carried with her aunt, Lady Avis, to the court of King Holum. An important stipulation of the contract is that the Princess will not be *forced* to marry anyone against her will. Of this we have been told," Lignin shared. "If she accepts you in front of an audience, there may be objections, but the two Kings would have to come together, and decisions will have to be made. Can they deny a prince of the land as her chosen suitor? It is a ploy, but you will be in a better position to get what you desire. Maybe it is time for us to come out of the woods and stand up for ourselves as people of this land."

"I heard in the tavern the betrothal ceremony for Princess Alaine is but two days away," Flecher advised.

"It does not give us much time to prepare," worried Delle. "He can't go to the castle dressed like that!"

"No," agreed Jute and Nocken, nodding their heads. "He certainly doesn't look like a prince," Flecher added.

"We will have to make haste to the tailor," Lignin demanded. "He will have to have new clothes and boots. In fact, we will *all* have to have new clothes. Holum's court is about to meet the seven Princes of the Forests. We will go with Carver and support him in a show of force!"

The ray of hope changed Carver's expression, then he frowned, "I can't buy new clothes. I don't have enough money. I had to buy food and pay for this room."

"Ha! We have plenty of their coins!" pronounced Bole, as he pulled a pouch of jangling coins from out of his vest and threw it onto the bed.

18
Plans Afoot

Late that afternoon at Irongate, with the aromas of roasting dinner meats wafting through the air, it was the quiet hour for Queen Hester, prior to the bustle of preparation for the evening. Her bath was being prepared and her banquet gown was being pressed and laid out by March, her dependable maid. The Queen sipped on a small cordial glass, filled with the fruity wine the Marquis brought to her in barrels from the vineyards on his estate.

"This is quite good, Felix. How long since it has been put up?"

The Marquis sat opposite the Queen in her cozy, private sitting room. He was relaxed and satisfied with the events of the afternoon. The impressions made upon the Hawthorn nobles seemed favorable.

"It is only five summers old, dear cousin," he replied, taking a sip of wine himself. "This is a blend made especially for you and your ladies. It is a light wine, but a bit too sweet for a dinner wine."

"How was your afternoon with Alaine?" Hester inquired, getting to the quick grasp of things. "Did Alaine meet your ridged requirements for a bride?"

The man took another sip of the wine, allowing a pause for thought prior to answering. The sun was lowering in the west.

Shadows were gathering in the room where the lamps were not yet lit.

"She is still very girlish, which is to be expected at her age, but she is poised, intelligent, and chaste. Her attire is rather plain, so a new wardrobe will be needed. Mother will see to that. The color of her hair is a brighter red than expected. I'm not in favor of having children with red hair, but I can only hope that their coloring will favor mine."

"You are getting ahead of yourself, dear one," Hester commented with affection, thinking of him as the younger brother she never had. "First the girl must accept you, so that must be our focus. As to the hair color, there are many stylish headdresses that can be used when she is in company. As you said, my aunt can assist you with her appearance. For any children, red hair may reinforce their royal linage, and remove any doubt of a male child's ability to lay claim to the Eastgreen Highlands throne upon the death of King Granth."

"Now who is getting ahead of oneself, cousin? Yet, you have made a good point. It would be a benefit to be the father of the heir to the throne."

"What about the tour of your ship? Did that go well?"

"I believe that they were overwhelmed at the size of the Galeecia. There were many compliments from their party. However, Alaine was quiet, with few words. I think she was somewhat intimidated with the thought of a voyage at sea."

"And the young Duke?"

"I found myself enjoying his company. He has the head of a seasoned soldier and the manners of a courtier. He is used to being in charge of things, despite his age. He is not to be underestimated. I feel that we are on an equal footing, other than my wealth, which I am sure he cannot match," the Marquis replied. "I did my best to promote myself as a man who would be a suitable match for the girl."

Then after a brief pause, "You cannot question the Duke's sense of duty for Alaine's protection. A rather odd occurrence happened while we were at the Byway Shops with the ladies."

"Oh?" the Queen prompted, with curiosity.

"The Duke Morr-Leigh and I were passing the time while the ladies were looking through the shops when he suddenly jumped up and ran out the nearest doorway to the street. He must have seen something through the shop window, or someone. He never said; but he was obviously disturbed. He mentioned something of a possible kidnapping plot and wanted to get the Princess back to Irongate as soon as possible. I don't know what it was that abruptly caused such fears.

"He didn't mention anything of it once we collected the ladies and herded them into the coach with all of their packages. He was brooding all the way back to the castle."

"Kidnapping?!" exclaimed the astonished Queen. "Could that be possible? Should I alert Holum of a threat?"

"I'm not sure that there *is* a threat," replied Felix. "The Duke seemed to think that the Princess would be safe, once here at Irongate."

"This is alarming," Hester declared, pensively, wary of a disruption of her carefully laid plans regarding the betrothal of Alaine to her cousin. "I think I must relay this issue to the King. He may wish to alert the castle guard, at the very least."

"That might be wise. I don't take the Duke Morr-Leigh as a fool, and not a man to jump at conclusions without cause. Whatever he saw at the shops was enough for him to take action for the protection of the girl."

Kent left the dining hall, giving his apologies to his mother and Lady Charlyn, leaving them in the care of Duke Seaken-Char. Going to the footman, he demanded a lantern and made his way out the front door and onto the gravel path leading to the old guardhouse and stables. The two-story stone structure that predated Irongate Castle was closer to the sturdy front walls and massive castle gates of the Irongate compound.

The driveway was deeply rutted from horse and carriage traffic, so Kent tried to keep to the smoother center of the path. The sound of a fox echoed through the bushes. Trees ran between the guardhouse and the primary road that led to the front doors of

Irongate. Like the west side of the castle grounds, the greenery was unmanicured and allowed to grow freely, which disguised the guardhouse and stables. As Kent approached the structure, he was surprised to see that it was fortified by ten-foot stone walls, which were not seen from the front road. However, one of the two gates stood open, so he entered the courtyard with the great building straight before him.

There were two fiery torches on sticks staked before the wide, wooden porch with its central door. The air smelled of horses, a familiar odor for Kent, and at a closer look, he saw two long stable blocks, one on each side of the enclosed courtyard.

As Kent approached the portal, a guard appeared out of the shadows of the porch and came to stand before him. The man's initially aggressive manner changed when he saw Kent's formal attire, realizing this was a man of some substance.

"Hail, sir. Who is it you seek?" the guardsman asked, as Kent came towards him.

"Two of my men from the Morr-Leigh Garrison are temporarily housed within. I have need to speak with them. I am their captain."

"Wait here, Captain," the guardsman replied, entered the building.

After a few moments, an older soldier opened the door and motioned for Kent to enter. The man had crinkly, dark eyes under bushy eyebrows. A thick, wide mustache covered most of his upper lip. He was slightly shorter than Kent, but of a robust stature. His shirt was untied at his throat, and a thick belt hooked at his waist held up his pants.

"Good evening, sir. I'm Captain Foy, the Captain of King Holum's Guard. I'll take you to your men. It's been a good story Lieutenant Miles told of the garrison's forays north of the country."

"Yes, the weather was with us, and the campaign was successful. For now, as you probably know, we are here as escort to the Princess Alaine of Hawthorn; therefore, I must speak with my men."

"Is anything wrong, Captain?"

"No, no. It is just concerning arrangements for tomorrow. I need them to be on hand early."

"I believe that they remain at the table finishing their meal. Come this way."

Kent followed the man through the main hall, noticing what appeared to be the armory, through a wide doorway and past a stairway going up to the second story on the way. The soldier led him to a long room whose purpose was depicted by extensive tables with benches. Miles and Covey sat across from each other, both with goblets in their hands.

"Here they are. I'll just leave you to it, sir," the soldier said, excusing himself and doing an about face.

Covey, surprised to see Kent and fearing the worst, jumped to his feet. Miles, whose back was to Kent, turned to see him, and also stood up. Kent motioned for them to sit and came to take a seat next to Miles.

"What's wrong?" Covey insisted, anxious to hear the reason for the visit.

"Do not distress," Kent waved, trying to relax their concern. "I just wanted to speak to you about tomorrow, as well as some other things I have on my mind regarding the Princess."

"Is she alright?" Covey asked, still worried.

"She's fine. We just finished dinner and there is a play going on for entertainment. But that's not why I'm here. It seems the Princess agreed to go on a horseback ride with Prince Brannon in the morning. We'll be going outside the castle gates, and I want you both to come along as an escort."

"When and where?" Miles asked, going for the details.

"At breakfast time, at the front steps of the castle. Tell the grooms to bring two well-trained horses for Prince Brannon and the Princess and another one for me. Don't be late."

"Is that it, sir?" Miles questioned.

"No, there is one more thing. You both remember the lad with the dog that warned us about the highwaymen following our company? The one who turned out to be of the forest clans?"

Both men nodded their heads, wondering where this was going, as their Captain continued. "I was in Harbortown this afternoon with Marquis de Locke and the ladies when who should walk by the window but Carver Vale. At first, I couldn't believe it. When I ran out of the shop to follow him, he and his dog had disappeared. It's been bothering me since it happened."

"Does the Princess know of it?" Covey asked.

"No," Kent replied, his hand brushing hair from his forehead. "I didn't mention it to her. I just rushed to get the ladies back here to Irongate."

For a few moments the three trained soldiers sat in silence, pondering the worst that could happen regarding Carver Vale.

Kent rested his elbow on the table, and continued, "We know that the forest clans live in different regions throughout the land and almost exclusively stay to themselves. They have their own language, governing, and ways of living. We rarely come across any of them. Yet our visit to Middleoak gave us a glimpse into their society. They have strong family ties and marry among themselves. So, I asked myself, what is Carver Vale doing in Harbortown? Finally, I'm worried about Alaine. Carver came from Hawthorn Village, as did we. Now, we are here with the Princess and so is he. Did he follow us? What are his plans? All I can say to you both is to keep an eye out for him and let me know if you see him. And Covey, be around the castle when Alaine is about the lower floor and grounds."

"Should we enlist the King's Guard, sir?" reasoned Miles.

"Not now," answered Kent. "I have nothing to offer as a threat other than my own suspicions. Just be on the alert."

"Can you have a cup with us, Captain?" Covey offered.

"No, I need to get back. I'll see you first thing tomorrow morning."

"We'll walk back with you," Miles offered. "The guardsmen may take you for an intruder. They are jumpy with all that is going on at Irongate. Captain Foy put them on alert, but we're not sure why."

"We are all a little jumpy. I will be glad when the betrothal ceremony is over, and Alaine has made her choice."

For Alaine, the busy day was over. She sat before the ornate mirror at the dainty dressing table in her room at Irongate. Two ribbons were being tied under her chin, securing the lacy sleeping cap found at the Byway Shops. After she returned from the lengthy dinner and after-dinner play, put on by the Queen's theater group, Alaine quickly threw off her gown and pulled all the pins from her hair, allowing it to fall. With a sigh of relief, she put on a new linen nightgown, with long sleeves and embroidered, lilac sprigs on the bodice – also from the shops. Walking barefoot on the floor, the coolness on her feet reminded her of her tower room at Hawthorn. It was a fond memory that she would tuck away.

Familiar voices were coming from the sitting room, so she wandered in to find her aunt and Nana in conversation on the comfortable couch. Genna was pouring milk from a pewter pitcher into cups.

"The kitchen was quiet, so I was able to warm the milk and add some honey and nutmeg," the maid mentioned, as she continued to fill the stoneware.

"Alaine, see if Charlyn would like some warm milk," requested Lady Avis, referring to the girl who remained in her room.

Soon the bevy of females, including Genna and Charlyn, were sitting around the fireplace, sipping the sweet, warm liquid from the mugs in their hands.

"Nana has brought some news, Alaine, that you may wish to hear, so that you will be better prepared for the betrothal ceremony," advised Lady Avis.

All turned their attention to the plainly dressed, but no less respected nurse, awaiting her words, while embers crackled at the fire.

"I've been spending most of my day in Mistress Ronan's sitting room," Nana began. "She kindly offered it to me, as it is much larger than my bedroom and goes unused most of the day. We have been having tea in the afternoon, before the preparations for dinner. I think that she gets lonely and speaks fondly of her old home at Hawthorn Village, with a desire to return there. Anyway, we got onto the subject of the Marquis. You know that he is the Queen's cousin, and from all that is said, is very rich. According to Ronan, it seems that the Marquis and Queen Hester have put their heads together and the plan is…," Nana paused, to make sure that all were listening, "the Marquis is going to ask for Alaine's hand at the betrothal ceremony."

For a moment, no one spoke. Charlyn took in an audible breath. Alaine's expression went from one of interest to a grimace. An additional burden had just fallen upon her shoulders. The news was not unexpected, based upon comments that had been made at dinner and also from the Marquis himself on the ship today. Alaine knew if she chose not to accept the man, it could be taken as an insult to Queen Hester's family; yet the thought of him as a husband was oppressive.

Lady Avis, always suspicious of Queen Hester, was sure that, in the end, there would be something in a successful match with the Marquis for the Queen herself. This was just the type of thing she and Queen Iris anticipated from Hester. On the other hand, the man *did* have much to offer Alaine.

"He is not a prince," Charlyn wondered, "so how can he propose marriage when Alaine is of a higher rank?"

"The marriage contract requires the man be of the nobility, but does not stipulate that he be a prince," Lady Avis responded. "Is Mistress Ronan sure of this, Nana? Is King Holum aware of the plan, and is he agreeable?"

"Of that I am not sure," Nana responded, "but the rumor is afoot throughout the castle. When I asked Ronan when the Marquis would present himself, she said that it would be at the betrothal ceremony."

"There is nothing to be done about it," Alaine admitted. "The Marquis is one that I will have to consider along with the others. What else can I do without causing an affront?"

Then, weary, "I'm going to bed. I have agreed to a horseback ride with Prince Brannon in the morning. The man seemed surprised to think that I could ride. Are horses not ridden by women of his country?"

The question hung in the air unanswered, as all of the other women's minds were focused on the upcoming betrothal ceremony and what to expect. All had their own thoughts as Alaine went off to her bed.

Carver escaped into the cool, misty, night air, with Astra by his side. The day had been filled with emotion, and he felt a need for some time alone. Time to oneself couldn't be had with all of his brothers and himself crowded into the two-bedroom cottage rented by Bole. They found the place on a tip from the bartender at the tavern. It was one in a row of cottages usually rented by sea captains when they came to shore and their ships were moored at the harbor. Luck was with them, since one cottage was empty and for let. Harbortown was full of visitors arriving for the Queen's garden party and staying for the betrothal ceremony. Those not staying at Irongate needed to find lodging in the town.

It was getting late, but Carver could hear the noise from men still working on the docks at the harbor, as the sound seemed to echo through the thick, damp air. They were probably loading last minute cargo and supplies into ships, planning to sail on the morning tide. Carver went with quickness toward the far end of town, with Astra bounding along to keep up with him. He had become accustomed to the usual activities of Hawthorn Village, but never a town as large as Harbortown. There seemed to be no quiet here, even at such a late time of day. He quickened his pace away from the din of the town, as he longed for the quiet of the forest.

Prior to settling into the small house, Bole insisted on a visit to the tailor's shop - the very same shop where Carver bought a new shirt that morning. The shopkeeper was beside himself when all seven of the brothers invaded his store, quickly pulling articles from the shelves. Lignin took charge, telling his siblings to get in line and let the tailor take one man at a time. The tailor called in his apprentices, and they set to work. Lignin made sure that Carver was the first to get attention and insisted on more than one set of clothes suitable for nobility. By the time they left, the measurements were taken, the orders were placed, and the gold coin was paid. Hats and boots would need to be purchased at other shops.

Carver sped along and Astra followed. Harbortown was left behind as the byway wove its way along the seacoast. Carver thought of the earlier lectures of his brothers. He felt foolish to think that he could just ask Alaine to marry him, and she would just come away with him. If she did agree, would her father and King Holum agree? Where would they go and where would they live? Lignin was right. He had really not thought things through. He was living in a dream world and had not considered any consequences. Yet now, there was a plan. Now, he would do what was needed and hope for the best.

He stopped in his tracks. They had come a long way. Astra walked to him and nuzzled his hand. They could hear the rhythm of the waves as they hit the rocks along the shore. Carver sighed into the darkness, feeling better.

"Come, Astra. We have to go back."

Near midnight, within the castle, the dining hall was long since empty. A few noble guests were still in the great parlor room, where a play had been performed as after-dinner entertainment.

Duke Seaken-Char, plagued by wakeful nights, was among them. King Holum, also having a late night, saw the Duke sitting alone and approached his old friend.

"Rengard, I see that all of your ladies have deserted you for their beds. Would you like to come with me for a nightcap?"

"That would be appreciated, Sire. I was just gathering the strength to go upstairs," quipped the older man, taking the time to get out of his chair.

"Follow me to my hideout…"

The Duke's curiosity was piqued as the King led him out to the main hall and turned into a narrow hallway beside the east staircase. The passage was a dead end with a discrete door on the left.

"Stenson calls this my closet," Holum called to the Duke, over his shoulder. "It's a place I go when I want some time to myself or wish not to be found."

As the King opened the door and proceeded into the irregularly shaped room, the Duke agreed with the boy – it felt like a closet. Firstly, Holum lit a lamp, as the interior was pitch black.

With some light, the older man noticed that the ceiling of the room sloped from very low at one end to very high at the other. It was a hollowed- out space under the grand east staircase. The interior was sparsely furnished. A long, low cabinet holding the lamp, scrolls and loose papers took up the wall at the high end. There were two armchairs with leather buttoned backs separated by a small table. The royal was busy pouring drinks from a bottle into glasses, then, handed one to the Duke as he took his seat facing him.

"So, it is the Lady Avis, is it Rengard?"

"Oh, I know what they will all say at court – an old goat with a pretty, younger lady; but she makes me laugh. She makes me happy. The funny thing is that I've known her since she was a girl. She and the Duke were always at the Hawthorn court before he passed. I respected the man. I never thought of Lady Avis as a companion until I took a dinner feast to the escort party when they were camped on my land… It was then I had a chance to talk to Avis. In fact, we talked all through the night. I hated to leave her. So, after much thought, and the approval of my sons, I decided to try for her hand."

"Good reason to show up here out of the blue," laughed Holum. "What can happen, but she says 'no'? She is a beauty for her age, with all of the grace and wisdom of a mature woman. I am in your corner."

"I have no delusions about my age, which makes the time I have more precious. Why should we both be alone?"

Then, after some quiet moments and a few sips of brandy, "What of Hester? Has she recovered?"

"Yes, she's doing well. It's been almost five years since we lost the last child – a baby girl. Hester was so devastated we decided not to try for more children. The loss of three royal babies was enough. Hester spends her days running the household and meddling in the intrigues of the courtiers. It keeps her going. I think about it sometimes," Holum relayed, pensively. "It seems that the villagers have their houses bursting at the seams with children, yet Granth and I have only managed to produce one royal heir each. Not that our queens were unwilling. We were just not fortunate," the King lamented.

The Duke, trying to move to a happier subject, "How is Stenson doing? He has certainly sprouted up."

"He *has* grown up so fast of late. The tutor is working out well. The man's traveled south for a home visit during the warm season, but he'll be back before the leaves turn. Stenson is learning his Latin and Greek. He enjoys history and all he can learn of far-off places.

The boy pours over the maps and is itching to go on a sea voyage with the Marquis – not yet he's still too young. I have him sitting in on the Council meetings and audiences. It is good for him to know the kinds of issues that come before a king. He has a desk in the scribe's office and has learned a lot there," Holum went on. "Stenson is so serious, though. I would like him to have more recreation with boys his own age."

"What do you think about Alaine and her choices? The poor girl has quite the dilemma. No matter which man she chooses; she is destined for a life in far off lands."

"It appears to be her lot in life," the King commiserated. "Alaine has turned out well, unspoiled and intelligent. I believe that she is ready for a match. Sturgrom is a good man," Holum went on, "eager for a young bride. I believe that he would treat her well. Unusual clothing, though - too much braid, buttons, and fur, but I guess that is the style at his court.

"Prince Brannon I would not advise for Alaine. I hope that she is not charmed by his good looks and realizes his shallow personage. He has a handsome face but nothing in the head behind it. Typical third son of a king. He's a gadfly with the ladies of the court, and none seem too old or too young. The man has certainly taken advantage of my table, as he craves rich foods and wine. He has been here through two full moons. I will be happy to see the back of him."

The old Duke chuckled at the King's animation of Brannon, "If it were a match, they would be certain to have beautiful children."

"Beautiful and poor," Holum proposed. "The story is that King Ryan approached Granth with the suggestion of a marriage. It seems his coffers are running low, and he is looking for an infusion of gold at Alaine's expense. I'm not sure why Granth went ahead with the invitation. Brannon has two older brothers, both with families. He will never see the throne unless he could somehow wheedle his way onto Granth's throne through an underaged male heir."

"The Hawthorne Council would never allow it," Rengard stated, firmly. "I'm afraid that would be a cause for war."

"Then, there is the Marquis, Hester's all too rich cousin who is in the market for a bride."

"The Marquis? You must jest, Sire."

"No, it is not a jest. Don't get me wrong. I have no dislike for the man. He is of good character. Alaine could do worse with Brannon," Holum surmised. "I was surprised when he showed up earlier than usual this year with his huge ship in the harbor. I believe that Hester may be behind it somehow. Felix plans to make a proposal to Alaine. Hester thinks that I don't know of it, but *of course* I know of it. She forgets that I live here, too, and have my own sources for information. If Hester pulls this off, it will be quite an upset. Granth and Iris will be taken aback."

"One way or another, Hawthorn will lose our dear Princess. Sad, really…"

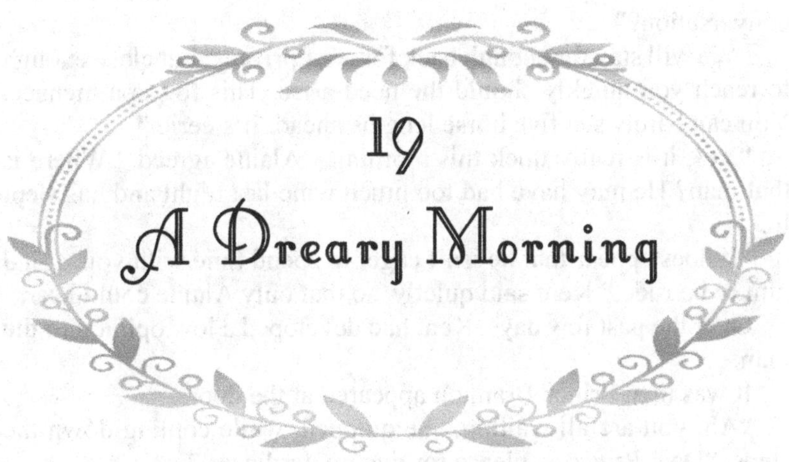

19
A Dreary Morning

Getting ready for her horseback ride with Prince Brannon, Alaine picked a plain, brown gown with a high collar, long sleeves, and a very wide skirt that would cover her legs during the ride. She sat on the bed and pulled on the long, woolen leggings Nana had knitted for her to be worn beneath her underskirts, to protect her legs while riding. She was thankful to have them. When finished, she took a final look in the little mirror. Her hair was up and knotted in a net at the nape of her neck. She wore her hat with the pheasant feathers, tightly pinned to stay in place.

She wore no jewelry, the only decoration being a small row of lace around the neck of her gown going up to her chin. She was ready, but not greatly enthused. Charlyn was just up from her bed, and Lady Avis was still abed. She grabbed her oldest cloak and left the comfort of the suite.

Alaine was to meet Brannon outside the front doors of the castle. Two horses were saddled, awaiting riders, being held by a groom. Kent was also off of his horse, but Covey, Rand, and Lieutenant Miles were mounted and ready to leave.

"Captain, why are so many going with us?" Alaine asked Kent.

"You will be riding out from the castle grounds, Princess. So a small escort is warranted."

"How will the Prince and I have any privacy of our conversation?"

"We will stay far enough back for your privacy, but close enough to reach you quickly should the need arise. This fog is a menace. You can barely see five horse lengths ahead. It's eerie."

"Yes, it is really thick this morning," Alaine agreed. "Where is that man? He may have had too much wine last night and has slept in."

"It does appear that he isn't eager to spend time with you. I find him to be rude," Kent said quietly, so that only Alaine could hear.

Over the past few days, Kent had developed a low opinion of the man.

It was then Prince Brannon appeared at the doors.

"Ah, you are all waiting," he quipped, while coming down the steps. "Dear Princess, please forgive my tardiness."

Alaine had already picked the black stallion and was ready to mount without delay.

"We have not been waiting long, Prince Brannon," Alaine answered aloofly. Ready to mount, "Captain, will you assist me up?"

Presently, the small troop rode off toward one of the wide dirt roads that wove through the castle complex. As they went off the gravel drive, they found themselves on a rather straight pathway that ran along the back side of the Queen's garden. The high, spiked, wooden wall on one side and the tall hedge rows on the other, filled with the low hanging fog, gave the effect of a mystical tunnel. Alaine's horse balked and snorted his displeasure with the sense of confinement coming from both sides.

Once beyond the hedges, they came to the large kitchen gardens. It was clear how the wagons came this way for their deliveries to the castle cooks. Prior to reaching the back walls they came to poultry coops and pens. A fulltime job it would be to care for the variety of birds in separate coops.

Alaine pulled back on the reins, bringing the stallion to a stop before the back gates. She was surprised to see a complement of eight armed guards – four on the scaffold running above the massive gates made of wood and iron, the other four on the ground.

Outside the castle grounds, the fog inhibited the view of the adjacent countryside to such a degree that, until one was on top of things, there was little detail. The trees, those that could be seen, were ghostly sentinels. The reddish outline of the royal dairy barn was sitting back from the roadway. There was a wide dip in the path where the milk cows constantly crossed from the fenced meadow on their way to the barn for their milking. Alaine picked up the pace by kneeing her horse into a trot.

Brannon quickly matched her pace.

"You sit a horse well, Princess. How long have you been riding?"

"I used to spend the summer days at Duke Morr-Leigh's Juniper Lodge from the time I was a toddler. One day when his mother and our nurse were not watching, he set me on his pony. Fortunately, I learned to enjoy riding before I could be afraid to get on a horse. My father keeps a robust stable, as you can imagine. I have my pick of mounts - some are my favorites."

"In my country, the men ride the horses…very few women," the disparaging man remarked.

"What do the women do in your country?"

"They run their houses, care for their children, and tend their gardens. Our ladies are known for their fine needlework and lacemaking," he bragged.

"Sounds invigorating," Alaine remarked, with sarcasm.

"We could always ask my father's permission for you to ride."

"Ask permission?"

"King Ryan has strong expectations of the members of his family and his courtiers. Actually, that is why we are here, is it not? Our fathers approved a possible match for us, and we were both sent to Irongate, regardless of our own wishes."

"You do not wish to be here, Prince Brannon?"

"I was not consulted on the matter, Princess. I was told to get on the ship – so here I am."

Alaine looked at the handsome Prince riding beside her. Unlike Prince Sturgrom, or even the Marquis, this man didn't seem to care what impression he made upon her. She put her knees to the horse's sides and let him have his head into a full gallop.

It felt good to feel the mist on her face as the horse sped through the thick fog. It was like flying through the clouds. She heard the men yelling behind her, but she paid no attention. The feeling of freedom had captured her. Suddenly she saw something in the road ahead. It was coming up fast – two figures. At once she tried to rein in the stallion. The well-trained horse came to a halt so quickly that Alaine was almost unseated. Only her riding experience and her good balance kept her on the horse's back.

The two men waited on the side of the road. Flecher, with a bow hanging from his shoulder, stepped forward and assisted Alaine with her dismount.

"It is good to see you again, Princess. May I present my younger brother, Jute." Both of the men bowed.

"Another brother? Yes, I can see that he does resemble Bole. What are you doing here, so far away from your woods? Not hunting the King's cows, I hope?"

Both of the men shared a laugh with Alaine.

"To answer your query, one of our family required assistance, but you are right in that we prefer to stay in our familiar places."

Alaine was about to ask Flecher about Carver when Prince Brannon brought his horse to a stop just in time. He quickly joined her on the ground.

"Are you all right, Princess?" Brannon asked, as he came to stand at her side.

"Yes, I fare well. I came to a stop when I saw these men in the road. "Flecher, Jute, this is Prince Brannon from the land of Mirth, across the sea."

The woodsmen bowed with respect to the royal.

"We have heard of your father, King Ryan," Flecher acknowledged.

"You *know* these men?" the Prince inquired of Alaine, with surprise.

"We had delays on our travels to Irongate due to rain and flooding. Flecher guided us through some difficult terrain. We are indebted to him and his family," Alaine explained.

Brannon had no time to ask any further questions as Kent and the other men came up and brought their horses to a stop. The Duke was immediately off of his horse, not happy with Alaine for galloping ahead. Then he realized who the two men were.

"Flecher," Kent remarked, "I am amazed to see you here!"

His look relayed a demand for more information from the woodsman. "We are on our way to the harbor. We have business there which cannot be denied. I was just telling the Princess how we would prefer to be in the forest," Flecher explained.

"These are King Holum's private pasture lands. His guard patrols this road," Kent advised.

"We strayed here in the fog and happened upon the road. We will leave and head back across the fields. Fare thee well, Princess," reassured Fletcher, raising his hand in a wave.

"It was good to see you again," Alaine called, waving back, wishing she could have asked about Carver.

"That was odd," Covey remarked, still on his mount, with Miles nodding his head in agreement.

Kent was even more suspicious of seeing the woodsmen, especially after seeing Carver Vale in Harbortown just the day before.

"Princess, I think that we should head back to the castle. This mist is never-ending and does not allow for viewing the countryside. Do you mind, Prince Brannon?" asked Kent.

"I must agree with you, Duke. It is best to head back. Hopefully the fog will lift before the Queen's garden party."

Alaine didn't raise objections. Seeing Flecher had brought Carver back to her mind. The time with Prince Brannon was enough to find him as uninteresting as he seemed to find her.

Lady Charlyn was in her room, with gowns pulled out of the trunk and laid on the bed. In the afternoon, Queen Hester was having a garden party to which many nobles were invited. The girl pulled back the curtain at the small window to see an army of servants hastily working in spite of the mist, preparing for guests in the formally trimmed shrubbery and lawns. Then, after checking on the weather, she returned to her dilemma. It was always the challenge for ladies.

What should she wear? Unlike Alaine with her two trunks tightly packed with gowns, Charlyn had one trunk and a much smaller selection of dresses. So which of the three gowns on the bed would be best for the garden party? She knew that Kent had already seen them all. Maybe she could wear her hair in a different manner, she mused. Lost in her thoughts, she heard Genna in the outer rooms answering the hall door.

"What is it, Genna?" Charlyn heard Lady Avis call to the girl.

"It is a message from Duke Morr-Leigh, milady,"

"Well, bring it here," Lady Avis instructed.

"It is for Lady Charlyn, ma'am."

"Oh? Take it to her, then."

Charlyn reached her doorway at the same time as Genna. She took the tightly folded paper and turned back into her room prior to opening it. Unfolding the note, she quickly read the small, neat lettering:

Meet me at the bottom of the stairs.
I'm waiting for you.

~Kent

This was not a request, but a command. It appeared to be urgent, as he was willing to wait for her. Charlyn glanced down at her morning dress, which was not her best, and her hair was still hanging in its long braid; yet it couldn't be helped. She would have to go as she was or keep him waiting.

"I'm going down to the front hall," she called, rushing to the outer door, not allowing a chance for questions from the surprised Lady Avis.

Once in the hallway, she walked as quickly possible. Kent was pacing below as she came down the stairs.

"What is it?" she asked a little fearfully, before reaching the bottom steps.

Kent turned to look at her, his face filled with concern. Charlyn saw that he was casually dressed in his garrison vest, pants and boots.

"Where is Alaine?" he demanded.

"She is taking a bath after her ride with Prince Brannon."

"There is something strange afoot and I think, as Alaine's close companion, you may have some answers about it."

Confused, Charlyn said nothing, but waited for him to continue.

"You remember that man with a dog that was at the inn on the first night of our journey? The next day, he warned us of the highwaymen following us. His name is Carver Vale. He went on his way, and the next time I saw him he was leading Alaine through the woods, turning out to be a member of the woodland clans. While we were with those people, I noticed that he and Alaine seemed to know each other. But how? I asked myself. He never showed up at the dinner at Middleoak, but Alaine came to the treehouse the next morning still wearing her evening clothes. She was very upset and continued in a foul mood all the way to the seacoast."

Charlyn was beginning to understand what Kent was getting at - Carver Vale – the man Alaine had confided about that day in the bath tent. Charlyn knew that something had happened the night of the dinner at Middleoak, and she suspected that Alaine had seen Carver. Yet, Alaine had never spoken of the woodsman again. In fact, the subject seemed to be unwelcome, so Charlyn hadn't asked any questions.

Kent continued his story in a louder voice, "When we were at the byway shops yesterday, the same man walked by the window, followed by his dog. I was surprised to see him. What was he doing there? He was gone before I could speak to him. Then, this morning, while on our ride escorting Alaine and Prince Brannon, who should step out onto the road but Flecher? You remember him - Carver's brother, and our guide through the forest? He had yet another brother with him today. And again, I ask myself, what are they doing here? We know that these people rarely leave the woods or associate with people outside of their clans. And yet, here they are!

"I've been thinking to myself, what reason would any of these woodsmen have for being here? What is happening *here* that would draw them? The Princess of Hawthorn is choosing a husband, that's what! I *know* that this has something to do with Alaine. Have you seen her with this man, Carver Vale?"

Based upon what she did know, Charlyn thought that Kent was right to put the two of them together. If the woodsmen were here in Harbortown, there might be something to Kent's concerns for Alaine.

"Charlyn, have you seen him?" Kent repeated.

"No, I have not seen him since that night at the inn," Charlyn answered, truthfully.

"But you *do* know something about this, don't you? Is there a plot for Alaine and Carver Vale to run away together? Or are these men here to kidnap Alaine?" Kent demanded, his voice rising.

"What?!" she exclaimed with distress. "I don't know of any such thing!"

"Charlyn, I think that you know *something* of this man, Carver, don't you?!"

"I cannot say," Charlyn responded, the redness coming to her face, offended by Kent's abusive tone of voice.

"If you know *anything*, you must tell me! This is not a jest, Charlyn. Alaine may be in danger!" Kent yelled, his voice echoing through the hallway.

Charlyn had quite enough of this. She raised her chin in defiance. She was now angry with Kent's treatment of her. To her dismay, tears flooded into her eyes.

"I have nothing to say, sir!" Charlyn stated adamantly, as she turned to go back up the stairs.

"Is anything amiss?" came a strong voice from behind them.

Charlyn and Kent spun around to find King Holum standing a very short distance away. They were so intent in their argument; they had not heard him approach. Both wondered how much he had heard, as they bowed before the King.

Holum came to stand next to Charlyn. He took in the girl's high color, and gently wiped a tear from her cheek.

"My dear, you must go up and finish your preparations for the garden party. My Queen has gone to great efforts having the garden readied for the guests," the Monarch said gently.

Charlyn realized that she was being dismissed, and once again curtsied to the King, before turning to rush up the stairs.

"Beautiful girl, even in tears," Holum remarked. "Now, come, Duke Morr-Leigh. It's time that you and I have a talk."

The King led the embarrassed younger man to his nearby hideaway.

Genna was stunned when she opened the hall door after hearing a light knocking. Queen Hester herself was standing at the threshold, with packages in her arms. The maid curtsied, widening the doorway, allowing the royal to pass.

Queen Hester entered the cozy sitting room, and the surprised Nana and Lady Avis immediately stood and curtsied. Charlyn came out of her room, composed after the hour to herself, dressed and ready for the garden party. She quickly bowed, also startled to see Her Majesty. The last to come into the room was Alaine, fresh from her bath, wearing only a thin, wraparound dressing gown. She, too, was amazed to see the Queen standing there.

"Aunt Hester," Alaine stammered, in a curtsy, "I apologize for my dress. I took a bath after my ride with Prince Brannon."

"How did that go?" Hester inquired, with curiosity.

"It was thick with fog which made it hard to see much of the countryside."

"I meant, with Prince Brannon?"

"I'm not sure, to be honest. He does not seem to be very enthusiastic regarding a match. He blames his father for going forward without concern for his wishes in the matter."

"Hmm," the Queen paused, "Though he is older than you, possibly he is too immature to understand the responsibilities that go with a royal title. I was engaged to your uncle at fourteen and had nothing to say in the matter. It is the price we pay, as you well know."

"May we offer you a cup of tea, Your Majesty?" Lady Avis interrupted, remembering manners.

"No thank you, Lady Avis," Hester answered, turning toward Alaine. "I am here to bring gifts, possibly to be used at this afternoon's festivities. The Marquis told me that you were rather rushed away from the byway shops yesterday. My royal dressmaker works closely with the shop owners and found out that you were looking at a particular fabric for a gown before you left. So, I had this made up for you. I hope that you like it," Hester said, handing Alaine a package wrapped in a thin paper.

Unwrapping the package, Alaine discovered a blush-rose bundle of material.

"Oh, this *is* the fabric that I was looking at - the pink of spring blossoms. It is wonderful!" Alaine exclaimed, holding the gown up to her body. "Thank you, Aunt Hester."

"You will need your layered underskirts, as the skirt does billow out," Hester advised. "Here is a little something to go with it," she said, handing Alaine a small box. "Your uncle and I wanted you to have it as a remembrance of us."

Alaine opened the box to find a tiny, rose-colored stone with a golden loop to allow for a chain or ribbon. It was a clear, multifaceted stone, cut in the shape of a heart.

"It is a ruby, perfect to wear on a ribbon at your throat."

"This is beautiful and goes so well with this gown. I will wear it today. Thank you, Aunt Hester, and please thank Uncle Holum. I will treasure it."

"Also, I have not forgotten you, Lady Charlyn. The King said that you were having a difficult morning. I hope this will cheer you up," Hester remarked, handing another package to Charlyn.

The girl quickly unwrapped the gift, to reveal the soft fabric that was a shawl with a pattern of white flowers with green leaves woven on a gray background. Charlyn had chosen her forest green gown trimmed in white lace for the garden party. She put the shawl around her shoulders and twirled around.

"I'll wear it with my dress!" Charlyn exclaimed, "It is elegant! Thank you, Queen Hester."

"You are welcome, my dear. We have been very pleased to have you here."

Then Hester turned to address Nana and Lady Avis. "Lady Avis, I hope that you are planning to join us this afternoon? I don't think Duke Seaken-Char will be happy unless you are there."

Lady Avis laughed, as did Alaine and Charlyn.

"Yes, of course I was planning on it. I'm looking forward to seeing the decorations in the garden," the Lady replied.

"Nurse McNiven, Ronan has told me that she has been sharing her sitting room with you. She has enjoyed the company."

"It was very kind of her to have me. It's a lovely room with plenty of light for my knitting," Nana responded.

"I would like to invite you to the garden party. Don't worry about your attire; this is a much less formal occasion. The Marquis has invited some of the merchants he deals with, and a few of the nobles are bringing their children. It should be a happy time for all, and you are welcome," Hester proclaimed. "And one more thing," after turning to take her leave, "Alaine, would you mind going down with the King and me? There are still several of my courtiers who would like to meet you."

"Yes, of course, Aunt Hester."

Once the Queen left, "*That* was unexpected," breathed Lady Avis. "I guess we had all better get ready to go down. Genna," she called, "help Alaine dress and fix her hair. She must be ready when Holum and Hester return!"

20
The Queen's Garden Party

The fog had lifted over the Queen's garden and the rays of the sun warmed the sea air. The garden was crowded with participants of all ages. Alaine received compliments from the King and the Queen on her new gown. The dress was made in the style of gowns being worn at the Irongate court: a swooping neckline, billowing sleeves, cinched waist, and full skirts. To please her aunt and uncle, she wore the ruby heart at her throat, held snugly in place by a pink ribbon tied at the back of her neck.

The Princess spent the required amount of time with her hosts, being introduced to many more people whose names she would never be able to remember. Prince Stenson had cleverly made his escape from the royal line and was at the lawn bowling alleys with a group of young people. Looking around, Alaine had to admit that the garden had been transformed into an outdoor fair. There was a booth with a puppet show for the children, jesters parading in costumes with bells, and a magician going from spot to spot with his tricks. A fortune teller sat in a little peeked tent, and a line of excited young ladies were waiting their turn with the forecaster.

Finally, after taking a moment to herself, Alaine found the drinks table and noticed Covey hovering nearby for the second time. Kent was behind it, she knew, but she ignored it. She carried her drink over to the great stone pad which was currently occupied by a group of musicians playing folksongs, near where tables and chairs were set out. Lady Avis, Nana, and Duke Seaken-Char were enjoying the atmosphere. Alaine joined them at the table, glad for a chance to sit down.

"How is it that you are alone, Princess, with all of these handsome young men wandering around?" Duke Seaken-Char jested.

"It seems that Prince Sturgrom and Prince Brannon are otherwise occupied. Even the excellently dressed Marquis is nowhere to be found. So I am on my own, except for Covey, of course. He has been hanging close by, probably on Kent's orders."

"We've seen Prince Sturgrom with his entourage," Lady Avis added. "It seems he has developed many friendships since he's been here. The courtiers all admire him."

"Good for trade. Good for Hawthorn to have relations with his northern country of Swerd," the Duke stated, referring to diplomacy.

"Yes, but all of the courtiers around him are at least ten years older than me. I am sure that he looks upon me as a child," Alaine surmised, woefully.

"Prince Brannon always seems to be surrounded by the young ladies. I'm not sure if he is pursuing them or they are trying to entice him. He's certainly taking advantage of his visit to Irongate, not to mention his enjoyment of the wine," put in Lady Avis, her disapproval of the man barely hidden.

"I don't care to think of this any further right now, with tomorrow's betrothal ceremony hanging over my head. Though my choices for husbands are few, more numbers of suitors would not make the decision any easier," Alaine expressed, with some sorrow. Changing the subject, "Where is Charlyn? I have not seen her. Is she with Kent?"

"No, she came down with us and is here someplace," replied Nana. "Something happened between Charlyn and Kent this morning which I have still not sorted out," Lady Avis relayed.

"While you were in the bath, Alaine, she received a note from Kent and suddenly went out of the rooms. Returning a short time later, Charlyn seemed upset. I believe she was crying. Speaking to no one, she went into her room and didn't come out until Queen Hester's visit."

"A lover's spat, no doubt," the Duke guessed, taking a draught of his ale. "It is clear they are taken with one another."

"Dear me, I feel I have been so focused on myself that I haven't been a good friend to Charlyn, especially if she is in distress. I will try to find her," Alaine declared, leaving her chair. "Where *is* Kent, anyway?"

"No one has seen him," his mother replied. "Maybe you *should* try to find Charlyn. I don't like the idea of her being miserable and feeling alone. Irongate is a long way from Darkwood Lodge and her family."

"I will check the rooms first and come back down if she's not there," Alaine assured her.

True to her word, Alaine hastily made her way to their suite. Genna was there, bored at being left alone again, wishing to leave to meet with Rand. But Lady Avis was adamant that their rooms not be left unattended, so she sat by the fireplace doing some sewing on one of Alaine's slips.

"Have you seen Charlyn?" Alaine demanded, short of breath after running up the stairs.

"No," Genna answered, wondering what was going on. "She left with your aunt and Nana and hasn't been back."

"No one else has been here?" Alaine probed, thinking of Carver Vale and the wooden feather that was left on her pillow previously.

"No, milady, I have been alone here."

Alaine left Genna to her tasks and rushed back down the stairs. At the side doors leading to the garden, who should be waiting, but Covey!

"Good afternoon, Sergeant. You are certainly underfoot today," she addressed the man, while holding up a hand to deter his comment. "Don't tell me. It was the Captain that told you to keep an eye on me. Where *is* he?"

"Last I spoke to him, he was going into Harbortown," Covey answered.

"Harbortown! Why would he go there today?!"

"He did not say, Princess. He was out of sorts and had something on his mind."

"Oh, never mind," she said, dismissively. "Have you seen Lady Charlyn? I'm trying to find her."

"No, I've not seen her since she came down with Lady Avis."

"All right. I'll keep looking. She's not in the rooms, so she must be in the garden."

Alaine went out onto the steps, where she had a view of the full length of the garden. The smell of food was in the air. More tables had been set up on one of the larger lawns, and the serving tables were laden with platters. People were moving toward the food. Alaine began searching through the people, looking for Charlyn's blonde head and green gown. It was then that she saw Prince Stenson coming up the steps toward her.

"I have a message for you," the Prince blurted out, when he reached her.

"What?" Alaine asked, with surprise.

"It was odd," the young Prince relayed. "I was over at the archery bales with a friend. A couple castle guards are helping the ladies use the bows and arrows. Then a man came up to me. He looked like a noble, but I've never seen him before. He asked me if I could fetch you because he had an important message for you."

Carver Vale, Alaine thought at once! "Did he have a beard?"

"No, now that you mention it. Do you know him?"

"I'm not sure, but I must see him."

"Come, I'll go with you," Stenson offered.

"I can't go. Sergeant Covey is watching my every move. He would follow us."

"Not if we get in the serving line with the rest of the courtiers."

"I can't eat right now…"

"No, we'll go get in the line. The Sergeant will think he knows where we are, and then we'll slip away when he's not looking."

Alaine smiled, "You are a devious young man."

"I have to be, around this place. Come on," he urged.

Following Stenson's plan, they were able to get away, and strode to where the archery bales were set up at the back of the garden.

There were several nobles taking their shots. Shouts would come up whenever someone's arrow hit the target.

In the background, by a large cypress bush, a man lingered. He wore a gray hat with a maroon feather at the band. His cloak, tied with a thick cord at his throat, was a deep purple and pulled back over one shoulder. His light shirt was covered with a green vest. His pants and high boots were shades of brown. Alaine knew at once that it was not Carver Vale.

"Wait here," she told Prince Stenson.

The man saw Alaine and rightfully assumed that this was the Princess. He started walking toward her, as she went to him. They both stopped a few feet apart, taking a moment to appraise one another.

Alaine didn't know exactly who he was, but her instinct told her of his family. The man was shorter than Carver, his hair was the same color with some white strands, and there was the similarity with Carver and Flecher. As with all of the woodsmen, his face was free of facial hair - no beard. His mouth was wide, with thin lips closed as he studied her. As with most of the people of the forest clans, the eyes were large, gray, with flecks of blue under thick lashes. There were lines at the corners of the eyes and near the mouth indicating a more mature age than Carver.

"Another brother?" she guessed. "How many of you are there?"

"Yes," his soft voice replied. "There are seven of us. I am Lignin. I'm next oldest to Bole, where Carver is the youngest." He paused. "My brother seems to think that you would be willing to take him as a husband. That would be quite unheard of among both our peoples. Yet my brothers and I are here to help him. He asks that you do not make a choice of husbands until he can speak with you."

"He will be too late, I'm afraid," Alaine said, with regret. "There is a ceremony tomorrow, in front of the entire court of Irongate. I must make a choice for a husband. It is my duty to my parents. I am a princess and cannot marry whomever I choose."

"Do you love my brother?"

"I don't know him well, but I must admit that I am drawn to him and wish to be with him. It is as if we have known each other for a long time. I don't really know what love is, but my heart is with him, and I will never forget him, no matter whom I marry," Alaine confessed.

"That is enough for me to know," Lignin announced. "You must do what my brother asks and not make a choice until he can speak with you. We have a plan. Also, he asked me to give you this key, and says to keep it with you tomorrow. Have a restful night, Princess, because tomorrow will be a memorable day."

"Alaine!"

The Princess heard Kent's voice calling to her. She quickly tucked the small key on a string into her bodice before turning to see him and Covey approaching with wide strides. Prince Stenson took a quick path away, predicting trouble from the Duke's tone of voice.

"Who was that man you were speaking with?" Kent demanded.

"He is a noble, I believe," Alaine answered, as if they were speaking of the weather.

"Where did he get off to? Covey, go try to find him. I wish to speak to him."

Alaine turned to look, but the man was nowhere to be seen. Quickness seemed to run in the family, she thought. Alaine knew Covey's search would prove fruitless. Unfazed, she could hold her own with Kent.

"Where have you been all day?" she demanded. "And what did you say to Charlyn to upset her this morning? I haven't been able to find her, and your mother said she was crying."

"I have been in town on the business of *your* protection. And here you are, speaking with strange courtiers without a chaperone."

"Prince Stenson was with me. I am safe enough here in the Queen's garden, I think. Besides, what is in Harbortown regarding my protection? I know no one there. If there were anyone to fear, they would be here, today, risking the wrath of King Holum."

"I wished to find Flecher in Harbortown, to ask him about his business here. He knew of our plans and our reasons for coming to Irongate. I am fearful that he may have plans that somehow affect your betrothal. Alas, my hunt was fruitless. I couldn't find him."

"I believe that you are overwrought, cousin, and are chasing ghosts. You cannot assume that the woodsmen's business in

Harbortown has anything to do with me. By the end of the day tomorrow, I will be engaged," Alaine remarked, with dismay.

"Have you made your choice?"

"No, I have not, but whomever my choice, I am destined to leave behind all that I know and love."

Alaine's words struck home. For the first time, Kent understood her dilemma. He had been so focused on getting her to Irongate safely that he had missed the point that she would be leaving, possibly not to be seen again as she resided in a faraway land. Maybe she was right about chasing ghosts, when the real issue was that she would choose a husband and soon be gone. A sadness overtook him as he realized how much he wished not to lose her from his life. As troublesome as she was at times, she was family.

Meanwhile, Alaine pressed the hidden key to her breast and held onto a thin sliver of hope. What did Carver have to say, she wondered? Would he be too late? How could it possibly change anything? If he did come, at least she would see him one more time, and have a chance to say goodbye.

Charlyn sat in a room that looked like a library, having shelves lined with scrolls of parchment and rare books. Colorful maps were draped over wooden stands. Her chair was padded, placed next to one of the windows overlooking the castle parkland. The rays of afternoon sunlight spiked their way through the treetops. There was little movement in the landscape - only an occasional bird fluttering from here to there.

Earlier, she had come downstairs with Nana and Lady Avis. The tall doors were all open, leading to the garden, which was transformed for the day's activities. They were quickly joined by Duke Seaken-Char, who must have been watching for them. They proceeded to make the obligatory stroll to the end of the grounds and back. Charlyn listened to the conversation but said little. Once they returned to the wide porch-like steps near the doorway, she gave a reason to leave, and excused herself. Kent was absent from the garden, adding to her concern about their budding relationship.

Was he avoiding her? What happened that morning was their first quarrel. Not that she hadn't seen him angry before, but the anger had never been directed toward her. She felt heartsick and just wanted to be alone.

Once inside Irongate, Charlyn wandered along the front hall, looking for a place to sit by herself. Never having previously gone as far as the second staircase that led to the west wing of bedrooms, curiosity overtook her. At the end of the hall were more tall, closed doors. She looked over her shoulder to make sure there was no one around, as she opened one to peek inside. So, this was the great hall, she thought. Its beauty had been spoken of at dinner. This was where the betrothal ceremony was to be held. It was an expansive, rectangular space with a polished stone floor, high, painted ceiling, and a raised dais at the far end holding the royal thrones. Extravagant windows lined one side of the room, letting in golden light. The center aisle was designated with wooden posts and thick velvet ropes. The room could hold a large crowd of courtiers, to be sure. Had Alaine seen the room where her fate would be decided? Charlyn wondered.

Feeling brave, she continued into the depths of the west wing, opening doors and looking into empty rooms. Finally, entering a room at the end of the hallway, she found a view of the outside park, with chairs strategically placed for reading or gazing out the long windows.

Now, looking out the nearby glass, she thought about going home to Darkwood Lodge. She did wish to see her mother but had no desire to take her place back in the suite of rooms shared with her younger sisters. On her return, she would request her own room, feeling far beyond any childish whims. There was no thought of the handsome squire, once pined for. With her heart on the verge of breaking over the loss of Kent's admiration – and could she say, love – Charlyn knew that she was a child no longer. Thinking of all the tender moments with Kent and how she looked forward to being with him every day, a future at Darkwood Lodge seemed bleak.

The afternoon passed, and gradually the sun dipped beneath the castle walls, and the light began to fade. Charlyn became lonely and restless. Putting aside the misery, she felt an urge to find Kent and make things right between them. Even if their friendship didn't end in a stronger bond, there was still time to find joy in each day, and the time left to be with him. Suddenly, in a hurry, she was out of the chair and out the door, with no looking back.

Soon, Charlyn paused at the top of the wide steps that led to the garden. There was a change in the atmosphere from earlier in the afternoon. Two footmen were going about, lighting the lines of torches that appeared less noticeable in the sunlight. The glowing pathways were being prepared for the night. The children were gone, rushed off for their dinners and early bed after the high-spirited day. The lawns in front of the steps were filled with tables of courtiers dallying over their food and drinks, in no hurry to be off. Music came from a distance, and couples paraded arm-in-arm up and down the walkways, enjoying the twilight. The soft murmur of voices floated in the air.

Seeing the table where drinks were served, Charlyn realized she was thirsty, and made her way there, all the while looking for Kent or Lady Avis. Even Alaine was not about. She saw King Holum and Queen Hester going from table to table, interacting with their guests. A minstrel ambled along the front walk. Accepting a small glass of cider from the server, she watched as Prince Brannon approached her.

"Lady Charlyn, how are you enjoying the garden party?"

"It is well done, I think," she responded.

"Where is the Princess and the rest of your party?"

"I'm not sure. I have been looking for Lady Avis and Duke Morr-Leigh."

While having his wine cup filled, he offered, "I will help you find them. Have you been down the walkway?"

"No, I just came out. I spent part of the afternoon inside."

"Come, we will search through the tables to the back of the garden. I've gotten a good look of the place since I've been here and know it well."

Charlyn followed Prince Brannon, stopping frequently at individual tables, but not finding her company. Then they went on some of the less-traveled garden paths where the light was fading, with fewer torches lit.

"Over in the corner there, behind those tall hedges, is an amphitheater with grass-covered benches. The ladies bring their cushions to sit on when there is entertainment. There is a statue of Old King Holmes, Holum's father. I was told King Holmes established a garrison of guards here long before the castle was built. That's why the guardhouse and stables are so large. They have been here for ages. This place was originally a fortress," relayed Prince Brannon.

"Why would there be a fortress here?" Charlyn asked.

"The harbor. It is a prime spot for an invasion. Ships can come in and offload their soldiers. The old King kept the coastline well-guarded. That's why three of the dukes have their castles on the seacoast."

"Interesting."

"Behind this row of bushes is another secret of the garden. There is a fountain and a small pool. One of the young ladies showed it to me. Evidently, they go there in the afternoon to practice their drawing. Do you draw?"

"Only a little and not very well, I'm afraid. My youngest sister is the artist in the family."

Falling into a silence, as they followed the pathway, Charlyn was beginning to feel uncomfortable, wanting to go to the more lighted part of the garden. Those she sought wouldn't be found in this desolate area. The Prince was obviously impaired by the wine. His gait was not steady; moving from side to side on the walkway, he had bumped into her more than once. What he was saying was making sense, but his words were sometimes slurred.

"I would like to go up to the flagstone pad where the music is playing. I believe Lady Avis and the Princess may be there," she bravely requested.

"We will go that way, but first there is one more place I would like to show you. It is just ahead, by those tall bushes. Come, there is a surprise at the center."

The Prince led Charlyn along the circular path which opened into a garden room with curved walls of hedge. A statue of a lady holding a basket of flowers stood at the middle of the space. Benches for sitting were placed around the perimeter of the circular garden space. The area was poorly illuminated by a couple of nearby torches.

"Here, sit down," the Prince suggested, while taking a seat. "I must rest for a while."

"Actually, there is not enough light here. I wish to get back," she complained, refusing to sit.

"Back to Morr-Leigh? Tell me, is it that you are engaged to the young Duke?"

"What? Oh no, no - we are not engaged. He is the son of Lady Avis and the captain of the garrison that traveled with us from Hawthorn Castle. Most of the soldiers are waiting for our return near Eckelform Hall at Leggot."

"You seem to be much in the Duke's company. Is there a romantic attachment between you?"

Charlyn was becoming more and more uncomfortable with Brannon, wondering if she should just leave the man sitting on the bench. She also disliked his line of questioning regarding Kent.

"We have not known each other very long but have been enlisted in our duties to Princess Alaine. We have become friends," she answered. Then, "I believe it is best for us to leave here and get back to the party."

"I enjoy the privacy here. I get tired of people watching my every move," he replied. "You are of marrying age. Do you have any prospects at home?"

Now Charlyn was annoyed and a little fearful. She had allowed him to lead her to a secluded spot. How could she leave without causing a problem? she wondered, as the Prince continued to ask personal questions.

"Do you have a suitor for your hand? Have you ever been kissed…?"

The courtiers had put up their bows and arrows due to the impending darkness. Alaine and Kent were on the path coming back from the archery bales. They walked in silence, both deep in their own thoughts. Torches were being lit, shining intermittent, golden circles on the path.

Suddenly a lady's screams cut through the evening's peace. Kent was immediately aware that the cries of distress were coming from a nearby hedge grove. He pulled the Morr-Leigh dagger from its sheath at his belt and rushed towards the ongoing commotion. Alaine, not to be left behind, ran after him.

As the two came around the opening in the hedge, they saw Charlyn pushing Prince Brannon away from an embrace. Kent was transfixed and shocked to see the scene before him. Alaine quickly realized the situation. She knew Kent and his temper could get to a dangerous level in an instant. Her cousin would have no problem running the man through with his dagger - Prince or no Prince.

Alaine ran to Charlyn, standing in front of her and the stumbling Bran- non.

"Kent, no!" she yelled in panic. "Put that away! He's drunk!"

"I'll have his liver!"

Charlyn let out another scream, this time in fear of what was happening before her.

"Kent! Stop! Think about what you are doing!" Alaine called, remaining in front of Charlyn and Brannon, as Kent charged forward.

"What is going on here?!" came a strong, demanding voice.

All stopped in place and turned to see King Holum, backed by the Marquis and several noblemen. Holum quickly gathered as much evidence as he needed.

"Sheath that blade, Morr-Leigh! There will be no killing here tonight!" the King commanded.

Alaine bent and retrieved Charlyn's shawl from the ground and handed it to her distressed Lady. Charlyn quickly put it over her bare shoulder, covering where her dress had been torn. More nearby courtiers poured into the circular space. The garden statue bowed her head looking at her flower basket. There was a silence in the ring as all present awaited Holum's words.

"Prince Brannon, dare you accost a Lady at my court? Has King Ryan raised you with no manners, sir?" Holum asked but allowing no time for the Prince to answer. "I have grown tired of your overindulgence and bad behavior. My guards will accompany you to your rooms to pack your belongings and leave the Irongate grounds tonight! And they will carry a letter from me to your father, to be delivered by your ship's captain. You will leave this land on the morning's tide. Be gone with you!"

Two guardsmen who had responded to the ruckus, took the chastised Brannon by each arm and led him away.

"Lady Charlyn, are you alright?" King Holum asked.

"Yes, Your Majesty. I am so sorry for the trouble," the girl replied, in a weak voice.

"You have nothing to be sorry for, my dear," Holum assured, in a comforting manner. "The man is a lout, trying to take advantage of your good nature. It seems that the stars have been aligned against you today. Princess, would you escort your Lady upstairs? Duke," the King ordered Kent, "find Lady Avis and apprise her that her charges are in need of her. I fear that the evening's festivities have come to an early end."

At the sight of Brannon being hauled away, the news of what had happened spread like wildfire through all those courtiers left in the garden. It became clear that the Queen's garden party had come to an end.

21

An Anxious Night

The King soon left the scene of the skirmish, followed by the courtiers, after Alaine hurried off with Charlyn. Kent remained, taking a seat on a bench, with his head hung down. The scorching anger had dissipated. The Marquis, who had remained behind, felt for the man and came to stand by him.

"Come, we will find Lady Avis," he persuaded, placing a hand of sup- port on Kent's shoulder.

"This was all my fault. Charlyn and I argued this morning…again, at my prompting. I was worried about Alaine and went on an errand to Harbortown to question a man we met by chance on our ride with Prince Brannon this morning. He is a recent acquaintance whom, I fear, may have unfavorable plans related to Alaine and the betrothal ceremony. I couldn't find him. I *should* have remained at Irongate. I *should* have stayed with Charlyn and escorted her to the garden party. This would have never happened if I had stayed."

"You saved the girl from any real harm. Don't blame yourself. I've been watching Brannon throughout the time that I've been here. There is no doubt that some of the other noble ladies have fallen into his trap. He is a spoiled, selfish cad, so it is good to be rid of him.

He would have never made a fit husband for the Princess Alaine," the Marquis related.

"Come, man, let us find your mother and the Duke Seaken-Char before they hear of the events from another source."

Learning of the incident with Prince Brannon and Charlyn from her distraught son, Lady Avis left him in the company of Duke Seaken-Char and the Marquis, the last of which delivered a cup of whiskey for the younger duke.

The Lady hurried to the east wing, apprehensive over what she might find once she reached the rooms. Entering the chamber, she saw much fussing from Nana, trying to console the sobbing Charlyn, with Alaine sitting beside the girl, holding her hand.

"Take a few sips of the wine, dear," Nana requested, thrusting the silver goblet into Charlyn's free hand. "It will calm your nerves. I'm sure that all will be well tomorrow."

"It will not," choked Charlyn, between sobs. "I'm a disgrace at court. My father will hear of this. All will be speaking of me with disfavor tomorrow."

"Charlyn, I'm still unsure of what happened between you and Prince Brannon, and I need to know so I can support you," Lady Avis asked, as she took a seat. Then, "Nana, where is Genna?"

"I said that I would remain in the rooms so she could spend some time with Rand. I thought that it would cause no harm," the nurse replied.

"That is fine," replied Lady Avis, giving Charlyn some time to compose herself. "Charlyn?"

After a moment, Charlyn began her story.

"I spent most of the afternoon inside because I was out of sorts over the quarrel I had with Kent this morning. Later, I came out to the garden, trying to find him, desiring to make things right between us. Prince Brannon approached me and offered to help me search for you and Kent. All was well at first, as we walked through the garden. The Prince was pointing out some of the garden attractions, but I soon became aware that he had drunk too much wine and asked to return to the front of the garden.

"He said that he had one more thing to show me and led me to a secluded circle of high hedges. I wanted to leave, but he ignored my request. It was getting dark, and I became fearful.

"All at once, he stood up, grabbed me by the shoulders, and tried to kiss me. The more I tried to push him off, the more determined he became. I was frightened and desperate for help. I began to scream, hoping that someone would come to help me. Kent and Alaine must have been nearby because they were the first to arrive. Kent had his blade drawn and went after Brannon. Alaine was yelling at Kent, trying to stop him from harming the Prince. Then the King, the Marquis and some other nobles came to my aid.

"King Holum must have seen my torn gown and accused Brannon. Before the man could answer for himself, the King banned him from the court, saying that Prince Brannon must leave tonight! Two guards took him away.

"I was so foolish to go with the man alone. I should have seen that he'd had too much to drink. I put myself in a shameful situation. Now, I am disgraced, and I've brought dishonor to my family," Charlyn finished, and the tears began anew.

"Put away your tears, Charlyn," Lady Avis advised. "You are not disgraced, although you will probably be the talk of Irongate for the next few days. There is nothing the courtiers like more than a juicy tale. King Holum is the hero of this story in that he defended you. No one will dare go against him. Now, sip your wine. You have had a narrow escape."

Then to Nana, "Go down to the kitchen and ask for a maid to carry up some broth and rolls for the girls. I doubt that either of them has had much to eat since breakfast. They should have something in their stomachs before they go to bed. Tomorrow will be another demanding day. We must make an early night of it."

The seven brothers sat around the kitchen and main room of the small house they rented in Harbortown. They finished a meal of bread, greens and broiled sausages. Each man held a cup of varied contents between wine, mead and cider.

Carver had eaten little.

The mad rush to obtain clothes and boots appropriate to present themselves at King Holum's court was complete. The nearby shops would need to restock their shelves of the finery bought with Bole's gold coin. Surely, the tailor and his apprentices would catch up on their sleep tonight.

Two carriages with horses were hired for the next day. Lignin believed that they would be able to gain passage onto the Irongate grounds. With so many nobles flocking to the castle for the betrothal ceremony, there shouldn't be a problem, especially once they were dressed in their elaborate new clothes, to pass as the nobility that they were.

Carver sat alone, listening to bits of conversations among his brothers. He was quiet, with nothing to say. He thought that so many things could go wrong the next day.

What if King Holum denied their entrance to the hall and sent them away? The main question was, would they arrive in time, before the Princess chose a husband?

If they were in time, what if Alaine *didn't* say 'yes' to his proposal? All these things circled through his head as he absentmindedly petted Astra.

Astra! What should they do with her? He would have to fetch her a bone and leave her in the house with the hope that they didn't end up in the Irongate dungeons.

The gift Carver had made for Alaine sat in the middle of the table. He had worked late into several nights to finish it. A soft velvet was purchased to line the inside shelves and drawers. He had stained the wood with the brown juice of forest mushrooms, bringing out the grain and detailed crevasses in the wood. The hinges were of polished brass, as well as the small metal lock that hung from a ring in the latch. Specifically made for her, he hoped that Alaine would be pleased with the gift.

"You are very quiet tonight, Carver," Jute commented, interrupting his brother's thoughts. "Are you having second thoughts?"

Jute, closest to Carver in age, spent many years at their father's manse during their growing years. Soon after, he had taken up his heritage of managing the expanse of woodland in the north of the Hawthorn land mass. Though dissimilar in looks, Jute and Carver were close, and supportive of each other in the face of the band of older brothers.

"No, no second thoughts about Alaine. I have loved her for a long while. I am just fearful of the outcome at Irongate. If I get there in time to ask for her hand, I believe that she will accept me. Then what? *That* is the question."

"Soon we will all know. King Holum knows of The Treaty of the Trees. And he knows of our clans residing in the forest lands. He holds the key as to how this will turn out, as does his brother, King Granth. Either of them could forbid the match. Put your fears away for the night, at least. We will all be there with you tomorrow."

Carver had come to agree with Lignin. The proposal to Alaine must be done in a proper manner if he had any hope of peacefully gaining her hand. Tomorrow would be the most important day of his life. Was he ready? he asked himself.

Lady Avis shooed both the girls off to their rooms once they had eaten, and neither complained.

Alaine undressed and sat cross-legged on the bed in her nightgown. Her gown for the ceremony hung from the top of the wardrobe, already steamed free of wrinkles, lustrous in its cream-colored fabrics and seed pearls. Genna had laid out all but her jewels, including the delicate slippers, embroidered with tiny flowers over the arches. The royal sash of the Hawthorn Kingdom hung by itself over the back of a chair. The day of the fateful decision was upon her.

Her gaze wandered to the little key on a string resting on the dressing table. An urge came over her to, once again, see the tiny figurines Carver had given her. Going to the trunk where they were hidden, she rummaged for the bag tucked into the lower front corner.

One by one, Alaine pulled the little figures out of the canvas bag: the rabbit, the dog - Astra, the fawn, the feather, and the little box with the heart stained red. She carried them back to the bed and placed them in a line on the bedside table near the candles, where the detail could be seen. Then, studying each one, she remembered Carver with the small, curved knife in his hand, working on the fawn. Alaine sighed. She thought of his hands, his touch, and his embrace the night he kissed her by the lake. Her thoughts were interrupted as a tapping came from the closed chamber door.

"Come in," Alaine called.

Charlyn entered, also dressed in her nightclothes, hair streaming down her back. She closed the door and came to the bed.

"I couldn't sleep," said the girl, with eyes still puffy from crying. "Oh, is that the dress?" she exclaimed, seeing the hanging gown.

"Yes, that's the dress. Mother designed it. Days were spent sewing on the pearls around the bodice and the bottoms of the sleeves. I must have tried it on ten times while they were trying to get the length and the fit right."

"It's wonderful. I've never seen such a beautiful gown."

"You must wear your lovely, rose gown tomorrow and stand with me. I cannot bear to be alone."

"As you wish," Charlyn agreed, smiling. "What are those?" she asked, noticing the figurines on the bedside table.

"Carver made them and gave them to me. The last one, the feather, I found here on my pillow, the night of the banquet. So I knew that he was nearby. Genna said that no one entered the rooms that night. I have no idea how it came to be here."

"Maybe he paid a servant to bring it. They come in and out of the rooms."

"Yes, maybe," Alaine said, trying to envision it. "Tell me, what was it that happened between you and Kent this morning?"

"He sent me a note calling me downstairs. When I met him, he began asking questions about Carver Vale. It seems that he saw Carver in Harbortown yesterday. Then, this morning, he met Fletcher on the ride with Prince Brannon. Kent is suspicious that their being here has something to do with you. He even mentioned a kidnapping plan. He wanted to know what I knew about you and Carver."

"What did you tell him?"

"I told him that I hadn't seen Carver since the night at the inn and that I knew nothing of any such plans. Kent was being quite loud in the hallway when King Holum came and interrupted us. The King dismissed me. What happened after that, I am not sure."

"I *do* feel that Carver is in Harbortown," commented Alaine, "as well as some of his brothers. One of them came to the garden today during the party. He sent Stenson to fetch me. He gave me this key and hinted at a plan for tomorrow. He urged me not to make a choice for a husband until Carver could speak to me. I told his brother that it would be too late, as I must make a choice at the ceremony."

"When have you seen him since the night at the inn?"

"I met him the night we were camped in the field at the little bench overlooking the pool. I saw him again the night of Genna's wedding and went with him to a small treehouse in the woods near where we were camped. He guided me through the woods the day Kent and his men went to find the soldiers who hadn't returned from the hunt. Carver's brother, Bole, was holding them captive when Carver and I arrived. At my request, Bole released the men and had them led back to the road. We stayed behind at Bole's treehouse, and Flecher was also there. It was then that we learned of the Old Road that went through the forest, and on to the seacoast. The two older brothers agreed to ask permission from their clans to allow us to use their road. And, well, you know the rest.

"I met Carver again after the dinner at Middleoak. That night I will never forget," she spoke wistfully. "I believed that he loved me."

"But you were so angry for days after and have not spoken of Carver."

"Yes, I was angry with him. It seems that every time I met with him; my jewelry went missing. First, the broach, then the amethyst necklace, and lastly, the emerald necklace the night at Middleoak. Alas, I have fallen in love with a thief! Yet, I don't understand it all and I can't get him out of my mind. Tomorrow, I must choose between Prince Sturgrom and the Marquis if the gossip is true, and he comes forward with a proposal. This key on a string is my only hope, and only a wisp of a hope it is. What does Carver think he can do?"

"Lady Avis has told me that you cannot be forced to marry against your will."

"That may be true, but I believe if I refuse, I must have a well-founded objection. What would that be? Both Prince Sturgrom and the Marquis are good men who have much to offer me as a husband. If they make an honest proposal, I have a duty to my mother and father to make a choice. There is no escape from it. I will leave my heart here by the lake at Middleoak when I go off with my new husband."

"Oh, Alaine, I am so sorry. I wish that I could be of help. I know that my father will have much to say when I marry. I can only wish that it will be someone that I love."

"What of Kent?"

"I do love being with him and look forward to seeing him every day, but he hasn't spoken any words of love or made promises pertaining to the future."

"Sometimes he is detached when it comes to women. Yet I have never seen him so enticed since he met you. I believe that he won't want to lose you. Right now, I think that *I am* his main concern. He must answer to my father."

"It is my hope that you are right. I think that my father may approve a match, but only time will tell…"

Irongate's rooms were filled to the top beams with guests awaiting the following day's ceremony. The kitchens would be bustling throughout the night with food preparations for the celebration. Many villagers were hired to help with the festivities. The Majestic Hall was cleaned and draped in flowers and garland, ready for the influx of nobles.

The evening in the garden had ended earlier than planned on the order of King Holum. He had gone to his study to write a letter to King Ryan. It was to be delivered tonight to Prince Brannon's ship captain, with a note demanding that they depart on the morning tide.

Queen Hester stood with the Marquis in the thinning reception hall, listening to his story recapping the events in the garden.

Hester smiled with pleasure at the news of one less prince in the line of prospects for Alaine.

"Holum never liked the man, and both of us hoped that Alaine would not be taken with his handsome face," she commented.

"I agree that he did not seem to be a good match for her, if I do say so myself."

"This puts you in a stronger position, Felix. Is your proposal prepared? Do you have an engagement gift ready?" Hester asked.

"Of course, I have taken care of all that. I believe that she will like the gift, as it cost much coin. I chose it with great thought, thinking that it must be fit for *my* wife. It is a necklace with a golden chain and a pendant of jade. The pendent is a dragon surrounded with flowers. I bought it from a trader who brought it from the Far East. It is uniquely carved jade stone and is said to bring good luck. To go with it is a bolt of light-green silk for a gown."

"That sounds exquisite. It should show her that she can expect to live well, should she choose you as a husband."

"I don't think there will be any objections from her family. You and Holum have supported me, and I have gained a good rapport with her aunt, Lady Avis, and Duke Morr-Leigh," Felix surmised.

"Well, we shall soon see. Prince Sturgrom certainly has his merit with the promise that Alaine will one day be a queen, and their children will be heirs to the throne. That is something you cannot offer.

"Even though I have tried to speak of it, the girl withdraws and shows no interest in discussing it. It is unknown what is going on in her head. You must do your best tomorrow."

"I will, cousin. I bid you a good night and will see you in the morning."

In her room, behind the closed door, Alaine was not the only person searching the bottom of her trunk for something of importance.

Lady Avis was trying to find the scrolled Marriage Contract that will need to be agreed upon prior to any marriage ceremony.

At last she found it, next to King Granth's Will of Succession. The latter she would deliver to King Holum with its seal unbroken prior to leaving Irongate.

Avis believed that once Alaine made her choice, the Marriage Contract would be needed. Alaine's choice of husbands must meet the requirements of the contract.

Also, the proposed husband had a right to know of the dowry that would come with the marriage.

The Marriage Contract would need to be signed by Alaine and the proposed spouse and witnesses.

The Lady sat in the bedside chair as she untied the ribbon and unfurled the document containing King Granth's royal seal.

There had been much discussion at Hawthorn between King Granth and Queen Iris prior to the final approval of the terms.

Lady Avis shifted in her seat to catch the candlelight as she began to read the flourished script of Squire Dilford:

Contract for the Marriage of Princess Alaine of Hawthorn

Let it be known prior to the marriage of the Princess Alaine of Hawthorn that the husband of the Princess will not have a claim to The Throne of Hawthorn of Eastgreen Highlands. Male heirs of the Princess will have claim to The Throne of Hawthorn with the majority approval by the Council of Hawthorn in accordance with my Will of Succession. So says I, King Granth of Hawthorn.

Let it be known that Alaine, Princess of Hawthorn, shall not be forced to marry against her will.

Let it be known that the prospective spouse to the Princess Alaine will be of noble blood and will provide evidence of nobility.

Let it be known that the dowry of the Princess Alaine will consist of the following:

- 500 pieces of gold to be paid by the Hawthorn Monarchy upon the marriage.
- 100 pieces of gold to be paid on the day of the summer solstice, 50 pieces of which are to be for the personal use of Alaine to maintain her household.
- All personal clothing and jewels belonging to Alaine. Jewels to be held in the personal possession of Alaine throughout her lifetime.
- 100 crates of sheep wool and 10 crates of goose down.

- 200 rabbit pelts, 50 beaver pelts, 25 deer hides, and 25 bear skins.
- 50 lugs salted, dried meats, 50 wheels assorted cheeses, 1-barrel pickled eggs 100 bags fine ground wheat flour, 100 bags fine ground oat flour.
- 10 boxes fine white salt, 10 boxes assorted spices and herbs 50 barrels dried nuts and berries.
- 20 barrels honey, 20 barrels tree syrup.
- 2 trunks fine linens for table and bed, one gilded looking glass.
- 20 silver plates and spoons, 2 silver candelabras, 10 silver candleholders.

Commodities to be delivered prior to the first summer solstice after the marriage.

Signed by Proposed Spouse: Signed by Princess Alaine:

_______________________   _______________________

Signed by Noble Witness: Signed by Noble Witness:

_______________________   _______________________

So says I, King Granth of Hawthorn. So says the Council of Hawthorn.

Lady Avis could not prevent the tears coming to her eyes as she furled the document and replaced the green velvet ribbon. It was all so formal, and so final. How could she say goodbye to this child? Never again to see her at Juniper Lodge. Never to see her children playing in the garden. As for her sister and Granth, what a hole in their lives Alaine's loss will leave. Things will never be the same…

She took hold of her wine goblet and drank. The Lady knew that she must get some sleep before the fateful day ahead.

As two girls will do, Alaine and Charlyn talked into the night. They spoke of the men. They discussed love and what it is. They spoke of their fears that love would be lost for them. Both had tasted its nectar and longed for more, yet it was fleeting and just out of reach. Then, when all topics were exhausted, Charlyn went off to her bed, leaving Alaine to herself.

Alaine was physically and emotionally exhausted. It seemed such a long time since she had dressed that morning for her ride with Prince Brannon. In fact, the busy few days at Irongate merged into a long blur. Not that she wasn't thankful that her aunt and uncle had done everything to make her time at Irongate memorable.

Stenson. Alaine was so proud of her cousin and happy for the chance to know him as he matured. She believed he would make a fine king one day. Then there was Kent – more like a brother – she would miss him. She hoped he would see that he could pick no one better than Charlyn for his bride.

The candles waned on their pedestals, to be blown out by the girl in the bed. For now, not a princess. Just a girl with one last night to think about the one with the green eyes. She was still propped against the pillows, as her eyelids drooped in the darkness. She fought against sleep, not wanting the night to end; but, at last, sleep overtook her.

Soon she was lost in dreams. They were clear and in color as she moved through them from one scene to another. At first, standing alone in a bedroom at Hawthorn Castle, the rug on the floor and the quilt on the bed were familiar. It was morning, and the golden light came in through the small windows cut into the castle's exterior wall. She knew that this was *their* room, holding all of the possessions of their life together. By the wall, under the window, was a

cradle, with its head and footboards elaborately carved with leaves and small forest animals. Yet, as she walked towards it, her focus was the wrapped bundle *in* the cradle. It was hers and his.

Walking with him in her garden, they went to the bench at the far end and sat down. It was afternoon; shadows were beginning to climb up the walls, and a breeze blew in through the open arches on one side. He played at his pipe. The notes of music were accompanied by the gurgling from the fountain in the background.

In her dream, Alaine saw the moss faeries flying before them. It was dark, but the little beings knew where they were going. She did not need to look at him to feel his presence beside her, a hand in his. Walking along the fern-lined path, they came to the clearing. There, hanging from a thick limb on ropes was the carved bed. It was a refuge, where they could lie and watch the sky through the branches of the tree. This forest was also their home.

Suddenly the dream was disturbed. Not wanting to leave him, she was being pulled away. Her eyelids fluttered as her consciousness returned. She opened her eyes, and Genna's face was before her.

"Come, Princess, you must get up now. It's time to bathe and dress. I have brought you a warm tea of mint. It will take some extra time to fix your hair today."

So the day had dawned with all of its trepidations.

22
Preparations

King Holum was up early the morning of the betrothal ceremony, knowing that the day would place many demands upon him. As he dressed in temporary clothes, rather than the robes of the monarchy that he would wear later, he had tasks to complete before most of Irongate stirred from their beds. He peeked into the bedroom where his Queen remained in her slumbers. A wave of compassion came over him. He hoped that the day would not bring too much distress when the girl failed to choose Hester's cousin, Felix, for a husband. Based upon what he observed and the activities he had recently been made aware of, all pointed to the Queen's disappointment as her plans went awry.

He fastened the last button on his tunic and proceeded downstairs to meet with Sir Foy, the Captain of his guard. After some discussion, Foy assured the King that his instructions would be followed, and that his men would be in their proper places. Extra men would be placed outside the front doors and in the receiving hall, in case of any disturbances. Irongate was prepared to welcome noble visitors.

Foy was alert, as expected, and had tasks in hand. He reported to Holum that the ship of Prince Brannon had sailed and cleared the harbor on its return journey. The disgraced Prince Brannon was on board, probably sleeping off his indulgences of the previous day.

Holum had some worries that King Ryan might take affront and find a need to retaliate against Hawthorn for banishing his son. He carefully worded his letter to King Ryan alluding to the young man's behavior.

Surely, the father knew what the son was about. Holum had not told Hester about information recently learned. Brannon had already taken a mistress back home who had borne him a child. King Ryan had refused to allow his son to marry, as it would bring no profit to his court. He would prefer the dowry of a princess. Had the Princess Alaine set her sights on the man, Holum would have advised Alaine, as well as King Granth and Lady Avis.

Now there was no need. To be sure, the trade between the two countries would be strained for the next few years.

Once he was finished with Foy, King Holum met with Corith, the head footman of the castle. Corith and his pages were responsible for all of the pageantry of the betrothal ceremony. Again, somewhat unusual instructions were given by Holum. Corith was a master of regal gatherings in Majestic Hall. The plan for the royal procession was discussed, as well as the presentation of the suitors vying for Alaine's hand. Corith thought the list of suitors had been narrowed to the remaining Prince Sturgrom and the Marquis, until the King threw uncertainty into the flow of the program.

There was much detail that Holum was unsure of, but based upon what he already knew, he expected the unexpected and made preparations for it.

Maids scurried up and down the hallways and stairs of Irongate, carrying trays back and forth from the kitchen. The morning was in full swing. Some of the noblemen had taken their breakfasts in the dining rooms, while the ladies preferred to break their fasts in the privacy of their rooms. Chamber pots were being emptied and fresh water delivered for morning bathing. The women would focus on their dressing in order to be well groomed for the day's assembly. The hour before noon, the great doors of the hall would be opened, and the audience would be admitted according to their rank. Prime spots in the room would soon be filled.

Alaine was very quiet as Genna helped her into the gown, tying the laces at the back, pulling the bodice and waist into a close fit. She sat still at the dressing table as Genna brushed out her hair in the usual way prior to the braiding. How Alaine wished that she could allow her hair to fall to her shoulders and wear the delicate copper circlet around her forehead and hair. The jewels for today sat upon the dressing table before her, retrieved from the trunk just this morning. The sides of her hair would be braided and secured to the top of her head. In front of the braids would be the tiara of golden peaks studded with seed pearls. The rest of her red locks would be restrained in coils tucked at the back of her head, held in place with a gold-colored netting, also alight with pearls. At last, when the arduous process was complete, Genna reached for the rope of creamy, smooth pearls and fastened it at the base of Alaine's neck, adjusting it so that the oblong center pearl, hanging from a golden filigree triangle, was suspended precisely below the hollow of the throat. Alaine attached the two matching, but smaller, pearls set on their golden wires, to each earlobe. When finished, both maid and mistress stared into the small looking glass, Genna with satisfaction, Alaine with disbelief at the reflection.

Alaine got up from her chair and found the chain belt with its dragonfly and fixed it around her waist. The bejeweled insect hung down at her right hip. Genna helped her place the royal Hawthorn Sash, going from her right shoulder, across her front, ending in a point at her left hip.

"Are you sure that you wish to wear the dragonfly belt, milady?" Genna asked, after adjusting the dark green sash.

"The gown was a gift from my mother, the belt and sash are from my father. I represent them both today. I am the Princess Alaine of Hawthorn," Alaine stated, taking hold of her emotions.

"Have you made a choice, milady?"

"No, Genna. I am torn. We will see what the day will bring and what the men have to say for themselves. I must consider my parents' wishes and my duty to the people of Hawthorn," Alaine replied in all seriousness.

When Genna wasn't watching, Alaine secured the small key on a string at her wrist beneath her long sleeve. She gave a heavy sigh, as it was her last hope in her heartfelt feelings for Carver. "I am as ready as I will ever be. Let us go out."

In the process of dressing, the seven Princes were running into each other. None of them had slept well, as is typical, trying to adjust to a bed away from home. With the shortage of beds in the small cottage, the coach and chair in use, it was a pillow on the rug for Flecher.

There were sausages, eggs, and wedges of cheese for breakfast, all cooked by Delle. He enjoyed cooking and could produce the most delicate flatbread and fluffiest eggs. His short, corpulent figure gave evidence of his love of food. Astra was in her element, going from one man to another gleaning all that she could. Carver wasn't hungry and ate little.

The coaches and their drivers arrived at the door and the brothers pre- pared to load in. These rented modes of transport were certainly not of the level expected for the nobility. Basically, they were crude boxes on wheels, only one of which was painted, but they would have to do to go the short distance to Irongate.

Fletcher would have preferred to go on foot, but that might not have gotten them through the front gates even when wearing their fine clothes. He was wedged into one corner on the wooden plank of a seat with Delle next to him. Lignin was in the opposite corner, deep in his thoughts of the politics related to their undertaking. Bole was about to climb aboard when he heard a dispute coming from the other coach.

"I should have known better than to put those three together," complained Bole to the older set of brothers, on his way to deal with the youngsters.

"You can't bring her. There's no room in here!" yelled Nocken, squeezed into the corner of the more compact coach.

The carved gift for Princess Alaine sat next to him on the seat. Jute was tucked in the opposite corner and Carver was outside, encouraging Astra to jump into the narrow space between the seats.

"What is the matter?" Bole demanded.

"He's insisting on bringing Astra. There's no room in here and we shouldn't bring a dog to the court," insisted Nocken.

"I can't leave her here alone," Carver argued. "What if we don't get back before night? The Princess knows and likes her. I think that it will be all right."

"All right, load in. Carver, it will be on you if it proves a disaster."

"What's wrong?" Fletcher asked, as Bole climbed into the front coach.

"He's bringing the dog," Bole related, resigned.

"That's Carver for you - him and that dog," replied Flecher.

"Let's just get there," Lignin said, with impatience. "It's to Irongate, driver! Move on!" he called out the small coach window.

The doors of the great Majestic Hall were open, and courtiers were being led in by the red-suited pages. Those of highest rank were being shown to the front areas of the room. The hum of excited voices filled the air. At some point, when the room was full, the doors would be closed, awaiting the announcement of the King and Queen's entrance.

On the dais, the gilded thrones of the monarchs had been moved to one side for today's ceremony. On the other side of the stage was placed a decorated chair with a high back for the use of Princess Alaine. The flag of the Lower Kingdom of Weston Mareview Lowlands and the flags of the five dukes of the kingdom lined the back of the platform.

Duke Morr-Leigh, Duke Seaken-Char, and Lady Avis were already escorted to a front-row viewing spot directly in sight of where Alaine would sit. Kent had assured that Sergeant Covey was in the hall, off to the side of the dais. Prince Sturgrom and the

Marquis de Locke were also in their places at the front, on opposite sides of the aisle.

Meanwhile, King Holum and Queen Hester waited in an anteroom near the great hall with Prince Stenson, Alaine, and Lady Charlyn. King Holum was now dressed in his full royal regalia. He wore a sedate black cassock with gold buttons that went from his neck to his knees. The sash of the Lower Kingdom of Mareview slashed across his chest. He wore a full-length robe with a black silk lining and a deep purple exterior. The robe had a long tail that would trail after the King as he walked. The King found the garment bothersome but dealt with it on the occasions it was required. On his head was a golden crown, overlaid with golden ships on both sides and one oval-cut sapphire in the center at the front.

Alaine was surprised to see Queen Hester in her formal attire. On any day, Hester would change clothes several times, wearing gowns of radiantly dyed materials and rare, colorful silks. She was the center of fashion at her court, influencing all who came to Irongate. But today, all frivolity was gone. Hester wore a high-necked, long-sleeved, straight gown that flowed to her feet. The blue of the dress reflected the same blue as in the Mareview flag. Her long robe was lined in the similar color silk, with an outer navy-blue velvet. As with her husband's, the robe would flow behind her as she walked. From her neck hung a golden chain with a medallion depicting the royal seal of the land. Her lustrous ebony hair was drawn back in a tight coil, and upon her head was a delicate golden crown beset with diamonds and sapphires in the front. It had been a gift from Holum after the birth of Prince Stenson.

While Holum and Hester reflected calm, Stenson was pacing around the small room, impatient for the action to begin. His lanky frame was also dressed differently. He wore a long tunic that went to his knees, with a row of shiny brass buttons. The Mareview Crest appeared on a patch over his heart. His lower legs were covered in black hose ending in short, black boots. He also wore a matching cape with a clasp at the neck.

Charlyn wore her rose gown as the Princess had requested; but it was Alaine who was the light in the room among all the somber colors. Her serious facial expression highlighted her features.

Her aunt and uncle complemented her appearance. Her cousin teased her, saying she looked too grown up.

As they waited, Sir Foy of the guard entered the room. He came directly to the King and whispered in his ear. Holum nodded, and the man left.

"What was that about?" inquired Hester of her husband.

"Just an expected report from Foy. I met with him earlier. Everything is coming along as it should."

Then to Alaine, "Don't fret, Princess. We will be going into the hall shortly."

Lignin was surprised at the ease with which both of the homely coaches made their way past the gatehouse at the castle. True, there was a long line of carriages with courtiers trying to reach the Majestic Hall before the doors closed. Possibly that was why the guards at the gate appeared a little lax on this special day.

The brothers piled out of the coaches on the side of the castle where the gravel drive was extended and was a parking space for many other coaches. Lignin signaled for them to move toward the parkland on the west side of Irongate, where they gathered under a tall maple tree. Astra loped along, unfazed by all the people and excitement. Jute carried the gift for the Princess, as Nocken continued to complain to Carver about the dog.

Carver was not listening. All of the color seemed to have drained from his face. He felt sick.

"Carver, what's the matter?" Flecher asked, putting his hand on Carver's shoulder.

"There are so many people here…" he voiced, weakly.

"Carver, get ahold of yourself. This is no different from the large ceremonies we have at Middleoak. You knew there were going to be a lot of people here. That's the whole point of this. The Princess will make her choice in front of the Irongate court," Bole consoled. "This is their custom, just as we have ours."

Lignin put it to his brother, "Do you want to go back to Harbortown and return to the forest? You must decide now."

"No, I can't go back without knowing if she would accept me. I would regret it the rest of my life. I love her and I want her. I must do this," Carver answered, trying to fortify himself.

"Good. I will go up to the castle and see what I can find. Wait here," Lignin said, and headed toward the front doors.

Soon all seven brothers and Astra were sitting or walking about in a small, well-furnished room somewhere on the first floor of Irongate. They had been led there by a lad in a red suit and told to wait there until he returned.

Delle took a bite from an apple he found in a fruit bowl sitting on a low table. Flecher paced behind one of the two couches, feeling trapped. Lignin stood by two pitchers of water on a shelf, counting out the seven clay cups - seven cups. His suspicions slipped into a complete thought. Everything about getting into Irongate had been too easy. Someone *knew* they were coming! The question was, was it friend or foe? Had they walked into a trap?

Previously, he had left the driveway, thrown his cape over one shoulder, and straightened the befeathered hat on his head as he proceeded up the front steps of Irongate. Once inside, Lignin took in what was happening, as courtiers were milling about, awaiting their turns of being led into the hall by the pages. He gathered himself to his full height and approached, with authority, one such page returning from the hall.

"Good man, I am Prince Lignin of the Staghorn Woods. I have need to speak with the head footman if you please."

The man was surprised, and almost panicked. Another prince, he thought to himself? If the man *was* a prince, a page could be dismissed from his job if he didn't handle the situation correctly.

"Wait here, sir. I will find Mister Corith to attend you."

The man scurried off into the crowd. Lignin realized that more than one of the nearby courtiers were looking him up and down. He removed his hat and bowed to the nobles, who then turned away.

Moments later, the young footman returned, followed by an older man, dressed in a more elaborate red outfit, with white hair and a closely trimmed beard.

"I am Corith, the head footman here at Irongate. May I be of assistance, sir?"

"Yes. I am aware that you are very enlisted at present, but I must speak with you in private…"

After a brief conversation, during which Lignin supplied the man with a small scroll of paper, the woodland Prince found himself following the young man in the red suit back out to the driveway, collecting the rest of the group, and being led through a side door, away from the crowds, into a quiet room.

Lignin said nothing about his thoughts, not wanting to raise alarm, especially with the already nervous Carver. Flecher continued his pacing. Bole sat still, seemingly deep in thought. Possibly they, too, were suspicious and sensing a possible trap. The outside foyer was quiet. Had the betrothal ceremony begun?

"We all must be ready to be escorted into the hall. Straighten your clothes and hats. Bole, help Carver fix his cape - and where is my crown? Carver, you must take care of it," Lignin advised, as Carver placed the metal ring on his head. "I am only lending it to you. It was just lucky that I had it with me, having come from the Assembly.

"Let's talk about how we will present ourselves when we are led into the ceremony," he continued. "I provided the head footman with a list of our names so that he can announce us. Bole, Flecher and I will enter first, then Delle and Nocken, followed by Jute and Carver. Jute, you will carry the gift for the Princess."

"What about the dog?" Nocken asked, still annoyed that the animal was there.

"She'll be at my side," answered Carver, forcefully.

Suddenly, the door to the room opened and the red-suited man motioned for them to follow.

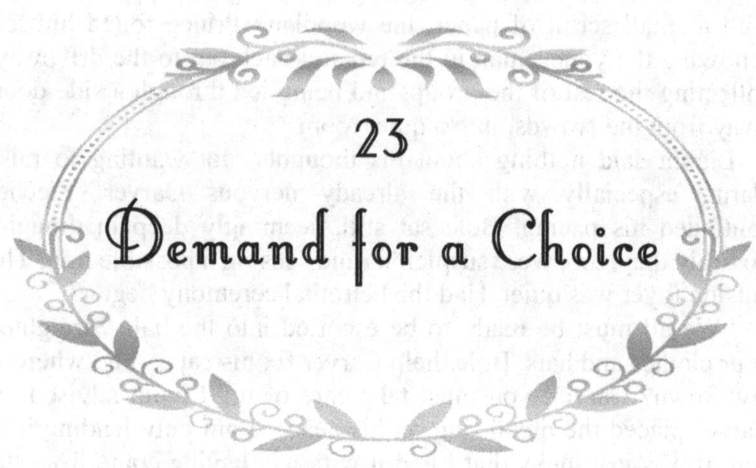

23

Demand for a Choice

At last, Corith opened the doors of Majestic Hall and strode to the end of the aisle. The man banged his long stick on the stone floor three times in an attempt to silence the great room. He waited a brief moment and banged his stick again. Courtiers turned to look toward him with expectation, and the hall became quiet.

"Hail to you, noble countrymen and honored guests!" the footman's strong voice rang out for all to hear. "Give your respect to His Majesty, King Holum Targ, Monarch of Weston Mareview Lowlands and Queen Hester de Locke."

Then the footman stepped aside as King Holum slowly led his Queen down the long aisle, to the music of a flute and drum.

The man again banged his stick and called out, "Hail nobles and guests! Give your respect to Prince Stenson Targ, heir to the throne of Hawthorn Weston Mareview."

Stenson followed his parents, awkwardly trying to match his pace with the beating drum. And so it went. King Holum reached the dais and led Hester to her seat, prior to taking his throne. When

Stenson came onto the stage, he took his place, standing at his father's shoulder.

The stick banged again, "Hail, nobles and guests! Welcome from the Hawthorn Eastgreen Highlands, the daughter of Duke Noeman of the Walls, Lady in Waiting to the Princess Alaine, the noble Lady Charlyn."

A flute and the strings of a fiddle played as Charlyn took her turn to walk. She carried a hawthorn branch with green leaves. The girl's cheeks blazed pink, fearful of her reception after the turmoil at the Queen's garden party the previous evening. She had not gotten far when a nearby noblewoman clapped her hands as Charlyn walked past. Soon more in the crowd picked up the applause in a show of support. The noble girl straightened her shoulders and held her head high. Charlyn thought Lady Avis had been right, in that there was support from those who had heard the story of her and Prince Brannon. The courtiers embraced Charlyn as one of their own who had been wronged.

When Charlyn reached the front of the hall, she turned and looked to the front of the crowd, searching for, and finally finding, the all-important face. When their eyes met, he smiled a small smile, and a sense of relief flooded through her. Maybe all would be right between them. The Lady could not wait to speak to Kent; but first, there was her responsibility to Alaine. All must wait until after the ceremony. So she gracefully mounted the stage and took her place, standing next to the chair reserved for a princess.

Now it was Alaine's turn to stand at the end of the aisle, awaiting the footman's announcement. Golden light filtered into the room through the rare, tall windows. The crowd had turned toward her with anticipation.

Corith banged his staff three more times. "Hail nobles and honored guests! Give your respect to the Princess Alaine of the Hawthorn Eastgreen Highlands, daughter of His Majesty, King Granth and Queen Iris."

The music of the flute and the strings of the fiddle began again. Alaine clutched her hawthorn branch and began to walk. There were murmurs of appreciation from the audience as they caught a glance of her. She reached the front, climbed the steps, and walked to the chair. When she turned to face the crowd, applause and cheers filled the room.

She scanned the front row and saw Kent smiling, seemingly filled with pride. Lady Avis was also smiling, taking a handkerchief from Duke Seaken-Char to wipe a tear of happiness. How the Lady wished that her sister, Queen Iris, could be here to see her daughter looking so lovely.

After the audience settled, King Holum stood to address his flock. "Welcome all. You will be glad to hear that the Irongate kitchens have been working through the night to fill the dining rooms with a delicious luncheon for us all," he announced, and the crowd answered him with the twitter of laughter. "But first, we have an important event to witness. Today is a day of celebration for the Upper and Lower Kingdoms of Hawthorn. Our beloved niece, Princess Alaine, is here to begin the journey of taking her place in the world by leaving her home and choosing a nobleman to be her husband. So, without any further delay, who here will propose for the hand of Princess Alaine?"

"I will speak for the Princess!" called out Prince Sturgrom, as he stepped forward. The audience broke into applause and cheers.

"Come forward, Prince Sturgrom, visiting from the snow-capped Kingdom of Swerd," King Holum called out, and then took to his seat.

The Prince took his place in front of Alaine and began his speech, "Dear Princess Alaine, please accept this small gift from the people of Swerd, who would welcome you as my wife and future queen."

Sturgrom's man brought forward a box and set it before Alaine. She lifted it onto her lap and opened the lid.

"Oh, it's beautiful!" Alaine exclaimed, as she lifted the white fur hat adorned with a spray of clear crystals at the front. "This would be perfect for a winter's day."

Prince Sturgrom bowed to the Princess and resumed his place in the front gallery.

Holum stood again and began to speak, "Prince Sturgrom, we have so enjoyed your visit to our court, where you are always welcome for future visits. Now, would anyone else wish to address Princess Alaine?"

"I would!" called out the Marquis, from his place in the gallery in front of the Queen.

"Come forward, Marquis de Locke of Raydon," invited King Holum.

Holum took his seat as Alaine watched the tall Marquis move to stand before her. Charlyn, Alaine and courtiers waited for the man prepared to make his case.

"Dear Princess, as my wife, I cannot offer you a royal court or a future crown. But I *can* offer a warm, majestic villa by the sea, where you would want for nothing. And with my ships, I can promise you will not say goodbye to Hawthorn but will be able to make visits to see your family. So I humbly request your hand in marriage.

"To show my great admiration, I have brought you a gift. I have searched for the perfect present for the lady who would be my wife. Allow me to present you with this small token. It has traveled a long distance from the Far East, where it was made. It is said to bring good luck to whoever wears the stone."

Charlyn came forward and took the small, silk-covered box from the Marquis and handed it to Alaine. Opening the box, Alaine gasped upon seeing the contents. She couldn't resist running her fingers across the cool jade stone – a carved green dragon surrounded by tiny blossoms. It was a pendant on a delicate gold chain.

"Dear Marquis, this is truly a rare and beautiful gift," she said, sincerely impressed. "I thank you."

Murmurs were running through the crowd. Who would Alaine choose? The audience was in a jolly mood. On-the-spot wagers were being made among the courtiers. The ceremony was almost over, with the promise of good food and drink at its end. Yet, the people on the stage were quiet. The Queen smiled at her cousin, who returned to his place in the front gallery. Stenson fidgeted with his buttons, bored with the ongoing program.

King Holum nodded his head to Corith and sat quietly as he waited for what he knew was to come.

Sure enough, the stick banged three times on the stone floor. Gradually the audience turned their heads from the front to the back of the room, as the stick sounded for the second time.

"Your Majesties, Princess Alaine, nobles and honored guests, give your respect to the seven Princes of the Hawthorn Woodlands." The man in the red suit began his list of names, "Prince Bole of Oaks Forest, Prince Lignin of Staghorn Woods, Prince Flecher of Owlbrook Treehold."

The footman paused to allow the three Princes to begin their walk toward the dais. There was no music, and the audience grew silent taking in the change of program.

Corith continued, "Prince Delle from the Trees of the Lake, Prince Nocken of Hollybranch Forest," as Delle and Nocken began their walk behind their brothers. "Prince Jute of Lancehold Forest and Prince Alfred of Elder Tree Forest."

The seven princes, dressed in their finery, made their way forward, and the murmurs within the crowd grew. Surely this was objectionable. They waited for the King to speak and put an end to this disruption. All had the same question on their lips - who were these unknown princes? The Duke of Leigh gave an audible groan and shot a look to Covey to be on alert.

"What's happening?" Lady Avis asked, in a panic. "Kent, did you know of this?"

"I suspected something was afoot, but I could not get any answers. That was why I went to Harbortown yesterday. It is too late now," Kent whispered back.

At the same time, Hester was alarmed at this breech in protocol. "Holum, who are these men? How can they be Princes of Hawthorn?"

"I will explain later, Hester. Be still and see what comes of this," Holum advised his Queen.

The Princes reached the front of the hall and formed a line before the royals. Charlyn looked from one to another of the men, only knowing Bole and Flecher by name. She switched her gaze to Kent, who seemed distressed, while Lady Avis appeared confused. Duke Seaken-Char was quiet, yet seemed to have some knowledge of what was happening, with his long awareness of the forest clans. Covey, always Alaine's protector, moved closer to the end of the dais.

Alaine was as surprised as anyone else. On the verge of a demand for her choice of husbands between Prince Sturgrom and

272

the Marquis, the timing of this interruption could not have been better planned. She had all but given up any hope of ever seeing Carver again, despite what his brother had said the day before in the garden. Now he stood before her.

The men bowed in unison before the royalty. For Alaine, the sight of all seven brothers at once was stunning. She remembered most of the faces that she had seen at the dinner at Middleoak. Yet, there was never a mention of their nobility among the forest clans. Never had Carver told her anything that would imply that he was anything more than a member of Bole's clan. Then there was the name, Alfred. How formal it sounded, rather than Carver.

Standing last in the line, Carver certainly looked every bit the Prince that he claimed to be. Taller than his brothers, there was a serious expression on his face. His light hair was down, near his face. He wore a metal crown on his head, not elaborate, but a clear symbol of rank. His eyes were on her, probably trying to judge her reaction. His off-white silk shirt was covered by a golden long vest that hung down over his tan trousers. He wore tall brown boots. Carver's wide cape flowed below his knees, as was the style, lined in brown silk, with a heavy, green fabric on the exterior. This was not the Carver Alaine knew, usually in his rustic clothing and long, woven robe. Then Alaine noticed Astra sitting next to him, and she had to smile to herself. Who but Carver would bring a dog to court?

At this point the audience was talking freely among themselves. The noise in that hall was becoming louder. They wanted answers about these strangers. King Holum stood again and called for quiet from the crowd. He waited patiently as silence finally prevailed.

"Who will speak for the Princes of the Forest?" he asked the men before him.

"I will speak," answered Lignin in a strong voice, as he stepped forward, removing his hat and bowing before the King.

"Does the Assembly of the Groves know that you are here at Irongate today?" Holum asked.

"No, Your Majesty. We have not had time to inform them."

"And your father, King Alfred, is he well and still residing at Elder Tree Forest, near Hawthorn Village?"

"Yes, Your Majesty, he is well."

"Why have you traveled from your forest homes to interrupt our ceremony?"

"We have come to be with our brother, Alfred, as he wishes to speak to the Princess Alaine."

"Prince Alfred," called the King to Carver, "did your father give his approval for you to be here today?"

"He gave his permission to follow the Princess on her journey to Irongate, Sire," Carver answered, in a strong, clear voice that could be heard by the courtiers.

"Did he give his approval for you to come here *today*?" the King insisted.

"No, Your Majesty, but as a Prince of Hawthorn, I would ask your permission to speak to Princess Alaine."

The King took his time in answering, which heightened the attention of the audience.

"Due to the fact that your father and your people have held to The Treaty of the Trees since the time of my grandfather, Arden the Great, there has been peace between our peoples over two generations. Since you are a Prince of the Forest, I will grant you permission to speak to Princess Alaine."

Again the crowd broke into exclamations of surprise, refusing to be hushed as King Holum held up his hands. Queen Hester gave her husband a look of disbelief. He appeared to be indulging these men.

Stenson, on the other hand, was trying to get the attention of the dog. He had always wanted a dog of his own, so to see one at court was a treat. Pulling a sausage from his pocket, the young Prince called to Astra, "Here dog!"

When it came to food, Astra had a long, specialized nose, and bounded onto the platform with no further encouragement, going straight to Stenson. Hester let out a scream of alarm which did nothing to deter the animal. Astra went straight to the boy and took the sausage, chewing it to bits as Stenson stroked her head.

"Stenson, a sausage in the pocket of your new clothes?" the father admonished.

"I thought that I might get hungry. You know how these things go on," Stenson replied.

"Get that dog away!" yelled his mother.

Alaine got up from her seat and called the dog, "Astra, come here!" she commanded sharply.

The audience quieted, interested in watching the drama on the stage. Now, finished with her sausage, Astra ran to Alaine, greeting her with a lick on her hand.

"Astra, sit," and the dog sat. "Now, lie down here," Alaine said, pointing to a spot next to her chair.

The dog obeyed, and Stenson quickly moved to that side of the dais to be near the dog. The Queen was surprised at Alaine's ability to control the large animal.

"Prince Alfred, you may speak to the Princess Alaine," King Holum ordered, as a hush fell over the great hall.

Carver stepped forward to the edge of the platform, directly in front of Alaine, and began to speak. The audience went silent, straining to hear what was said.

"A few winters past, I came out of my woodland home to visit the Village of Hawthorn. I made friends there and brought my wood carvings to be sold at the blacksmith's shop. I saw you one day in the lane, laughing with some of the village children. It was later that I learned who you were: The Princess of Hawthorn. I always longed to speak to you, but never had a chance.

"Recently, I heard that you were leaving to be married, traveling to Irongate Castle. I asked my father, King Alfred, if I could follow you. He believed that it was a useless pursuit but gave his permission.

"I thought, I am a prince and should be able to speak to a princess. So, I did. Thanks to a spell of bad weather on your journey, I was able to spend some time with you. Now, I am here as a Prince of Hawthorn to ask for your hand in marriage."

The quiet courtiers erupted with shouts and jeers. Objections came from those supporting Prince Sturgrom and those supporting the Marquis. The Queen was appalled. Holum stood again and lifted his arms to signal the crowd to be quiet.

"Dear people, this all may sound strange to you, but these men *are princes* from our land of Hawthorn. Their forest holdings span both the Upper and Lower Kingdoms and have been there for untold winters. It is their clans that were the original people of Hawthorn and helped to save the land from foreign invasions. They have protection by law under The Treaty of the Trees. Please give Prince Alfred your respect. Prince Alfred, you may continue."

"Princess Alaine, I have brought you a betrothal gift. I know that you need a safe place to keep your jewels, as you seem to be somewhat careless with them," Carver said, with a quirky smile.

"Really, *Prince Alfred*?" Alaine responded, with sarcasm in her voice and stressing the name she was not previously told.

Jute climbed the two steps and placed the square wooden chest on Alaine's lap, then quickly retreated to his spot next to Carver.

Whispering resumed in the audience, but Alaine paid no attention. She was captivated by the carving on the lid of the chest. It was a familiar scene, as if standing on the main road in Hawthorn Village, looking up to the gates and walls of the castle, with the keep and towers in the background. A pang of homesickness washed over her for the many times she had taken the same view for granted.

On the front of the box was a brass plate with a lock. Knowingly, she grabbed the string hidden in her sleeve and pulled out the small key.

Inserting the key that she thought she would never use; she opened the lock. Alaine lifted the latch and the lid.

With a gasp, the Princess saw the carving on the *inside* of the lid. In great detail was a relief of her little garden, as if one was looking in from one of the open arches. There was the kitchen door, the pathway, the fountain, and the bench at the far end. She looked up at Carver. He knew of her garden. He had to have been there, she thought. She remembered the many times sitting on the bench and dozing off, thinking she heard the music of a pipe playing somewhere nearby.

Charlyn, standing next to Alaine's chair, leaned over, looking into the chest. "Look Alaine, isn't that your lost broach?"

Indeed, nestled in one of the square compartments on the top shelf of the small cabinet was the opal broach Alaine thought she had lost in a farmer's field.

"Yes, it is!" Alaine whispered to Charlyn.

Continuing her search, Alaine lifted the two trays with small compartments that opened up and out on little brass hinges. Then she saw it…sitting on the black velvet at the bottom was her emerald necklace glistening back at her. He *had* taken it! Closing the trays, she pulled out the uppermost of three drawers, and as suspected, there was her amethyst necklace laid out on the velvet.

"Yes, Prince Alfred," stated Alaine, now addressing Carver, "I *do* have great need for a chest to keep my jewels safe from light fingers that would steal them away. This one is well suited.

"As to your request for my hand in marriage, why is it you think I would consider your offer? I am a Princess of the Fields, and you are a Prince of the Forest."

"You will accept me because you love me, as I love you," answered Carver, in all seriousness.

A rumbling was heard from the spectators. Queen Hester, visibly upset, was amazed at the man's audacity.

"A princess does not marry for love," Alaine professed. "A princess must marry for what is best for the people of her realm."

"What is better for those of the Upper and Lower Kingdoms of Hawthorn than to bring together the people of the fields and the clans of the forests? It could begin with us," Carver retaliated to her challenge.

Alaine put aside the jewelry chest and stood up in front of her chair. "Unifying the peoples of Hawthorn, after many years of separation, would certainly be a noble cause. In that case, I will *accept* your offer of marriage, Prince Alfred."

Carver's face relaxed into an exuberant smile. He bounded up the steps to stand next to Alaine. He took her hand in his. Astra quickly joined them. The crowd erupted. The King and Queen were both on their feet. Sensing possible danger from the disgruntled courtiers, Sergeant Covey and Kent moved to stand in front of the platform facing the outraged nobility. The six remaining forest princes quickly turned to face the crowd and prepared for confrontation, joining the young Duke and Covey. Astra barked at the melee.

King Holum raised his arm, and guardsmen entered from the side door at the front, with more coming in through the great doors at the back of the hall followed by the small army of pages.

"Noblemen and women," the King called out, "quiet! I demand quiet!"

Slowly the crowd calmed. The addition of the guards and the pages was helpful, one providing a show of force and the other a reminder of the required courtly manners.

"Friends, the Princess Alaine has made her choice," the King proclaimed. "The matter is yet unsettled, as the match must be approved by two kings who are not here today. It will fall upon me to make further arrangements. So, as your King, I ask you to follow the pages out of Majestic Hall to the dining rooms. I will ask the Marquis de Locke to stand in for me and Queen Hester as host, so I can address urgent matters. Enjoy your luncheon!"

The guards moved from the front of the room, encouraging the people out the back doors as ushered by the red-suited pages. Lady Avis and Duke Seaken-Char didn't leave with the others. Lady Avis was in complete puzzlement, having never *seen* this, Prince Alfred. At least she couldn't remember him from the dinner at Middleoak. She remembered Bole and Flecher but had no idea that there was nobility among the forest clans.

Queen Hester was livid over the current events. And, rightfully or wrongly, she blamed her husband. How could he let this happen!? Obviously, he had known something about these forest men. Stenson became a nearby target of her wrath.

"Stenson, go get your lunch," the mother yelled at the boy, who was still petting Astra. "We have important affairs to discuss."

Recognizing his mother's tone of voice, the young Prince escaped through the side door. Hester was going to speak to the King, but before she could get a word in, he began speaking to those remaining in the hall.

The King called out to the head footman, who came to the front of the hall with the pages, "Corith, have the pages carry Alaine's gifts and escort Lady Avis, Princess Alaine and Lady Charlyn to their rooms. Lady Avis, please retrieve the marriage contract and return to the Map Room with my footman."

Alaine squeezed Carver's hand, giving him a look of assurance. "I will see you soon," she promised him, then followed the King's command.

Once the ladies had left, the King addressed Carver, "Prince Alfred, there are many issues to be resolved regarding your proposed match with Princess Alaine. It's an unusual situation that could impact the entire land of Hawthorn. There is much to discuss. Will you pick a representative for the deliberations?"

"My brother Lignin will represent me," offered Carver.

"Fine. You and the rest of your brothers may return to Harbortown and await the outcome of our discussions," Holum ordered. "And take the dog!"

All of the Forest Princes and Astra filed out of the hall, leaving Lignin with the royals and nobles, some openly displeased with the events of the day.

"Rengard and Duke Morr-Leigh, you can follow us into the Map Room, where we can decide what should be done next," Holum instructed, somewhat weary of the current dilemma.

"I wish to come, too," Queen Hester interjected. "I still don't understand where these men came from and how Alaine can be betrothed to *this…this…stranger*."

"Yes, Hester, you may come with us. You need to know what this is about."

24

Engagement in Doubt

Lady Avis was trying to keep up with the long strides of the king's footman walking along the upstairs hallway to their suite of rooms. Alaine and Charlyn lagged behind, followed by two pages carrying the gifts from the betrothal ceremony.

Avis was in a state of confusion. The unthinkable had just happened right under her nose. Young women were so unpredictable, she thought, dismayed. One handsome face, all common sense is lost, and well laid plans go astray. Oh yes, she had seen it many times over the years at court, usually leading to disastrous results.

At the rooms, Lady Avis held the door open, allowing the girls to file in. The pages placed the carved jewelry chest and the other gifts on the long table by the door.

"I will wait for you here," Corith reminded, as Lady Avis was closing the door.

Alaine and Charlyn stood before the dark fireplace. Alaine was radiant with excitement, grabbing and holding Charlyn's hands. Nana had gotten up from the couch and was eager to hear about the ceremony.

"Can you believe that he is a prince!? He was a prince all along but never told me!" Alaine exclaimed, finally allowed to express her joy. "That means he is noble, and we can marry!"

"She chose Prince Sturgrom?" Nana asked.

Avis rushed to the girls, "Alaine, who *is* this man? How is it that you came to know him? How can you accept a stranger for your husband?"

"He is no more a stranger to me than Prince Sturgrom or the Marquis. You remember, Auntie," Alaine reminded, using the name she called the Lady from her childhood, "the first night of our journey, at the inn, the man with the dog."

Lady Avis thought back and she *did* remember the strange man with the dog.

"I remember he looked like a highwayman! Could that be the transformed Prince Alfred?" Avis demanded.

"Who is Prince Alfred?" asked Nana, more confused than ever.

"Yes," exclaimed Alaine, dreamily, "that was the first time I saw him. I didn't know it then, but he was following our journey to Irongate. He had seen me in Hawthorn Village and always wanted to speak to me."

"She chose a prince, but not Prince Sturgrom?" Nana asked, trying to keep up.

"He camped near our company during the rains," Alaine continued. "I spoke to him. Remember when Kent went to find the men who didn't return from their hunt? Well, it was Carver, I mean Prince Alfred, that led me and Covey through the forest to Bole's hamlet. We found Kent and the men, and first met the forest people. After Bole released our men, we had a meal with these strangers, who seemed to mean us no harm. They asked about our travels, and later showed us a map of Hawthorn with villages and roads through the forest that were unknown to us. It was then that we asked to use the Old Road through their forest to avoid the flooding. Kent and I were both surprised when Bole said that they would ask their Assembly for permission for us to pass," Alaine explained.

"So, this Prince Alfred is one of the forest people?" Nana asked.

"Yes, Nana," Lady Avis answered. "He claims to be a prince and at the betrothal ceremony asked Alaine to marry him in front of the entire court!"

"What!?" Nana exclaimed.

"When I saw him again after the dinner at Middleoak, I knew that I was drawn to him, but thought I would never see him again once we left the forest," Alaine related. "He never said that he or his brothers were princes of the forest clans. I couldn't believe it when they all appeared at the ceremony today. I still can't believe it! He is the man whom I wish to marry!"

"Alaine, I am sure that this is not what your parents were thinking when it came to your marriage. You don't even know this man. What will I tell them?" pleaded her aunt.

"*I will tell them!*" Alaine responded adamantly. "We are perfectly suited. I will tell them that I have made my choice."

"Does that mean she's marrying someone from the forest people?" Nana questioned, still grasping for understanding.

The conversation was interrupted by a banging at the door.

"Oh, I must go. The King wants to see the marriage contract!" Lady Avis exclaimed, rushing to her room to retrieve the document. On her way back to the door, clutching the roll of paper, "Girls, stay here in the rooms. Nana, please stay with them. I will return as soon as I can," the Lady called on her way out the door.

"Come, Charlyn and Nana. You must help me out of this dress. Nana, don't worry, I will tell you all about what happened today. Charlyn can tell of anything that I forget."

The afternoon sun was coming around Irongate on its usual journey, and its rays poured into the Map Room. Holum, Hester, the two Dukes and the strange Forest Prince were already beginning discussions by the time Lady Avis arrived, clutching the rolled marriage contract. She quietly took a seat nearest the door.

Holum was standing beside a wooden rack where the oversized map of Hawthorn hung on display. The Upper and Lower Kingdoms were defined, as well as the boundaries of the landholdings of the seven northern dukes and five southern dukes. Swaths of land, undefined, were painted in a green wash.

Holum was speaking, "Hester, I have tried to explain The Treaty of the Trees several times in the past, but because it has little influence on your life here at court, you dismiss it. Yet, it is the law of our land and has great impact over what happened in Majestic Hall today."

Hester began to speak, but Holum held up his hand to discourage her, and continued with his thoughts.

"After the war years and the squelching of the ongoing invasions from abroad, an agreement was made between the forest clans, who were the original people here, and King Arden and his people who wished to settle the land of Hawthorn. The forest people, who helped King Arden win the wars, didn't want to give up their old ways or leave their forest homes. They wanted to remain separate from our society.

"So the land of Hawthorn was divided. This, of course, was before the time of my father, King Holmes, and Hawthorn was not yet split into the Upper and Lower Kingdoms. It was agreed in The Treaty that the forest lands would continue to be held by the people of the forests. If you regard this map, you will see these green spaces, where no villages or roads are shown. These remain the land holdings of the forest clans to this day.

"King Arden was concerned, thinking that his people would need wood for building and daily living. So it was also agreed that this large, northeastern forest would be part of King Arden's kingdom," Holum said, pointing to the large green expanse at the top of the map. "The lands awarded to the Dukes of Hawthorn were allowed to grow their own trees for their use, but the major lumber production was controlled by the King's Forester, currently Duke Noeman of the Walls.

"Overall, I would say that The Treaty has worked well. Oh yes, there have been occasional disputes where Granth or I have received notices from the Assembly of the Groves, when action was needed against one of our dukes or tenants, but it is rare. Wouldn't you say, Prince Lignin?"

Lignin was sitting apart, in a chair by the large map table with his back to the window. The afternoon light came in from behind, giving him an almost mystical aura. His eyes were attentive, and his expression was serious. All in the room turned to look at him and awaited his words.

"I am a member of our Assembly of the Groves, and I can affirm that there have been no major conflicts under The Treaty over time. Our clans know that any complaints can be brought to the Assembly, and we try to resolve them within our community, at times giving up small parcels of forest lands in order to be good neighbors and maintain the peace. If there is a major issue that we are unable to resolve, a letter is sent to the King's Council, either of the Upper or Lower Kingdoms. This does not happen often and has always resulted in supporting the law. The dukes have their own guardsmen and have been helpful in enforcing borders between the forests and the farmlands."

"How many of these clans are there?" asked Queen Hester, surprised to hear that another seemingly large population of people inhabited the land.

"We have over fifty clan families living in different hamlets within the forests. Some have remained in the same place for over a hundred winters," Lignin added.

"So many?" Hester replied in astonishment. "How can we not know of these people?"

"We *do* know of them, my dear," Holum answered. "The twelve dukes of the land all have seats at our Council tables. Rengard can probably speak to times going back to my father's reign when matters concerning the forest clans were discussed at Council, and actions were taken as needed. So far, peace between our peoples has prevailed since the signing of The Treaty.

"But for today, we must discuss the betrothal of Princess Alaine to Prince Alfred," Holum insisted, changing the subject.

"Yes! That is what I want to know," Hester interjected. "How does Alaine even *know* this man? How did she meet him with no introduction? The whole thing seems very informal. How can this be appropriate for a royal princess? This engagement *must* be set aside."

Hester's words were not accepted well by those in the room. Lady Avis, who thought of Alaine as almost her own daughter, could not totally dismiss the girl's happiness with the betrothal.

Also, she took affront to the implication of impropriety reflecting on Alaine, and also upon herself as the girl's guardian. Duke Seaken-Char could sense the sudden chill from Lady Avis, who was taking the Queen's words as an insult. Kent also stiffened in his chair, feeling he had done all he could to safely escort Alaine to Irongate. As far as he knew, Alaine could be headstrong, but would never behave in a manner that would dishonor her or her parents. Prince Lignin also felt insulted, not only for his brother, who did nothing more than fall in love with the Princess, but for the Queen's demeaning tone towards his forest people in general.

"Hester, that is not helpful. Alaine's choice was made in front of the entire court. If the betrothal is set aside, it will be by King Granth or King Alfred," Holum insisted. "For now, we need to move forward."

"Holum, you can't be in favor of this match!" the Queen persisted. "It is almost as if you knew this was going to happen."

"I did know enough to make preparations," Holum told. "The day before the garden party the tailor sent his son to deliver Stenson's suit. When I asked where his father was, I was told a tale of men coming into the shop requiring fine clothes needed for court in just two days. When the shopkeeper brought Stenson's new boots, again I was told of a group of strangers needing new boots. One of the guardsmen told of his mother renting a cottage to seven men with no beards and strange clothes. It was the butcher who told the cook about the man with the dog coming to the tavern.

"The morning of the garden party, I had a rather long discussion with Duke Morr-Leigh. He detailed some of the obstacles they met on their journey to Irongate and their accidental encounter with the people of the forest. At the request of Princess Alaine, the forest clans agreed to escort her across their lands to the seashore, rather than continue to be delayed by the flooding at Leggot. The guide used the Old Road that runs along the River Falls through the forest. Once at the seacoast, they traveled south on Shoreline Byway while in disguise, which explains why they arrived in farmers' wagons instead of a royal coach.

"The day in Harbortown with the Marquis, Duke Morr-Leigh saw Prince Alfred on the byway. He had no idea of the man's plans but was very surprised to see him here. The morning of the garden party he ran into two more of the clansmen on the road behind the castle, which included the guide who led them to the seacoast. He became concerned, rightfully so, that trouble might be afoot concerning Alaine and the betrothal ceremony, and these men of the forest," Holum explained.

"I, too, started putting things together. Unlike Duke Leigh, I had knowledge of King Alfred and his hamlet in Elder Tree Forest near Hawthorn Village. I also knew that he had several sons who controlled the various forest plots. I agreed with Duke Leigh that the men being here at this time could have something to do with the betrothal ceremony. So, I made a few arrangements in case they showed up at court. Sir Foy reported to me this morning when they arrived and Corith carried out my instructions. Now, Lady Avis, may I see the Marriage Contract approved by King Granth's Council?" the King demanded.

Lady Avis brought the rolled document to Holum. He unfurled it and began to read.

"It seems that Princess Alaine cannot be forced to marry against her will, which supports her choice of Prince Alfred, as she has the right to refuse any marriage. This document also addresses succession to the Eastgreen Highland throne, denying it to Alaine's husband, but allows her male children to apply for the throne, with the approval of the Council. Prince Lignin, would Prince Alfred be agreeable to that stipulation?" Holum asked.

"Carver, I mean Prince Alfred, has never been interested in politics, but is aware that he will be expected to manage the Elder Tree Forest hamlets upon my father's passing. He has already represented those clans at the Assembly. He is the seventh son, with few ambitions, other than to marry the Princess Alaine, so I don't believe that he would disagree with that part of the contract," answered Lignin.

"The Contract also requires proof of nobility. Is there documentation of this for Prince Alfred?" Holum further questioned Prince Lignin.

"Our father would speak to that. There is no question that Alfred is our King, and there is no doubt that Prince Alfred is his son. Each clan family keeps its own archives and lineage tablets. When I send a message to my father, I can inform him that these records are needed."

"Actually, we must send a messenger to King Granth *and* your father," proposed King Holum. "I suggest a meeting of the Kings, including King Alfred, at Hawthorn Castle. I will escort Alaine and the ladies back to Hawthorn. We can plan a meeting at Hawthorn, in say, ten days hence. I will send a scout on ahead so that there is time to prepare. Is the plan agreeable to you, Prince Lignin?"

"Yes," answered Lignin. "I will join my brothers and we will quit Harbortown for our homes. Alfred will go to our father, and I will call a meeting of our Assembly. My brothers will spread news of the events to our clan families. Ten days would be time enough for us."

"So be it. There is much to do," said Holum, ending the discussion with some direction.

The next day, Irongate was in a frenzy. It was announced that Princess Alaine would be leaving, and that King Holum and Queen Hester would be taking her home to Hawthorn Castle. Initially, Holum planned to go without the Queen, but Hester refused to be left behind. After much non-regal shouting, which was either heard echoing through the halls or whispered about throughout the castle, the King relented to Hester's demands. Yet, Holum did win part of the battle. Hester would be limited to one maid and two traveling trunks. He said that she would have to make do. If she wasn't ready to leave at first light in the morning, she would be left at Irongate! Then he strutted off to his own apartment with some measure of pride. Such is married life, even for the royals.

Genna went from room to room helping Alaine and Charlyn repack their trunks. Soon, the trunks were closed, and clothing set out for the morning long before the dinner was brought to the rooms. The maid was eager to get home and begin her married life with Rand. Since their rural wedding, they had seen precious little of each other. She had not had much time to revel in being a new bride.

Nana, too, was ready to leave, with thoughts of her comfortable room and bed at Hawthorn Castle. Mistress Ronan stopped by to tell her she would be traveling with them to Hawthorn. King Holum agreed that she could visit her sister and family in Hawthorn. The housekeeper was in a twitter preparing for the trip, and quickly waved off, leaving Nana happy for a travel companion.

Alaine spent the morning arguing with Genna as to what should go into which trunk, while drifting off into daydreams about Carver, reliving the events of the betrothal ceremony.

Meanwhile, Lady Avis made arrangements with Seaken-Char to escort Alaine to return the betrothal gifts to Prince Sturgrom and the Marquis. The Duke arrived just after luncheon.

Prince Sturgrom welcomed them into his suite in his usual genteel manner. There were no hard feelings for not attaining Alaine's hand. In fact, his mood was very jovial as he offered them wine. He said that he was also in the process of preparing to leave Irongate – and not alone.

When Alaine failed to accept his proposal, he promptly asked another to be his bride. She was the Lady Charlotte, the daughter of Duke Labsum, probably ten winters older than Alaine, and frequently seen in the company of admirers around Sturgrom during his stay at Irongate. His trip to Hawthorn was not in vain. Charlotte was tall and thin and would make a stately queen for the land of Swerd, with plenty of time to produce the desired heir. Alaine could picture the white fur hat that she was returning on the Lady's chestnut curls. Alaine was truly happy for the Prince as she said goodbye.

At first, the next meeting with the Marquis, to return the jade pendant, was not as friendly. The man was cool, his ego bruised with Alaine's choice of husband, which appeared fanciful to him. He took the girl's age into account, blaming romantic notions rather than practicality. Duke Seaken-Char did much to appease the man, using his tenure of diplomacy to bring the Marquis around. The Duke convinced the man to travel along with the nobles going to Hawthorn, promising an introduction to King Granth and the other dukes of the Upper Kingdom. There was the possibility of trade deals to be made. The old Duke appealed to the Marquis as a merchant and the chance for profitable opportunities. Alaine voiced her support, calling him a part of the royal family, who, by improving trade, would benefit all concerned. She flattered his great ship and praised the amount of goods that it could transport on his visits to Hawthorn. The Marquis' mood improved as he considered the benefits, and finally agreed to make the journey to Hawthorn Castle.

While Alaine took care of these duties, Charlyn felt trapped in the rooms with Lady Avis, Nana and Genna. There had been no note or word from Kent. She wished to speak to him and longed for the closeness they previously shared. She hoped that there might be a chance to see him at dinner, only to learn that a cold supper would be served in the rooms. The kitchen and the castle staff were in a bustle, preparing for the early morning departure of the royals.

That evening Charlyn retired to her room early, wishing to be alone instead of trying to make polite conversation. She suffered from an anxious melancholy, having not spoken to Kent since the morning of the Queen's garden party, and *that* had ended in an argument. She could feel their budding romance slipping away. All too soon she would be at home in her forest clad lodge, alone, but older and wiser about the world. She sat on the bed as forlorn thoughts nagged her.

It was getting late. The dinner dishes had long since been taken away. The fires were lit, the chamber pots emptied, and the beds turned down for Alaine's last night in Irongate Castle. She sat alone in a comfortable chair by the fireplace, with the heavily shadowed room surrounding her. One small lamp sat upon the low table, casting dim light. Her feelings were confused in an anticlimax after the excitement of the previous day. Sleep was far from her mind.

Over dinner, Lady Avis, focusing on their departure in the morning, had nothing to say about the betrothal between Alaine and the Forest Prince. She seemed to believe that much more was left to be said by King Granth. The engagement was in doubt, and Avis would not encourage Alaine, only to see her hurt in the end. The Lady retired to her room early in the evening after a second glass of wine. Slightly depressed with the state of things, the good aunt felt she had done all that she could to promote a successful match for her niece, only to deliver the current dilemma to her sister and King Granth.

Nana and Genna left for their rooms shortly after supper, Nana saying that she must pack her things and prepare to leave. Genna made similar excuses, but Alaine knew that she was off to meet with Rand.

Charlyn had also gone to her room. Alaine felt sorry for her friend, who was pining over the lack of contact with Kent but knew she could do little to relieve the situation. The two would have to find each other.

Alaine sat deep in thought when a tapping came from the outer door. Rushing to answer, she imagined improbable thoughts of Carver waiting on the other side. But no, it was a porter bearing a small scroll of paper tied with a string. The man was somewhat surprised to recognize the Princess herself, answering the door.

"I am sorry to bother you so late, Princess, but I thought that it would not wait until morning. This was delivered for you by a guard from the gatehouse."

On the way to her room, she grabbed the small lamp, wishing to open the little roll of paper with assured privacy. Once seated on the bed, she untied the string and unfurled the parchment. A wooden pipe with its intricate mouthpiece and round little holes along the shaft fell onto the bed. It was the pipe Carver used to play music at Middleoak. A scratched penmanship put a message on the page.

My Love,

Keep this pipe for me until we meet again. All is well. I go to my father to demand his support for us. I promise our reunion in Hawthorn. My thoughts are only of you.

— Carver

Tears came to Alaine's eyes. It was the first time he had written to her. It was a promise of his love and their future together. It was the hope that they would find a way to be married. This was what she needed to keep her strong in the days to come. Now she could go to bed and wish for dreams of her love.

25

Homecoming

By the next evening, the royal party was having a greatly desired meal at Brighton Towers. It was a long day on Central Road as, true to his word, the king's coach left Irongate at first light. They did not make a stop for rest and water until the sun was high at midday. Unfortunately for Alaine and Charlyn, they shared the ride with the King and Queen Hester. The Queen was intent on changing Alaine's mind regarding her choice in husbands. She said that, once at Hawthorn Castle, Alaine may feel differently about her choice, and that it was not too late for her to change her mind.

The one thing that added some levity to the day was Stenson — the stowaway. As the caravan of coaches and wagons stopped for a break, Stenson snuck out of a wagon to get a drink, only to be spotted by the Marquis, who was on horseback, riding with the men and guards. The Marquis quickly dismounted and marched the boy forward to where his parents were on foot by their coach. His mother exploded in a tirade of parental anger, with the boy's excuses falling on deaf ears. The Queen threatened to send the errant Prince home with a guardsman. Fortunately, his father interceded on his behalf, allowing him to continue on the journey. Stenson probably wished that he was back in the wagon with trunks, rather than spending the rest of the day sitting between Alaine and Charlyn under his mother's stern glare.

Brighten Towers was a great stone and wood edifice, its two block towers jutting high into the sky, threatening to the observer, while actually being a bed and breakfast for travelers along the road. Duke Brighton, the richest among the Lower Kingdom dukes, provides meals and a bed for a small fee. Constant are the commuters along the Central Road through all seasons, so the Duke was a welcoming host. Tonight, the suite of rooms held separate for King Holum would be in use. Duke Brighton and his Lady attended the Betrothal Ceremony at Irongate. They now traveled home with the royal company, but a runner was sent ahead the night before. When they arrived, a hot meal was waiting, and the bedrooms prepared for the night.

Alaine and Charlyn sat together at the end of one long table. The supper of cold fowl, pickled eggs, roasted lamb, and farm vegetables was well received by all. Alaine could not resist another buttered slice of the sweet, brown bread.

Now the company was breaking up for the night. King Holum, Queen Hester and almost all of the ladies had already left the table for their beds. A group of men gathered around another table, where bursts of laughter would break out from time to time as cups of wine were consumed. Charlyn noticed that Kent and his lieutenant were among them, so she dallied over her food. Not a word had passed between her and Kent during the day of travel.

Finally, Alaine pled weariness and rose to go upstairs to the room that she would share with Charlyn. Being a Princess had no bearing when it came to available sleeping space. Charlyn also stood to leave, but instead of going upstairs, she wandered through the lower floor rooms of Brighton Towers until coming upon doors leading to an outside terrace and garden. She followed her urge to explore and get a breath of night air.

Outside, Charlyn was rewarded with a fine summer night. There was only a slice of a moon and a few puffy, gray clouds in the sky. The air was balmy and smelled of grass. A chorus of crickets were making their chirps, calling to one another. Charlyn walked along the smooth pavers to the far end of the stone porch, standing still in the darkness while taking in the night. Then, footsteps were heard on the stones, and Charlyn watched as a figure walked through the door and out to the lawn. For a few moments the crickets were silent, sensing his presence.

Charlyn stood very still…barely breathing to avoid any sound. The dim light highlighted the black of his silhouette – the forehead, the straight nose, the familiar mouth and chin. His hair was tied back so his clean-shaven jawline was outlined against the garden beyond.

"Charlyn?" a soft, masculine voice pierced the silence.

"I am here," she returned, stepping out of the deep shadows.

Kent turned toward her, and with a determined stride, closed the distance between them.

"Charlyn," he repeated softly. Putting his hands on her waist, Kent bent his head to kiss her lightly on the forehead.

Placing her faith in him, Charlyn stepped forward, closing the small space between them. That was all of the encouragement Kent needed from her, as his arms embraced her, and his lips found hers. It was a kiss so long, so desired by both, that they emerged breathless.

"The last few days have been torture," Kent said, with emotion, as he held her close. "I have so wanted to speak to you. I am sorry for being a brute the morning of the garden party. Nothing was your fault. That night when Brannon assaulted you, I truly wanted to run him through with my dagger. Thank goodness that Holum was there. I was not even thinking that I could have started a war between Hawthorn and Brannon's country. It was then I realized the depth of my feelings for you."

Kent stopped speaking, to take a breath. Tears of relief flooded into Charlyn's eyes.

"I couldn't speak to you the day of Alaine's ceremony, and yesterday my mother appeared to be holding you captive. I tried writing you a letter, but there was so much to be said and I couldn't get it right. I want to tell you everything and get your thoughts. What you may think means much to me. I want to be with you every day.

"I've been thinking of the future and decided to hand over the Garrison to Miles. I will promote him to captain. The Garrison will remain housed on my lands, ready for service at the command of King Granth. Then I will be free to take up my position at court and manage my landholdings. I need you with me. Charlyn, if you will have me, I wish for us to marry."

After a brief pause, "What say you?"

"Yes, I wish that too. I have missed you. Even though it has only been days, it felt much longer," she answered, the tears now rolling down her cheeks, while she took in what he said. "Do you think your mother will approve of our marriage?"

"Are you jesting? She is already seeing the grandchildren playing in the garden at Juniper Lodge. What about your father? Will he give his permission when I ask him for your hand?"

Charlyn laughed, "With three daughters to marry, I am sure he will agree to a Duke of Hawthorn."

"Then it is settled. We will have a quiet pledge between us. When we reach Hawthorn, I will seek out your father for his consent, and allow him to make the announcement. I will tell my mother, and you may tell Alaine, swearing her to secrecy. In the meantime, here is the Morr-Leigh badge for you to keep until we are wed. Then you shall have my grandmother's ring."

Kent handed her the familiar round metal pin usually attached to his cloak. She laid her head against his shoulder, and they held each other close, while the crickets sang their song.

Holum was restless with the slow pace of the coaches and wagons. He encouraged some of those on horseback to ride on ahead. Other than a picnic lunch in a roadside field, the horses were pushed from sunrise to sundown. Alaine and Charlyn changed coaches, much to Alaine's relief, so Stenson rode alone with his parents. Duke Seaken-Char came to the girls' rescue, offering room in his carriage with him and Lady Avis. The interior of the Duke's coach was as plush and comfortable as the King's. Lady Avis reported that she had spoken to Nana, traveling with Mistress Ronan, Genna, and March, the Queen's maid; and the nurse had no complaints other than the long hours on the road, and its effect on her "old bones".

The next stop for the caravan was Leggot and nearby Eckelform Hall. Kent and Miles met up with the Morr-Leigh Garrison that was camped there, waiting for them. The cooks made sure that all of the men, including the King's Guard, were well fed and settled for the night. The royal party made their way on to the Hall, with the high-pitched slate roof for which it was known. A hearty supper of lamb stew and venison pies was prepared for the guests. Barely finished with the food, most were off to bedchambers, because the King demanded another early morning departure.

A night in tents could not be avoided, since the next stop was Seaken Hall, too far a distance to travel from Leggot in one day. The caravan quit early to allow for setting up camp before sunset. Once again, Annie and her girls, along with Smyth, found themselves responsible for preparing a large meal for the company. Having traveled with fresh meat and vegetables from Leggot farms, they met the challenge. After dinner, Stenson was sitting around a fire circle with his father, the Marquis and other men, enjoying every minute of the camping experience. Later, small lanterns glowed inside the many tents, going out one by one, as the travelers settled in for the night.

Seaken Hall, located several miles off the Central Road, was set in the countryside, surrounded by farmland. The winding road traveled alongside apple and nut orchards. Green pastures led to the large farming village of Char, where various shops and townhouses lined the high street. Not far from there was the great gatehouse, leading to Seaken Hall. A massive guardhouse was the first structure after the main gates. Alaine was surprised to see that the guardhouse, stables, and horse corrals were as large as her father's holdings. The rural driveway leading up to Seaken Hall was lined with mature oak trees that provided shaded passage all the way to the circular front courtyard. The two-story building itself was made of gray block, covered with clinging vines, in many places climbing to the roof. Two imposing doors were set back in the center of the blocks, that were otherwise windowless along the front of the building. There were several other large homes dotting the nearby landscape.

Alaine had heard talk of Seaken Hall from time to time at her father's court. The old Duke rarely raved of the place, allowing others to pay it justice. There was talk of its great assembly room and vast dining hall with high, decorated arches.

The weary travelers filed into the great entry foyer, with its various staircases leading to the second floor. Next, the royal party flowed into a room called The Painted Salon. This was a comfortable, great room with long couches, tables for card games, and overstuffed chairs where one could doze. Yet, what made the room famous were the walls painted with scenes of famous landmarks of the land of Hawthorn. Landscapes included old Craig Castle, the steep cliffs along the Strait of Meteran, and the lighthouse tower at West Dunes Keep, among others. Alaine came to a full stop before a depiction on a wall, next to one of the fireplaces. There she saw a detailed picture of the waterfall at Middleoak, as viewed from a spot near where Carver kissed her. Whoever painted this must have been there to give so perfect a replication of the falls and the surroundings. She knew that Seaken Hall had stood for over a hundred winters, built in the time of her great-grandfather, King Arden. Is it possible that the painter was a friend of the forest clans, she wondered? The panorama could have been painted before any division of the land and forests.

With these thoughts, Alaine entered the dining hall, following Duke Seaken-Char, Lady Avis, and the King and Queen. The long table was lavishly set, surrounded by the Duke's family, awaiting their patriarch prior to taking their seats. Rengard quickly made introductions of his two sons, their wives, and their five children, now fully grown with spouses of their own.

It was after dinner, when all had filled their stomachs, that Duke Seaken-Char rose from his seat at the head of the table to offer a toast, "Your Majesties, Prince Stenson, Princess Alaine, Marquis de Locke, guests and loved ones, it is a pleasure to have you all here tonight. It has been over sixteen summers since I lost my beloved wife, Matrecia. Since then, I've been shuffling around this great hall, expecting to live the rest of my life alone. Since the boys have taken over managing the lands, my only obligation has been to King

Granth and his Council. With little demands on my time, I must admit that I fell into bad habits of rambling between my cozy den and my bedchamber, sometimes not leaving the house for days at a time. My dear daughters-in-law would frequently coax me out for dinner at their homes, but most of the time I was here alone.

"I must thank our lovely Princess Alaine, because her journey south to Irongate gave me a purpose to leave home. I have to admit, with apology, I wanted to check on how Duke Morr-Leigh was doing with his role as a royal escort for the Princess. Bringing food for all, I was pleasantly surprised when I entered their encampment. It was one of the happiest days of my recent life, thanks primarily to this enchanting noblewoman," motioning to the woman at his side, "the Lady Avis. After a long discussion with my sons, I decided to follow the fair Lady to Irongate.

"Now, I am happy and no longer alone. I have put aside my stick and walk more every day. Fortunately, tonight, thanks to the Lady's good grace, I can announce our intent to marry. That is, as soon as we can get all of these young nobles settled down," he quipped, as laughter went around the table. "Will you all raise your cups to the Lady Avis Leigh, my future bride!"

Best wishes and happy thoughts floated around the table as a dessert of honey cake with clotted cream and strawberries was served.

The caravan arrived at Hawthorn Castle after midnight on the fifth long day of travel. King Granth and Queen Iris hastily rose from their beds, in robes and night caps, to meet the wilted travelers. The two Kings embraced each other, as it had been several years since their reunion. Queen Iris pleased Hester with a warm welcome and compliments regarding the sleepy Prince Stenson, now standing taller than his aunt. Queen Hester introduced her cousin, the Marquis, who promptly thanked the King and Queen for their hospitality in accepting his visit at the invitation of the Princess. The offer of food was rejected by Holum, explaining that they had stopped for a meal and to rest the horses at Crossroads Inn. It was then Holum decided not to spend another night on the road, so they pushed on to Hawthorn Village. Queen Iris led Holum and Hester to the best suite of guest rooms, promising time to talk on the morrow.

After a heartfelt reunion with her parents, Alaine quickly requested a change in bedchambers, wishing to be near her Aunt Avis. She also requested Charlyn to have the room next to hers. Her mother was surprised at the requests.

"What about your beloved tower room, Alaine?"

"Give it to Prince Stenson, mother. He will enjoy it, as well as having some distance from his parents. His mother was displeased with him for stowing away on the journey," Alaine explained.

Iris laughed, "I will see to it. The lad is certainly welcome. It will be good to get to know him. He was so little the last time he was here."

Later, Alaine changed into her nightclothes and settled into a large bedchamber next to her Aunt. Queen Iris, not wishing to wait for the next day to speak to her daughter, knocked on the door and entered, carrying a cup.

"I've brought you a small draught of port to help you sleep," her mother said, bringing the wine to the bed where Alaine was propped up on down pillows.

"Oh, mother, it is so good to be home!" she said, giving a long sigh. "There were times in recent days I believed never to see this castle again, or you and father."

Queen Iris took a long look at her daughter, realizing that this was not the child that left only a couple full moons before. The girl had matured into a young woman in what seemed to be overnight.

"Your father received a rather long letter from Holum, telling of the betrothal ceremony and your unexpected choice of husbands. I must say, dear, that we were very surprised. It has led to circumstances that couldn't be predicted. Tomorrow your father will meet with Holum and others to understand all that has happened. He also called for a meeting of the Council."

"I will have my say, too, mother. I love Prince Alfred and will have him as my husband, or none other. Not only is it the best for me and Carver - I mean, Prince Alfred - but I am convinced that it is the best for the land of Hawthorn. It is time for all of the people of the land to come together. It will take time, but there will be a beginning, with our marriage," Alaine professed.

"How can you be so sure of him, Alaine? None of us have met this young man. How well can you know him over such a short time? Marriage is a bond that will hold you for the rest of your life. It is very serious for you and for our country," Iris reasoned.

"He has shown his love for me, risking all to have a life with me. I love him and I know that we are destined to be together. It is our desire to marry."

"Well, it is very late. We will speak more of this tomorrow. For now, take your rest and be assured that your father and I love you and want only what is best for you."

"Please don't close your mind to him, mother. I don't think anyone could love me more than he does. Once you meet him, you will love him as I do. We will need your support."

"All right, but for now, you look tired. Get some rest and know that we are glad that you are safely home."

Iris rose from the bed, caressed her daughter's head, and left Alaine to her own thoughts.

Townspeople living along the main thoroughfare leading to the Hawthorn Castle gates, were awakened in the middle of the night to the sounds of horses, carriages, and wagons passing by their homes. There was no sleeping through the commotion.

The next day, it was learned that Princess Alaine had returned home. Coming with her, to everyone's surprise, was King Holum and Queen Hester. It had been many seasons past since the Lower Kingdom royals visited Hawthorn. The status of the betrothal of the Princess was unknown, but it was said an unknown nobleman traveled with the royal party.

If there was one thing the people of Hawthorn Village didn't like, it was not knowing what was going on at the castle. Huddles of housewives stood outside the shops and at their fenceposts, swapping whatever tidbits of news that could be had. Their usual informants, friends or relatives who worked at the castle, were also in the dark over what was really going on. Speculation was running high in the village.

After Alaine's return home, King Granth had a long discussion with Duke Morr-Leigh and Duke Seaken-Char. He came away with a sense of what had transpired on the journey to Irongate and what happened once they had reached Harbortown. He particularly wanted to know everything about the encounters with the forest clans and the time at Middleoak. Most of all, he wanted any details concerning Prince Alfred, or Carver Vale, as he was known. Kent gave a detailed account.

King Granth spent the next few days gathering information. He spent the afternoons closeted with King Holum. The brothers discussed any events remotely related to the deep forests of the land and the forest clans. They poured over maps of Hawthorn dating back to their grandfather's time. These maps had been drawn up long before the division of the land into two kingdoms, and possibly prior to the signing of The Treaty of the Trees. The castles at Hawthorn Village and Harbortown had not yet been built. Craig Castle was the only castle on the maps. Only a few of the strongholds of the dukes were shown from that time.

However, these maps did show things that were not charted in future maps. All of the eight forest regions were clearly defined. Old roads and paths, many times, went directly through the forests. The maps also showed the Central Road, already in use as the main artery going from north to south. Holum compared the list of names of King Alfred's sons, and the names of the forests they claimed. Many of the forest names were the same or similar to the names on the old maps.

The royal brothers also discussed The Treaty of the Trees, which, so far, had served them well. There had been a long peace between the peoples of the land. Both Kings were concerned as to how a marriage between Alaine and one of the Forest Princes could affect the peace and the longstanding agreement.

Granth knew that he needed to understand the girl's decision regarding a union with the Forest Prince. Her mother was unable to sway the girl from her convictions or prepare her for possible disappointment. It was late in the day that King Granth came to Alaine's room, ready for a father-daughter talk.

"So, this is the jewelry chest that you spoke of. It does show real craftsmanship," he said, while running his hand over the relief on the lid of the wooden case. "How could he know our village so well as in this carving?"

"I believe that his home is near here. Carver - I mean Prince Alfred - told me he comes to the village often," Alaine answered.

"If he visits the town, then people must know him. I will put out queries for us to learn more about him."

"I have learned all that I need to know," Alaine persisted, defiantly.

"There is no harm in gathering whatever is known about him prior to his father arriving," the King defended.

"His father is coming?" Alaine asked, suddenly alert with this new information.

"Yes, a visit is expected in two days' time. A message was received by Squire Dilford. Your uncle and I will meet with King Alfred," the father responded.

The discussion with her father ended in a congenial but noncommitted manner. King Granth remained skeptical.

After her father left, Alaine couldn't help but feel heightened worry. Will it be possible for the three kings to agree on the marriage, she wondered? There would be little peace for her until the matter was settled.

As King Granth sought information from townspeople, he found that Prince Alfred and his dog were well known in the town - not as a prince, but as Carver Vale. The reports were favorable. It seems the royal butcher always saved bones and meat scraps for Carver's dog, after the lad made a cupboard for storing salt for sale with meats he sold. There were several references to a shop at the front of the blacksmith's cottage where carved boxes, chairs, and other items were for sale, all made by Carver Vale.

"Jones, send two men to the blacksmith in the village and tell him that King Granth wishes to speak to him," the monarch ordered.

Hewitt, working at his forge by the cottage, was astounded when the king's men showed up, summoning him to the castle. He begged for time to remove his heavy apron, wash, and put on his best shirt and jacket. Finnie was in a dither, wondering what King Granth would want with her husband.

Soon, Hewitt stood before King Granth and King Holum, his head bowed, and his hat in his hands.

"I have been told that you and your wife are friends with a man named Carver Vale," the King began. "I also heard that he stays at your cottage when he comes to the village. Is this true?"

"Yes, Your Majesty."

"How long have you known him?"

"About four winters."

"Do you know where he comes from?"

"I think he lives with his father in the nearby countryside."

"Does he speak of his family?" the King questioned.

"At times he talks about his brothers. I believe there are a lot of them. From what he says, I don't think they live around here. He has never spoken of a mother, and I have never asked, sensing it was something he didn't wish to speak of."

"Has he ever spoken about the Princess Alaine?"

"He rarely speaks of her, but I know that he has a great admiration for her."

"How do you know that?"

"Just a feeling, really. He will go out of his way to catch a glimpse of her when she comes to the village."

Hewitt wouldn't mention what he thought were Carver's nighttime trips to the castle.

"Did you know that he followed her when she recently left on the journey south to Irongate Castle?"

"Yes," the man answered, humbly, beginning to understand the reason for today's summons.

"Did he tell you why he would follow her?"

"He said that he needed to know what happened to her."

"Did you know that Carver Vale is really Prince Alfred of the forest clans and that his father is King Alfred, ruler of the forest people?"

The blacksmith stood awed with silent disbelief. He reviewed in his mind what the King had just said. This was the Carver Vale that rolled on the floor when he played with the children. Could he possibly be a prince? Hewitt thought.

"Can he really be a prince, Sire? His clothes are rough, and he appears to have no wealth. That is, he cares nothing about what his woodworks sell for. My wife puts aside the coins for him. I must say, he does have good manners, and I thought it unusual that he can read and write. He's teaching my boy letters."

"I assure you that it is true. At Irongate, he appeared with his six brothers before King Holum's court and asked for the Princess Alaine's hand in marriage. She accepted him, so we are in a quandary. Soon his father will meet with us to discuss the match."

"Finnie will never believe this," Hewitt mumbled to himself.

"What did you say?" asked King Granth.

"It's all just a little hard to believe…Carver being a prince."

"Yes, many of us feel the same disbelief right now."

Hewitt left the castle and walked toward his home, not knowing what to think. The King asked him to keep the talk of Carver and the Princess to himself. He'd have to tell Finnie if he wanted to get any sleep that night. She would have to be sworn to tell no one.

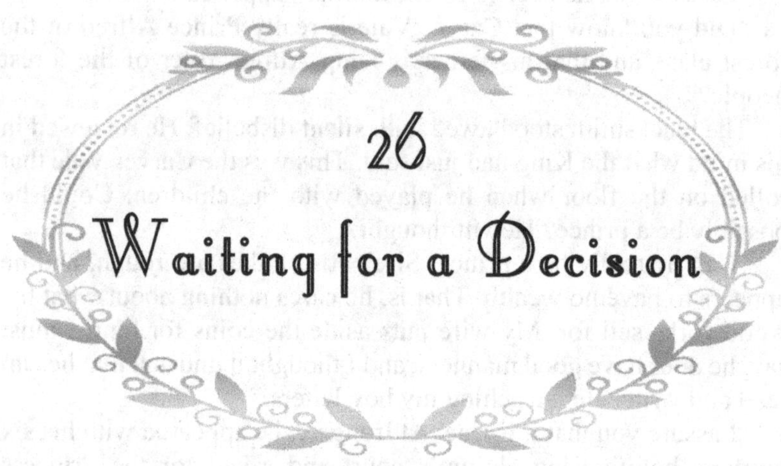

In the days after the homecoming, King Granth and King Holum were closeted away, putting their heads together. They discussed the dilemma before them concerning Alaine and the Forest Prince. One by one, they met with the Dukes of the King's Council soliciting opinions. There were no strong objections to the match. The men of the Council didn't think that the marriage would lead to any great change to the society of the northern kingdom, however they did believe that it would bring more attention to the forest clans that occupied the forests.

Although Alaine was very glad to be home at Hawthorn Castle, the approval of her betrothal to Carver Vale was always at the back of her mind. Yet there were other demands upon her, such as assisting her mother in the entertainment of the Irongate guests during their stay. Queen Iris and Alaine, along with Lady Avis, planned outings, afternoon ladies' gatherings, and banquet dinners for royalty and visiting nobles. Queen Iris, for the sake of good relations, did what she could to allow Queen Hester to be the center of attention as an honored guest, doing her best to meet Hester's needs.

One day, an outing of Iris, Hester, Avis, and the Marquis was to a nearby woolen mill, where sheep and goat wools were transformed into durable textiles used for clothing. Hester considered herself somewhat of an expert on fabrics and was interested in visiting the mill that followed the process of spinning the wool into thread. The busy loom vault held many different sizes of looms, all staffed by experienced weavers. Envisioning the prospects of a multitude of clothing items, the group returned to Hawthorn Castle with so many bolts of cloth, a wagon was borrowed to hold the purchases of the day. Queen Hester was thinking of colorful woolen gowns for foggy, winter mornings at Irongate. The Marquis de Locke bought textiles to transport home to Raydon as a gift for his mother.

In honor of Queen Hester's visit, Queen Iris held a formal luncheon, inviting all of the ladies of the Hawthorn court, as well as their daughters. The event allowed the ladies to show off the best of their fair-weather attire. A meal of spring greens and chilled pheasant with mushrooms was followed by plates of cheeses with rye bread. Dessert was cherry tarts with sweetened butter cream. Several local wines were served with the meal, causing some of the younger maidens to fall into giggles and bouts of laughter. Hester, in a jovial mood after several glasses of wine, thanked Queen Iris for such a delightful afternoon.

That evening, Alaine retired to her new bedroom with green rugs on the floor and plush, burgundy bed coverings. Pleased with the accomplishments of the day, her mind was too busy for sleep. Carver and his green eyes always filled her thoughts at the end of the day. She would wait for the castle to quiet prior to making her way to the kitchen and the doorway to her garden.

"Come to bed, Iris. There is no point standing at the window," King Granth urged, while putting out the bedside lamp.

"I thought sure that she would go down to her garden tonight. Alaine has darkened circles under her eyes, so I know she isn't sleeping," assumed the concerned mother.

"She will be fine, my dear. We know that Alaine has never needed much sleep," Granth replied.

"I have tried talking to her. I've never seen her so determined as she is about this young man," Iris lamented, as she climbed into the high bed.

"Yes, she is determined, but she is also a princess of the realm and knows that she must bow to duty. It is yet to be decided as to whether the match can go forward," the King reminded. "I must say, I have been questioning all who know of the man and have heard nothing that would raise alarm. The thing is, no one other than the blacksmith seems to really know him. Oh yes, they recognize the lad and his dog, and many have spoken with him, but he has managed to keep his true identity a secret from the villagers. He stays with the blacksmith's family when he is in town, but the poor villager was speechless when I told him the person he knows as Carver Vale is really Prince Alfred of the forest clans."

"Hester still believes Alaine should marry the Marquis. Handsome and rich as he may be, there doesn't seem to be an attraction there," Iris mused.

"Except for the Duke of the Walls' youngest girl. Closin, is it?"

"What?"

"The Marquis, or Felix, as Holum calls him, appears to be entranced by the girl. He persuaded a change in table seating at dinner tonight so he could sit beside her."

"Granth, she is but a child. She has just put her hair up this winter. This is her first visit to court, and her mother keeps a watchful eye. No, she is far too young for a pursuit by the Marquis."

"You are probably right. I was just surprised to see it," Granth relented, with a yawn.

"What does Holum say about Alaine and Prince Alfred?" Iris asked, changing the subject.

"Holum and I are of like mind when it comes to this match. At Irongate, Holum spoke with an older brother who is involved with the Assembly of the forest clans. He was to take the news of the betrothal to their council. Holum and I worry of any unrest or conflict with the forest people. Holum says a couple of the Lower Kingdom dukes have coveted the forest lands bordering their landholdings for years. We would not want a war. We will have to wait to see what King Alfred has to say, and how a marriage would impact The Treaty of the Trees."

"Poor Alaine. I fear that her heart will be broken if things don't work out. It is her first love."

"We can't resolve this tonight, Iris. Go to sleep, now," returned the sensible King.

When Carver showed up at Hewitt and Finnie's cottage expecting to have dinner and a pleasant visit with the family, he was in for a surprise. Instead, he was met by the couple standing together in a cool reception. Their four children, excited to see Carver after the time away, were told to go outside, their mother's arm up with finger pointing to the door.

"Prince Alfred?" Hewitt demanded.

"I came to tell you about that," responded Carver.

"After all this time?" asked Finnie. "Did you not have trust in us?"

"Of course! I trust you both. I would have been lost without all that you have done for me," Carver replied, hanging his head.

Finnie's heart softened, seeing Carver contrite and sincere.

"Come, sit at the table and tell us about it," Finnie urged, as she moved to the only dining space in the cottage. "Now, why didn't you tell us who you are?" she probed once they were seated.

Carver began his story, "My people of the forests don't associate with the people of the fields. We stay to ourselves and guard our privacy. That's how we are brought up. We have our own ways, our own language, and we have our own system of communication and leadership. To leave the forest is frowned upon, especially for the son of the King. Because I'm my father's son, I was prepared to represent the clans of Elder Tree Forest at our Assembly. Like my brothers, I was taught the language of the kingdom by a wise old tutor, who spent his younger winters among your people. My father believes that we must be able to speak with you. Our senior folk all speak the language and many of the young ones.

"Other than my lessons, I had much freedom. My father is aged, and my brothers were grown and left the homestead. From the time I was small, I would wander in the forest, always coming closer to the edges. From the trees, I used to watch the horses and the wagons going along Central Road, coming and going from the village. My curiosity grew as I strayed closer and closer to the town. Gradually, I started coming to the stone bridge, where I could sit and watch the activity of the village and the children playing in the street. One day, at your Winterfest, I brought some of my little animal carvings and handed them out to the children. That was how it began, and, well, you know the rest."

"What about the name, Carver Vale?" Hewitt asked.

"Being the last child, I was named after my father, so there were two 'Alfreds' in the family. My next-older brother saw that I enjoyed carving pieces of wood and started calling me Carver. Soon, others were using the name. The name Vale is close to a word we use in our language which means 'an open space in the woods'."

"What about Princess Alaine?" Finnie asked. "Is it true that you are betrothed?"

"I first saw her on an early visit to the village. I was attracted to her and had a longing to know her. I knew I was a prince, so I reasoned we were of similar rank. My father and I spoke of it, and he tried to dissuade me, but by that time, I was going up to the castle at night to be near her when she went to her garden.

"I became sure she was the one I wanted for my bride. During the journey to Irongate, I managed to meet with her when her company was camped by the woods. She seemed to like me and that gave me the hope to continue my aspirations. My brothers followed me to Harbortown, supporting me in my quest. They went with me to Irongate, where the betrothal ceremony was being held. It was a surprise to all when she accepted my marriage proposal. Now there is much ado among our people and yours. All of the kings of the land are involved. It remains my hope that we will wed soon."

"Is your father in favor?" inquired Hewitt.

"He says that he must hold council with the other kings, so I must wait until then to know the outcome," Carver relayed, with dismay.

At this time, the nosey children began coming back into the house, bringing Astra with them.

"You must all clean your hands!" Winnie ordered her brood, "Dinner is almost ready, and Carver will be eating with us."

Carver smiled, relieved he was forgiven and once again welcome in the family.

After dinner, Hewitt and Carver sat before a low fire in the grate, as Carver recounted all that had occurred since he left Hawthorn to follow Alaine. There was a certain freedom, now that he could speak of details that included his being a member of the forest people. Hewitt spoke of his summons by King Granth, and the questions about Carver's life among the villagers. The cottage became quiet as the children went to sleep in their beds and Finnie retired to her room.

Carver took his leave, with Astra settled in her old bed near the forge. Hewitt knew that Carver was off to a visit at the castle. With a pat on the shoulder, he cautioned Carver to be careful.

Except for an occasional bark of a dog, the town of Hawthorn was quiet. The houses had gone dark and there was no movement on the side streets. With speed, Carver made his way on a familiar route to the castle. He climbed the high stone wall and surveyed the castle grounds for any motion, prior to jumping to the ground and deftly making his way toward the back of the castle, seeking the limestone walls surrounding Alaine's garden. Rather than taking his usual place by the back wall, Carver trekked around to the open arches in the side wall, climbing up, over and into the plot to await the girl he knew would come. The garden was silent, with no sounds of the night. Even the small fountain sat stagnant. So Carver took a seat on the bench where the Princess normally sat during her nighttime visits. He would wait for her.

The night went on. No light was coming from the castle's tower slits or windows. At last, the small door at the other end of the garden opened and a cloaked figure came through to the yard. Carver stood and softly called her name.

"Alaine!"

At once, Alaine was surprised, then relieved, and suddenly filled with joy as she hurried to join him. His arms welcomed her in an embrace, as he held her to his chest. Alaine could hear his heart beating, while taking in the faint scent of the forest on him. They were both so happy to see each other. "How did you get here?" she asked, as they settled themselves close together on the bench.

"I had to see you, and hoped that you would come to the garden," Carver said, with a small laugh, not revealing that he had come to the garden many times before. "The walls of this stronghold are not enough to keep me away. I missed you so much, and I feared that you may not still want me as a husband."

Now it was her turn to give a laugh as she reached to hold his hand, longing for his touch.

"You must not fear. I have thought of nothing but you and our possible life together. For instance, where shall we live? And I'm wondering if your people will accept me. I must learn their language, so that I can speak with them. You must teach me," Alaine prattled on.

"Where we would live is a good question. I have responsibilities to the nearby forest clans. My father has a very roomy manse in the trees, but he favors a smaller cabin nearby, enjoying his solitude. So there is a place for us in the woods. I have come to enjoy Hawthorn Village and the townsfolk. I believe it would be good to split our time, living in both places."

"What did your Assembly say to our marriage?" Alaine asked, fearing the answer.

"I traveled with Lignin to the council meeting where my brother presented the idea to the members. Much discussion was had. There are always those that wish for no change in the situation between our peoples. Some expressed the fear of the loss of our woodlands – that is a long-held apprehension. So easy it would be to light fires and burn us out, one forest at a time."

"That is a very frightening thought," Alaine agreed.

"Some of the younger people would like to have more interactions with those outside the woods. Most of the members who saw you at Middleoak were in favor of the match, reasoning that the joining could be beneficial. In the end, there was no agreement, putting the decision onto the shoulders of my father."

"What will happen, then?"

"It is up to my father to speak with the kings of Hawthorn. He agrees that he must come here to meet with them. He has sent a letter to your father," Carver informed.

"Yes, my father spoke of it. Father refuses to give me an answer about his decision. I hope that your father comes soon."

"You must not be dismayed. We must be patient. I have faith that we will be together," consoled Carver.

"That is my hope, too" Alaine said, wistfully.

Alaine searched his face in the darkness, enjoying the unexpected time with him. He casually twisted a lock of her hair in his fingers, never getting enough of looking at her. Slowly, he bent his head forward and gave her a gentle kiss that became more ardent as she responded to him. Holding each other in the darkness, the night passed by too quickly. There was no further need for words, the closeness being enough for them both.

Alaine, Charlyn and Genna sat in a circle on the rug around Nana's chair in her sitting room. It was a little room off her bedroom, where the nurse spent much of her time. The low fire was burning in the little iron stove, as the older woman was always cold. They were making warm jackets for the children of Hawthorn Village, a usual summer project, to be handed out at the Harvest Festival. Since the girls were free for the afternoon, Nana enlisted them for help.

"Where is your mother, today?" asked Nana, pulling down feathers from the crate in the center of the circle.

"She and Aunt Avis have taken Hester for a ride in the country and to the village to visit the shops. I fear Aunt Hester will not be impressed after seeing the stores in Harbortown. Then, they are to have luncheon at the hostel. I think mother is running out of ideas on how to entertain Hester," answered Alaine.

"Last night's dinner must have been exciting, especially for you, Charlyn. It was the talk of the castle this morning. When will be the wedding?" inquired the nurse.

All focused on the fair Lady, and Charlyn felt a blush come to her face. "My father insists that it will have to wait until after the Harvest Festival. He thinks there should be a proper engagement period, especially after what happened with Esbeth of late," Charlyn answered, stuffing soft feathers into sewn pieces of wool.

Ears perked up for the story about Charlyn's sister.

"What *did* happen with Esbeth?" Alaine asked, having heard some whispers among the maids.

"You remember I told you about Will, the squire who came to Darkwood Lodge to train with my father's guard?" Charlyn began her story. "I believed that he had feelings for me, but as soon as I was out of sight, he transferred those attentions to my sister, Esbeth. The two were discovered by one of my father's mill managers at a storage shed. The man reported them to my father, who was outraged, as was my mother. Father called for the mayor of Darkwood Village to come to the lodge and demanded that the couple be married at once!"

Gasps were heard from Nana and Genna. Genna had some sympathy for the girl, having faced a similar situation. The stuffing of the feathers into the jacket shells temporarily stopped as they all looked to Charlyn, awaiting more details.

"Closin said they were married *that day* without a chance to even change their clothing. There was no wedding feast in the lodge that night, just tears. My father instructed mother to pack up all of Esbeth's clothes and belongings. The next morning, Esbeth and Will were loaded into a wagon, and sent to the squire's father in the next county. Father sent a letter demanding the man take responsibility for them, and said there would be no dowry, since the young man had taken advantage of Esbeth's innocence."

The sitting room was quiet, no one knowing what to say. Alaine thought of her clandestine meeting with Carver the previous night. Her mother and father would probably not be pleased, should they know of it.

"Well, in my long years, it is not the first time to hear such a tale," Nana added at last. "We can only hope that they will be happy together. How is your mother doing, losing two of her three daughters to marriage in such a short time?"

The story told, the stuffing and pinning of the jackets resumed.

"Mother and father are not getting along. Father blames mother for Esbeth's behavior and the shame she brought upon the house. Mother is upset that father has denied any sort of dowry for my sister," explained Charlyn.

"At least your father accepted Kent's request for your hand in marriage," Alaine reasoned.

"Kent said that the meeting with my father didn't start out well. Father was in a temper toward all young men. Kent had to convince him that he had developed a deep love for me during our journey and the time spent at Irongate. Kent told him of his mother's impending marriage to Duke Seaken-Char and her plan to move to Seaken Hall. Kent promised that I would become mistress of Juniper Lodge as soon as we marry. Upon some further persuasion, father gave Kent his consent."

"Your father seemed very happy when he announced the engagement at dinner last night," Alaine reminded. "In fact, almost everyone is approving. You are the talk of the court."

"I believe both of my parents are happy about the match. It's just that it comes so soon on the heels of the events with Esbeth," Charlyn added.

"I, for one, am so happy that Kent has found such a wonderful girl," Nana crooned. "It is time for him to stop running around with those soldiers and settle down."

"I heard that Kent and Duke Seaken-Char took the Marquis to the distillery, yesterday. Did Kent tell you?" Alaine asked Charlyn, while pinning a jacket seam, ready to be sewn.

"Yes, Kent said they all had a good time tasting the whiskey," Charlyn giggled. "Kent still smelled of it when he returned. I refused to kiss him. He said the Marquis hired five long wagons to transport all of the barrels he bought. They are on the way to Harbortown to be loaded on his ship. The liquor is made with barley and cannot be found in his country. The Marquis stands to make a fine profit."

"Where is the Marquis today? With Kent?" Alaine asked.

"That is another interesting story," replied Charlyn. "It seems that my father offered to take the Marquis to see the tree syrup farm. I went once when I was younger. The men tap the trees and collect the sap. The liquid is boiled down in big vats to make the thick, sweet syrup. Then it is put up in barrels and sold. The place is north on the road, so they will be gone all day."

"That sounds like a good day. Maybe the Marquis will buy some syrup barrels to take home," suggested Nana.

"What's interesting is that my father asked my mother to go along, but she refused. So he asked Closin if she would like to go, and she was thrilled at the prospect. The girl is infatuated with the Marquis. She believes him to be the most handsome man she has ever seen and does nothing to hide her admiration. You should have seen them sitting together at dinner last night. Mother says that father is encouraging it, and Closin will be in the depths of despair when the man leaves. Mother says that she is too young for marriage."

"Previously, when you spoke of Closin, I thought her to be a young girl, yet she is quite mature, and is taller than me. Her looks are very fair," Alaine observed, "with her hazel eyes and those little curls around her face."

"She is but fourteen last winter," stressed Charlyn. "I tell you; I do not look forward to the coach ride back to Darkwood with mother and father at odds, and Closin in misery over her lost Marquis."

"Worry not," said Nana. "Soon I will be knitting baby blankets for all of you young ladies."

"Sooner than you think, Nana. It is early days, but Rand and I may have a little babe after Winterfest," Genna announced. "Mother is very excited, but it is too soon to put the news out."

"Oh, Genna!" exclaimed Alaine, reaching to hug the girl.

The good wishes and conversation went on among the ladies. There was so much to look forward to. As happy as she was for Charlyn and Genna, Alaine hoped that *her* future would soon be as bright as she wished.

Queen Iris was determined to speak to her daughter, who appeared to be avoiding her. Nana pointed the Queen toward the girl's room where, at last, Iris found her.

"Alaine, I must speak with you," Iris called, entering the bedroom.

"What is it, mother?" Alaine asked, putting away clean clothes.

"Come sit down. We must discuss what will happen if there can be no approval of the marriage with Prince Alfred."

"I am hoping there *will* be an approval, mother."

"I know you are, dear; but I think you must prepare yourself for a chance of disappointment."

"Have you had news?" Alaine asked suspiciously, fearing her mother may have heard some bit of information.

"No, no there is no news. Your father is trying to keep an open mind. As King, he and your uncle must think of the people and their wellbeing. I'm sure you would not want to be the cause of bloodshed or war."

Alaine thought of the things Carver had told her the previous night.

"No, I don't want that," Alaine had to agree.

"I'm just asking you to understand that this is no ordinary proposal. If things do not go the way you wish, you are still young. After a time, your father can find other prospects for you."

"I don't want other prospects, and I don't wish to speak more of this, mother," Alaine announced, feeling put upon. "I will not give up my hope for this marriage."

"Alright," Iris said, not wishing to argue. "I ask you to just think about your future, whether it is what you wish or not."

After her mother left the room, Alaine felt her eyes filling with tears. She knew that her mother was well-meaning. She also knew that if it came to unrest or possible war among the people, Alaine would have no choice but to sacrifice her love.

27

The Three Kings

The elderly, stout man used a tall walking stick as he sped through the forest. Though aged, he was thankful to have not lost his quickness. He could still pass at such a pace so all that was heard was the crack of a fallen branch and the twitter of moving leaves.

He stopped at the edge of the woods, seeing the Central Road in the nearby distance. The surrounding landscape was deserted except for the squirrels chasing about. The oddly dressed figure made his way to the road, knowing his final destination wasn't far beyond. The hem of his regal raspberry colored cloak dragged along the ground. His fawn skin cap was tilted to one side of his head over long, lanky locks of white hair. Not fond of trousers, Alfred wore a long tunic of the finest woodland fabric, with a sheen that gave it a bronze color. The only mark of a king's rank was a gold, oval amulet, embossed with an ancient yew tree, hanging on his chest from a copper chain tarnished with age. His ankle-high boots were soft-soled and lined with fur.

Alfred slowed his walk, knowing he was now on the land of the people of the fields.

Before long, a wagon came along. Horses were reined to a halt as the driver took pity on an old man so far afield from town.

"To where do you travel, good sir?" the waggoneer called.

"I go to the castle at Hawthorn," the elder said to the driver.

"Hop on the back of the wagon. These melons and vegetables are for the castle kitchens."

Alfred took advantage, climbing onto the loaded cart. As they moved on down the road, he had a chance to view the countryside he hadn't seen for many summers. As they crossed the stone bridge and came onto the main street, Alfred was surprised to see the once tiny farming hamlet was now a well-built, busy township. He saw many townsfolk afoot and gathered in small groups. This man of the forest looked at the current styles of clothing the people were wearing, as they returned stares at the strange old man riding on the back of the wagon.

The roadway widened and became steeper going up to the open castle gates. Traffic was coming and going on foot, on horseback, and in wheeled vehicles. The guards waved the wagon through, with barely a glance at the wagon's driver or the man riding on the back. So it was that King Alfred came to King Granth's castle courtyard.

Once on his feet, Alfred found his way around the massive stone building to the front, where steps led to the expansive plank and iron doors. Well-dressed nobles clustered in small groups on the long portico gave looks of curiosity as he climbed the steps, his stick in hand and his pouch slung over a shoulder. One of the two castle doors was propped open, allowing free passage into the great foyer with its high ceiling. Slightly overwhelmed, the King eventually wandered into what looked like a large receiving room. Finding a high-backed chair, he propped his stick, deposited his satchel, and took a seat. He watched as people ambled through the room to who-knows-where.

Odd place, he thought. Were there no footmen or stewards?

Stenson happened to walk through the room on his way to the foyer leading out of doors, when he saw the strangely dressed man sitting in the chair. The old man seemed somewhat lost.

"May I be of help, sir?" Stenson asked the man, as he stopped before the chair.

"If you don't mind, I've had a long roaming and could do well with a drink," Alfred replied.

"I will get you something," Stenson assured, as he walked off toward the kitchens.

The lad returned shortly, with a large flask of cool cider which he handed to the traveler, who drank deeply.

"What is your name, good fellow?" Alfred asked.

"I am Prince Stenson," the boy answered. "We are on a visit to Hawthorn."

"Ah, King Holum Targ's son. Last I heard, you were but a babe. Now, here you are, taller than myself."

"Do you know my father?" Stenson asked, trying to remember if he had seen the man before.

"No, we have never met," Alfred replied, "but I am here to meet with your father and your uncle, King Granth."

Stenson's eyes grew large as he realized that his father and uncle were waiting to meet with the King of the Forest clans about Alaine's betrothal.

"Are you King Alfred?"

The man smiled and nodded.

"I saw all of your sons when they came to Irongate for Alaine's betrothal ceremony."

"Did you? What do you think of them?"

"Well, there were a lot of them. I did like Prince Alfred, and his dog. I wish I had a dog. Alaine says that she wants to marry your son."

"It is a complicated matter. That is why I'm here," Alfred confirmed.

"Allow me to take you to the Tapestry Room; then, I will tell my father you are here."

Stenson carried the man's bag and led him across the foyer and down a long hallway to the most impressive room of Hawthorn Castle.

Upon entering, King Alfred looked around the grand hall, admiring the stone, wood, and window glass. He strode over to the nearest tapestry hanging on the soaring wall. Stenson's uncle previously explained the history belonging to each of the three large, woven drapes, portraying important events of the royal House of Hawthorn.

"That one is at Craig Castle, before this castle was built. That is my great-grandfather, King Arden, signing The Treaty of the Trees," Stenson said, pointing to the character at the center of the mat.

"This is a very good telling of the scene; however, it was not so perfect at the time. That day was rainy, and Arden was a large, handsome man, but not so finely dressed. This person is supposed to be me, when I was much younger, ready to sign The Treaty. Oh, it was so long ago," Alfred said, with feeling.

Stenson looked closely at the forest King, trying to see any resemblance to the tapestry. Could he really be *that old*? the boy wondered.

"Have a seat at the council table, Your Majesty, and I will fetch my father and uncle without delay."

Stenson ran through the castle, trying to find his father, thinking he would be with his uncle, King Granth. He finally found them at luncheon in a small dining room off the kitchen.

"Father, Uncle Granth, you must come at once!" the boy exclaimed, after bursting into the room. Both men looked up from their food, startled.

"What is it?" Holum asked, imagining an emergency.

"He is here! I didn't know what to do with him, so I took him to the Tapestry Room. He is waiting for you!"

"Who is waiting?" questioned King Granth.

"King Alfred. The king from the forest," Stenson stressed.

The brothers exchanged a look and stood at once, the unfinished meal dismissed.

"Go get the marriage contract, Holum. We may have need of it," directed Granth. "I will summon Squire Dilford, as we may have need of his pen, as well. I'll meet you in the foyer."

A short time later, Holum, Granth and Stenson entered the Tapestry Room through the east doorway to find the King of the

Forests sitting in a chair, flask in hand, gazing out the windows. He stood as soon as he saw them.

"King Alfred, welcome. I'm sorry, but no footman told us of the arrival of your coach," King Granth said, in greeting. "I am Granth, and this is my brother Holum. It seems that you have already met Stenson."

"He is a fine lad, who kindly fetched me a drink after my journey and brought me to this elegant room. No footman is at fault, as I came to your castle on the back of a wagon bringing a delivery. The good man stopped on the road and gave me a ride."

The younger kings couldn't help but stare at the ancient man. His short, round figure was not what they had expected. To come on foot from his forest to the castle was unheard of, especially for a king.

Squire Dilford came rushing into the room, with rolled parchment tucked under his arm, and a quill and inkwell in his hands.

"I've invited my royal scribe in case there is a need," King Granth explained.

"Dilford is known to our people," King Alfred said, nodding to the man. "His mother belonged to one of our local clans, many winters past."

King Granth and King Holum were both surprised to learn such an important man to the King's Council had roots with the forest people.

"Stenson, you may leave us, as we have much to discuss with King Alfred," Holum ordered.

"Please allow the boy to stay," Alfred requested. "It will be he who makes the decisions long after we're all gone."

King Holum nodded his consent to Stenson as they all took their seats around the heavy wooden table. Before talks could begin, the old King pulled up his bag from the floor and removed a highly decorated metal tube, aged green in the grooves on its surface. Alfred opened the round lid at one end and pulled out a thin, leather skin, unfurling it onto the table. Squire Dilford, who recognized it from the legends he had heard from his youth, let out a gasp.

"This is the original copy of The Treaty of the Trees, written in our forest language, a language older than the language of the

Kingdom," Alfred explained. "It is held in a vault in high forest caves, where it is kept safe from fire, flood or disaster. I'm sure you have seen the other copy in your language. Here is the mark of your grandfather, King Arden. He signs with a large first letter."

Granth and Holum stood and bent over the table for a closer look at the skin, examining the odd characters etched into the hide, and their grandfather's mark. Both men recognized the mark, having seen it previously on other documents.

"This is my mark, here," Alfred relayed, pointing to the peculiar marks representing a name at the bottom of the angular script.

The brothers were stunned that the old man announced that it was *he* who signed The Treaty. They had previously seen the original copy in their own language, signed by Arden and a representative of the forest clans.

"I was told the nobility of my son, Prince Alfred, needed to be proven, but it cannot be established without evidence that I am, and have been, the monarch for my people."

Granth sat quietly while looking at Alfred. The man would have to be over a hundred winters in age to have signed The Treaty of the Trees with their grandfather. Alfred *was* surely of great age. His hair and eyebrows were white; otherwise his face was free of any beard, as was usual among his people. His skin was thin and tracked with fine winkles, looking almost translucent, but his deep blue eyes and expressions were sharp. When he spoke, his teeth appeared grayed with age; his lips were pale, but his voice was strong.

Again, Alfred reached into his bag. He pulled out thick sheaves of parchment-like paper, cut into a long ledger. The tan textured pages were covered with columns of angular characters. The brother kings were quiet, respecting Alfred, allowing him time to explain what was brought forward.

"During the seasons of spring and fall, our people have ceremonies at Middleoak, requiring all newborns to come from across the forest lands, for what is translated into your language as 'choosing day'. It is an important, sacred rite of our people. The child is given a name of the parents' choosing and enlisted into the family clan. This choice is recorded and remains with the child for life. If the parents are of the same family clan, there is no issue. If the parents are of different clans, they must decide into which clan the child will be registered, usually the mother's clan. The name of the child, the parents' names, and the time of birth are recorded," King Alfred explained. "This is the record for my family, and the names of my children and grandchildren are listed here. Alfred was a child of my older age, a time when I didn't expect to have yet another son. Here is the recording from his choosing day," Alfred said, pointing to a particular inscription on the textured paper. "Alfred, who is also called Carver, is my son and a prince among our people. So, if my nobility is accepted by you, my son's nobility should also be accepted. My son, Lignin, told me proof of nobility was required by the marriage contract."

"Yes," King Granth agreed, "that is a requirement. I thank you for providing this validation. Actually, the primary concern regarding the marriage of Prince Alfred and Princess Alaine is the possible unrest between our peoples. Our people have had hardly any contact and know little of the forest clans and their customs. Will they accept Alaine's marriage to an unknown forest prince? On the other hand, will the clans accept an outsider as a bride to one of your princes? Has your Assembly agreed to the match? Could the match lead to discord?"

"According to my son, our Assembly is divided on the idea. There is no strong opposition, just apprehensions. They have left the decision to me. As far as *your* people are concerned, my understanding is that the nobility was willing to accept your dear Princess marrying a prince from a far-off land, to leave the country of Hawthorn forever. At least, if she were to marry a forest prince, she would remain a Princess of Hawthorn."

"That is a good point," offered Holum. "It would be greatly desired to keep her here."

"So, what are your feelings about the match, Sire?" asked Granth, of the old King.

"My son is devoted to the Princess Alaine and has great love for her. He is willing to give up all to be with her. We have all tried to dissuade him at times, challenging him with potential problems, but he remains steadfast in his desire to marry her. I would like to see the girl and talk to her before I make my decision regarding a marriage. Would that be possible?" Alfred requested.

322

Granth and Holum gave each other of a look of agreement with the reasonable request.

"Stenson, go find Alaine and tell her to come at once," ordered King Granth, and the boy ran from the room. "In the meantime, we will review the marriage contract with you, King Alfred."

Alaine was with Charlyn and Genna, choosing gowns for the evening's dinner when Stenson knocked on her bedroom door and entered without waiting for Alaine to answer. He announced the arrival of King Alfred. Excitedly, he told Alaine that she was wanted at once in the Tapestry Room.

"Oh, my!" Alaine gushed with alarm. "Quickly, Genna, I must put on a better gown before I go down. Which one should I wear? Stenson, wait for me outside while I change."

It was Charlyn who chose a two-toned blue velvet dress from the cupboard, as Genna rushed to untie the laces of the morning gown. Agreeing with the choice, Alaine dressed as quickly as she could. The lace scarf covering her braids on the back of her head would have to do, as there must be no further delay.

As soon as Alaine entered the Tapestry Room the three kings stood, and her father made the introductions. The Princess curtsied to the old King. The man motioned to the chair next to him, wishing for Alaine to sit with him, then gave a look to the younger men. Granth and Holum realized they were being dismissed, so they quietly retired to Granth's nearby workroom.

Alaine felt no fear of this man. She could see some of Carver in his face and eyes. They began their conversation. The wise man had many questions for her, which she answered one by one. They spoke of serious things and also laughed together at times. Alfred could appreciate that Alaine was not only beautiful, but intelligent. Her eagerness to learn about the people of the forest, learn their language, and take part in their customs, impressed him. Her feelings for better communication among all the peoples of Hawthorn was idealistic, but a good premise for the future of the land. Who better to lead the change than a Prince of the Forest and a Princess of the Fields?

Finally, Alaine invited the King to her favorite place in the castle – the kitchens. Once there, Annie was so impressed upon being introduced to the Forest King, she did what was her place, and presented him with a plate of freshly grilled trout, steamed greens with walnuts, and a fresh, soft roll and butter. Alaine took a roll for herself as they ate and discussed food common to the forest clans. A dessert of tea and strawberry scones with lemon curd finished the unexpected meal.

Alfred had heard tales of Alaine's limestone garden from Carver and asked if he could see it. Alaine was only too happy to show off her outside sanctuary. She led the King through the low portal into the garden. They strolled down the path and naturally found themselves seated on the far bench. There they talked away the dwindling afternoon. Alfred spoke of the clans and the past. Alaine spoke of the land of Hawthorn and her hopes for the future. As the light dimmed and twilight was upon them, Alfred mentioned how much he had enjoyed the afternoon, but it was time for him to leave. Going back into the kitchen, he gathered his stick and bag, and left, unceremoniously, through the kitchen door.

Alaine went to find her father in the large gathering room, with King Holum. Iris and Hester had returned from their day out and were curious to see the Forest King that their husbands spoke of. Having drinks before dinner, the Marquis and Duke Noeman were also wishing for a glimpse of the man. Charlyn and her mother joined the group, wanting to know if a decision was made about Alaine and Carver.

"Where is he?" Granth asked, surprised to see his daughter enter the room alone.

"He has gone," Alaine replied, as all in the room stopped their conversations to look at her. "He will return in two days' time with his son. Mother, you will finally have a chance to meet Carver. Once everyone has met, a decision will need to be made regarding our marriage. A decision, not only for our sake, but for the sake of the land of Hawthorn."

With that, Alaine excused herself in order to dress for dinner.

The next two days went by slowly for Alaine. Every night she went to her garden, hoping to find Carver waiting for her, but he didn't come. On the day King Alfred was expected to return, Alaine spent the morning choosing a gown and carefully styling her hair.

True to his word, as the sun rose high in the sky, King Alfred and Carver climbed the steps of Hawthorn Castle. King Granth, assuming the visiting king and his son would once again come on foot, stationed Squire Dilford at the door to await them.

Once they arrived, Dilford led them to Queen Iris's tearoom, where Granth and Iris, King Holum and Lady Avis were looking forward to the meeting. Alaine was filled with anticipation. Queen Iris noticed the change in her daughter when Prince Alfred, or Carver, as Alaine called him, entered the room and was introduced. Iris was impressed with his clean-cut form, and the look of assurance that he gave to Alaine. Unlike his father, Carver's hair was tied back, and he wore clothes that would be accepted at the Hawthorn court. He was soft-spoken and his manners were polite.

Carver came with gifts for Alaine's parents. He presented Queen Iris with a small wooden box which, when opened, revealed an irregularly shaped smooth, yellow stone attached to a chain.

"I believe the stone is called amber in your language," Carver said. "It comes from the ancient trees and is highly prized by our people. It is thought to bring good luck and long life, as it holds the essence of the forest."

Iris was surprised to receive a gift and pleased with the sentiment behind it.

"I have brought this for you, Your Majesty," Carver said, turning to King Granth. "It is rare and also from our oldest of trees. It was ground and polished by one of our craftsmen."

King Granth took the leather sheath, opened it at the top, and withdrew a polished stone handle and blade of a hand's length. The multicolored woodgrain ran along the handle and blade. The blade itself was finely honed to a sharp edge.

"Petrified wood," King Granth informed, showing it to the ladies. "It is wood so old that it has hardened to stone. It is a stunning piece of workmanship. I thank you, Prince Alfred."

"Call me Carver," the young Prince requested. "It is the name used by my family."

Carver was pleased that his gifts were well received. It was then that King Granth suggested the men go to his workroom for discussions. As Alfred had wanted to speak with Alaine, Granth wanted time to speak with Carver.

Iris and Lady Avis sat at a table sipping from cups. Alaine walked around the room with worry, awaiting the return of Carver and the three Kings. Would there be a decision about the marriage? those remaining wondered.

After a time, Carver and the Kings returned to the room where the ladies were waiting. The women were eager to hear what had transpired behind closed doors, and the decision concerning Alaine and Carver. The facial expressions of the men were sober, causing a shiver of fear to run through Alaine. She tried to prepare herself for bad news. Queen Iris and Lady Avis went to stand with the girl in the case that support was needed.

"We have come to an agreement," King Granth announced. "The Kings of Hawthorn will support the marriage of Princess Alaine to Prince Alfred."

Carver, standing with his father, gave Alaine a smile as she raised her hands to her mouth, letting out a sob of relief. Whatever Carver had said to plead his case to the monarchs, he had managed to convince them. Iris and Avis quickly embraced Alaine in the excitement of the moment.

Alaine, not to be contained, ran to her father and gave him a thankful hug. She grasped the hands of her Uncle Holum as he bent to kiss her cheek, which was moist with tears of happiness. When she turned to give her thanks to Carver's father, the old King grinned and placed her hand into the hands of his son. The couple stood together.

"I will call the Council together, and once they are informed, we will make a public announcement," King Granth declared.

And so it went. After the approval of the Hawthorn Council the news of the engagement went out. The castle guard and the King's musicians were sent to the Hawthorn Castle gates. Rumors of an announcement had circulated in the village, and the people quickly gathered. The king's Proclamation was read with fanfare by Jones, the Council Footman, dressed in his official attire. The decree told of the marriage of the Princess Alaine of Hawthorn to Prince Alfred of Elder Tree Forest on the day of the upcoming full moon. The declaration also invited the people of Hawthorn to join in the wedding festivities to be held at the castle. A new excitement filled the air.

It was three days since the visit of Alfred of Sylvan. King Holum and Queen Hester would be ending their visit and leaving in the morning; so, a family dinner was called for on this last evening.

Rather than at the end of the table, Granth sat in the middle on one side of the long dining table, opposite his brother Holum. Iris was on his left, and Alaine was seated on his right, across from her aunt, Lady Avis. Kent sat next to Alaine, sitting across from Duke Seaken-Char. Queen Hester, dressed in a newly stitched, woolen gown, sat opposite Iris, and next to Holum, with the Marquis at her other elbow. Charlyn was dismayed to be at the other end of the table, far away from Kent, between the Marquis and Prince Stenson. Across the table from Stenson was Closin, looking the radiant maiden that she was, seated beside her mother. Duke Noeman sat across from the Marquis, with whom he had developed good relations, and between his wife and Queen Iris.

The roast was carved and served, the wine flowed, and the mood was pleasant. These were the evenings of late sunsets, when the breeze was warm, and the air held the scent of flowers and blooming trees.

Granth and Holum could rest easy regarding their discussions with King Alfred. The three Kings had identified the need to improve communications between their peoples. King Alfred offered the land deeded to the forest clans by Duke Morr-Leigh to be common ground, used by all the people. King Holum, impressed by Prince Lignin, extended an invitation for him to attend his next council meeting, so that the Dukes of the Mareview Lowlands could speak with him and possibly open communications with the clans' Assembly of the Groves. Not to be left out, King Granth offered his next council meeting to Prince Jute, Carver's brother, who held forest lands in the north of the Eastgreen Highlands, west of Duke Noeman's forest lands.

Lastly, the monarchs looked forward to the marriage of Alaine and Carver. The young Prince and the Princess of Hawthorn would be the first ambassadors for their people. When the palace made the announcement in Hawthorn Village, townsfolk were confused about the Prince. Who was this person marrying their Princess? Was it not the rich noble who traveled to Hawthorn with King Holum and his family?

Under the agreement, Carver would be allowed to visit Alaine every five days prior to the wedding for chaperoned courting. On one of these days, the couple was walking down the main street of the village, with Astra loping along, for a visit with Hewitt and Finnie. Carver wanted Alaine to meet his adopted village family. Once word got around in the village that the engaged Prince was the lad with the dog and the one that carved the furniture, the villagers were surprised to learn it was the familiar face. Not only were the people accepting, but housewives were bragging about the cupboards, spice boxes, and cradles that had been carved by the Forest Prince.

The wedding would be held at the castle, which would be open, with everyone invited. Preparations for the wedding had begun and the anticipation of the townsfolk was high.

Sitting at dinner with the royal families of Hawthorn, Kent listened to the light conversation around the table. He glanced across at his mother and Duke Seaken-Char. Their heads were leaning together in quiet talk. Kent spent the last two days taking his mother to Juniper Lodge, where she packed most of her clothing and personal belongings. The trunks were now sitting in the castle courtyard, where tomorrow they would leave for Seaken Hall. The Duke and his mother were to be married upon their arrival at Seaken Hall, and Lady Avis would live with her new husband as Lady of the household. By this time, Kent was agreeable with the match for the sake of his mother's happiness. The man was loving and respectful, and at times would tease Avis, making her blush. As a wedding gift, Rengard promised to make over a suite of rooms for the Lady's personal use. The couple were a portrait of mature love.

However, Lady Avis wouldn't give up her comfortable room at Hawthorn Castle. The couple would be frequent visitors when the Duke was called to King Granth's council meetings, and Avis would visit her sister. Soon, they would be returning to the castle for Alaine's wedding at the time of the next full moon. The lady would also have a room at Juniper Lodge, where she had resided for so long. Avis was happy with the plan for Kent and Charlyn's wedding after the Harvest Festival. Then, there would be a new Duchess of Leigh.

Prince Stenson, ready to return home, was using this time at dinner to convince his father to allow him to have a dog. Holum refused to make any promises, not sure if the boy was old enough to responsibly care for a pet. The King knew that Hester would never allow an untrained animal within Irongate Castle. Maybe at Winterfest, Holum thought.

Hester was in her glory, monopolizing the conversation at that end of the table. Now that is was decided that Alaine would marry the woodsman, the Queen had moved on. Amazingly, the Marquis secured a betrothal to Duke Noeman's youngest girl, the Lady Closin, who became Hester's new protégé. It was agreed that Closin, at the age of fourteen summers, was too young to marry. So an arrangement was struck. Felix would return to Raydon as usual but would come back in two summers to claim his bride. In the meantime, Hester would host the girl at Irongate over the next summer. Who better to tutor Closin in the traditions and sensibilities of the Raydon court than a former Princess of Raydon? And, of course, all new clothing would be required for the bride of a Marquis.

As for the Marquis, he was in love, and was not sure how it happened. Thankful that the plans with Alaine hadn't worked out, he sat quietly, gazing at the beautiful maid who would be his bride. Closin had ash-blonde hair with tiny ringlet curls surrounding her face, heavily lashed hazel eyes, which seemed to change color with the color of her gown, and perfect lips that he could hardly wait to kiss. At the base of her creamy neck hung a gold chain with a jade dragon, a gift he thought was made for her. His trip to Hawthorn Castle was a success. He had met the royalty of the land, made trade inroads, and found the perfect bride. He was suddenly eager to have a wife and give his mother the grandchildren she wanted. Felix would busy himself with preparations until his return to Irongate in two summers. Charlyn sat quietly next to the Marquis and across from her sister and parents. She knew Closin would prefer to be sitting where she was, closer to Felix, as the younger girl had begun calling him. Closin and Charlyn would be traveling in the morning, on the way to Seaken Hall. Closin convinced their mother to allow her to go along, hoping to spend more time with the Marquis before his trip home. Selfishly, Charlyn hoped to spend time with Kent.

Lady Noeman was completely taken aback with this visit to Hawthorn Castle. She came reluctantly at the urging of her husband, still distraught over the abrupt marriage and departure of Esbeth. Charlyn came back from her journey to become engaged to Duke Morr-Leigh, and soon to be wed. Now, Closin was betrothed to the Marquis. So quickly she was losing all of her children. She always knew it would happen, but not so soon. She wasn't ready.

Duke Noeman of the Walls was pleased with the world, and after a few cups of wine was prematurely missing his daughters. He was happy that Charlyn and Closin had made such good matches. Now, dowries were on his mind, one needed at the Harvest Festival, and another one for Closin, two summers hence. Sadness came to him when he thought of all his girls married and gone. He leaned over and took his wife's hand and bent close to her ear.

"We must have all our girls home for Winterfest," he whispered. "We will invite Esbeth and Will. She will have her dowry. After all, she *is* the daughter of a duke. We must hold them all close while we are able."

Lady Noeman looked at him and saw the change of heart in his eyes. "That is a wonderful idea, love," she replied, giving him a tender smile and a squeeze of his hand.

Queen Iris sat quietly next to Granth. In the morning she would travel with the party going to Seaken Hall. She would chaperone Duke Noeman's girls there and back. Her husband and Alaine wouldn't travel. With a wedding upon them, and the entire village of Hawthorn invited, there were endless preparations. As the dessert was served, Queen Iris was pleased to hear that the visit of the royal family from the Lowlands was being praised by Queen Hester. Holum made a toast to their hosts. Granth followed with his own toast and good wishes for all of the impending nuptials, and to the engagement of Felix and Closin. The brother kings had come together in their goals for leading the land of Hawthorn forward. Overall, the visit had been a success.

great field was enclosed on the one side of the grounds of Hawthorn Castle. Originally, it was to be a place of refuge for the villagers in the chance of an invasion, war, or other catastrophe.

During this time of peace, it was used for the annual Hawthorn Games, usually held toward the end of summer. The dukes and their teams of squires would set up their tents, displaying their flags, and compete in trials of horsemanship, swordsmanship, and other games of strength and endurance. At the end of the contests, the King's feast is held, and the Hawthorn Trophy is awarded to the victors.

The field was also used on occasions when the castle gates were open to the public for Winterfest, the Snowmelt Celebration of spring, and of course, the Harvest Festival. Now the field was being prepared for the upcoming wedding festivities for the Princess Alaine, planned for the day of the full moon.

With Queen Iris away for her sister's wedding at Seaken Hall, King Granth was fully engaged in transforming the castle's great field into a welcoming place for nobles and countrymen alike.

Time was running out, as the cycle of the moon showed a fuller orb in the sky each night. So Granth enlisted all of his guardsmen, stable hands, local carpenters, and available strong lads from the village to bring forth his vision for the nuptials. Great tents were erected inside the tall perimeter walls, each with a designated purpose. They would be used for serving food and drink, and to hold tables for eating. A playground for the children was being constructed at one corner of the field, with its own castle with ramps for climbing and rope bridges for crossing. Swings and a tunnel maze were next to be set up. At the other end of the field, small booths were being built to house carnival games for all ages. The festive day should hold enjoyment for all.

With the backdrop of the limestone arches, a platform was built for the wedding ceremony outside of Alaine's garden. That was where the vows would be given and taken, with a vast space of standing room, for all to have a spot for viewing. Bleachers were being erected on both sides of the deck for the courtiers. King Granth's sleeves were rolled up as he moved from one worksite to another, supervising the progress.

Lentil Gull had been the head Housekeeper at Hawthorn Castle since Alaine was a young girl. She had watched the sometimes-willful Princess grow up. Her loyalty to Queen Iris was strong, and she wanted nothing more than to dress the castle for the wedding in a manner to make the Queen proud and Alaine happy. Lentil managed preparations for all types of castle events. She knew what was to be done to apply festive decorations to every window, fireplace, arch and doorway. The Tapestry Room would be the hall used for the traditional bride's dinner, where all of the courtiers would toast the newlyweds.

Alaine had grown to have great respect for the housekeeper and her abilities. She felt a bit ashamed of some of the previous entanglements between them over the running of the kitchens. Now, Alaine was happy to have given up those responsibilities, while looking forward to becoming a wife and partner to a forest prince.

Lentil welcomed the truce between them and took detailed notes of Alaine's wishes for the food and table at the prestigious dinner.

Then Lentil was off to speak with the gardeners. Ropes of garland were needed. The flowers would wait until the morning of the wedding, when the vases would be filled and appropriately placed.

Queen Iris, Lady Avis, Nana and Genna, who was holding a tray of hot tea and scones, were huddled outside the door of Alaine's bedchamber.

"What if she's still asleep?" whispered Nana.

"It is time for her to awake," replied the Queen. "There is much to do before the ceremony. She must be gotten ready."

"I have the girls heating water for her bath. Remember, it takes a long time for her hair to dry, especially after I twist it into curls," Genna reminded.

"Go ahead, Nana, knock on the door. We can't stand here all day," Avis insisted.

Alaine was awakened to the sounds outside the door before the feeble knocking. She looked over to the window, trying to guess the time of morning. Tonight was the night of the full moon. She sat up in the bed. By the end of the day, she would be a new bride. It was finally time.

"Come in," Alaine called, and then laughed to see her loved ones troop into the room.

The crowd flocked to the bed and delivered their hugs, as Genna carefully placed the tray on the top quilt. Around her they gathered, taking spots on the mattress, sipping the tea, with the giggles of happy girls, as crumbs fell upon the covers.

"My little girl …," Iris cried.

"Mother don't start crying or you will have us all in tears," Alaine implored.

"Yes, don't start her crying. We do not want a bride with puffy eyes," agreed Avis.

"Genna, is the gown ready?" asked Queen Iris.

"Yes, Your Majesty," Genna answered, jumping off the bed, running to the wardrobe and opening the door.

"Oh," exclaimed Iris, seeing the dress, "I can't wait to see it on you, Alaine." But first, there was time to finish the tea and scones.

Carver arrived early to Finnie and Hewitt's cottage on the morning of the full moon. He carried a satchel and his elegant cloak and was dressed in all of his finery, with Astra in tow. He took a seat at the table as Finnie put a cup of hot tea in front of him. He pulled his princely crown from his bag and sat it on the table before him. The children gathered around him, admiring the metal ring, and asking Carver to put it on.

Finnie had her hands full trying to keep all four children clean and neat in their new clothes, while running around after Astra. Finally, she gave orders for the youngsters to sit, and put the eldest in charge. The two younger girls continued their fussing with one another and giggling, but the older boys were obeying their mother lest their father get involved. Finnie rushed off to get herself ready.

Hewitt had rented a wagon for the day since they would not all fit in a coach. When neighbors learned Hewitt and his family would be taking the groom to the ceremony, they raided their summer gardens and decorated the rented cart with flowers and streamers along both sides. The fancy wagon sat outside the cottage, waiting for its passengers.

Carver was not nervous, but eager to get to his bride. He brought with him a humble copper ring for her finger. It was nothing like the jewels she was used to, but it had been passed down in his clan and provided by his father. Alfred had given it to him, wanting the girl to have something from the clans on her wedding day. Carver put it in his breast pocket next to his heart.

As he looked out the front window, Carver saw streams of townsfolk on foot, making their way to the castle. Carver knew that after today things would never be the same. Their lives would be changed, but together, he and Alaine would face the challenges. In his heart, he knew that this marriage was right and good.

The hustle of dressing Alaine for the wedding was taking place. Alaine had agreed to wear the gown made for the betrothal ceremony at her mother's request, along with the royal sash and dragonfly belt. Now Genna was giving her full attention to Alaine's hair.

Raisen, Squire Dilford's girl, had been in training with Genna since Alaine had returned from her trip to Irongate. She would be taking Genna's place as the lady's maid to the Princess, when Genna left for her new life with Rand. Genna's pregnancy was confirmed, so Genna, her mother, and Rand would be leaving their work at the castle to move to the countryside, just outside the village.

It seems that Sergeant Covey, with few expenses, had been putting away his coin for years. Now that he was no longer needed as Alaine's bodyguard, he decided to leave the life of the castle.

So he bought a small estate with a manor house, large barn and barnyard, and two additional cottages on the property. He was starting his own transport business, having two large wagons built, and buying teams of strong farm horses to pull them. Covey invited Rand to be one of his wagon drivers for a salary and the use of the largest cottage on his land.

Although Alaine knew that she would miss Genna, she was happy for her and Rand. Raisen seemed the perfect fit, as she was as eager as Alaine to learn the language and culture of the forest clans, since the girl learned that her grandmother was from a clan.

"Are you sure that you do not wish to wear the tiara with the pearls that goes with this dress?" Genna asked.

"No, today I will wear the copper circlet of the forest clans," Alaine replied, "and don't bother pinning my hair up."

Genna gave a disapproving look that Alaine saw reflected in the dressing table mirror.

"I know what you're thinking, mother will not approve, but I'm doing it for Carver. This is our day, after all. Let the courtiers whisper about it."

"As you wish, milady."

When Alaine was ready, and the time for the ceremony arrived, King Granth and Queen Iris escorted their daughter down the front steps of the castle, and around to the field. Music played as they walked to the platform set up for the ceremony. The mayor of the village waited there, wearing his finest robes and metal chain of office. The handsome Prince stood patiently beside the man. Alaine's gown drew appreciative hums from the crowds, but it was her hair that made everyone stretch their necks for a glance. Her red curls fell in waves onto her shoulders, defying the traditions of the day. A small copper band with circlets wound across her forehead and around her head, holding the masses of hair in place. Alaine was relishing her new identity, as she would soon be a princess of the forest.

In the front section of the boxes for the nobility, Lady Avis and Duke Seaken-Char sat close together. Next to them were Kent and Charlyn, excited for Alaine, and imagining their own upcoming wedding. Nana McNiven, not to be left out for this day was seated next to Lady Avis. Sergeant Covey was also provided with a place of honor. Along with the villagers, Genna and Rand stood in the front row, in full sight of the bride and groom. Next to them were Hewitt and Finnie, with Astra calmly sitting between the children.

The closer the royals got to the platform, the louder the cheers from the people. Soon the royal trio ascended the steps. The King and Queen walked the bride to the groom and took their seats, allowing the vow taking ceremony to begin. Silence came to the audience when the mayor joined the hands of the couple and began his words. The vows and pledges were exchanged, clearly heard by all present. When all was done, the newlyweds turned to face the people hand-in-hand. The cheers went up, to be heard all through the town and countryside.

Earlier in the day, no one had noticed the old man moving quickly along the road with his overly long cloak trailing behind him, using his tall stick to steady his pace. Not only were all of the villagers on their way to Hawthorn Castle, but people were coming from all over the countryside to see the Princess marry, and to join in the festivities. Long before reaching the castle gates, carts, carriages, and wagons were parked in every available space. Likewise, it was inside the gates where the noble coaches were jammed together, taking up one entire side of the courtyard.

The man wandered onto the vast field, following the crowds of nobles and commoners alike, to the platform before limestone arches, bedecked with wreaths of summer flowers amid hawthorn boughs. Chairs for King Granth and Queen Iris were on the platform, set off to one side. There, along with the Mayor of Hawthorn, stood Carver, awaiting his bride. The father took pride in his son, who knew what he wanted, would not be deterred, and pursued it to the end. The old King liked the girl straight off.

She appeared to be unspoiled, and as determined as Carver to share their lives and embrace her place among the forest clans.

After watching the couple make their vows, Alfred wandered over to the food tents, where he had a meat pasty and a cup of mead before ambling toward the gates. He took his leave without a word, knowing that a binding ceremony and a great celebration was in the works at Middleoak, set for the time of leaves turning. There, he would wear his crown and fine robes. He and his sons and families would host the masses of clans folk, who would travel from all the forestlands to see the marriage of their youngest prince. As was the custom, the daughters-in-law would make the bride's gown and prepare all the food for the feast. He laughed to himself to think that all of his sons had found a life partner except Flecher. He would need to encourage the boy.

With these thoughts in mind, Alfred wandered down the hill, away from the castle, toward his forest home. There were great hopes for the people of Hawthorn, both of the forest and the land.

The bright light of the full moon shone in the sky, casting silvery rays onto the private garden as the bride and groom entered through the low kitchen door. They stood by the trickling fountain as they gazed, arm in arm, at the moon and the stars in the cloudless sky. Alaine had changed out of her formal gown into a soft, comfortable morning dress. Carver's gold vest was cast aside, and his fancy shirt was untied at the collar. His trousers were untucked from the confining tall boots, which were replaced with his fur-lined forest shoes.

After the long, busy day, Carver could finally pull his Princess to him, lift her chin with a finger, and share a heartfelt kiss, their first married kiss, with the promise of many more to come.

Alaine gave a moan of pleasure as his lips strayed to the side of her neck and his hands caressed her back. She moved her body to him, thrilling in his closeness. They wandered to the bench and sat hand-in-hand, sharing yet another kiss in the moonlight.

"Are you happy?" Carver asked.

"I could not be happier. I love and feel loved."

"Our love will last forever," he murmured. "And every time we see the full moon we will be reminded of our love. From now on, there will be no sleepless nights for either of us."

"But we will still visit the garden, won't we?" she asked.

"Of course, whenever we can; and we'll bring Astra."

They both laughed.

The Happy End

Epilogue

The Hawthorn Castle belonged to the people now, where travelers would flock to renew their ties with the country's history. Festivities were still held at the castle: Winterfest, Snowmelting, and the Harvest Festival. There were tours offered by resident historians. Its library was renowned and open to scholars. Architects came to study its structure. The castle on the hill still dominated the northern commerce center of Hawthorn Eastgreen. What had been the monarch's landholdings near the castle had been transformed into a public park. The bustling township had sprawled out, encompassing almost all of the nearby countryside. Much of the forestlands were repurposed, leaving only the respectful groves of the Elder Tree Forest.

Decades of summers had gone by, but the summer Hawthorn Games went on in the county as an honored tradition. Teams would gather at Hawthorn Castle to vie for the coveted trophy. Hawthorn's monarch no longer lived at the castle, but the King traveled from the new palace near Leggot, to stay at the castle, and host the King's Feast at the end of the Games.

Today, two young cousins were on their way to the castle, walking from the inn where their families were staying. Both had brothers participating in the games, and their noble fathers were involved with the Duke's team. Their mothers agreed to have a long morning, so the girls were on their own. They stopped to rest on the old stone bridge in the middle of town, the one that crossed over the River Ways. Looking over the side, they noticed the water was low on the banks, but rippling along in the middle of the flow.

The bridge separated the hostels and inns from the business district of the town. In Old Town, as it was called, retail shops lined the cobblestone street, except for eating halls or an occasional tavern. The girls took their time going up the road toward the castle. They were very interested in the fashion of the day, so it was a treat to look at the latest items displayed in the shop windows. They agreed to come back and bring their mothers with their purses, and coin for purchases.

By the time they got to the castle, they were warm from their walk, and decided to go inside the great hall to cool off, and possibly find something to drink. Once in the wide foyer, where the air was cooler, they came to stand before a larger-than-life portrait, hung in a prime location on the high wall. The picture was of a young woman standing by a table, looking at the viewer. There was a brass plate below the picture:

"I wonder who she was," Cassie said, her head bent back, looking up at the portrait.

"My mother told me about this picture last year when we were here. Mother said that she was a princess who used to live here. It was a time when the land was divided into two kingdoms. My mother tells that King Stenson demanded that this picture be put here, and should remain as long as the castle stands," Laurel repeated from memory.

"King Stenson, the Unifier?" Cassie asked.

"Yes, he's the one. Mother said that they were somehow related. Stenson knew her before he became King, and before he brought the two kingdoms together as one."

"She has beautiful hair, and I like that little circlet that goes across her forehead. Her eyes are really blue, and her mouth is almost smiling," Cassie observed.

"I wonder if that stone in her necklace is a real emerald," Laurel pondered. "If she was a princess, it might be real; but the only ring on her hand is that little band without a jewel."

"That green gown *looks* like a gown for a princess. See those little designs in the fabric? They look like dandelion puffs. That dragonfly hanging from her belt has some jewels on it," Laurel pointed out.

"What's that she's holding in her hand? It looks like a little wooden statue?"

"I think it's a deer. No, it's a figure of a dog with long legs," Laurel guessed.

"Maybe it belongs in that carved chest on the table," Cassie pointed out. "Does your mother know what happened to her?"

"Mother says that tales of her are woven in with the tales of the forest clans, and she is not sure how much of that is folklore. One of the stories says that she married a forest prince. Once her parents passed on, she went to live in the forest and was never seen again."

"Well, we all have tales of the forest people in our families now. My father's grandmother was from the forest clans," Cassie reminded, dismissively.

"Mother thinks that it was a magical time, back then. We still use some of their words in our language. And Middleoak is still considered an ancient place for the forest clans. Mother says some people still live there. Those loyal to the beliefs make journeys there every year," relayed Laurel.

"It's too bad we don't know more about the lady," said Cassie. "The picture is beautiful and reminds me of the olden days."

The girls took a few more minutes studying the portrait before leaving to find a drink. Then they would go to the field to find their fathers.

Acknowledgements

To Page Turner Books, Inc., I am so excited to be selected as one of their first authors to publish under their Young Adult genre. I would like to personally thank Dr. Leanne Staback, president of Page Turner Books, Inc. who - one day, some time ago - convinced me that I could write a book. With her support and guidance, I have been able to write and publish books important to me and my family. Thank you for your patience throughout the years!

For his role in editing, I would like to thank Dr. Ray Cress. He brought new light to this rather long manuscript with all the corrections I didn't realize were needed. His assistance with grammar and improved word choices were greatly appreciated. He made me realize that I have no idea where commas belong…need to work on that! When I went off course, he brought me back. Thank you, Ray!

To Dean Sutton, Cassandra Katsoulis, Sloane Hybarger, and Leanne Staback at Page Turner Books, for their assistance with cover design - they are very talented, and I am thankful for all their work and input.

Lastly, thanks to my husband. The writing process can be messy, with computers set up in inconvenient places, lots of paper everywhere; and sometimes, going out to get food when I worked past the dinner hour.

Character Profiles
for
Alaine of Hawthorn

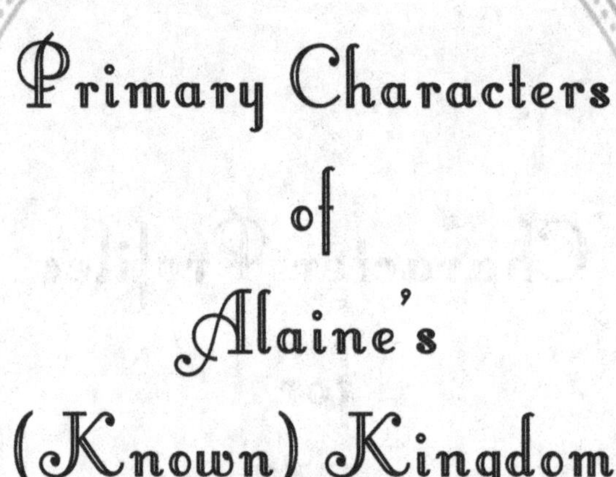

Primary Characters
of
Alaine's
(Known) Kingdom

*(Characters are listed alphabetically,
and not by order of importance)*

Captain Kent Morr-Leigh

Son of Lady Avis.
Nephew of King Granth and Queen Iris.
Cousin of Princess Alaine.
Veteran soldier.
Captain of Morr-Leigh Garrison.
Charged with escorting Princess Alaine to the Weston Mareview
Lowlands' Irongate Castle of King Holum Targ for betrothal.
Newly named Duke by the Council of Hawthorn.
Duke of Morr-Leigh landholdings.
Takes his father's place on the council.
Lands border King Granth's landholdings around Hawthorn,
orchards and grains.
Resides at Juniper Lodge.

King Holum Targ

King of Weston Mareview Lowlands.
Younger brother of King Granth of Hawthorn.
Son of King Holms of Hawthorn.
Uncle of Princess Alaine.
Resides at Irongate Castle at Harbortown.
Sponsoring Princess Alaine to introductions to noble suitors for
her hand in marriage.

Lady Avis

Older sister of Queen Iris.
Widow of Norbert Morr-Leigh, former Duke of Leigh.
Duchess of Leigh from Juniper Lodge.
Mother of Captain Kent Morr-Leigh (current Duke of Leigh).
Alaine's Aunt.
Charged by Queen Iris as chaperone for Princess Alaine as she
travels to Lower Kingdom for her betrothal.

Lady Charlyn

Daughter of Duke Noeman of the Walls.
Sister to Esbeth and Closin.
Squire Wilken Chason is her lost love.
Young lady-in-waiting and traveling companion for Princess
Alaine.
Developing relationship with Kent Morr-Leigh.

Princess Alaine

Sixteen year old, only child of King Granth and Queen Iris.
Princess of Hawthorn Castle.
At the age for marriage.
Journeys to Lower Kingdom for betrothal.

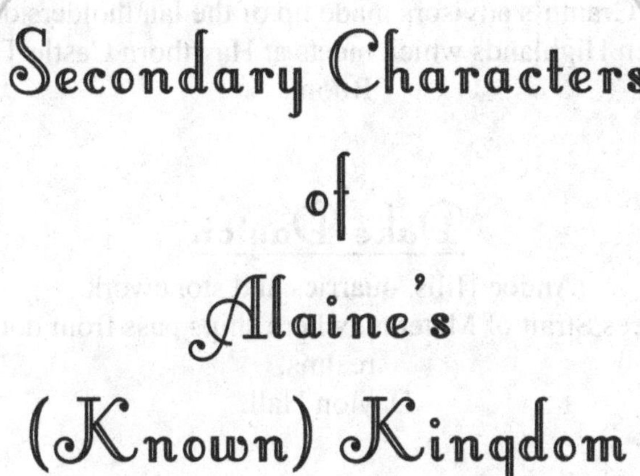

Secondary Characters

of

Alaine's

(Known) Kingdom

*(Characters are listed alphabetically,
and not by order of importance)*

Annie

Cook at Hawthorn Castle.
Charged with managing meals on journey to the Lowlands.
Helpers: Oween and Clara.

Council of Hawthorn

King Granth's advisors made up of the landholders of the
Eastgreen Highlands which meets at Hawthorn Castle Tapestry
Room.

Duke Dayton

Andoc Hills, quarries and stonework.
Oversees Strait of Meteran, where ships pass from northern
realms.
Dayton Hall.

Duke Eckelform

Resides at Eckelform Hall.
Holds lands south of Seaken-Char, farming and shepherding.
Andoc Hills, quarries and stonework.

Duke Filroy

Filroy Hall, northwest, near Seaward Pass.
Older advisor who served in King Holmes' army.
Farmlands.

Duke Gillis

Resides at Gillis Halls.
Holds lands south of Duke Leigh lands, raises horses and dairy
cows.
Older council member.
Friend of King Holmes.

Duke Noeman of the Walls

Boyhood friend of King Granth and his brother.
Father of Lady Charlyn.
Resides at Darkwood Lodge.
Forester for the upper and lower kingdoms.
Controls northern forested lands, in charge of lumber production.

Duke Rengard (Ren) Seaken-Char

Friend of King Granth's father.
Resides at Seaken Hall.
Powerful, older Duke.
Can raise 1,000 men-at-arms.
Lands provide grains and animal husbandry.
Journeys to Irongate.
Love interest Lady Avis.

Dukes of the Lower Kingdom

Duke Brighton of Brighton Towers
Duke Eastwick of Eastwick Hall
Duke Labsum of Sunset Manor
Duke Portwron of West Dunes Keep
Duke Shefelton of Ways Hall

Genna

Daughter of Ellen, kitchen worker.
Worked at Hawthorn Castle since childhood.
Lady's maid to Princess Alaine.
Loyal friend to Princess.
Travels with Princess to Lowlands.

Jones

King's footman to King Granth's Council

King Granth of Hawthorn

Grandson of King Arden, who settled the land from marauders and
signed The Treaty of the Trees.
Son of Old King Holmes, who divided the land making each of his
sons kings by dividing Hawthorn into the Upper and Lower
Kingdoms.
Older brother of King Holum Targ.
King of Eastgreen Highlands.
Alaine's father, House of Hawthorn.
Resides at Hawthorn Castle, seat of Eastgreen Highlands
government.

Lentil Gull

Housekeeper for Hawthorn Castle.

Mister Corith

Head Footman Irongate Castle.

Mistress Ronan

Housekeeper for Irongate Castle; formerly of Hawthorn Village.

Morr-Leigh Garrison

Soldiers led by Captain Kent Morr-Leigh.
Recently returned from battles to support neighboring kingdom,
now responsible for escorting Princess Alaine to the Lowland
Kingdom.
Lieutenant Miles; Scouts: Felter, Proden; Sergeant Ash.
Smyth is garrison cook and provides first aid.
Flag and shields – blue and gold on white background.

Nana McNiven

Older member of Hawthorn Household.
Former nursemaid to Queen Iris and Lady Avis; and then, Kent
and Alaine.
Travels on journey to Lowlands.

Prince Stenson

Twelve-year-old son of Holum and Hester.
In line for throne of Lowlands.
Unknown to be possible heir to Hawthorn throne per King
Granth's Will.
Cousin to Princess Alaine.
Tutor: Papopolis.

Queen Hester de Locke

Wife of King Holum.
Jealous of Queen Iris.
Elder cousin Marquis de Locke.
Former Princess of Raydon.
Opportunistic toward matchmaking for Princess Alaine.
Feared by Lady Avis.
Maids: March, Celia; Ladies: Lady Amy Sculpter.

Queen Iris

Alaine's mother.
Queen of Eastgreen Highlands.
Wife of King Granth.
Younger sister of Lady Avis.
Aunt to Kent Morr-Leigh, Duke of Leigh and Prince Stenson, son
of King Holum Targ.

Rand

Hawthorn Castle footman.
Driving royal coach on journey to Lowlands.
Love interest for Genna.

Sergeant Covey

Respected, veteran soldier chosen by King Granth as bodyguard to
Princess Alaine since she was a child.
Loving, adversarial relationship with Alaine.

Squire Dilford

Scribe, keeper of King's records.
Not well known that mother was of the forest clans.
Daughter: Raisen.

Sir Foy

Captain of King Holum's Guard.

Suitors for Alaine

Marquis Felix de Locke

Not a prince but an extremely rich shipping merchant from the
sun-drenched country of Raydon.
Cousin to Queen Hester who was a Princess of Raydon.
Handsome, persuasive, promises a life of great wealth for Alaine.
Name of ship: Galeecia.
Name of estate: Raydon Seaview.

Prince Brannon

Third son of King Ryan, from Mirth, a short trip across the sea,
whose father is demanding a royal match in order to bring wealth
to his kingdom.
Young, very handsome, flirtatious with women.

𝔓rince 𝔖turgrom

Prince that came from northern land of Swerd to obtain the hand of
Princess Alaine in marriage.
Kind, widower; intellectual, wardrobe too warm for Harbortown
climate.

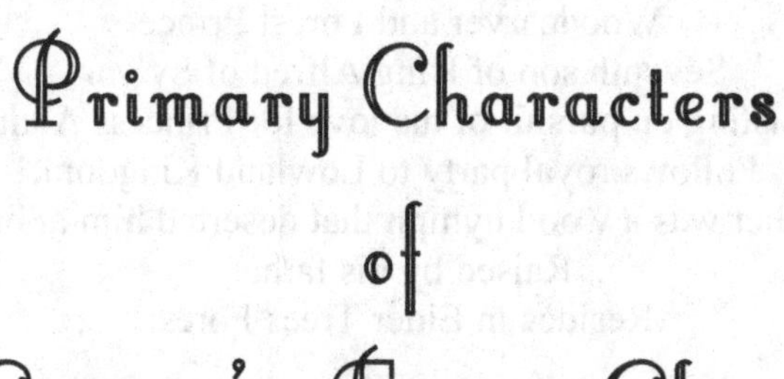

Primary Characters of Carver's Forest Clans

*(Characters are listed alphabetically,
and not by order of importance)*

Astra
Carver's dog and constant companion.

Carver Vale (aka Prince Alfred)
Member of the forest clans.
Woodcarver and Forest Prince.
Seventh son of King Alfred of Sylvan.
Insisting on pursuit of his love for Princess Alaine.
Follows royal party to Lowland Kingdom.
Mother was a wood nymph that deserted him at birth.
Raised by his father.
Resides in Elder Trees Forest.

Secondary Characters
of
Carver's Forest Clans

*(Characters are listed alphabetically,
and not by order of importance)*

Assembly of the Groves

The governing body of the forest clans made up of representatives
from each forest region.
Responsible for governing policies, resolving disputes, and
making decisions for the common good of the Clans.

Brothers of Carver Vale

Older sons of King Alfred.
All Forest Princes who have assumed their responsibilities for
tracks of forest lands and their family clans within the Upper and
Lower Kingdoms of Hawthorn according to The Treaty of the
Trees.

Bole

Eldest.
Forest land holdings border the Central Road and the landholdings
of Duke Seaken-Char.
Oversees Middleoak.
Resides in the Oaks Forest.

Delle

Loves to cook.
Stocky build.
Resides in the Trees of the Lake.

Flecher

Fourth in line.
The archer.
Good relationship as a guide with Princess Alaine and Duke Morr-
Leigh.
Resides in Owlbrook Treehold.

Jute

Closest in age to Carver, grew up with him.
Looks like father.
Sympathetic to Carver.
Resides in Lancet Forest.

Lignin

Second eldest.
Oversees Staghorn Woods clans.
Diplomat of the brothers.
Very active in the governing body for the Clans people, Assembly
of the Groves.

Nocken

Fifth in line.
Critical of Carver.
Resides in Hollybranch Forest.

Finnie

Hewitt's wife.
Runs shop and sells Carver's wood products.

Hewitt

Hawthorn Village blacksmith.
Friend of Carver.

King Alfred of Sylvan

Carver's elderly father.
Resides in his manse in the Forest of the Elder Trees near
Hawthorn Castle.
Monarch of forest clans.
Signed The Treaty of the Trees with King Arden.
Disapproves, but allows Carver to follow the Princess on her
journey to the Lowlands.

Towns and Cities
of the Land

*(Places are listed alphabetically,
and not by order of appearance)*

<u>Char</u>

Large, farming village near Seaken Hall, on Seaken-Char
landholdings.

<u>Eastgreen Highlands</u>
&
<u>Weston Mareview Lowlands</u>

The two kingdoms of the land of Hawthorn.

<u>Harbortown</u>

Busy seaside town where merchant ships come with their cargo
from abroad.
Location of Irongate castle.

<u>Hawthorn Village</u>

At the foot of Hawthorn Castle.

<u>Leggot</u>

Town on Central Road near the River Falls.

<u>Middleoak</u>

Secluded, capital city of forest clans in view of the waterfall and
lake at The River Falls.

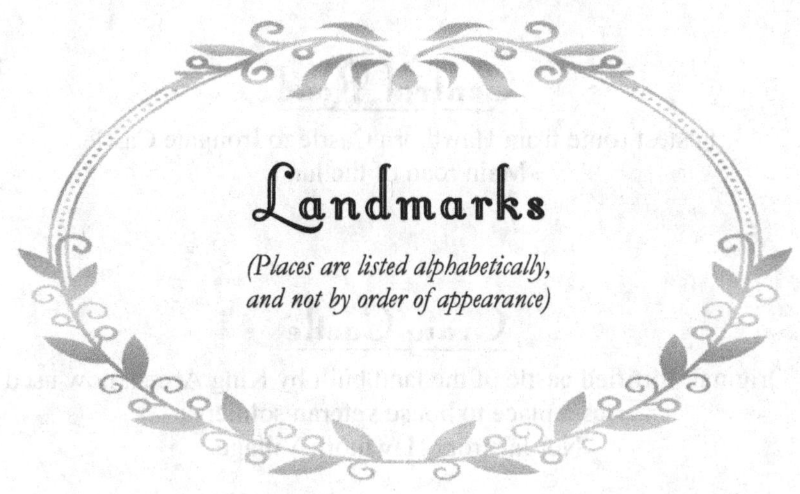

Landmarks

*(Places are listed alphabetically,
and not by order of appearance)*

Brighton Towers

Home of richest duke of Lower Kingdom, near Central Road.
Provides accommodations to travelers.

Byway Shops

Merchant shops lining Shoreline Byway in Harbortown.

Central Road

Fastest route from Hawthorn Castle to Irongate Castle.
Main road of the land.

Craig Castle

Original, fortified castle of the land built by King Arden, now used
as a place to house veteran soldiers.
Not far from Hawthorn Village.

Crossroads Inn

Large inn for travelers along the Central Road about a day's travel
from Hawthorn Village.

Darkwood Lodge

Residence of Duke Noeman of the Walls and his daughter, Lady
Charlyn.

Eckelform Hall

Home of Duke Eckelform, located north of Leggot.

Harbortown Harbor

Large stone harbor on the Shoreline Byway, near Irongate Castle.
Port of commerce and fishing for the land of Hawthorn.
Of strategic importance.

Hawthorn Castle

Seat of Eastgreen Highland government.
Residence of the King.
Alaine's home.
Holds Hawthorn Games annually.

Irongate Castle

Seat of King Holum Targ's government at Harbortown.
Old, stone guardhouse on castle grounds.
Originally a fort.

Juniper Lodge

Residence of Lady Avis, Duchess of Leigh, Kent Morr-Leigh,
Duke of Leigh.
Almost a day's travel from Hawthorn Castle.

The Old Road

Ancient road, known and used only by the forest clans.
Runs from the Central Road, along the River Falls, through
Middleoak, through forest lands to the seacoast.
Once used by invaders to the land of Hawthorn.

The River Falls

Runs from mountains of northeast, west to the seashore, much of it
through forest lands.
Waterfall at Middleoak.

The River Ways

Runs from high country, along Hawthorn Village, running to the
sea.

Seaken Hall

Residence of Duke Seaken-Char, seat of local government.

Shoreline Byway

Main road that runs along seacoast from Harbortown.
Three of the five Dukedoms of the Lower Kingdom along the
seacoast.

Stonelink Bridge

Crosses The River Falls on the Central Road near the town of
Leggot.

Strait of Meteran

Ships approaching the land of Hawthorn from northern lands must
pass through this waterway.

Timber Road

Runs from northeastern lands of the Duke of Noeman to transport
timber to the Central Road and lowlands.

Documents of Importance

*(Documents are listed alphabetically,
and not by order of appearance)*

Bole's Map

Detailed map of the land of Hawthorn, including details of forest clan holdings as well as those of the people of the fields.

King Granth's Will of Succession

Allows Alaine's male heirs to apply for the throne with the consent of the Council, otherwise Prince Stenson first in line to throne, which allows for the reunification of the two kingdoms of Hawthorn.

Marriage Contract

Details requirements for husband for Princess Alaine.
Discussion of succession to the throne of Eastgreen Highlands.
Itemizes dowry.

The Treaty of the Trees

Treaty between the original people of the land, the forest clans, and the new people wishing to settle the land for farming, etc.
Signed by King Alfred and King Arden.
Divided the land between the forests and the fields.
Put restrictions on the use of the forests given to the forest clans and restrictions on the way lumber is produced for use by the people of the fields.
Separated the people, the governance, the culture and lifestyles.

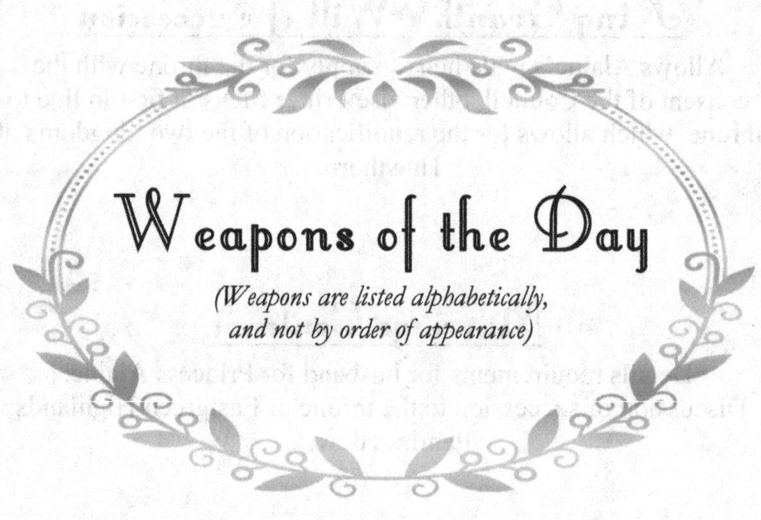

Weapons of the Day
(Weapons are listed alphabetically,
and not by order of appearance)

Cannon

Available > 13th century, initially used on battlefields.
A large, heavy piece of artillery, typically mounted on wheels.

Dagger

Short, pointed knife with edged blade.

Long Bow

Bent wood bowed with tight string at both ends.
Used with arrows for hunting game.

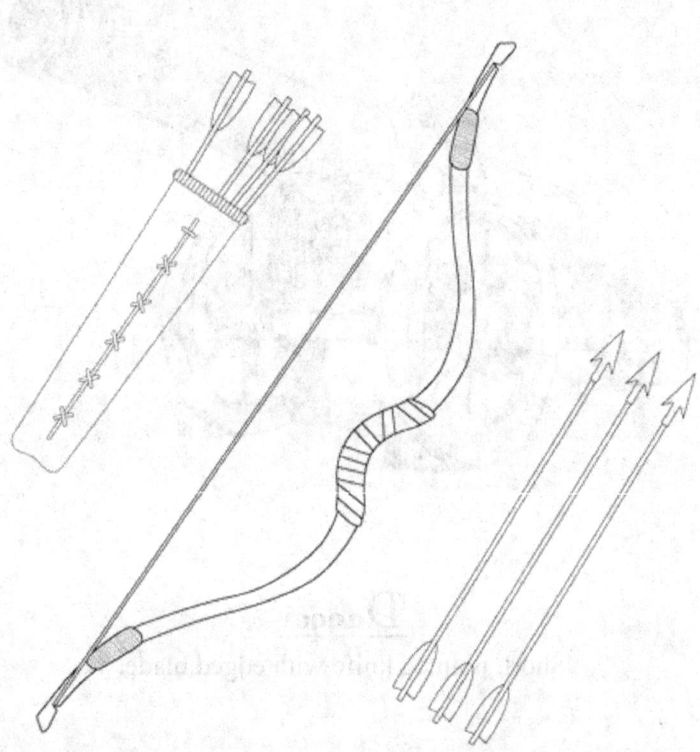

Long Sword

Long metal blade with point and honed edges, a hilt, and a handle.
Used in battle sometimes with shield.

Rapier
Thin, light, sharp pointed metal sword.

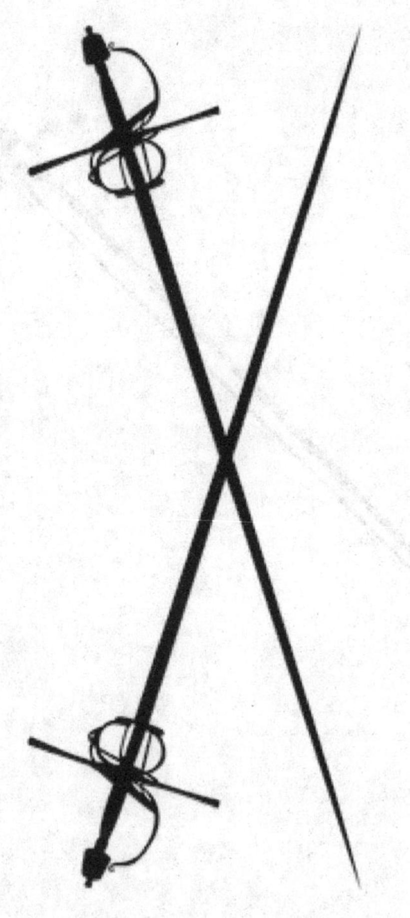

Sword Hilt Dagger

Metal dagger with a hilt and handle.
Morr-Leigh dagger.

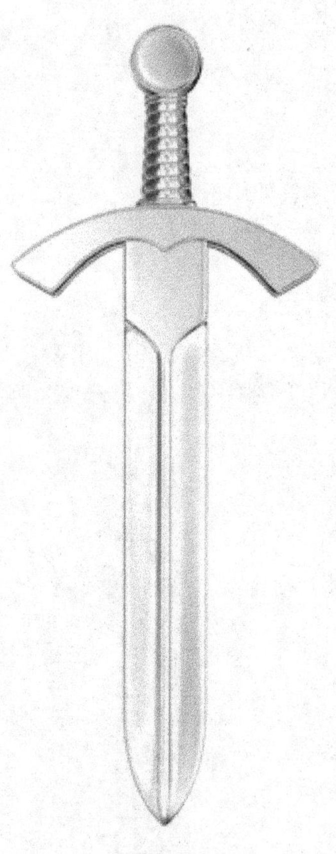

<u>Short Sword</u>

Similar to long sword, but shorter and more convenient to carry.

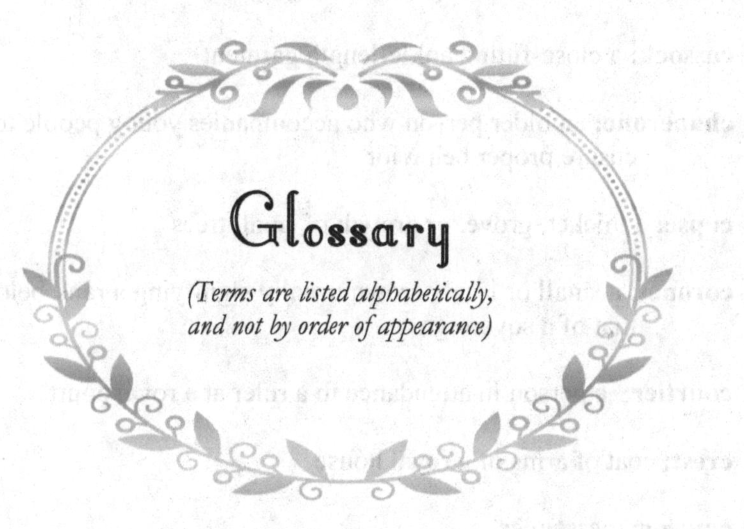
Glossary
(Terms are listed alphabetically,
and not by order of appearance)

anonymity: a state of lacking individuality, distinction, or
recognizability

anteroom: a small outer room that leads to another room and that
is often used as a waiting room

armada: a fleet of warships

blacksmith/blacksmithing/blacksmith's: a smith who forges iron

betrothal/betrothed: engagement/engaged to be married

cassock: a close-fitting ankle-length garment

chaperone: an older person who accompanies young people to
ensure proper behavior

copse: a thicket, grove, or growth of small trees

coronet: a small or lesser crown usually signifying a rank below
that of a sovereign

courtier: a person in attendance to a ruler at a royal court

crest: coat of arms of a royal house

courier: messenger

dais: a raised platform

dowry: the money, goods, or estate that a woman brings to her
husband in marriage

draught: a serving of drink

emporium: a store carrying many different kinds of merchandise

en masse (French): as a whole group

en route (French): on or along the way

faerie/faeries/fairy/fairies: an imaginary being usually having a
small human form and magical powers

farrier: a person who shoes horses

forge: to form something (such as metal) by heating and
hammering

furled: to wrap or roll close to or around something

gadfly: a person who stimulates or annoys other people especially
by persistent criticism

gnome(s): an ageless and often deformed dwarf of folklore who
lives in the earth and usually guards treasure

heritage: property that descends to an heir; something transmitted
by or acquired from a predecessor; or something possessed
as a result of one's natural situation or birth

impropriety: an improper act or remark

lady-in-waiting: a lady of a queen's or a princess's household
appointed to wait on her

lean-to: a wing or extension of a building having a lean-to roof; or
a rough shed or shelter with a lean-to roof [Lean-to
meaning only having one pitch or slope]
Liege: a loyal subject; or a vassal bound to feudal service and
allegiance

manse: a large, imposing residence

marauder(s): people who roam from place to place making
attacks and raids in search of plunder (jewels, money, etc.)

mead: a fermented beverage made of water and honey, malt, and
      yeast

morrow/on the morrow: tomorrow; the next day

***moss faeries:** small, kind-hearted faeries that live in the forest,
      sleep in groups in the moss that grows on the north sides
      of forest trees. Green glow when they fly. Lead the lost
      from the deep forest. [*Invented/Created by Eileen Raye
      specifically for *Alaine of Hawthorn*.]

mutton pasties: sheep's meat pie

noble: of high birth or exalted rank

nymph: any of the minor divinities of nature in classical
      mythology represented as beautiful maidens dwelling in
      the mountains, forests, trees, and waters.

page(s): a youth attendant on a person of rank especially in the
      medieval period; a youth being trained for the medieval
      rank of knight and in the personal service of a knight.

pavilion: a large often sumptuous tent

pixies: cheerful, mischievous sprites (aka fairies/faeries)

propriety: conformity to what is socially acceptable in conduct or
      speech

prudence: caution as to danger or risk

rapport: a friendly, harmonious relationship

sash: a large and usually colorful ribbon or band of material worn
      around the body, draping from one shoulder to the
      opposing hip and back up

smith: a worker in metals

smithy: the workshop of a smith

sprite(s): elf; fairy; and elfish person

squire: a member of the gentry ranking below a knight and above a gentleman

stronghold: a fortified place; a place of security or survival

tapped: to pierce so as to let out or draw out a fluid

trawler(s): a boat used in trawling [trawl: a large conical net dragged along the sea bottom in gathering fish or other marine life]

treachery: violation of allegiance or of faith and confidence

unfurl(ed): to open out from a furled state; unfold

verdant: green with growing plants

About the Author
EILEEN RAYE

A fifth book for Eileen Raye, "Alaine of Hawthorn" is written for young adult audiences, embracing historical fiction and fantasy lore with a modern-day twist. Ms. Raye is a supporter of the printed page, bookstores - new and used - and encourages reading for all age groups.

She currently lives in Boulder City, Nevada - near Las Vegas - with her husband. Her hobbies include reading, writing and attending a book club. Retired from a fulfilling career in nursing, Ms. Raye also enjoys gardening, jigsaw puzzles and a robust "Harry Potter" collection. Family, grandchildren and pets bring a sweetness to her life.

Bibliography

Andreykuzmin. "Old Paper Scrolls and Parchments Set Realistc 3D
Illustration Stock Illustration - Illustration of Isolated, Background:
91331451." *Dreamstime*, 27 Apr. 2017,
www.dreamstime.com/stock-illustration-old-paper-scrolls-
parchments-set-realistc-d-illustration-image91331451.

"Anonymous Definition & Meaning." *Merriam-Webster*, Merriam-
Webster, www.merriam-webster.com/dictionary/anonymous.
Accessed 21 Jan. 2023.

"Anteroom Definition & Meaning." *Merriam-Webster*, Merriam-Webster,
www.merriam-webster.com/dictionary/anteroom. Accessed 21 Jan.
2023.

"Armada Definition & Meaning." *Merriam-Webster*, Merriam-Webster,
www.merriam-webster.com/dictionary/armada. Accessed 21 Jan.
2023.

Begemot_30. "Fairy House in a Gated City Stock Illustration -
Illustration of Lake, Anxiety: 61313505." *Dreamstime*, 27 Oct. 2015,
www.dreamstime.com/stock-illustration-fairy-house-gated-city-
illustration-fictional-situation-form-collage-photos-
image61313505.

"Betrothal Definition & Meaning." *Merriam-Webster*, Merriam-Webster,
www.merriam-webster.com/dictionary/betrothal. Accessed 21 Jan.
2023.

"Blacksmith Definition & Meaning." *Merriam-Webster*, Merriam-Webster,
www.merriam-webster.com/dictionary/blacksmith. Accessed 21 Jan.
2023.

"Cassock Definition & Meaning." *Merriam-Webster*, Merriam-Webster,
www.merriam-webster.com/dictionary/cassock. Accessed 21 Jan.
2023.

"Chaperone Definition & Meaning." *Merriam-Webster*, Merriam-Webster, www.merriam-webster.com/dictionary/chaperone. Accessed 21 Jan. 2023.

"Copse Definition & Meaning." *Merriam-Webster*, Merriam-Webster, www.merriam-webster.com/dictionary/copse. Accessed 21 Jan. 2023.

"Coronet Definition & Meaning." *Merriam-Webster*, Merriam-Webster, www.merriam-webster.com/dictionary/coronet. Accessed 21 Jan. 2023.

"Courtier." Merriam-Webster.com Dictionary, Merriam-Webster, https://www.merriam-webster.com/dictionary/courtier. Accessed 21 Jan. 2024.

"Crest Definition & Meaning." *Merriam-Webster*, Merriam-Webster, www.merriam-webster.com/dictionary/crest. Accessed 21 Jan. 2023.

"Courier Definition & Meaning." *Merriam-Webster*, Merriam-Webster, www.merriam-webster.com/dictionary/courier. Accessed 21 Jan. 2023.

"Dais Definition & Meaning." *Merriam-Webster*, Merriam-Webster, www.merriam-webster.com/dictionary/dais. Accessed 21 Jan. 2023.

"Dowry Definition & Meaning." *Merriam-Webster*, Merriam-Webster, www.merriam-webster.com/dictionary/dowry. Accessed 21 Jan. 2023.

"Draught - Definition, Meaning & Synonyms." *Vocabulary.Com*, www.vocabulary.com/dictionary/draught#:~:text=A%20cold%20burst%20of%20wind,can%20be%20called%20a%20draught. Accessed 21 Jan. 2023.

"Emporium." Merriam-Webster.com Dictionary, Merriam-Webster, https://www.merriam-webster.com/dictionary/emporium. Accessed 21 Jan. 2024.

"En masse." Merriam-Webster.com Dictionary, Merriam-Webster, https://www.merriam-webster.com/dictionary/en%20masse. Accessed 21 Jan. 2024.

"En route." Merriam-Webster.com Dictionary, Merriam-Webster, https://www.merriam-webster.com/dictionary/en%20route. Accessed 21 Jan. 2024.

"Faerie." Merriam-Webster.com Dictionary, Merriam-Webster, https://www.merriam-webster.com/dictionary/faerie. Accessed 21 Jan. 2024.

"Fairy." Merriam-Webster.com Dictionary, Merriam-Webster, https://www.merriam-webster.com/dictionary/fairy. Accessed 21 Jan. 2024.

"Farrier." Merriam-Webster.com Dictionary, Merriam-Webster, https://www.merriam-webster.com/dictionary/farrier. Accessed 21 Jan. 2024.

"Forge." Merriam-Webster.com Dictionary, Merriam-Webster, https://www.merriam-webster.com/dictionary/forge. Accessed 21 Jan. 2024.

"Furl." Merriam-Webster.com Dictionary, Merriam-Webster, https://www.merriam-webster.com/dictionary/furl. Accessed 21 Jan. 2024.

"Gadfly." Merriam-Webster.com Dictionary, Merriam-Webster, https://www.merriam-webster.com/dictionary/gadfly. Accessed 21 Jan. 2024.

Garashchuk, Anastasiia. "Dragonfly Stock Vector. Illustration of Insect, Lengthy - 220684114." *Dreamstime*, 7 June 2021, www.dreamstime.com/dragonfly-ector-isolated-illustration-image220684114.

"Gnome." Merriam-Webster.com Dictionary, Merriam-Webster, https://www.merriam-webster.com/dictionary/gnome. Accessed 21 Jan. 2024.

"Heritage." Merriam-Webster.com Dictionary, Merriam-Webster, https://www.merriam-webster.com/dictionary/heritage. Accessed 21 Jan. 2024.

"Impropriety." Merriam-Webster.com Dictionary, Merriam-Webster, https://www.merriam-webster.com/dictionary/impropriety. Accessed 21 Jan. 2024.

Izonda. "Vector Gold Chain Stock Vector. Illustration of Military - 36476412." *Dreamstime*, 7 Jan. 2014, www.dreamstime.com/stock-photography-vector-gold-chain-file-eps-format-image36476412.

"Lady-in-waiting." Merriam-Webster.com Dictionary, Merriam-Webster, https://www.merriam-webster.com/dictionary/lady-in-waiting. Accessed 21 Jan. 2024.

"Lean-to." Merriam-Webster.com Dictionary, Merriam-Webster, https://www.merriam-webster.com/dictionary/lean-to. Accessed 21 Jan. 2024.

"Liege." Merriam-Webster.com Dictionary, Merriam-Webster, https://www.merriam-webster.com/dictionary/liege. Accessed 21 Jan. 2024.

"Manse." Merriam-Webster.com Dictionary, Merriam-Webster, https://www.merriam-webster.com/dictionary/manse. Accessed 21 Jan. 2024.

"Marauder." Merriam-Webster.com Dictionary, Merriam-Webster, https://www.merriam-webster.com/dictionary/marauder. Accessed 21 Jan. 2024.

"Mead." Merriam-Webster.com Dictionary, Merriam-Webster, https://www.merriam-webster.com/dictionary/mead. Accessed 21 Jan. 2024.

"Morrow." Merriam-Webster.com Dictionary, Merriam-Webster, https://www.merriam-webster.com/dictionary/morrow. Accessed 21 Jan. 2024.

"Mutton." Merriam-Webster.com Dictionary, Merriam-Webster,
    https://www.merriam-webster.com/dictionary/mutton. Accessed
    21 Jan. 2024.

"Noble." Merriam-Webster.com Dictionary, Merriam-Webster,
    https://www.merriam-webster.com/dictionary/noble. Accessed 21
    Jan. 2024.

"Nymph." Merriam-Webster.com Dictionary, Merriam-Webster,
    https://www.merriam-webster.com/dictionary/nymph. Accessed 21
    Jan. 2024.

Obsidianfantasy. "Fantasy Scenery with an Old Castle Stock Illustration
    - Illustration of Fairytale, Wizard: 17260179." *Dreamstime*, 7 Dec.
    2010, www.dreamstime.com/royalty-free-stock-images-fantasy-
    scenery-old-castle-image17260179.

"Page." Merriam-Webster.com Dictionary, Merriam-Webster,
    https://www.merriam-webster.com/dictionary/page. Accessed 21
    Jan. 2024.

"Pasty Definition & Meaning." *Merriam-Webster*, Merriam-Webster,
    www.merriam-webster.com/dictionary/pasty. Accessed 21 Jan.
    2023.

"Pavilion." Merriam-Webster.com Dictionary, Merriam-Webster,
    https://www.merriam-webster.com/dictionary/pavilion. Accessed
    21 Jan. 2024.

"Pixie." Merriam-Webster.com Dictionary, Merriam-Webster,
    https://www.merriam-webster.com/dictionary/pixie. Accessed 21
    Jan. 2024.

"Propriety." Merriam-Webster.com Dictionary, Merriam-Webster,
    https://www.merriam-webster.com/dictionary/propriety. Accessed
    21 Jan. 2024.

"Prudence." Merriam-Webster.com Dictionary, Merriam-Webster,
    https://www.merriam-webster.com/dictionary/prudence. Accessed
    21 Jan. 2024.

"Rapport." Merriam-Webster.com Dictionary, Merriam-Webster, https://www.merriam-webster.com/dictionary/rapport. Accessed 21 Jan. 2024.

Ravven. "Fantasy Woman Long Red Hair Dressed Brocade Medieval Gown Fur." *Depositphotos*, depositphotos.com/photo/fantasy-woman-long-red-hair-dressed-brocade-medieval-gown-fur-609722314.html. Accessed 10 Jan. 2023.

Ravven. "Handsome Fantasy Male Prince Long Blonde Hair Leather Armor." *Depositphotos*, depositphotos.com/photo/handsome-fantasy-male-prince-long-blonde-hair-leather-armor-196573582.html. Accessed 10 Jan. 2023.

Raye, Eileen. *Alaine of Hawthorn*. Page Turner Books, Inc., 2019. "Moss faery/moss faeries" are terms invented by the author for this manuscript.

"Sash." Merriam-Webster.com Dictionary, Merriam-Webster, https://www.merriam-webster.com/dictionary/sash. Accessed 21 Jan. 2024.

"Smith." Merriam-Webster.com Dictionary, Merriam-Webster, https://www.merriam-webster.com/dictionary/smith. Accessed 21 Jan. 2024.

"Smithy." Merriam-Webster.com Dictionary, Merriam-Webster, https://www.merriam-webster.com/dictionary/smithy. Accessed 21 Jan. 2024.

"Sprite." Merriam-Webster.com Dictionary, Merriam-Webster, https://www.merriam-webster.com/dictionary/sprite. Accessed 21 Jan. 2024.

"Squire." Merriam-Webster.com Dictionary, Merriam-Webster, https://www.merriam-webster.com/dictionary/squire. Accessed 21 Jan. 2024.

"Stronghold." Merriam-Webster.com Dictionary, Merriam-Webster, https://www.merriam-webster.com/dictionary/stronghold. Accessed 21 Jan. 2024.

"Tap/tapped." Merriam-Webster.com Dictionary, Merriam-Webster, https://www.merriam-webster.com/dictionary/tap. Accessed 21 Jan. 2024.

"Trawl." Merriam-Webster.com Dictionary, Merriam-Webster, https://www.merriam-webster.com/dictionary/trawl. Accessed 21 Jan. 2024.

"Trawler." Merriam-Webster.com Dictionary, Merriam-Webster, https://www.merriam-webster.com/dictionary/trawler. Accessed 21 Jan. 2024.

"Treachery." Merriam-Webster.com Dictionary, Merriam-Webster, https://www.merriam-webster.com/dictionary/treachery. Accessed 21 Jan. 2024.

"Unfurl." Merriam-Webster.com Dictionary, Merriam-Webster, https://www.merriam-webster.com/dictionary/unfurl. Accessed 21 Jan. 2024.

"Verdant." Merriam-Webster.com Dictionary, Merriam-Webster, https://www.merriam-webster.com/dictionary/verdant. Accessed 21 Jan. 2024.

www.ingramcontent.com/pod-product-compliance
Lightning Source LLC
Chambersburg PA
CBHW010546170726
48285CB00011B/2783